Also by Mae Schick

Lila

A Life of Her Own

Minna

Mae Schick

Dedicated to

My family and friends,

and especially

to the memory of the women who served
during World War II.

The efforts which we make to escape from our destiny only serve to lead us to it.
-Ralph Waldo Emerson

.

Contents

Acknowledgments

Rosie the Riveter is the iconic representation of roles filled by women during World War II. I am grateful for their stories which have given me insight into this period of American history.

Thank you to Janice Kooiker for her dedication and profound patience. Her insights and wisdom helped see *Minna* through multiple revisions.

Emma Winkelman encouraged the forays into alchemy and pushed the story an unexpected direction.

And to John, for his unflagging devotion, and for the ready glass of wine after a hard day's work.

Minna

Part I

One

"Minna's been out in the alley smokin'!" Fischer shouted, storming through the door of Schneider's Bakery on his quest for Saturday morning doughnuts and coffee. He jerked his thumb in that direction as he headed for the hat rack, not waiting for Lila to respond.

"Oh boy, here we go." Iris ducked below the counter, pretending to arrange coconut cookies in the case, certain she was the target.

He examined the pegs, choosing where to park his precious charcoal-gray fedora. *So some careless idiot don't knock it off.* Customers gawked at him from the tables, wary of what would happen next. He waved his hand over the hat's brim, brushing an invisible piece of lint before he turned around, enough time for Lila's icy stare to glaze over.

"We'll talk about this in the kitchen." She sounded breathy, somewhere between a bark and a squeal. She stepped from behind the counter and pointed him through the swinging doors.

"Anyone need more coffee?" Iris said lightly once the doors swung behind them. "Lovely day we're having." She tittered, relieved she hadn't been in the line of fire. She waved the pot toward the stragglers idling in mismatched chairs, chairs Franz had recruited years ago from secondhand shops, or rescued from alleyways. Five years earlier, when the Schneiders insisted she rename the bakery, Lila had balked.

Faithful customers advised her to jump at the opportunity. "A wise choice."

"Sounds more friendly," they suggested.

"Like putting on a fresh coat of paint," they told her. "Pump up the place."

She just smiled. Every corner of the business whispered, "Schneider."

People turned hot and cold like the seasons, Lila decided, but she wouldn't let anyone influence her decisions. The store was a success, and she wasn't going to tempt fate. The idea seemed as heartless as her brothers and sisters back in the Dakotas neglecting their mama's gravestone.

"I'll have some more." A burly fellow snapped his head up from his newspaper and called across the tables, waving his cup.

"Here it comes, Clyde. How 'bout another doughnut? Looks like you could use one," she joked.

"Ah, come on, Iris. How 'bout sweet-talkin' me?"

"In your dreams," she teased. "Anyone else?" Iris smiled at the cluster of faces. Fischer had disrupted their Saturday morning reverie. They shook their heads, returned her smile, and went back to reading their papers.

"I would like half a cup, please." A studious woman spoke. A few of the customers, but not this serious one, would put off the day as long as possible, avoiding the blast huffing down Higgins Avenue off the Rattlesnake.

"You got it, Stella. Another slice of rye, too?"

"No, no," the bookish woman said. "I still have half a slice, and one's my limit." She set firm her rosebud lips. She gave a circumspect glance toward the swinging doors.

"Did you get a good look at that guy?" A Montana State University girl giggled to her friend, both with striped scarves long enough to step on and choke themselves to death.

"He's really cute when he gets mad," the other said of Fischer. A fact he would relish if he heard it and wasn't in such a peeve.

Birdbrains! Iris said to herself. *His admirers are getting younger all the time.* Fischer was in an enviable position with so many young men gone. The boys the girls would usually play coy with were off and had been fighting in Operation Torch in Morocco, or at Midway.

"You knew about this, didn't you?" Fischer barked as he barged through the kitchen doors, shoving his face too close to Lila's and banging his knuckles on her worktable. She took a startled step back. Yeasty smells, pungent from predawn baking, hung in the air. As she opened her mouth to address the issue of Minna's smoking, he snapped, "S'bout those soldiers out at the fort! Who's mindin' this show, is what I'd like to know."

Oh brother. So he knows about that, too, then. "What about them?" She wasn't about to let him bully her. "She's sixteen and feeling her oats." She acted nonchalant, sucking in her breath and holding it.

"Pull up that long underwear, Clyde," Iris chortled on the other side of the wall. "Don't want no breeze where the sun don't shine, now, do we?" Clyde must have been getting ready to leave. Lila was torn between whispering a silent thank-you to her sister for distracting the customers from her former husband's behavior, and being perturbed at how she talked to them.

"Yeah, well, those boys are feeling something, too, Lila," Fischer growled, "and it ain't oats!"

She swallowed a smile. She couldn't help it. She sucked in her breath again, but this time he saw it.

"Oh, I suppose you think that is funny, then?" He glowered.

"Maybe...maybe not." The lines around her eyes were from going without a decent night's sleep since Minna started this business. *Minding the show. Ha!* She could squash that bug in a second since she was the one who enforced curfew and interrogated Minna, who came in at one o'clock in the morning, trying to sneak past her mother sitting on the edge of her chair by the living-room window. When it turned cold and Lila realized she was shivering, she pulled an afghan around her shoulders. Maybe the temperature had dropped, or maybe it was from anger or fear. She waited and watched, and as the minutes passed in painful lurches, she grew more anxious.

If she told him how *his* Minna begged for rides from anyone willing to take her out to the fort, he'd blow his stack. She had enough woes without his tantrums, and she wouldn't give him the satisfaction of being right. He would blame her for not keeping the girl home, where she belonged. If she let him cross the line, just a tad bit, it would be misery.

"If you hadn't run out on me back then," he'd start, "she'd be a good, upright girl now." Yes, to Fischer's way of thinking, Minna could be a saint! Any acting out on Minna's part was Lila's fault; after all, she had been the one who had moved out with Minna when she was a toddler and left him with a pot of soup simmering on the stove.

"Try a butterhorn." She put the tray, redolent of yeast and icing, under his nose. "I made them with raisins, just the way you used to like them."

"Mmmm." He bit the roll in half after licking the icing. He chewed with his mouth open and said with his mouth full, "Are you gonna talk to her?"

Talk to her? She turned away and bit at her lip. "You mean hurl ultimatums," she had the urge to say. Talk? He wouldn't know where to begin. It took two people to do that. "Yelling," she would have clarified, "is not the same as talking."

"You haven't, then?" she asked, grinning. Of course he had. Minna had whipped through the kitchen from the alley on Thursday afternoon after his encounter with her, making the back door screech behind her. When she was on the other side of the swinging doors, she spit out, "Jackass," intending Lila to overhear. His trigger mouth trailed him like his twin. It had earned him a fair share of enemies around town. He would not alienate a customer, though.

"You act like the goddamn saint, Lila, but everyone knows what you and my brother get up to." He motioned toward the upstairs. "Hell, Willy ain't no brother of mine." He couldn't get the venom out of his mouth fast enough. "And you pretendin', 'cause you live over there on Pine Street, you ain't crawlin' in bed with him?"

"Okay. That's it. You're not going to start this again." Willy had rented the apartment above the bakery when he moved back from Seattle years ago. Fischer brought it up in most of their arguments. Minna had made matters worse during the summer to get revenge on Lila for not letting her go with five soldiers up the Blackfoot to Seely Lake on a sweltering August day.

"Do I have to spend the whole day selling cinnamon rolls?" Minna had whined at ten o'clock that morning. It was the sixth scorching day in a row. The bakery was suffocating, but Lila was not sympathetic.

"Don't exaggerate," she said, wiping the sweat off her own forehead with her forearm.

Minna pouted. "I'm not exaggerating! It's hot as doughnut grease in here," she complained to deaf ears. Lila had scheduled Minna's time from her toddler days onward to protect her from that monster called idleness, whose giant jaw hovered overhead, waiting.

The less time the girl had to fill her head with strange thoughts and questionable activities, the safer Lila felt. Every hour filled with purposeful activity meant one less hour of worry. Minna envied the high school girls she served doughnuts to, students she sat next to in history and English classes. They roamed the stores after school, and during the summer, they stopped for vanilla Coca-Cola at the drugstore. In her freshman year, they asked her to go with them.

"I can't. Sorry," she'd say, hating the bakery.

"Hi, Minna," they greeted her when they came in for doughnuts. "What have you been doing this summer?" Not waiting for an answer, one described her train ride to the coast. "This is from there," she sashayed in her colorful sundress.

"Well, I was at Flathead Lake and about died when I jumped in that icy water," the other one said. "It was fun on the dock, though"—

she grinned—"with some cute boys!"

Minna smiled like she was having the time of her life standing behind the bakery counter and replied, "I'm not sure…yet, what I'll be doing." After the store closed, pans needed to be scraped and cleaned, floors mopped, and windows washed. Lila stuck with this agenda for Minna even after it started falling apart.

"If you think I'm letting you go with five boys to the lake, you need to have your head examined." Lila put her foot down.

"Aunt Iris would let me go," Minna argued. "She'd get it, Lila. That we're going *swimming.*" Lila squeezed the tray she was holding as if it would slip out of her hands. As a child, Minna called her Lila, and Lila preferred that; it maintained a separation that she needed. In adolescence, that distance became intertwined with antagonism.

"Your aunt isn't the one raising you, and if she was in favor of it, I think she should have her head examined, too!" Just once, she wished her sister could support her wishes about how to raise Minna. *If Iris had kids of her own…* but there was no point willing the impossible.

What galled Lila about her ex-husband's public outburst in the bakery was his sudden concern for Minna. Over the years, Fischer and Minna met by accident on downtown street corners, or in the drugstore. Except it was no accident. Minna was only seven years old when Lila started loading her down with deliveries, sending her out on Main Street with loaves of bread.

"Well, just look at you," people commented of the little girl lugging an armful of bread, and Minna pushed her chest out, proud. The sweet-smelling woman with the bright lipstick behind the counter at the drugstore sometimes gave her a nickel and whispered, "Honey, buy yourself a candy bar." Minna chose a Hershey bar with nuts and gobbled it down before she got back to the bakery.

When Minna started carting bread around town, Fischer came looking for her. He'd loiter in a storefront opposite the bakery, waiting for Minna to return from school. Fifteen minutes later, once she'd eaten her cookie and drunk a glass of milk, Lila sent her back out with her little arms loaded like she was carrying kindling. Sometimes Franz walked with her, helping her keep the loaves from falling. When he wasn't with her, if Fischer wasn't in the garage fixing a car, he jaywalked between cars along the street, noting the brown Buick and robin's-egg

blue Ford, never missing the make or color of a car, to catch up with her.

"Well, just look at that," he'd say. "Fancy meeting you here, girlie." He'd grin and take the top loaves off her pile.

"Hi, Fischer." She laughed. After the first time, she expected him. They were magnets from the time Fischer showed up at Iris and Paulie's wedding reception, and he took his little girl in his arms for the first time. She had waddled to him, navigating around the silk stockings and trouser legs, and when he lifted her into his arms, she stuck a familiar finger in his mouth.

"Probably best not to mention this to Lila," he said of their encounters. They thought Lila never found out about them.

"There's Fischer!" He showed up every year on Christmas Eve and her birthday. Minna waited for him to come.

"Not again," Lila muttered under her breath. "He has no idea what to buy a young girl." *When is he going to find someone else to bother at Christmas?*

He waited outside the bakery till Lila put up the CLOSED sign. He peered between the slivers of frost on the bay window and over the few remaining pies while Lila squeezed the mop out and took the last swipes across the linoleum. Lila pretended she didn't know he was there until he banged on the glass with his elbow. He was as proud as Saint Nicholas, announcing his visit. He couldn't knock because his arms were full of presents for Minna, boxes glittering with the free gift wrap from J. C. Penney's. The gold bows were as large as his fists.

He was Father Christmas appearing from the shadows of early evening, a silhouette against the wintry street lamp. He got so cold standing there, his nose became a leaky faucet. He clutched his packages with brown mittens thick as Lila's baking mitts. He pulled his red stocking hat down over his ears. *How many fathers would go through this trouble if they'd had their daughter yanked away by a conniving mother?*

"I'll never wear the ugly thing." Minna had despaired the previous year when he'd brought her a full-length gray coat with black buttons larger than silver dollars that a matron would consider perfect. She waited until he left before saying it, but he saw her gleeful face turn glum.

In an earlier era, he brought thick wool dresses with hems almost to the floor. He added dark woolen stockings, the kind his

mother had donned back in the Dakotas, a carry-over from the old country, for the daughter he chose to view as demure.

Minna hoped the impossible, that he would bring something she loved as much as she liked the cheery wrapping on the packages. She couldn't help but be downhearted about the gray coat. She'd hinted to him about an ice-skating outfit, in periwinkle, to match her Prussian eyes. She thought for sure he'd remember because she'd emphasized "*our* Prussian-blue eyes." She wanted to glide over the ice in a dainty flared skirt with white tights, if Lila would allow her to go to the rink. That was always the question, though, guessing if Lila would give permission. Minna turned so gloomy when she opened the gift that Fischer's face fell. He looked like someone had called his favorite dog an ugly cur. She tried to be kind. She smiled and thanked him after recovering from her disappointment, and as soon as he was gone, she put it out on the shelf in the alley.

"Give me a few hours," Auntie Iris said when she saw the gray coat and Minna's pinched face. She sewed Minna's desire up in a few hours with pink crinoline to give the skirt extra lift. "That pink sets off the Prussian blue," Iris noted.

"One time only," Lila let her go skating with the girls from her English class, maybe because the outfit was from Iris—not Fischer. A boy from her algebra class was there, too, twirling and skating backward. Minna was mortified when he asked her to skate with him. She didn't know where to put her hands or how to move with him on the rink. Or how to act toward him when they were in their next class and learning equations.

Two

"Ain't you even one bit ashamed of yourself?" Fischer continued his rant next to the butterhorns. The pastry didn't help calm him down as Lila hoped. He was again dredging up his favorite beef about Lila and Willy, the wound reopened by Minna in August.

"You can get that silly notion out of your head," Lila had snapped at Minna about the soldiers. Not a hint of breeze came through the screen door in the kitchen. "You're not going up to Seely Lake." She pushed a damp strand of red hair off her forehead. It was insufferable by the ovens, and the workday had only started.

Something clicked inside Minna then. Lila didn't recognize it at that moment, and when she did—but that was much later—it was too late. Minna was determined to get out from under her mother's control, and refusing to let her go that day ratcheted it up a notch.

Minna could hold her temper, unlike Fischer. He hadn't figured out that yelling made Lila more obstinate. Minna understood that brick wall, and she wasn't going to slam against it. She went about her work, despite the perspiration.

"Hey, Clyde." The back of her blouse felt clammy. He was puffing and red in the face. "You ought to take a dunk in the river. Cool yourself off."

"Well, that ain't gonna happen. I might melt. But I'll have three of them doughnuts," he pointed to the ones with powdered sugar.

She said to the pharmacist, "I don't know how you can drink coffee when it's so hot in here."

"The hotter the better. That's what I say. Can't live without it." His skin looked like paste.

After the bakery closed, Minna wiped down the counters with ammonia as she did every day. Lila was scrubbing pans in the kitchen when Minna threw the rag down on the floor and pushed it and a half-full bucket of suds with one foot, leaving puddles on the flecked linoleum. Then she walked out. Marched right out the front door, went across Higgins Bridge, and headed down Brooks Street. She didn't even notice the cooling shade from the generous maples on the way to Fischer's auto repair shop.

She scouted between ailing cars until she found him lying under the body of a forest-green Packard, his face half-covered with oil, wearing a satisfied grin. Fischer was in top form when he was working on a car or fingering his accordion. He was happy in the presence of a woman, too, if she behaved as he wanted.

"Lila's been in bed with Uncle Will." Minna spoke down at him under the car, without even saying hello.

"Goddamn bitch!" He pushed himself out from under that car like someone had dumped gasoline on him. "How'd ya know that?" For almost a second he regretted cursing, but then his daughter was speaking of things that he would not allow her to know—the things that go on between men and women.

"Fifteen years," he mumbled to the chassis. Fifteen years and every day since, he would've bet money on Lila and Willy doing those things behind his back. *She's a cagey one, and Will's just as cagey.* What Minna said was no surprise.

After Lila walked out the door that last time, taking Minna with her but leaving behind a pot of bean soup simmering on the stove and a plate stacked with thick slices of bread and squares of spice cake in the middle of the table, it took Willy about two seconds to pack up and move out to Seattle. Lila moved back in with the Schneiders, up to her old room above the bakery, and Willy stayed away for five years, working at some high-powered repair shop. Fischer couldn't figure out how they could be together, but he sure felt like something was going on, even if they were five hundred miles apart.

Will showed up five years later, hoofing it from the Milwaukee depot. They hadn't seen or talked to each other since he had skipped town. "I'm just here visiting," he said.

"Yeah, sure," Fischer muttered.

"Can we just bury the hatchet?" Will practically pleaded, putting his hand out for his brother to shake.

"Not on your life." Fischer shook his head, spun on his heel, and walked back to the car he was repairing. Will followed, talking to his back.

"Nothin's ever happened between Lila and me." That was 100 percent more than Lila would tell Fischer. "Look't here, Fischer. I didn't hang around Lila when she left you. I think I've proved myself 'bout that." He wanted to say he loved her, that he'd been in love with her ever since he and Fischer rode their horses onto her papa's place over in the Dakotas twenty years before. She wasn't married to Fischer anymore and hadn't been for years, and Willy wanted to court her. He wasn't about to ask Fischer's permission. It wasn't Fischer's to give, but he wished he could at least speak the truth out in the open.

"How 'bout I come back and work for you?" he added. He was bold. Fischer put up his hand, but Will continued, overriding the hand, "We worked well together. Remember?"

"You were sniffin' on her from the get-go," Fischer spit out. "I plain don't care if I don't never see your face never again." Besides, Fischer didn't need the help. He had a good fellow working for him. A family man who showed up early and stayed late and knew a lot about fixing cars. Not as much as Fischer, but enough to do good work and keep the customers happy.

Will wished he could say, "Well, since we ain't goin' to work together, I'd like to start seeing Lila, just to keep things on the up and up." Maybe he would have, but Fischer slid under the chassis of a maroon Mercury and vanished.

Lila was in the dark about Minna tattling to Fischer. Sure, Minna had acted sore since she'd been told flat out that she wasn't going up to Seely. Lila wasn't blind. She saw the change in the girl but thought it would pass. When Fischer started snooping around, making his pronouncements, Lila couldn't know it was Minna who had gotten him going.

"She's my daughter, too," Fischer, next to the bread rack, said with a huff. "I don't want them stinkin' boys sniffin' around her." Lila thought, *She's as stubborn as you are.*

"How in the hell are you raisin' *my* daughter, anyway?" Truth was, she was wondering that, too, these past months. She'd become her guard, not her mother. All she needed was a rifle and a barbed-wire fence, and she'd be like the soldiers out at the fort, standing guard over the prisoners of war.

She didn't ask, "When did you get it into your head to act like a parent?" She had enough on her mind without his drama. She wondered if customers would complain because he'd bust in the shop like he did. They came to relax on Saturday mornings and leisurely read the paper, eat her doughnuts, and drink her coffee. If Fischer was going to explode in the bakery, his tank too full of anger to keep the cork in, she was going to have to find a way to stop him. It was disrupting. When he was at his garage under a chassis, or straddled over its insides dissecting the guts, she could be calm. Sometimes he showed up during the week, when he walked over the Higgins Bridge to pay his electric bill at the Montana Power Company and counted out one silver dollar at a time.

He found Minna, Thursday afternoon in the alley, puffing it up with a soldier. "What the hell you doin' with my daughter?" he had said right into the face of the very handsome uniform.

Lila had found them kissing a few days earlier. "Do you intend on releasing my counter girl so she can get back to taking care of customers?" She was sure she'd seen the boy yank his hand out from under Minna's sweater. She was surprised at how calmly she spoke. She didn't give Minna so much as a glance. She had just come out to put up bread that hadn't sold on a shelf Will had built for her in the alley. It was high enough to be safe from roaming dogs, but low enough for the people who lived under the bridge or over by the tracks. Martha Schneider would be gratified. When she was running the bakery, she had hustled down Higgins looking for the cold and hungry at the end of the workday, and if she didn't spot them huddled in front of the Stockman Bar, she'd wander up Ryman Street or over to Front Street. She wouldn't come back until her arms were empty. If the weather had turned, she'd bring along a jacket left in the shop and not claimed in six months, or a woolly cap, or one of Franz's flannel shirts. Poor Franz. He had his favorite shirts, but when Martha got sick and tired of looking at the gray plaid day in and day out, she would give it a good wash and have it in the hands of a person she wouldn't have to look at every minute of the day.

Lila didn't speak one word to Minna when she came out to the alley with the bread. Didn't even look at her. *Lord knows I won't mention to Fischer where I saw that boy's hand. That kid still has his baby feathers, for goodness' sake.* He had a thick shank of golden hair and drawled when he answered her question.

"Yes, ma'am," he replied.

"Okay, then."

"Don't want to, though." He blushed slightly, with shoulders straight and tall, in all his Brylcreem boyishness. Minna would relish that response.

"What's your name, young man?" She was surprised at his cheeky nerve.

"Archie, ma'am."

"Well, Archie, she's sixteen."

"Lila," Minna cried.

He laughed. "Just the right age, then, ma'am. Where I come from, girls already have at least one baby by that age."

"Not where we come from. You need to get going now."

❧

"You know, Fischer," she said. He'd helped himself to another butterhorn, eating it near the ovens. He had to lean toward her because she spoke so softly. Chair legs were screeching in the shop. She heard the bells tinkle at the front door. A few customers with muffled voices remained, unwilling to let that frigid chill sneak up under their jackets.

"I wonder if you are blowing off steam because of Willy and me, or Minna. If it's about me, it's none of your business. If it's Minna, then you'd better settle down because your yelling is not going to make it any better. And"—she set her jaw—"if you want to tell me something, you do not barge into my shop and make a public announcement about our private matters."

"You're one to talk. You got some nerve, Lila. Always have to be the one in control. You get that girl straightened out, and wipe that cheap lipstick off her." He rapped his knuckles on her worktable on his way out the back door.

"All clear?" Iris hustled through toward the back door a few minutes later, an unlit cigarette dangling from her mouth.

Three

"Wanna talk about it, Lila?" Will was in his stocking feet, and she didn't hear him slip down the stairs. His big right toe searched like a periscope from a hole at the tip of his white sock.

"You heard him, then? Impossible not to, I guess." She shook her head. She'd clattered the trays and pans loud enough to put the fire department on alert. If she hadn't caught a glimpse of Will's T-shirt out of the corner of her eye, she would have jumped. Strands of red hair strayed from under the blue bandanna, and the front of her apron was blotchy and smelled of ammonia.

"Here." He took the pans she was lugging. "Let me do those." He carried them into the kitchen, turned on the hot-water tap, and waited for the water to get warm.

"Did you just get up now?" His tawny hair poked straight up like broom bristles. It didn't sit well with her that he was sleeping late.

"Not quite." His breath smelled of sleep, and he sneaked a kiss onto her cheek. She almost backed away, but he snapped his blue suspenders to show how happy it made him, and she relented.

"You're hopeless." She grinned and took a deep breath.

"Well, you're not," he retorted. "You are the best thing a guy could wake up to in the middle of the day." He laughed. "Good God, that wind was howling like a dog. Between it and Fischer, I'm lucky I got any sleep at all."

"Well, some of us don't have the luxury of sleeping in broad daylight."

"I know, I know." He knew she didn't like it, but he was no slouch and needed to explain. "I was workin' at the garage on a dang Cadillac till who knows when. Some guy had to have it for his job before morning."

"What time did you get back?"

"I dunno. Maybe 'bout one thirty. It was so dark I ran into the corner of a building. See that?" He pulled his hair back to show the red mark on his forehead.

13

"I see it." She almost kissed it but stopped herself.

"You shoulda seen this guy, Lila. Traveling salesman. Looked like Teddy Roosevelt with them little round glasses and wide as a bull. He had these fingers thick as cigars. Said he had to get to Butte or he'd lose his job, blabbing at me the whole time and leaning against the front fender." Willy was busy explaining and not paying attention to the washing. Bubbles from too much soap in the dishwater flowed over the lip of the sink.

"Watch what you're doing!" Lila threw him a dish towel. She hated unnecessary messes.

"I bet I had to go around that fat belly fifty times." He mopped up the water. "He kept waving a wad of dollar bills at me, too. Boy, oh boy, Lila, I could be a millionaire." He grinned. "Then you couldn't say no to me, no more."

"Says who?"

He stopped washing and looked at her but couldn't read her face. "He had this fancy suit on, see. Bet he was itching to get to some dizzy dame. I finally told him to put his money away. I'd get his car done for him. I had that V-12 engine purring so you couldn't tell it was even runnin'. He got in it and asked me if the motor was turned on. What a knot head!" He shook his head.

"So you got today off? Here all this time I thought you were at work." Lila slipped up behind him and wrapped one of Iris's fancy aprons around his waist. He twisted around, trying to catch her cheek and plant a peck, but she was too quick for him. "Not so fast, mister."

He scraped the hardened sugar from a pan. His forearms were taut. She loved how the muscles stood to attention when he worked. She didn't let him know, though.

He'd only say something stupid, like ask her, "Why do you like them so much?" and that would somehow diminish it. She found comfort when she thought of his hands, though. Sometimes she would be cleaning the kitchen when he returned from work. He would jump in and grab a pile of trays.

"No, no," she'd cry like she was in pain and grimace at the grease still clinging to his arms, thick under the fingernails. "Just look at those hands"—resisting the urge to kiss them—"I've got enough grease to contend with. I don't need somebody's motor oil on top of it!"

"So, what I'm wonderin' is"—he shook out the damp dish towel—"if you'd knowed I was up there today, you'da paid me a visit?" He winked at her. She didn't answer. "Yep. I was here the whole time.

Boss didn't want to help out last night. Said he had a party to go to. Told me if I got the Cadillac fixed not to come in today."

"You hungry then? Want me to fix you a sandwich or blachinda?" He was dancing around her wiping the pans and putting them under her worktable. She was scouring the metal top, punishing it till it screeched in agony from the wire brush.

"I'm hungry for something." He was coy. "Okay, break my heart, sweetheart," he said with mock disappointment when she handed him a plate with pork blachinda. It took him two bites to devour it. He grinned when she handed him a second one.

"You don't have to eat it all in one bite, you know." She tried to prevent the smile from stretching across her face. It warmed her right to the pit of her stomach, the way he ate her food. While she waited for sleep to come on sleepless nights, she pictured him, eating her food. His delight quieted the fears she kept at bay during the daylight hours, mostly for Minna. Willy wasn't a mindless turkey who gobbled his food. He tasted how flavors interacted on his tongue, the suggestion of a certain spice. On the odd rainy Sundays when Minna was off cutting cloth with Iris, he savored Lila in his bedroom above the bakery.

"Yeah, but who knows when I'll get another." He grabbed her around the waist, but she shooed him off with her dish towel.

"I'll never get finished here at this rate." She wanted to get home ahead of Minna, who was helping Iris meet a big order from the girls at Alpha Phi sorority for an important ball. Already they had finished ten gowns, and they had four more to do. Minna cut the materials from Iris's designs, and the two worked together to perfect the finished seams.

Lila envied the pair, how they worked together, the way they laughed. They giggled at each other's crazy jokes. She was less anxious when Minna was with Iris. Her imagination preyed on her otherwise, when she didn't know where the girl was or who she was with. The once dutiful if reluctant daughter had changed, it seemed, overnight, and she appeared to have one purpose—to oppose her. Lila watched the transformation unfold, still hoping the girl would come to her senses. But she couldn't shake the dread.

"What's wrong?" Willy was troubled when Lila frowned. She put the dirty linens in a bag to take with her.

"It's Minna," she said. "I'm not looking forward to going home."

"I guess I coulda figured that," he said softly. "I can go with you and throw in my two cents. For what it's worth." She shook her head sadly. "That would only add fuel to the fire."

❦

Iris was both a blessing and a curse. She had too much sway with Minna about what she wore. She even encouraged a little flirting with a hem or neckline. Lila wouldn't have it.

"I swear, Iris," she bawled her sister out after one particularly unpleasant weekend. Iris was stacking perfect loaves of white bread in a rack behind the counter. "She is sixteen. Why do you put such ideas into her head? You could see to China in that skirt you sewed for her. I made her go back upstairs and change it." Minna had looked at Lila like she wanted to bite her head off. It almost made Lila stop breathing, but she wouldn't back down, and Minna knew it.

Minna had stormed up the stairs. "I hate you!" Her eyes were steely when she came back down wearing a modest but pleasant dress. They bored holes into Lila that made the mother tighten her stomach. Lila held her shoulders rigid and glared right back.

Just like Iris. Her sister had been that stubborn when they were back on the farm in the Dakotas. They'd get into it, the two of them, like elk locking their antlers in rutting season, and neither would back down until they hurt each other.

"Just remember, I'm waiting up for you," Lila had threatened. She had sent her right back up the stairs.

When she came back down, she wore a lovely two-piece blue outfit. "Now you look nice," Lila complimented her.

"Right." Minna grimaced.

"Be home no later than midnight." Lila told her before Archie knocked. Minna shrugged but didn't flinch.

"If you are late, get ready for a bucket of cold water in the face at four o'clock." She didn't recognize this girl any longer. Her quick, bright daughter seemed careless, apathetic almost, like she didn't recognize or didn't care that she was putting herself in danger. Lila saw the warning flares exploding like fireworks in the night skies. Where had the little girl—running down Higgins, her coat askew, arms loaded with bread—gone? She didn't know or like this murky and undecipherable girl.

"I'll take good care of her." Archie was wily, and she disliked his overly enthusiastic grin. "I'll get her back by midnight," he assured her, but it didn't feel comforting. She would not be able to appeal to his better side if she told him her concerns. He only added to her string of worries. She would lose if she had to go toe-to-toe with him. Certainly she would be even further diminished in Minna's eyes.

"Fischer's right," she said to herself after they'd gone, much as she wished otherwise. She wondered how *he* would handle Minna. *Would he give her a black eye or lock her up?* Minna had always been determined, but she had found love from Franz at the very beginning. He had taught her the importance of being respectful, even when it disagreed with her feelings.

"*Liebe*," he counseled her, putting his paw over a scrawny shoulder, "you don't have to agree with nothin' you don't agree to," and chuckled, pleased how his words came out. "You just tell it to yourself like you was sayin' it to the other person, see? Like it's your secret. It works better that way." He'd tap her cheek with his finger. She had opinions all the time. He could see them coming before they got there. They were like thunderstorms coming across her face, and he'd smile at her when he saw them blowing through, and that was enough.

"*Du, du liegst mir im Herzen*," he sang in his deep baritone when she was fussy. He tapped his heart when he sang the word *Herzen*. She pushed him away as she got older, but he still could make her laugh if he started to sing. She was with him in the end, when he was dying. She held his hand, and when she saw his lips moving, she leaned over so he could talk to her. Instead, he weakly sang, "My Home's in Montana, I Wear a Bandanna," smiling with his eyes closed. His pillow was sopping when Martha replaced her at his side.

Lila continued to hold a firm, invisible line, regardless of Minna's apparent determination to run over it. It knocked Minna back, but she pretended not to care. She was unreadable. Lila needed a code book to solve her.

"Do you have enough to keep yourself fat and happy until Monday?" Lila had asked Willy before she left the bakery. She hadn't recovered from Fischer's outburst, but Willy had cheered her up. "I could bring over some soup tomorrow." Lila had tugged on one of his suspenders, wishing she didn't have to leave to face Minna.

"Just bring yourself, and I won't ask for one other thing. I can take care of myself, you know." He untied the fancy apron and handed it to her.

"You can?" She made a disbelieving grin.

"Yeah. I can. Big boy here." He poked his thumbs at his chest. "But I sure wouldn't mind the company if it's you." He pulled the bandanna off her head with one hand and twirled it in the air while brushing his other through the red hair that had been smothered.

"Fischer can be such a stinker." She took her own apron off and put the two in with the other laundry she was taking.

"So I heard. Can't sleep when that guy comes around and shoots off his mouth." He finished the other blachinda, and she put a doughnut and coffee at his elbow to work on later. "Why's he bent out of shape this time? 'Bout us?"

"He says it's about Minna. He caught her smoking in the alley."

"Yeah. I seen that myself. I told her you wouldn't like it."

"And, what'd she say? No, let me guess. Probably she told you it was none of your business, right?"

"Worse. Said she don't care what you think. Said she's just biding her time. Turned her back on me as usual."

"Biding her time till what, I'd like to know."

Will shrugged. He knew about biding time. How many times had he asked Lila to marry him? He hadn't let a month go by that he didn't ask her again. It was always the same answer.

"If I was to get married again, you know it would be with you." His stomach turned sour when she said it. She had worked something out in her mind that went against them being together. At first she'd answer, "I've got my reasons, Will."

He wasn't one to stick his nose in. She had her reasons, and he would live with that. But that didn't stop him from asking. Maybe she would get to the reason one of these times, and if she did, then maybe she would hear herself, and she would see that marrying him was not such a bad thing. But the real answer squeaked out once.

"I can't." She was angry.

"Why for heaven's sake not?" He pushed harder than he wanted.

"I'd be going against Fischer."

"What?" Willy cried. He couldn't believe it. "What's he going to do? Come after us with a gun?"

"It's not like that," she told him. "Can't we just leave things as they are? Don't we have more happiness than most people?" What was he going to say to that? He was tentative from then on. If he mentioned it, she said, "If you really want to get married, Will, you should find someone who won't turn you down. You're a catch, you know." That surprised him. She didn't believe in handing out compliments.

"There ain't no one else, Lila, and you know that." He'd said it so quiet she had to strain to hear him. He wore the disappointment on his face.

"Why do we need to get married anyway?"

"We wouldn't have to sneak around to do what everybody already knows we're doin'," he said as if she needed reminding. "We'd be setting the right example for Minna, too. Be parents to her. Instead of me being the uncle Fischer tells her, and she believes, stole you away from him."

"Minna would be just as snotty—if not snottier—to you if we got married." As it was, she barely acknowledged him. Unless Lila stepped in when he asked her a question, she ignored him.

Lila didn't tolerate disrespect. "Behave yourself, Minna." Minna shot her a frigid glare.

"Well, I bet if we talked about this with Iris, she could say something to Minna and make her come around. Iris likes me, you know." He winked at her, and they laughed.

"I know she likes *looking* at you." Lila smirked, not adding that Iris was partial to viewing his backside.

"Oh, Lordy," Iris remarked one day when she was working the counter; Will had walked out of the bakery after his lunch break from the Starr Garage. "Just take a long look at that."

He had eaten two beef blachinda and drunk two cups of coffee. "A third one, Iris," he told her, "will either make me fall asleep or wire me higher than a kite. Either way, I wouldn't get any more work done today." He waved at her with his wool cap and then gave her a big bow near the door and walked away with a little squiggle in his hips. She laughed aloud, which drew the attention of the only other person in the shop.

"I sure wouldn't mind measuring him for a pair of pants." Her husky voice carried right across the shop, even though she thought she had spoken under her breath. The pharmacist sitting near the window stopped with his last bite of cherry pie in midair. He wore a stern look, either from sniffing too many chemicals or from being too Lutheran.

"Oops." This time she did whisper.

Four

"*I*ris, I'd like to ask a favor."

"Well, for criminy's sake, Lila, you don't even need to ask," she exclaimed, but she wondered what she was promising. "What is it?"

"I want *Tante* Catherine to meet Minna. She's growing up and hasn't even met her great-aunt." Minna had just turned twelve years old.

"You want to drag that poor girl back to South Dakota for that?" Iris was mulish. She wasn't ready to let go of old grievances.

"Yes, I do," Lila said in a tone that meant she wasn't about to discuss it further.

"You're gonna take her out of school for that?"

"Yes. That's what I want to do. So would you be willing to hold down the fort for one week?"

"Why only a week?" Iris clucked.

Lila had counted out the days, one entire day on the Milwaukee there, and one back, leaving them five days to visit.

"How about eight days? Or maybe six?" Iris nudged her, jabbing at her sister's precise and predictable timetable. She stopped short, not wanting to discourage Lila. "Of course I'll do it. You go and have the time of your life." She doubted that anyone would enjoy a visit to Tante Catherine. It was gratifying that Lila was asking a favor, something that happened less often than a solar eclipse.

"I'm just worried it will interfere with one of your projects." Lila frowned. Iris was filling an order for a local society lady invited to an important tea party.

"I want to make a bold statement when I come into that room!" the matronly woman had declared.

"I am *not* a seamstress." Iris glared when someone came to her with some silly pattern they thought adorable and couldn't live without. "Do you know what this is?" She'd slam her palm at the pattern. "This is second-rate stuff," she'd answer for them while they stood with open mouths, wondering if they were expected to respond. "If there is something I cannot abide"—she'd glower and pause, letting them wait to be enlightened—"it is insipid designs made by illustrators funneled through design schools and molded into thinking like their second-rate teachers. They have certificates! Certificates!" she emphasized to her newest customers because inevitably, they would become her customers. "And"—another pause for emphasis—"they are confident that they are the cutting edge of fashion." She harrumphed.

She did not solicit business. Paulie supported them just fine. She was a walking advertisement, wearing her own designs. Unknown women came up to her, some of them quite brash.

"Where can I find that outfit?" A middle-aged woman with a too-large bosom and no hips muscled past another woman.

"She didn't even say a decent hello," Iris griped to Paulie. "Didn't introduce herself or say, 'Excuse me!' Like I was doorstop."

"You couldn't have bought that outfit around here," they would inform her in the ready-to-wear section of the Mercantile, or by the perfumes in the drugstore, at the florist shop in the Florence Hotel, or even next to the apple fritters in Lila's bakery.

"I don't repeat my work," she huffed when the woman found she was the designer and pleaded for one just like it. Iris was all the while sizing up the woman's shape, making notes of the attractive attributes the woman possessed, and then creating a design that would be right for her.

"However, I can make something that will suit you better," she'd sniff. She studied the shoulders to determine their breadth, and then she made a mental adjustment to add more or less shoulder padding.

"I'd like puffy sleeves," a woman with Brunhilda upper arms requested, and Iris acquiesced, but only whipped a hint of fabric into the design to satisfy the whim. If a woman had well-shaped legs, like her own, she added a high-low hemline with ruche.

"It is a formal occasion," one woman spoke solemnly, and since she was not yet old—but certainly no longer young—Iris created a lavender gown in metallic lamé with a daring open back.

"You must accessorize your gown with sling-back heels," she advised another woman, who possessed particularly pleasing ankles that should not be minimized by a classic pump. Iris didn't receive complaints. If she had, she would have dismissed "their ignorance" without another thought.

"Go to someone else," she would have told them. Her creations appeared and drew attention at university functions and fundraisers. Her name was circulated in whispers and only by word-of-mouth by those willing to share the secret.

Paulie turned the nursery into a sewing room, and designing and cutting fabric soaked up the spare moments she would have devoted to a child. She loved being at the bakery, too, though, because at home she could crack jokes to the sewing machine all day long, but no one was laughing back or turning red with embarrassment. She divided her time between the two places.

"Well, it will cut into my work time for one of my hoity-toity patrons," she said with a chuckle to Lila. "But hey, I would love to keep the bakery running." She was making a rose-flowered rayon dress, cut on the bias. She wanted it to cascade like a waterfall over the tiny breasts and almost invisible hips of a university professor's wife who would be attending her first university wives' luncheon. Iris sucked in her breath with each piece she ran under the machine needle. As with each of her creations, she got a knot in her stomach and ignored the fact that for the past fifteen years she had been creating sensational clothing. Each time was the first time. *How will that slippery fabric mold to that scarecrow frame? Will the orphan have the guts to walk into that room with her head on straight? God forbid if she grabs a piece of the skirt and twists it up.*

"Get the heck out of here," she yelled to the wall if she made a mistake on a piece of cloth. She tossed her misfits into a pile where Paulie had once imagined putting the first child's crib when he built their bungalow. Her disasters grew into a mound of green and yellow and orange and glittering blue.

"It's not like you're going to be gone forever," she said to Lila with a sniff. "And who knows, maybe the governor will show up while you're gone. Oh, I would love to get going on him." Lila rolled her eyes at the ambushes Iris would set for her customers.

"We'll leave in three weeks, then," Lila determined. Iris's brain took a spin right there, and she hatched a plan for Minna that very afternoon.

Iris worked three mornings a week at the bakery counter. Some hours crept by in spite of a steady line of customers filing in and out, tinkling the doorbell. She came to life if a quirky person arrived.

"Need some coffee, I see, to get that engine of yours slowed down," she crowed at a brassy fellow who was running his mouth in the queue to anyone who was willing to listen. He didn't stop even after they turned their backs on him. "Make that two chocolate doughnuts," he interjected between his other conversations. He probably didn't get the gist of her comment, but Iris was satisfied.

"Lila, I can just about stand to hear that bell ring so many times in one morning," she complained numerous times to no avail. "Can't you figure out something else?"

"The Schneiders put it on the door, and it's going to stay." Lila was adamant. "Besides, when I'm back at the ovens and the only one here, I've got to run out front to fill the order and ring up the sale."

"Here," Iris said, plopping a sticky cinnamon roll on a plate and passing it over the counter without seeing if there was an actual human hand reaching for it. If she wasn't intrigued by anyone in the line, she puzzled out complex sewing problems like how to fold in leg-of-mutton sleeves for a gown a lady wanted to wear to the Foresters' Ball.

The day Lila asked her to mind the bakery for a week, instead of going home at one o'clock as usual to "make my Paulie a delicious supper," Iris stayed and made work for herself. Everyone knew that Paulie prepared almost all their meals. Iris settled in at her sewing machine once she was home, and if Paul didn't remind her to come to supper, she would not notice.

"You're still here this late?" Lila came through with a bucket of suds to wash down the empty shelves preparing for the next day's rolls and doughnuts and tarts.

"I've got to get everything ready before you leave, don't I? Spic and span," Iris retorted, as if Lila would leave it any other way. "I won't have time to keep up with it all when you're gone." It was Minna's job after school to shift the wrought-iron chairs, the wooden stools, and the high backs to sweep under the tables. Lila followed behind and mopped with a smelly solution of ammonia that bit into the nostrils. "Phew!" Iris nearly gagged.

"The stronger the better," Lila huffed.

That afternoon, Minna strolled into the bakery cradling a lonely, battered textbook to find that her work had been done for her. "Let's go, missy." Iris grabbed her by the arm. Lila was in the back banging pans into their beds. Iris tossed aside the soggy rag. "We got places to go and people to see, Minny-girl."

Iris had wiped down walls, searching for any uninvited cobwebs while waiting for the last school bell to ring. All the while she was assembling ideas for outfits her niece should wear. "She'll make an impression on those hayseeds in Aberdeen! Empire dress, I believe, with flared skirt, and crinoline to add body, a bolero jacket, hmm," she

23

thought. "Maybe plaid, or burnt sienna, and a clutch coat to match." Her niece was only twelve but almost everyone would get that wrong unless they were nosy and asked brusquely, "How old are you?"

"We're going to knock their socks off, Minna." She laughed pulling her through the bakery door and across Higgins.

"Whose socks, Auntie Iris?"

"Oh, I love that one!" Minna squealed as she turned each page in the pattern books at the Missoula Mercantile. They'd already spent over an hour poring over Butterick and Vogue patterns for the right traveling outfit, the tops of their heads bumping now and again in their enthusiasm.

"Well, let's analyze this, Minna. We have to think about how suitable it will be for getting on and off the train and the bus, and in and out of the car. "Lord knows what *Onkel* Jacob is driving these days." Iris shuddered. "Then we have to decide on the material."

"That's the one!" They pointed to it at the same time as they flipped the next page. An hour later they were still picking out fabrics, and the store was going to close soon. Iris calculated and considered practicalities while Minna imagined what she would look like in front of the mirror. Iris, in her head, was altering the cut and the length, adding a surprise swatch of turquoise blue just above the waistline. She could not follow the directions from the first step to the finish of any pattern. It would only agitate her, and the material would fly out of her hands in exasperation. "Idiots," she'd bark at the wall in front of her sewing machine and stamp on the treadle.

"How do you know it's going to turn out when you don't do what the pattern tells you?" Lila never could follow where Iris was going with her designs.

"Well, how do you know your cakes aren't going to fall flat, Lila, or taste terrible when you throw in things that nobody would dream of putting in, like those pomegranate seeds? I don't notice you using a recipe." Lila threw out her own share of discards on the reject heap and did not set them out for hungry people who would not quibble over the quality of fare.

"Because I won't be satisfied until I get it the way I want."

"Ditto."

Five

"Oh, my Minna is going to look so grand!" Iris said aloud between the aisles of fabric.

Her blond niece, too soon tall, was two aisles away running her fingers over flashy cottons. Then Minna peeked around a corner and flashed a grin. "Hi," she said happily.

"Oh, shoot! I'm gonna miss that girl," Iris mumbled when Minna had slipped into another aisle with bolts of cloth. Iris muttered some math calculations, standing on her tiptoes peering over the gabardine and butcher's linen.

"Hey, it's only for a week," she reminded herself, still tickled about how she'd teased Lila about the exact schedule she'd made. Iris tugged the end of powder-blue broadcloth. She crumpled it and wrinkled her nose. "Too stiff to follow the lines of Minna's figure." She did the same with the limp viscose, which was already tired out and ready to give up on life.

"I might have known it was you," the clerk said behind her.

Iris jumped, turning around quickly. Ever since Papa had beaten her when she was a teenager, leaving an indelible scar that started on her cheek and ended at her collarbone, she could not abide anyone approaching her back without warning.

"You don't need to be sneaking up on me, Eunice," she snapped.

Eunice pushed her horn-rimmed glasses up flat to her face, as there were no nosepieces to hold them on the bridge. She didn't need glasses, only wore them to minimize the fact that she had one working eye. She'd had the tortoise-shell frames shipped all the way from England and delivered to the Mercantile so her plumber husband wouldn't know how much she spent. She had seen one other lady in town wearing that brand, a woman who had stayed for two weeks at the Florence Hotel, sporting a fine black-sable stole to match her glasses. She also had bright red hair, which perturbed Eunice to no end because she herself would not dare go home to her husband "looking like a siren." He'd throw her right out on the street. She did reveal plump cleavage where her broad collar fastened. She'd sewn a second hook and eye above the lower one, and hooked it shut in the mornings when she dressed for work before her plumber husband dropped her off at the curb by the Mercantile. Inside the store, after removing her coat, she unhooked that top one. At the end of the workday she'd hook it again before he picked her up in his dull-blue Chevrolet step van advertising PETERSON PLUMBING UNPLUGS! on both sides and the rear of the vehicle.

"Now, now, Iris. What are you carrying on about? Need any help?" She snickered. The semiofficial Mercantile uniform of navy-blue linen, white collar, and brown belt contended for the limited space at her waist. "I could hear you gabbing clear over there by my cash register. You must be cooking up something good, blabbing away like that." The trouble with Eunice was that you never knew if you were looking straight at her, or if she was doing the same back at you.

Iris shifted her head a little to the left, then to the right, trying to find the middle of Eunice's line of vision. "I wasn't gabbing *or* blabbing, Eunice. I was measuring fabric. I'd think you'd know that by now."

Iris talked out loud to her fabrics. "Now this is what needs to happen," she'd explain to the fibers what she required from them to allow for the adjustments to her brainstorms.

"Here's a handy thing to know," she instructed Minna, measuring three feet of fabric without a yardstick, using the end of her nose and stretching the fabric out to the end of her arm. Minna nodded. *She's no dumbbell.* Iris mused. Why couldn't Lila see that?

Iris wasn't crazy about Lila hauling Minna back to the Dakotas, what with the drought scorching the middle of the United States. It had already turned thousands of workers into hobos who were riding the trains searching for any kind of job.

There was that other business going on in Germany, too. She didn't waste time worrying about what could happen since most of the time it didn't, but then Paulie got jeered at and was called a "wop." Like Paulie, she and Lila had accents because they had learned German at home first, before they started school.

"America is not going to go to war," she tried to assure Paulie, trying to soothe her own fears. That crazy nut was on the other side of the ocean. "We're safe as two barnyard cats." She brushed against him. But when the name-calling grew worse, she wondered.

People mostly dismissed the belligerent little loudmouth in Europe. He was a strange barking guy with a mouse of a mustache.

"He'll never last," people persuaded each other, shaking their heads in the early thirties. "Too ridiculous to lead Germany," someone else added, while Hitler's audiences grew in size and violence mushroomed. From a distance, it seemed inconceivable he could touch the deepest, the most hidden of feelings. He admonished German citizens, criticized them for becoming victims. He pierced their outrage, their wounds gorged with pus, to make them explode. He lifted them up, called them the master race, and then tore them down, chiding them for letting an inferior race run over them. He was brash, he said what they feared saying out loud and kept buried behind their daily faces.

Iris was a realist. German Americans had been terribly mistreated during the Great War. She'd heard her parents whisper about it through the paper-thin walls at night. She dreaded that, because of Hitler, this could ever happen again. Minna peeked around the bolts of material and made a funny face.

"What do you think of this, Auntie?" she held a forest-green wool next to her face.

"Look here, Minna," Iris said to her niece, who had circled past the muslins and her favorite fabrics, the taffetas and velvets, before returning to her aunt's elbow. "You don't even have to take the bolt off the shelf, and you already know if it will work with your design." Minna had made some good choices with colors and textures. For a twelve-year-old to understand basic construction, well, the only thing that could have made Iris any happier would be if Minna were her daughter. She felt Minna's breath on her neck as she leaned closer, concentrating and absorbing how her aunt used classic patterns to transform cloth into masterpieces.

"Figuring it out, are we?" Eunice buzzed past them. She was not herself a seamstress. Her talent was in sales. She memorized the patterns that changed in the books from year to year and knew her stock blindfolded. She directed her customers confidently to the precise bolt of fabric required in a pattern. If the customer was confused or uncertain about what to wear for a certain occasion, Eunice had just the pattern the woman needed. She was the only female salesperson in the store to achieve outstanding employee of the year at the annual Christmas buffet, and be presented with a brooch watch with FOR FAITHFUL SERVICE inscribed on the back. Without fail she pinned it to the right lapel of her dress daily. It was her medal as well as her timepiece, only her bad eye couldn't focus on its face, so it did not perform a functional purpose.

She explained to Mr. Peterson, following the award ceremony, that the brooch meant she was an outstanding employee. "Can't figure what a clock's got to do with that." He was organizing lengths of galvanized iron pipe into the back of his van, positioning them between valves and elbows.

"It's a watch, not a clock." She stamped her foot and explained how she could get a customer in and out of the Merc in less than thirty minutes! "Don't that mean something? And more than that"—she raised her voice to overcome the clang from his pipes and stems, stealing the attention she deserved—"I can send them on their way spending two times more than they expected when they walked into the store."

Mr. Peterson, being a man of common sense who counted his cents, told her, "That don't sound so good to me. Ain't you fleecin' 'em?"

Eunice adapted her style to her customers' preferences so as not to miss a sale. "Don't need your advice," Iris told Eunice the first time she met her, and Eunice stretched her customer smile farther than normal to accommodate her.

"Is that going to be it, girls?" Eunice looked toward them as she finished measuring and folding their purchases. She must have been looking at them as there were no other customers at the cash register.

"It'll just be a minute," Eunice told the pair when she tucked the cash register receipt and Iris's dollars into the pneumatic canister. It was sucked up into some ethereal part of the store. Iris knew what her costs would be, arriving at the dollar amount before Eunice put the figures into the adding machine.

While they waited for the canister to make its return trip with the change, Eunice asked Minna, "You're about fourteen now, aren't you, honey?" Eunice looked in the general direction of Minna. The girl shrugged, Iris bumped her with her hip, just enough to knock her off balance, and they tried not to start giggling.

"You're lucky to have an aunt who loves to sew," Eunice went on, her one eye watching for the canister, not the faces that tried to hold back their laughter.

"Eunice, how many times to do I have to tell you? I don't sew. I *design!*"

"Well, I am sure, Iris, that means something very special to you, but don't you sit in front of a sewing machine just like every other lady who comes in here to buy cloth and who calls it *sewing?*"

Iris shook her head. Eunice's head was stuffed with cabbage, and so was the rest of her body. She did have those slender legs, though, and if the store manager—and her plumber husband—would not have kicked up a fuss, Eunice would have come to work in sling-back heels. And she would have her hair dyed red. Iris imagined the perfect outfit for Eunice and her expensive-looking legs while they waited. She couldn't help imagining what she could make for the clerk, but Eunice would never know how good she could have looked.

"Three weeks," Iris prompted herself, to get Minna's wardrobe completed. Between the bakery and filling another customer's order, she required at least two fittings with Minna. She tried to keep her feet from doing a dance while they waited for Eunice's pneumatic cylinder. She kept her tongue, or she would have said, "Eunice, when did you get to be such a genius?" She tapped her fingers on the back of the engraved brass cash register, humming "Little White Lies" and rolling her eyes at Minna, who giggled.

Iris walked Minna back to the bakery and playfully nudged her with her hip, but without the usual banter. "You seem sad now, Auntie," Minna noted.

Iris had been in high spirits as they rummaged through cloth and dreamed up designs for Minna's travel. But the dread had returned.

"I'm just fine, sweetie." Iris smiled. "I'm going over the patterns in my head is all." She couldn't shake her apprehension. The most recent news was of prescient Germans packing suitcases filled with valuables and heading for the borders.

"Why does he have to shout so loud?" Paulie had whispered in a flickering newsreel that came before Charlie Chaplin's movie, *The Great Dictator.*

"Because he doesn't have anything good to say," Iris whispered back.

"Shh!" came from a man behind them. "I want to hear this fella even if I don't get a damn word of the German."

For those who didn't speak German, Hitler seemed a vulgar, angry man you would go out of your way to slide past in a dark alley. Charlie Chaplin mimicked him, making him seem silly and inept. Hitler and Mussolini and spaghetti—clever Chaplin, portraying a monster evolving into a peace lover. There was still time—and hope—that the momentum would hit an immovable force.

"All he asks for is absolute obedience," Iris protested, not wanting to give into her anxiety. "Like my goddamn Papa," Iris swore when they were back in their cozy bungalow.

Paulie didn't like her to talk like that. "Iris, Iris, please. Please use other words." Those hurt his ears and his heart. He would genuflect at Saint Francis Xavier at seven o'clock the next morning and feel ashamed that God had to suffer disrespect.

Six

"Anything you have, missus." Six or seven men a day knocked on the bakery's back door in the middle of the crippling Depression. The bakery stayed solvent because of Lila's firm hand.

"You can't be runnin' to the door to feed every Tom, Dick, and Harry." Willy fretted because she wouldn't turn anyone away.

"That could be me. Or you," she said of the guys who hadn't seen a razor in quite some time. Most wore sorry-looking jackets closed with twine, the soles rotting away on their boots. Sometimes a big toe stuck out. Willy was concerned for her safety and had the smart idea of installing a shelf out in the alley.

"Thank you, ma'am. You're very kind," a man with a punched-down hat that had gone too many rounds said, not looking at her.

"It's not right, Willy." She was torn. "I can't refuse someone when Minna and I, and you," she added, "are eating well and sleeping warm."

She waited for the government to figure things out. "It has to," she insisted to Willy. "That Roosevelt is going to give them jobs," she nodded in agreement with herself. But the men kept knocking. Once in a while, it was a woman with hollow holes for eyes. Lila would have her hands in dough, or boiling pie fruits, or spreading icing over cookies. If they came at ten o'clock, she was assembling fillings for blachinda. She put a bin inside the back door for the blachinda that didn't sell. She smeared peanut butter on slices of leftover loaves.

When they were young girls, Mama had sent Iris and her off to school with hard-boiled eggs in their lunch pails, saying, "So you can use your heads to learn your lessons good enough for the teacher."

Lila added protein to stave off the hunger pangs so the hobos could clear their heads, too. Bread would make them feel full faster, but the protein would sustain them until they took to the rails again and headed to the coast or to Butte to find work. She didn't like to hand out sugary foods like cinnamon rolls or cookies, but if there were leftovers, she did so.

"Everyone has a sweet tooth," she consoled herself, "and needs a treat once in a while."

Six days a week, four o'clock in the morning, Lila started the day. When her bread dough was ready, she made cinnamon rolls. Then she rolled out piecrusts and the dough for blachinda. She had a fine selection of cookies, including chocolate nut with a hint of coffee flavor and balls dipped in egg white, then rolled in nuts, with a thumbprint for homemade jelly.

"What's that one?" a kid from the university asked Iris. Lila always had three varieties of doughnuts on Saturdays, powdered sugar, maple, and chocolate dipped.

"Hmm." Iris squeezed her eyebrows together. "Looks like chocolate to me, but what do I know?" she said flatly. "I just sell 'em. You want one or not?"

"You work too hard, Lila," well-meaning customers told her.

"I'm sure you're right." She'd smile and continue to stack cookies in the case.

"Get out and go dancing," Clyde encouraged her. He stuffed a whole doughnut in his mouth before he got to his regular table. He smiled at Stella, but she was spreading butter on her rye.

"Come to our party," a couple from the Wilma apartments suggested.

"I wouldn't be caught dead doing that," she told Willy.

"Wanna go to the movies at the Roxy?" The too-young reporter winked.

'Who would complain the loudest"—she pressed Willy—"if they got to the bakery, and it was closed? You think they'd want to miss their favorite roll and coffee because I went dancing and didn't get up at four?" Though she did manage to make time to take Minna to see Clark Gable and Claudette Colbert in *It Happened One Night*, to see if it was as good as everyone was saying.

"A waste of time and money," she told Willy afterward, "and ridiculous." Minna laughed the whole way through it and said she wanted to be like Clark Gable. Lila didn't relish her daughter eating a carrot while sitting on a fence by the side of the road, waiting for a ride. Colbert played the rich man's indolent daughter who didn't have a job and spent her energies on frivolous adventures.

Franz objected when Minna, at age four, was perched on a stool at the sink scrubbing the bread pans. "Lila, she's only a baby."

When Minna was five, Lila trained her to roll cookies in powdered sugar. At eight, she was getting acquainted with the rolling pin. At ten, she helped fill the trays in the shop cases. At twelve, she swept the floors every afternoon after school, cleared tables, wiped them and the chairs down with ammonia, and helped wash up in the kitchen. They ate their breakfast at the bakery before Minna left for school. Two pieces of fresh toast for each of them with thick pats of butter.

"Don't forget to pack the bacon I fried for your lunch," Lila reminded her. Minna helped Lila stock the counter and put the baked pies in the shop window. Lila brewed the coffee, and they each had one cup, Minna's with half cream. When Minna headed out the door for school, Lila put up the OPEN sign.

✑

"Why are you doing Minna's jobs?" Lila asked the week before the scheduled trip to the Dakotas. She had hung a notice at the door explaining that the bakery would sell bread next Monday and Tuesday only. She didn't announce she would be gone for the week, only that the store would be open only from eight till noon.

"If they ask why"—as Lila knew they would—"you may mention I've gone to see my ailing aunt." It would be folly for Iris to step in and take over the baking.

"Why are you still hanging around doing Minna's work?" Lila asked again. Iris was waiting for Minna so she could do a fitting. "You're not doing Minna or me any favors, Iris."

"I got a confession." Iris didn't look at Lila when she told her about the travel wardrobe she was making for Minna.

"Oh, so that's what you've been up to. I might have known. I just wish you wouldn't hide things from me," Lila said evenly. She didn't like deception. She couldn't complain about the cleanup work because Iris had been seeing to it while she herself had gotten engrossed in baking quantities of cookies that would fill the shelves while she was gone. She had reviewed the inventory to make sure she would have everything she needed when she returned. Lila did notice that Minna seemed cheerful, which she attributed to the excitement of the upcoming trip.

"You're right." Iris hung her head. "I shoulda told you about it. I wanted it to be a surprise."

Lila pressed her lips together. "You should ask me, Iris. You know that." It set a poor example to Minna to do things on the sly. But she didn't want to argue with Iris. All the plans were in place, Iris would manage the shop, and although it went against all she believed, Lila let the matter drop.

"Yeah. I know. I was thinking I could get Minna interested in

32

making her own clothes," Iris offered, which would have been a reasonable argument another time.

"That's one way to look at it." Sometimes Lila felt she was raising two girls, not one, only Iris was not going to do any more growing up. Her sister had a wonderful talent, and despite her own genius as a baker, Lila was envious when Iris bubbled into the bakery carrying a new blouse or jacket or dress for Minna, and Minna's face glowed.

The rivalry between the sisters had changed from when they were growing up on the Dakota homestead. Lila had the stronger arms and could wrestle Iris to the ground. But Iris was strong in her legs. They were like two tomcats in the kitchen. Iris balked at Lila's commands, although she was secretly relieved that Lila did all the cooking and baking. Lila was cool. She held her temper because she knew Iris wanted a brawl. Iris knew exactly when Lila was ready to blow. That's when she'd push harder.

It was Lila who brought the bandages and ointment to the barn after Papa had beaten and disfigured Iris, cruelly taming her as if she were a wild horse. Iris didn't flee the homestead as Lila did. She turned docile and obedient until she came to her senses two years later. That's when she took the train to live with Lila and Minna in Missoula. They put aside their rivalry and lived in tight quarters. Iris got a job as a waitress at the Florence Hotel and met Paulie. Lila moved back in with Fischer for a time and suffered a miscarriage. Iris was the one who did the nursing then. She got a cookbook and learned to make vegetable beef soup with beets and fresh pea and carrots and dill. She mothered Minna and tried to smother Lila's sadness with garden vegetables and an overdose of Paulie's gladiolas.

The rivalry sidled up next to the sisters because of Minna. It lay between them like lazy fog that should have, but would not, burn off the Clark Fork River. It planted itself the moment Minna touched Iris's scar with her baby finger. That scar tunneled into the soul of Iris and was the thoroughfare to her despair and her joy. Iris recognized the envy in Lila's gestures.

"I made you a pair of slacks," Iris tried to make up for the awkwardness, handing Lila a wrapped package. There was no sense making a fancy dress for Lila. "You can wear these in the garden. See how I did the waist? Easy for bending over." She was proud because they would show off Lila's shapely waist.

"Oh, and I brought you some aprons." To the aprons, with flowers and birds and apple trees embroidered on them, she added ruffles on the hems and contrasting ties. It was the only way of replacing what she took from Lila for being dear to Minna.

"That's pretty," or "thank you," Lila mustered when Iris sneaked up behind her at the counter, untied the apron she wore, and replaced it with a one of a kind. Lila got even without having to wrestle Iris to the ground. She wrapped the aprons around Willy when he helped out.

"Ain't I beautiful," he joked and flitted between the sink and worktable, swishing it like a tutu, circling Lila. She put the slacks atop an unused pile accumulating in a bottom drawer and pulled on her faithful Levi's.

Iris could not make the score come out even. Once an idea lodged in Lila's brain it required more than pretty things to change it. Iris brought fresh flowers to the bakery, put them in small jars on the tables with a daisy and a marigold, or an aster or carnation. Iris was the mother with no child, Lila the mother whose child was not her own.

"She knows the ins and outs of the bakery from you, Lila," Iris praised her, hoping Lila would forgive her. "She can practically run the shop at the age of twelve." She laughed, dreading the words she feared, that Lila would refuse to let Minna sew with her.

"I try my best," Iris reported to Paulie. She didn't have to tell him. He could see how much effort she put into trying to stay in the background when the three were together.

"It's not your fault," he consoled her. "You can't control Minna."

"I know, I know." She sighed. It happened on its own. Someone would say something funny or make a stupid gesture, and Iris forgot to hold back. Then Minna would start laughing.

"It just never works with Lila," she told Paulie. "I try to get her laughing, too. I guess that's pretty stupid." Iris wanted Minna's attention, and in one way, she was relieved that Lila didn't fight for it. Iris needed Minna, and Minna needed Iris, but Iris wanted her sister, too.

"I don't know how to fix it," she confided to him.

"You have to live your life. Let Lila live hers." He was homely but wise, she decided. But what could she do when Minna looked straight at her and asked in front of Lila, "Can I stay at your house tonight? I love coming to your house!" She couldn't pretend she didn't hear, and she wouldn't say no just so she could ease the disappointment on Lila. They behaved like two giggling teenagers behind the counter waiting on customers, and Lila barked at them to behave, there was a business to be run.

"You spoil her, Iris. Now you're doing her jobs for her. You bring her something nearly every time you see her." She'd made that same argument to Franz when Minna was small. He scoured the secondhand stores, went through the trash in the alleys, always looking for what he could bring to "his Minna."

"She lets you do her work for her. She should be doing things for you—and me! If this goes on, this will become her habit. She'll slack off and let someone else do her work for her. I don't like it."

"But she's learning to make her own clothes. She's working, Lila." It was true, even though it seemed like play.

"I'm going to let it go this time, Iris." Iris gave a relieved sigh. "But"—Lila had more warmth than she wanted in her tone—"the next time you get it in your head to do something like this, ask me first. I'm not letting Minna off the hook because you get a notion in your head. And she needs to take care of her work at the bakery, as usual."

"Okay, Lila," Iris agreed. She felt like Mama had caught her sneaking precious sugar from the bowl.

Seven

"Gonna be a beautiful day for the girls to start their trip."

Paulie waved to the teal-blue sky. The sun smiled as if a customer from the bakery had ordered miles of views with cultivated fields, mountains with scrappy pine trees, rouge-and-ochre cliffs, and Indian reservations inhabited by ghosts.

"Just look at you, wearing a hole in your trousers." Iris would scold him if she caught him there by the car. "You know, Paulie, how much I hate mending things." He was pulling the chain bob on his watch out of his front trouser pocket again and again with his right hand. He was certain they would be late to the station. He kicked a pebble back and forth between his two-toned loafers outside the Pine Street house leaning against his black four-door sedan Ford.

"For the girls," he told Iris of the peach gladiolas he'd wrapped for them. He cradled them standing next to the car for fear they'd droop if he neglected them on the car seat.

Paulie had the firm conviction that his gladiolas could transform a less than perfect world. He had begun cultivating them when it became apparent he would not be raising children of his own. He nurtured the corms into glorious specimens. He believed his gladiolas were key to Lila's recovery following her tragic miscarriage. Iris had worn a path to the hospital with his violet and yellow and orange gladiolas' heads jostling over her elbow.

It was Iris who, during that frightening time, got him thinking about bringing glads to other sick patients. "I don't have a gripe about white as a color. But when that's all you see, it's all wrong," she said, referring to the sterile hospital. "I don't see how anybody can get well in that place."

Paulie was, at first, met with resistance when he arrived with an arm full of multicolored flowers. "That seems sinful," a fresh young nun with overwhelming credentials sniffed. "Too permissive, and it would undermine our authority."

"I don't think I agree," an older nun countered. "I can't see how flowers would interfere with our authority." She remembered Lila and the gladiolas, and the garden flowers that Willy brought her. They didn't pull Lila out of her blue depression, but they had lifted the nun's spirits. Lila's pallor matched the sheets, and she moved as if she were already in her coffin. The nun who nursed the distant woman favored that room while Lila was there. Lila should have stayed longer, but Fischer, complaining about how much it cost him "to keep them black crows fussin' over her," packed her in the car and took her home.

The nuns needed several meetings concerning Paulie's request. They negotiated. The older nun countered objections with, "Why not agree to the gladiolas if this little man is willing to do Hail Marys in the chapel with each of his deliveries?"

"How can we know he will do what we ask?" the dissenter demanded.

"Let it be between him and God," another stated, and that brought an end to it.

He took it personally, though. He didn't say so to Iris, but she guessed it. "Sin of pride?" she whispered to him. "That's what you're thinking, aren't you, Paulie? They don't want you to be too proud of those beautiful flowers."

"Yeah." They worried he would be puffed up over it. "Without God and Mary there would be no flowers at all," he said dutifully. They put his bouquets at the nurses' station and in the lobby, among distraught people who waited on hard chairs in rooms without any windows for whatever bad news was coming to them.

When he was jeered at for being Italian and came home with his shoulders dejected, Iris said, "Someone must have called you a stupid wop again." She could read him from the other side of the planet.

"It's that damn noisy Hitler," Iris grumbled as Paulie began getting more threats. He had been putting up with their taunts for years, even before he married Iris and was living on the North Side in his rented room, still learning the railroad job—back when the Italians took over where the Chinese left off.

"You talk funny." They bunched up their fists. "You're a damn lousy foreigner. You ain't one of us." He was an inch taller than Iris, and brown-skinned with eyes the color of coal. He didn't cower, he insisted to Iris. "They didn't have no good mama like me." He tapped his chest with his thumbs. "Mama taught us to respect people and treat them like we wanted to be treated."

"Do they know," he demanded, "about my glads?" Those flowers perhaps had cheered one of them, or a hospitalized relative. His gladiolas should have erased any misconception about him, and more than that, revise their notions about prejudice.

"I ain't seen no one off on the train before," he confessed to Iris when he brought his flowers for Lila and Minna. He suffered actual stomach pain watching others say good-bye to loved ones, each kiss and each embrace like ulcers. But it didn't escape his keen observing when a man sending his loved one away crushed the bouquet against the woman he kissed, who wore maroon lipstick and rouged cheeks.

"First of all, what sort of a man in love would choose such awful flowers?" he implored Iris.

"Not everyone's as romantic as you are, Paulie."

"Even bad flowers shouldn't be crushed," he complained. The assortment appalled him. It should have spoken what the lover couldn't express in words. Instead, those lackluster flowers got smashed when he fumbled to find her red lips, knocked her robin's-egg-blue cloche cockeyed, and got his nose snagged in her curls.

"Not a bit of horse sense," he muttered to himself as he waited at the curb of the Pine Street house for Lila and Minna. He had the good fortune of having married into a wonderful family, but as a railroad man, he could not fathom females who didn't keep to schedules.

"It's time, Minna," Lila barked up the stairs, but Minna was in front of the mirror swirling her skirt and pulling her bolero around her shoulders. "Hurry up, Minna," Lila repeated, running from the kitchen to the bottom of the stairs.

By the time Minna appeared, making grand strides as she entered the kitchen, her head high and looking faraway, Lila was too busy doing her own fussing to notice. "Did I give you all the keys?" she asked Iris for the third time. She started going over the instructions again.

"I've got it, Lila. I had it the very first time! I had it *before* the first time," Iris declared. "Go on, now. You're going to miss your train, and then Paulie will blame himself, and we'll all have to listen to him for the next three weeks boo-hooing that it was his fault."

Iris nearly swooned as Paulie had driven off toward the train station, and she parted company with them to go the bakery. "That girl is something." She pictured Minna walking to the coach as though the train would wait for her to stroll from the depot to their seats.

"Oh!" Minna gasped when hot vapor hissed at her alongside the train, and she jumped. She flipped her head around to see if anyone had seen her flinch.

"Honestly, Minna. Would you hurry up?" Lila rushed up behind her with their tickets in one hand, her black purse dangling on the same arm, and the bulky gladiolas in the other. Uncle Paulie had dashed ahead of them and turned to see if his goslings were at least attempting to follow him. He cocked his head to indicate their car and, out of breath, shoved their two suitcases through the open car door.

"Here we are." He tipped his hat to Lila and tried to give Minna a kiss on the cheek, but Minna was impressed with the uniform of the conductor, who was steering her up the three steps. He held her arm at the elbow until she was secure on the punched-steel landing.

She looked him in the eye and asked, "How do you like my orange quilted skirt?"

"I beg your pardon, young lady?" He glanced at Lila.

"I made it myself," she said, holding the edge of the hem in her right hand and swirling round to make it flair.

"It's very nice, honey," he said with a measured tone and tipped his hat.

"Good-bye, Lila. Good-bye, Minna," Paulie shouted after them. He walked parallel with them on the other side of the train windows until they reached their seats. "Have a wonderful time." His heart raced, and his cheeks looked like they'd been painted with rouge. He had imagined a much grander departure, smiles and hugs, and kisses that held a Saint Christopher blessing planted on their cheeks. He stayed by their coach until the train chugged down the tracks and waved after them until the caboose curved around the bend and they were gone.

"Minna, shame on you," Lila whispered as she shoved their two bags above their seats, planting the glads between them to keep their budding heads vertical. *May Tante Catherine still have enough sight to enjoy them.* She didn't look forward to nurturing them for a thousand miles.

"Why?" Minna cried. "What did I do wrong now?"

"You know perfectly well. The way you were with that young conductor. Honestly, Minna. Aren't you in the least embarrassed?"

"Isn't it all right to tell someone I made my clothes? Aunt Iris would think so, and so do I!" She pushed her head back into the fresh white napkin protecting the blue tweed. The train snaked between the canyons imitating the route carved out by the river. "Oh!" Minna whispered, going through the first tunnel. She watched the train's engine curving ahead when they came out the other side and hoped for another tunnel. The dark had surprised her, and it happened so fast.

"I'm starving," Minna declared just after Garrison, Montana.

"Well, for goodness' sake," Lila said. "I knew you didn't eat enough breakfast." She'd nibbled at her eggs and the edges of her toast. "I told you to eat something."

"I wasn't hungry then." She'd wanted to get dressed, to see how she was going to look in her outfit.

I brought a picnic." Lila was pleased with herself. She'd packed roast beef sandwiches with onions and mustard on crusty rolls.

"This isn't the place for a picnic." Minna felt embarrassed. She remembered sitting in an ant pile under a pine tree and yelping from the highways of tiny creatures running up her legs.

"Lunch is now being served in the dining car," the conductor strode through the coach. Minna flashed a smile, and he tipped his hat to her again. She wished she could try on his hat, but Lila would glare at her for a week and not say one word directly to her. He opened the door to the next coach, and it sounded like Eunice's pneumatic canister, sucking up the air on its way to the top floor of the Mercantile, only a lot louder.

"Why can't we eat in the dining car like other people?" Minna wanted to crawl under the seat when Lila opened the sack smelling of fried onions.

"Why do you think?" Lila said flatly, unwrapping the dill pickles from the wax paper. Minna scanned the landscape looking for another tunnel and pretended she wasn't traveling with her mother. She ignored the sandwich Lila handed toward her and instead watched as the Anaconda smokestack rose proudly in the distance. "So that's what it looks like!" she whispered in awe to the window. "Just wait till I tell the kids at school."

Minna could not avoid the hand with the pickle because it didn't disappear as the roast beef sandwich had when she refused to acknowledge it. Minna flipped her head toward Lila. "I don't want...Lila?" She looked at her mom. "Lila?" The world famous smokestack slipped out of view.

Lila heard Minna's voice ricocheting inside her head. "Lila?" Minna asked again, and this time, Lila handed her the pickle, and she took it.

But it was a flashback, and it was thirteen years earlier. Instead of Minna, Lila handed that pickle to Fischer. She and Fischer were on their honeymoon, moving to Montana. "Look 'at you just did!" Oh, Fischer got mad that day. His hands gripped the steering wheel of the roadster so tight they had white splotches on the knuckles. They had been married only a few days, and she had already felt a twinge about the real Fischer.

So here it comes now. Lila steeled herself. Before the wedding, in the dark upstairs bedroom at Tante's, she had brushed aside the doubt and let herself be caught up in the flurry of wedding preparations. Still, a small voice raised itself about what kind of man she was agreeing to marry.

They had stayed with her cousin in Mowbridge for several days after the wedding when the roadster broke down. When they said their good-byes, they were two dancing colts champing and ready to bolt across the open fields. The pickle incident was before they crossed the border into Montana, her red hair tousled by the breeze, and she feeling free as a tethered ball cut from its post. She'd started gently tormenting Fischer because he'd turned all business about potholes on the uneven road. She teased him but didn't recognize she was testing his mettle. They had married in haste, running from their troubles. She pushed the pickle between his teeth while he avoided jumping the ruts. "Cut it out," he yelled when the pickle brine dripped down on his pants.

She tested his temperament that day, all right, him sitting in wet, stained pants until they stopped for the night. "First impressions, Willy, is what counts," he advised Willy, who emulated his older brother. Fischer shone like a star when they performed at their barn-dance gigs. Willy figured out later that maybe second—or even third—impressions were necessary to make things stick.

Lila unnerved Fischer. He didn't like being spooked. Even before the pickle juice, he saw things he didn't like. Already he was brooding, worried he might have married someone who dared to mess with him. He wanted to take revenge, to dump her by the side of the road after she messed up his pants, wearing her fancy wedding dress and dainty shoes. *Give her something to think about, by God.* They hadn't passed another car for two hours.

"You're going to get it on my skirt." Lila heard her, but for a second she could have sworn it was Fischer.

"Oh, here." She pulled a clean cloth napkin from the lunch basket and covered the quilted orange pattern.

Eight

*L*ila hadn't ridden the train before, but her bakery goods made the trip regularly. She fixed meals for the railroad men to take in their lunch buckets. A brakeman from Butte had started it. The Schneiders still owned the shop at the time he got interested in her stuffed prune cookies. "Hey," he asked, following his first bite, "could you make pasties like them Irish women do for the miners to take down in the pits?" He explained that dough was wrapped around a filling. "Some kinda meat stuffing. Think it's pork."

"That sounds like blachinda," Lila noted and soon began selling the pastry made in the German way, with dough wrapped around pumpkin with a lot of coarse pepper. But the men turned their noses up. "Well, that didn't work," she said to Martha and moved on to experimenting with ground pork. She found it worked well as the basic ingredient, so she decided to try ground beef, which also did the job. To make the product more interesting, she included available ingredients that seemed intriguing, like dried tart cherries, cranberries, raisins, cinnamon, and slivered almonds. If huckleberries were plentiful, she added them. When the frigid north winds blew off the mountains, she added apples with onions and sage for comfort for the workers getting off and on the trains, their fingers stiff and white from the chill. The men ingested flavors foreign to their taste buds without knowing what was inside their blachindas. They did not think to tell her they liked them, but they lined up when a new batch came out on the trays.

The train rocked and swayed. The constant clacking was a sleeping drug for Lila who wanted to stay awake. The familiar and important things, the ovens, the counters, the pans, even the customers, felt faraway. She was curious if she would recognize any landmarks from the honeymoon. She pictured Tante Catherine running after the roadster, a plump lilac ball of dress fabric huffing and sputtering like she was on her last drop of fuel. She stopped abruptly, Lila's final glimpse of her aunt whose bread loaf legs could run no farther. Instead, she pulled out her white hanky and waved it as if in surrender. The hanky grew smaller and smaller until Lila could not tell if it was real or if she was imagining a white spot in the distance. She soon drifted into a sleep from the steady jouncing and dreamed of those warm, doughy arms of her tante encircling her. She could smell her tante's embrace, the scent of allspice and bay leaves and the heat that radiated the same comfort of a stoked stove.

When Lila woke, the fields of stubble and rich dark earth she remembered from that hopeful September day when she wore her fabulous dress, yellow hair ribbons toying with her face in the breeze, were shockingly different. They seemed squeezed and cheated out of life. Ashen soil with twisted sparse plants begging for a sip of water survived.

"So this is what it looks like now. No wonder the men are outside the bakery door looking for something to fill their bellies." Tante's letters were full of grim news of the drought that seemed to never end. Because there was no moisture to hold down the top soil, huge dark clouds hovered over the Midwest. Onkel Jacob wrote Tante's letters for her since her eyes could not decipher letters, let alone clouds engorged with dirt.

Tante's eyes had stopped seeing. Had that thief also stolen the sprite who lived inside her buoyant aunt? Tante needed an operation, Onkel said. He must have agonized, asking Lila to find a way around Aunt Catherine's resistance. He'd mentioned it in his shaky handwriting, in the next room, away from his wife who might not be able to see, but still had the hearing of a bat. "There ain't no point writing to her about it," he told Lila. "She'd pretend she didn't hear it." He didn't ask Lila to come back to convince her in person directly. He said he was happy to be his wife's eyes but feared what would become of her if he was not there to help her.

Lila and Minna caught a bus from Mowbridge. Lila had hoped to stay a day with her cousin, Peter, and his wife so that Minna could come to know them. They went to his house, but another family lived there now. With the crop failures and so many farmers deserting their unyielding fields, her cousin, who now had two children, had left for Chicago, where he had found a job. He was luckier than most, but then Peter pleased anyone he met.

The bus lumbered into her home village of Hoffen after they passed near Papa's farm. Hoffen's pride had been bruised by the drought, and no passengers got off. The bus went by the lane toward the cemetery, where Mama lay. Minna was starting to get cranky, and Lila suddenly had a splitting headache, which she blamed on a garrulous rotund salesman at the rear of the bus who sucked on his cigar, exhaling it down the aisle.

"I hate that stinky smell." Lila groaned, and she and Minna moved five seats forward. Her nose was running, and her eyes watered. Her stomach was churning, and she couldn't keep her legs still under her. She pushed the soles into the floor like someone was holding a pillow over her face. "Open the window some more," she told Minna.

"I already put it down as far as it will go."

Lila grabbed the cushion seat with both hands. "Let me off!" She muffled the scream in her throat and quickly glanced to see if anyone was looking at her. No one was. *Why did I agree to come back here? Why was I the one Mama sent into the root cellar for cabbage heads for sauerkraut?* The spiders lived on the rafters and hung two inches from her head. If her brother Irv, or Iris, or one of the other kids slammed the door above her, she would be in pitch black. She held in another scream.

They drove past the Hoffen granary and then the general store. The wooden sidewalk planks had been replaced with cement. In the park opposite, the trees that once lined the perimeter were dead or clung for life to a smattering of reluctant leaves. The bus passed a farm about four miles outside of town. It had the same smirk as Papa's farm. What jolted her was the way the windmill lurched in the stifling air. She saw the skeleton when it was still a mile off and did not take her eyes off it until it had been swallowed up by the distance they put between them and it. She wanted to see it fall off the landscape behind but couldn't make herself turn around. Its squawking must have been drowned out by the baritone hum from the engine of the bus. Still she was sure she heard it, that forlorn sound that nags to remind you that there is only you and God and the bare dirt under your feet.

"Next time," she said to the cigar smoker leaving the bus, "you might think about how that stinky cigar bothers other people." Minna looked at her mother, amazed. It was like Iris talking, except she wouldn't stop with that comment. She'd say, "Unless your brain is already addled." Minna waited for Lila to do so, to pause like Iris, like she expected him to respond, and once he started, she'd add, "In which case, it's too late, and there's no point sayin' more about it."

Minna was astonished. Lila was one to carefully imprison and guard her words. She viewed it as an asset, particularly in the bakery, to not give words free rein. She'd had ten years to observe how Martha kept her tongue, the little ways of expressing disgust or dissatisfaction, a sniff here, a click there. Before Lila inherited the business, she'd gained acumen that could not be passed along through a legal document.

The years of heavy lifting had taken their toll on the older couple's strength and reserves. Too many racks of bread pans, baking sheets, and plump bags of flour and sugar had worn them down. Lila mourned the ending before it came and was careful not to be obvious as she took on more of the duties.

Franz would become confused and shake his head. "Marta, I'm a old fool. You don't have to agree, neither." He put his hand up to stop her. "Either that, or I'm losin' my mind." The flour bins were already filled, and he thought he still had it to do. It was fair play on both sides because the Schneiders plotted on her behalf behind her back, utensil by utensil, codicil by codicil, willing the bakery a piece at a time into Lila's name until one morning she woke up to a business she entirely owned.

Franz's hands, thick and brawny by nature, were puffy, as were his ankles, and in his heart he felt dread for what was happening in the world. He wanted to make a last adjustment in the will, "just in case," he told the lawyer, "that business gets nasty for us Germans again"—he paused—"like what happened in the Great War. I don't trust that damn guy over there."

"Watch your language," Martha whispered as if Franz needed reminding. "He's the lawyer."

"Lila will get mushy about us two old fools," he told Martha when they decided it was time to move forward on their decision and pass the business to Lila. He couldn't shake the memory of the German Americans like themselves who had been humiliated, and sometimes much worse.

"You're worried, aren't you, you old fool?" Martha asked. "Lila won't like it. She won't want to hurt our feelings."

"Well, dang it, Marta. We ain't gonna give her no choice. Maybe we should change the name of the bakery while we is sittin' here," he tapped his finger on the lawyer's desk. "We got to think of Minna, too." His hands shook.

"When the people get riled up, they go looking for someone to take it out on," he educated the lawyer, who was too young to remember that far back. "We won't let that happen to Lila. We couldn't bear it." He slapped his old paws together and then raised the palms upward to hurry the lawyer along. Franz wrinkled his already crinkled brow. He whispered to Martha, "Let's call it somethin' American. I know. Lincoln's Bakery. That's the idea."

"Don't you go being silly." Martha kicked him under the table. "We will go on just as we always have." She nodded to the lawyer and said to Franz, "And let Lila decide for herself when the time comes." They were wasting too much time, and consequently too much money, discussing it in front of the lawyer who would bill them for each minute they spent with him.

"There's dem Germans who come to the States after the Great War." Martha glared at him. If Franz got started talking about those professional, middle-class people who now lived in the large cities, who had kept their noses clean and heads low until Hitler's star rose from out of the political pack, it would be another hour in the lawyer's office. The lawyer would sit there and add up the dollars and cents while Franz disclosed his facts about the secret group that had suddenly become quite visible.

They'd blossomed like night flowers, cheering for the fuhrer across the ocean. "Fritz Kuhn," Franz informed the lawyer. "Da name of their leader." He had been a chemical engineer from Munich, and he'd fought for Germany until he migrated, became an American citizen and those with similar backgrounds flocked to him. "You know what they call dis guy?" Franz asked loud enough that the secretary in the outer office heard him. "They say he's der American fuhrer. Dat's who."

"Sorry." The lawyer shrugged. "I haven't heard of him. Guess I'd better read up," he said, playing with his watch fob.

"Well, that's a good idea," Franz told him. "Otherwise, you could be marchin' in goose step, too."

Martha's voice quavered. "Franz, don't scare the poor man." The lawyer decided to use the moment to fill his fountain pen from the fancy inkwell.

"They say, 'We love America!'" Franz peered at the lawyer. "But then they go ahead and say they hate Roosevelt. They call his programs the 'Jew Deal' and call him 'Franklin Rosenfeld.'"

"We will watch," Martha promised Franz, hoping he had spoken enough of his piece to be satisfied.

"Wit our eyes wide open," he stressed, aware that history has the habit of repeating itself. "We watch *gut* now," Franz agreed. By the time the lawyer had the will drawn up and ready to sign, Fritz Kuhn had organized the German American Bund and avowed it wasn't an official Nazi organization. "We swear our allegiance to the United States. We only do what is necessary to keep America strong." Kuhn encouraged America to remain neutral when Hitler's army slammed into Poland. "We've got our own work to do here. Get aggressive about keeping our own country free from Jewish communist plots." He tossed jazz into that mix as well, and the out-of-control black musicians.

"Ach!" Franz moaned. Minna and he listened to Louis Armstrong. She turned the radio on in the bakery and danced around the worktable while Franz whistled.

"What's wrong now," he demanded of Martha, "that they going after dese black guys? Just because of der skin color?"

Nine

"So we get to meet our little Minna at long last." Onkel extended his hand in the old-fashioned way. He'd formally hugged Lila, wiping away his disobedient tears. Not a single one of Tante's plump calories in the last thirteen years had found their way onto Onkel's frame. A turbulent dust bowl storm could carry him off, if the reports of their power and velocity were accurate.

"Don't rush me to that graveyard just yet, Lila," he pleaded when she grabbed one of the suitcases Onkel was aiming to carry. He hustled ahead of her with both pieces of luggage. "That'll happen plenty soon enough." He spoke over his shoulder. "Let the old man be a gentleman."

"Of course. I'm sorry," Lila murmured, babying the gladiolas that she carefully laid on the seat of his maroon Plymouth roadster. She gave Onkel a big smile as they drove off, like a child to a parent she adored. Minna caught her mother's girl-look, coddling the flowers, too, smiling reverently at him. She was a stranger peeking into the window of an unfamiliar house. Lila didn't ever look at her that way.

"Peculiar family," Iris had said to Minna who stood on a stool while Iris pinned the hem of the skirt. She talked around the straight pins between her lips, providing the few details that would make any sense of the family Minna was going to meet.

"I used to be sassy." Iris had her hands on her hips, hitching the right one to show how she flirted with the boys on the softball field. Mostly, her voice sounded like she was walking over gravel, but there were days she could get high-pitched. Iris did not mince words when relating how her papa had beaten her, or her stepmother's sly cunning, playing on emotions and using innuendos to manipulate and control.

"Don't laugh, Minna." Iris shook her finger at her, starting to laugh too. "I used to be a character." She'd taken the shears to her mahogany hair by the upstairs mirror in Papa's room after she had seen a movie with a starlet wearing a bob wave. "You should have seen the look on your mother's face when she walked into that room." She grinned. "You'd a thought it was Armageddon. The floor looked like I had gone into the fur-trading business with all that hair piled up around my ankles.

"So I had this bob, see, and then I put all my hems up to my kneecaps." She pointed to that place on her knee. "They were doin' it in New York. And then I ordered pants from the catalogue. Just to get the boys to jerk their heads around." She cackled.

"I wish I had been there." Minna sighed.

"Well, honey, I even sneaked cigarettes with the boys behind the barn. That's between you and me, though. Okay?"

"Okay. I wish I was like you."

"Not if you are getting walloped," Iris cried. "Not when your papa drags you across the yard, pulls your hair out, and beats the living daylights out of you." She fingered the ravaged side of her face, the eternal reminder of her sass.

"After that, I hid out. I don't recommend it." She chuckled. "I couldn't think clear 'cause everything went black for a while after that. I ducked into the fields and stayed there pretty much for about a year. See, I was ashamed and afraid. I don't ever wanna be scared like that again." She pounded her fist on the kitchen table and made the red soup in the half-empty bowls spill over the soda crackers.

"I won't go meet him," Minna promised of the grandfather who still lived in the Dakotas, demonstrating her loyalty. "I'd tell him what a coward he is. I hate him," she added because he had buckled under to the stepmother who had torn the family apart.

"She sicced him on me. And he went after little Johnny, too. Just for good measure, I guess," Iris declared with thinly veiled hatred.

"What happened to Johnny?" Minna pictured a rail-thin, blond boy, cowering in the corner of the kitchen, watching the ruckus unfold, then slipping out to the barn to curl up in a ball with his cats for comfort.

"That's a very dirty shame what happened there." Iris shook her head. "Just a rotten dirty shame. He lives in Aberdeen now, and Tante and Onkel watch out for him 'cause he can't be on his own. Not right in the head." Iris tapped her temple and sighed. "If something happens to those two, Paulie wants to bring him here to live with us. That's Paulie for you, Minna. He's never even met my brother." She wrinkled her brow in wonder.

A long drag on a cigarette was the only way to calm herself when Iris looked back instead of forward. She carried a pack of Lucky

Strikes, her choice because they toasted their tobacco to protect the vocal chords. "That's what the ads says," she said to Paulie. "So my voice won't get raspy."

He knew it wasn't true. She tucked them into the special pockets she sewed for her aprons. She had a pack in the pocket of her cashmere clutch coat conveniently on a hook by the back door, but she kept her early promise to Lila not to smoke in Minna's presence. She had gotten in the habit of lighting up in the alley during breaks when she worked at the Florence Hotel before she married Paulie. These days she took her breaks in the backyard along the fence where Paulie babied his glads. She feared a stray spark would burn a hole in her fabrics if she smoked inside.

"I want to go home right now," Minna was about to say to Lila after the maroon car pulled up beside a white two-story house with lace curtains. But she couldn't get her mother's attention. Lila was laughing in a merry way, not her usual tight grin, and chirping and clapping her hands.

"Everything is just the same!" she rejoiced inside the cozy house, except for the overhead light that startled with brilliance. There was a hint of nutmeg and vanilla that prompted her to say, "Someone made vanilla pudding, didn't they?"

It smelled of old people, dank and sour, for Minna. The lace curtains in the parlor were thick and old-fashioned, holding out the sun. Visibility was cut by half again behind heavy beige drapes.

"I'll heat up Tante's borscht with some nice bread and butter." Onkel turned on the electric stove and nodded at them. Minna shook her head. She hadn't spoken to him yet. Iris had green-blue drapes with gold filigree in her living room. They didn't block out the world. The radio in Iris's kitchen blared to keep company with the ironing board waiting for when she breezed in from her design room to press down seams, hems, and facing. Iris's feet slid and hopped back and forth, following the nose of the iron and humming along with her favorite musicians. She sashayed her hips and belted out in her tenor, "It don't mean a thing if it ain't got that swing." She had to put the iron down for this song because she needed her hands to help her sing along.

Minna didn't see a radio in this kitchen. She wanted to be in Aunt Iris's kitchen, sitting next to the ironing board and eating a bowl of Campbell's tomato soup with saltine crackers, listening to Duke Ellington. She didn't want borscht. Iris could sing even with her mouth full, and she'd make a face and roll her eyes if she dribbled like she was decrepit. Minna didn't try that with Lila.

"Did Tante make the borscht herself?" Lila was surprised.

"She stands right next to me here"—he pointed to the spot of linoleum by the stove—"and tells me what to do first, and she knows when I've done it backward, too." He laughed. "She can tell when I'm cutting up beets, and if I'm not chopping the carrots the way she thinks they should be, she'll tap my hand and say, 'Now, Jacob, you didn't do that quite right, did you?'" He smiled sadly to Lila. "She catches me every time. I shoulda had it figured out how she done it all those years."

"I can hear you yakking out there, you know. Jacob, you're an old gossip!" Tante cried out from the parlor. "Come in here, *lieblings*. Come in. I want to see my girls." She was out of her rocker and aiming toward the kitchen her arms stretched out ahead of her, tottering. She didn't have her cane, and Lila ran to move a chair.

"*Ach, meine Tochter,*" the unsighted woman sobbed when they hugged. Tante's familiar lavender scent transported Lila back to age twelve. Tante's springy silver curls had not been informed that over a decade had transpired. Her eyes, behind the Ball jar glasses, still discerned silhouettes. Tante could follow shapes, which gave the impression she was seeing what everyone else did. It was disconcerting, as if Onkel had been misleading, except for the subtle stare that revealed a near blackness. Lila's fear of a dissembled spirit, overwhelmed and flustered by handicap, was for naught. It was very much intact.

The radio on the side table next to Tante's rocking chair was shaped like the windows of Saint Paul's Lutheran Church. Lila rubbed her glove across it when she was seated on a chair with a plump cushion at her aunt's side. The glove came away clean, just the way she wanted it to, the way it would be in the bakery after she helped the last customers wiggle into their coats, and pulled the blinds down so late buyers who remembered they were out of bread at home would not rap at the door to disrupt her cleaning. She replaced the baker's hat and shop apron with the navy-blue bandanna and wraparound, and went to work. After the counters sparkled, she aimed a mop at the floors. Even the walls and the photos from Professor Elrod of Glacier and the Mission Range were subject to a good swipe from a damp rag. She was gentle with the stained glass lamps that the Schneiders insisted she keep, but the brilliant pieces of color still got their fair "lick and a promise." No customer could complain about grime or that their food was served from a dirty dish. She hadn't expected Tante's house to be clean since she couldn't get around to find the dirt. That the rooms were being cared for meant someone was helping and watching out for them. But who would that be?

"*Liebe kind*," the blind woman addressed Minna, "now I want to know all about your first train ride. I have not been on one yet, but Onkel says it's only a matter of time. It didn't go too fast, did it?" She stretched out her arm. That wrinkled brow was remembering one particular day when the galloping horse she rode got it into its head to scare her to death. It would have thrown her if she hadn't held onto the reins with all her strength and squeezed her legs into the beast while sweat frothed on its flanks. She was a redheaded tomboy back then.

Onkel laughed. "Your tante hasn't gotten used to the auto yet. She's waiting for the world to slow down to normal and listen to her common sense once again." Minna was still standing, looking through the lace at the window. She wasn't some silly child. They didn't see she was nearly grown up. Lila glared at her, motioned with her eyes for Minna to move near to let Tante touch her.

"It was fine." Minna shrugged.

"The farms are suffering terribly." Lila jumped in. "Just like you said in your letters. It isn't so bad over in the mountains, but it was awful to see the fields like skeletons." She glared at Minna while she talked. "Tante, once you get your eye operation you can come and visit us. Then you will see what I've told you about the rivers and lakes. Onkel, you will love it there."

"Hold on, Lila. What is this, liebling, about an eye operation? What has Onkel been telling you?"

"Now, now, Catta. You think I been a troublemaker, do you?"

"I know you worry like a old fool. What's he gone and told you, Lila?"

"Catta, we can talk about it later. We need to feed these girls. They sure look like they could put some fat on their bones."

"I am not a blind old bat, Jacob. Hmm. Lila, has this old onkel got you riled up for no good reason? You don't want to make a commotion over these tired eyes. They see good enough to know you're not keeping enough meat on. Neither with the girl. You're working too hard, liebling, I can hear it by the way you walk."

Lila had been rehearsing her argument. Onkel warned her that Tante would say it was too much fuss over nothing. She'd set her jaw in the same way Lila did and say, "I have never been happier, Lila. Other people might be missing out on something, but it ain't me. That's for sure."

How many times had she told Jacob, "I see better now, old man, than ever before. Leave me alone about this operation nonsense."

Dr. Charles Thornton, who came over from the hospital for his regular cinnamon roll and black coffee, had advised Lila. "There are two methods, Lila"—he mulled the other pastries on the counter—"to remove the cataracts. The one that's more successful makes an opening in the capsule around the lens to pull it out." He paused for a moment to consider, and Lila waited for him to go on. "Sometimes, though, it might take another surgery to get the empty capsule removed." He ordered a blachinda to take back to the hospital for his lunch. "But a British surgeon is putting a tiny plastic lens inside the eye during surgery, and that procedure seems promising."

"Tante, I think Onkel is right. All the way here my mouth was watering for your borscht and bread. Do you think we could have some now?" She stood up and put her arm over her aunt's shoulder. "Let's talk about the other thing later. Okay?"

"Meine liebe. I hope you didn't come to see me because of these ridiculous old eyes. Tell me you didn't because otherwise I am going to get upset. I see as much as I need to. Ask your onkel if that's not so. If the dear Lord in heaven wanted me to see better, he would make it happen. I'm not going to argue with him. What I am worried about is that you show up and are nothing more than a bag of bones!"

"Now, now, you two. Are you gonna start going on about who's in worse shape? Catta, let's get these girls fed, and I'll get 'em settled upstairs. They must be about dog tired from all those miles they covered since yesterday."

Ten

"Wait! Don't go!" Minna caught the shadow figure just beyond the parlor that bobbed in and ran out.

Minna ran after it through the kitchen. "Wait, don't run away. Please!"

"What the dickens!" Onkel jumped up out of his chair forgetting he was an old man.

"What is it?" Lila reached out to steady Onkel, who teetered like he would fall back into the chair.

"Ach. I forgot about Johnny." Onkel hurried out after Minna.

"Mein Gott," Tante added. "Well, it's all my fault. I didn't remind him this morning you was coming. Go after him Jacob. Go!" But Jacob was already through the kitchen. "We got so worked up with you coming, and Jacob fussed about being late to the bus stop. We plain forgot to tell him." She put her hand over her mouth. "Poor boy is scared now."

"I'll go talk to him," Lila said.

"No, no, Lila." Tante put out her hand. "It's better if Onkel gets him calmed down first. He'll be tickled when he realizes you've come home." She patted Lila's hand. "Don't worry about that. Let Onkel sort him out first."

"He didn't know it was me, did he? When he came in now? I didn't even get a chance to see him."

"That's hard to know." She shrugged. "Maybe he did. Maybe he didn't. He'll be all right after Onkel explains it to him. He can't keep things in his head from one day to the next. We've talked about you coming several times." Tante patted her hand again. They felt like velvet gloves on Lila's own. One of Tante's silver curls was caught on a spindle on the back of the chair. Lila tucked it back and ran her hands over the curls to tame other stragglers.

He had to duck to miss the door jamb. He was that tall. Lila wanted to stare at him, but held her eyes at half mast, afraid he might run again. *He's so blond and handsome.* His neatly ironed blue shirt matched his eyes. His eyes. They were so clear and deep, and so innocent she choked back tears. Like a pristine lake. Minna and he were holding hands. He grinned at her, and she returned the smile.

Minna patted his arm. "It's okay. See? We're all here. Your family. Come sit with us, Uncle Johnny." She brought him to the davenport. "Didn't you know we came especially to see you?"

He giggled but didn't sit. "Did you see my cat?"

"No, I haven't," she said gently. "Have you lost him?" He started laughing with his mouth open and then couldn't stop. Onkel came over and put his hand on his shoulder. "It's okay, Johnny. Look over there. It's your sister. It's Lila, Johnny." Onkel handed his handkerchief to him to wipe the drool off his chin.

"My cat"—he was still laughing—"is red. Like that," he said and stopped laughing, pointing at Lila. Then he added, "My sister...sh-she-she used to have red hair."

"That is your sister, Johnny. That's Lila," Onkel reminded him. "See. She still has red hair."

"No. She went to the barn, and she didn't never come back." He looked at Minna and asked, "Do I know you?" He squinted down at her but didn't wait for her to answer. "Do you want some of my vanilla pudding?"

"He made it this morning. Didn't you, Johnny?" Onkel reminded him. "You wanted to make it because *Lila* would like it. Isn't that right?" Onkel smiled at Lila.

"Where is she?" Johnny asked. "She's gonna come and eat my pudding, but she went to the barn. She ain't comin' back." He was getting agitated.

Minna hadn't let go of his hand. "Come on, Uncle Johnny, let's go look for her. Maybe she's coming back from the barn right now. Then we can give her the pudding. Okay? Can I have some, too?"

"All of it. You can have all of it 'cause she went to the barn, and she went for good." His shoulders hunched as Minna led him back toward the kitchen.

"Uh-oh," he cried when a spoon fell from the bowl and landed in Minna's lap on her orange skirt. He had been very careful while dishing the pudding out. "Don't want to make no mess," he told her in advance.

"That's all right, Uncle Johnny. Look, it comes right off," Minna assured him.

He shook his head and repeated, "Don't want to make no mess. No mess. Do it right, Johnny boy, or you gonna get a good whippin'.

Yessir. A good whippin'." He was shifting back and forth from one foot to the other and looked as if he might start to cry.

Onkel came up behind and patted him on the shoulder. "How's that taste, Minna? Johnny sure makes a good pudding, don't he?"

"No mess. Don't make no mess," he continued, still shifting back and forth.

She smiled at Onkel for the first time. "It's the best pudding I've ever had, Uncle Johnny," she enthused, and he grinned like a cat. "Where's your cat?" she remembered to ask.

"In the garage, ain't he, Onkel?" Then he looked puzzled.

Jacob said, "That's where he is. That's where I saw him when I went to the bus station."

"What's your cat's name?"

"Oh look," Onkel exclaimed. "Here's Lila. Here's your sister, Johnny, come home."

"Did she come back from the barn?" He squinted at her.

"Hello, Johnny." Lila was tentative.

"Don't be afraid," Onkel whispered in her ear. Lila reached out for her brother's hand. He jumped back.

"You ain't her. You ain't my sister." He was only ten when she left home.

Their stepmother had told them to forget about her. "She ain't ever coming back," she'd roared. He hadn't forgotten her, but he didn't remember her either.

Onkel said, "Look. Don't you remember her hair? It's the same red hair. Remember?"

He was puzzled. "You're a naughty girl," he said, laughing awkwardly while trying to sort out his sister from the confusion roiling in his brain.

"Why's that, Johnny?" Lila asked.

"That mean woman said, said…"

"She said what?" Lila asked. Johnny started shifting again. Onkel put his arm on Lila and whispered, "Easy now. Take it slow."

"She said you was very bad." He continued to shuffle as though the stepmother might come through the door at any time. What else could they have said about Lila? She'd been ready to kill Papa in the barn if he had come one step closer when he was ordered to beat her. Then Fischer had jumped out of the shadows and surprised them. Maybe Johnny was right, maybe she was bad. She would have crushed Papa's skull that day, bringing an end to the threat, with the rusted wrench she had hidden. She would have hanged for it. But she would rather die than let him damage her as he had Iris and Johnny.

"Uncle Johnny. You like me, don't you?" Minna interrupted as he tried to sort out this person they kept telling him was Lila.

"You smell nice. And your orange…" He grinned, trying to remember the word for skirt. He nodded eagerly. "I like you." He kept his eyes on Minna and pointed behind him toward Lila. "but she is bad. Very bad."

"It's not true," Minna said startling Lila. "Somebody told you wrong, Uncle Johnny. Lila is not bad. See, look at me." He hadn't taken his eyes off her. "Now look at her." He was reluctant to shift his eyes, glancing quickly in Lila's direction. "She's my mother, so she can't be bad. Can she? And she will make you a very nice pie. Would you like that?"

"What kinda pie?" Johnny asked, abruptly stopping his shifting. Onkel chuckled.

"What kind of pie would you like?" Minna asked.

"I want her to make kuchen." Lila gasped. He did remember her! He remembered her kuchen.

"She fixed my leg," he whispered to Minna. They sat elbow to elbow at the kitchen table. Lila heard him say it. He did remember that night in the barn! He was such a fragile boy then, not like this larger-than-life man confiding in her daughter.

The days spent in the Dakotas were like gusts of wind. Johnny and Minna spent hours in the kitchen working so close together they seemed attached by their shoulders. He taught her his secret for making vanilla pudding, and she showed him how to decorate cookies that Lila baked. They giggled, and he teased her, and she teased him right back.

"You put too much vanilla in." He bossed her.

"Did not." She sassed him back.

"Did, too." The banter went on till they got tired of it.

In the afternoons, they walked hand in hand to the drugstore. Onkel gave them each a nickel that they spent on mystery packages wrapped in pretty paper in a bin. They debated their choices, rattling and feeling all of the boxes. Minna picked large boxes, one of which had lilac bath talc. Johnny was delighted with his giant orange comb. He ran it through his hair so many times Onkel hinted he was going to make it fall out.

"Does it look better now?" he'd ask Minna each time he combed his thick hair.

"It looks just fine now, Uncle Johnny," she answered each time.

He refused to let Minna help him with his chores for Onkel and

Tante. *So that's why the house is tidy,* Lila determined. Minna tried to take the mop he pulled out to scrub the floors to help him, but he barked, "No. That's my job."

"But I do it at home," she told him. "And I'm good at it."

"I'm better!" he retorted. "You go rake leaves." Onkel laughed when Johnny directed her away from his work, wanting her out of the house in the hours he did all his cleaning. The trees Onkel had been able to keep alive through the dry conditions hadn't shed their leaves, so Minna peeked around corners and stayed out of her uncle's way.

He wouldn't let her dust or iron or clean his stove. The burners were wrapped in aluminum foil and he got fussy if anything got spilled on them. He was very precise with the ironing and told Minna she could not do it because there should be no wrinkles left. Lila didn't understand her daughter, who was volunteering to do the work. In Missoula, she bucked at the ironing. Lila and Johnny were alike; she expected the white linens from the bakery to be perfect.

Johnny remembered her *Pflammenkuchen*. "Lila," he shouted excitedly for that was when he finally believed she was his sister. He caught a whiff of it when he and Minna returned from the drugstore and ran to his sister as if he was ten years old, calling her by her name for the first time. "Lila, Lila!" He laughed.

"Yes, Johnny." She cut the first piece for him. Tante was at the table, keeping Lila company, and then Onkel came in. "It's a party," Minna declared, and so it was.

"It's not a party until Lila fills my coffee cup with that brew of hers," Onkel corrected.

"Oh, Onkel. You haven't forgotten."

"How could I, liebling?"

Before the party began, Lila talked to Tante while she prepared the dough. "I can't get out of my mind how we rushed around here, you and me, getting ready for my wedding." Tante had been an engine, running from stove to table to counters.

"You're wearing the linoleum out," Onkel had cautioned her. Even then she was bumping into chairs and edges, in part from haste but also because of her failing eyesight.

Fischer had praised Tante's stew. "The best I ever had," he pronounced, waving his spoon as an exclamation point in the air. Tante, not one to be bought by words, half smiled, torn between his charm and her concern for the future of her favorite niece.

Lila missed her aunt's nonstop bustle and her silver curls bouncing to the rhythm of their own beat while she chopped and diced, but she was comforted being in her aunt's presence again. She hadn't realized how much she had missed it. Franz and Martha had given her refuge and a career, and they doted on Minna and cared for her, but she was home with Tante. She had left Tante's with a basket of unrealistic hopes and fears. She felt nourished once again.

Tante listened as Lila mixed flour and yeast, punched around dough, smacked it out on the table, and rolled it out. Lila released a decade of stored feelings she had tucked away like her jars of pears and peaches and tomatoes in the basement fruit room on Pine Street. As she stirred the custard for the kuchen, watching so it didn't scorch, Tante said, "I see," or "oh my," or "Meine liebling." Whether she was sighted or blind, bustling or stationary, Tante comforted Lila as she nudged the threads of history from the lips and heart that had kept them hostage.

Eleven

"So what's the business about Willy?" Tante poked. It was a gentle prod. Iris remembered their tante as nosy. Lila had blossomed the year she stayed with Tante and Onkel in Aberdeen for catechism at age twelve. When it was Iris's turn to go, she bristled and sulked her year away. She missed the fields where she romped and pouted and made secrets with neighboring farm boys.

"I don't know, Tante." The unruly halo of silver ringlets about the old woman's head was as independent as the soul it crowned.

"What?" Tante rocked, nodding the upper half of her body, and cackled. Then she said, "I was a red-haired devil once, too, you know." Lila didn't miss the intent of Mama's name for Lila whenever she was angry with her.

Tante erupted in a giggle like the young girl she had once been, galloping her pony, untamed red hair flying behind her. She giggled again and said, "Between you and me"—she leaned on the table and whispered—"and the kitchen sink, I could've been Iris." She slapped the table with her palm, giggled again. She blinked both eyes and looked like she was winking. Lila could not imagine how Tante was in any way like Iris!

"Well, that's enough of that nonsense," Tante said, tucking that statement into a pocket of her heart. "Now where was we? Oh yeah. About Willy."

"I don't know," Lila mumbled trying to imagine how Tante was like Iris. It was as improbable as tying the two ends of the world together. "I don't know," she said again quietly.

"Does that mean you don't love him?" Lila had mentioned him while she thumped the dough. She'd meant only to dip her toe into that water. She should have known that it would be like diving into the deep end. The blind aunt tapped her fingers on the table. "I knew it, I knew it," Tante cried out when Lila brought him up.

"Well, there is this man. Willy," she'd said.

"Of course there is!" Tante chirped. She hurried to ask, "Who's

Willy?" peering through her cloudy obstructions. They had been talking of Fischer, whose antics could fill both an afternoon and a book. Then Tante said, "Now, if I was your age, mein Gott, liebe, I wouldn't close no doors."

"He wants to marry me."

"Yeah, and…"

"And…" She shrugged. "I'm not ready, I guess. It doesn't feel right."

"Humph!" Tante huffed. When she found out Willy was Fischer's brother, she said, "Humph!" again.

"You can't measure them by the same stick, Tante."

"Why not?" Tante drummed her palms on the table. Lila divided the dough and patted it between two rectangular pans and one round one. She smiled picturing Willy wearing her fancy apron and dancing around her. Fischer, if he caught sight of that, would mock him, and Willy wouldn't care at all. He wasn't about to let his brother drain him of his happiness.

"He doesn't push me to decide. He's funny. He doesn't give ultimatums like Fischer did. He went away for five years, and when he came back…well, it was like he'd never left."

"And you live like you was man and wife?" Asking as if she was checking the weather forecast, she stared into the dark space between them. If anyone else had asked, Lila would be irate.

She nodded slightly to her blind aunt, who saw it through the eyes of her heart. "Liebling." She was very quiet. "This life is not just for hard work. Stop a minute"—she waved her hand in the air—"and listen to me." She chuckled softly, and Lila sat next to her.

"There's more than enough work in this lifetime. I, myself, if I wasn't a wrinkled old woman, and I didn't have Jacob, yeah…I would no sooner marry again than eat a snake!" Then she grinned and wrinkled her nose at both ideas. "I can only speculate about that." She sighed. "But I think I would want a man around sometimes, too, but not for the cookin' and cleanin'." She laughed. "I done a lifetime worth of that already for Jacob."

"When I'm with him, Tante, we sit and talk like you and I do. After Minna's gone to sleep he comes to the back door, and I make him a cup of coffee—"

"And a piece of kuchen, I bet."

"Yeah. That or…Tante, I make blachinda for the railroad men. They take it on the train in their lunches. Willy loves it, too."

"Those men eat the pumpkin?" She scrunched up her nose again.

"No, no. I'll make it for you the way I do it, and you'll see what I mean."

Johnny and Minna barged in through the back door. They had their surprise packages from the drugstore. "What'd you get, Uncle Johnny?" He unwrapped his gift, a checkered dish towel, and Minna made a face. "Ugh. I'm glad I didn't get that one."

"It's for the supper dishes," he explained, hugging it to him.

Minna pulled the stopper out of the Eau de Paris cologne that came in a blue glass bottle. She sniffed it. Then she put a few dabs behind her ear before doing the same for Lila. It was unexpected, and Lila had to stop herself from pulling away.

"Here, Uncle Johnny, try this." Minna went after him chasing him with the perfume bottle.

"No, Minna." He turned on her, ready to burst out in tears. "Don't do that."

"I was just teasing, Uncle Johnny." She backed away. He wouldn't look at her. "I'm sorry."

"Don't ever do it again." He put his palm up in front of her like a stop sign. She lowered her head and put the bottle away. "Promise me!"

She promised. "Shall we go look for your cat now?" Minna asked hopefully. He nodded. "I know he's in the garage." And they went out the same way they had arrived, hand in hand.

"Iris was like her," Tante said. Lila wished it weren't so, but she knew it. She tried to keep it pushed down and out of sight.

"With her, it ain't gonna to be easy."

"It hasn't been easy with her up till now."

"But Iris turned out pretty good in the end." Feisty Iris, whom Lila once disliked and envied and then later pitied because of the horrible beating. But Iris survived. She lived with her scars and laughed at her disfigurement. Lila didn't fault her anymore, but she begrudged her because Minna found in her sister an oversize heart always waiting for her.

Iris discovered her sauciness again because of Minna. It didn't come back all at once. It was like the winter sun peeking out from frosty clouds. Paulie and Minna believed in her, accepted her, and helped her unclog the artery dammed up by fear and hate, mostly fear.

Iris was aided through the singular touch of a baby's fingers, and the adoration of a swarthy, diminutive foreigner. The obnoxious laugh Lila had so despised on the farm sounded almost like music when it once again rumbled from the belly. Iris yawned like no one was watching and even farted again. She didn't hide anything from Paulie. He didn't like two things, and he told her so at the outset.

"Please speak kindly of our Lord. I don't like it when you use his name in vain." The second habit was her cigarette smoking. He failed miserably getting her to curtail either of these habits, but Paulie wasn't one to shake his finger, or wag his head in disgust. He murmured, "I love you so much," for he knew her actions hurt her more than anyone else.

Iris fumbled about inside herself to uncover the remnants of a mouthy girl who played softball back in South Dakota a decade earlier. The one who hooked up with the farm boys in the fields and shared cigarettes, wiggled her hips at them, and teased them with half-closed eyes. That girl was buried, the one who wouldn't back down, who stood toe-to-toe to defend herself; she'd stood over the grave herself. That girl who wouldn't let anyone decide what she should think or how she should act. It returned to full bloom, her sauciness and sass, the evening she and Paulie became engaged, the evening Fischer taunted Paulie, calling him names.

No one says mean things to my Paulie if I can help it. She'd stood up to Fischer and found Iris again that night, but wasn't able to prevent Paulie from getting a fist to the nose that knocked him out.

And Minna needed her, didn't she? She wasn't helpless, not even as a baby, but Iris knew without knowing at all, that what she had to give Minna no one else could give her. She stored in her cavernous heart, pints and quarts of goodwill and kindness. No one knew, when Minna was twelve years old, that time might be dripping like sand through an hourglass. That the hours already might be sipping the life from Iris a swallow at a time.

"You and Iris," Tante asked, "you do better now between you, ja? No more fighting like before?"

"Yes, Tante. We do better." Iris had nursed Lila for months after she lost the baby. Day after day, Lila stared past the fickle sapling that swung with the breezes. Willy brought flowers and sat with her in the hospital when she said nothing for days and stared out at Lolo Peak, and he listened to her heart whimper.

"And Iris knows about this Willy? Ja, of course she does," Tante answered herself. "And Minna. What does she know?"

"He is her uncle. She should treat him better than she does. Willy and I are careful."

"Ja. Probably not enough, though, ja? She knows something."

"You think so?"

"She's quick. Look at how she is able to take care of Johnny, and he doesn't know it. She doesn't want to know, but she does."

"Tante, can we talk about your eyes now?"

"You can talk about them. Ja. But you can tell that I see better than before."

"Onkel worries about you."

"That old man. He's an old woman, the way he fusses. And him with that borscht. He is going to stop my heart with it."

"You won't do it, will you?" Lila sighed.

Tante laughed. "Lila, sometimes you have to put your trust in the dear Lord. He will take care of all things. I don't go to bed with all those worries in my head. I don't want you should do that either. We will let things be. All right? And watch for what comes." Tante reached toward her niece and patted her arm. She tapped so lightly Lila wanted to close her eyes. "All is gut, liebling," the aunt counseled.

Twelve

"It's so hot a pig could pickle his toes on the dang sidewalk," Clyde said at the bakery counter one day. Minna exploded in laughter, which made Iris start giggling. It could get completely out of control, the two of them laughing so hard sometimes they were bending over and crying, "Oh, my ribs, my ribs." Any farcical remark pulled Minna to Iris.

"If that woman ain't nuts"—Fischer shook his head to Minna about Iris—"and I'm pretty dang sure she is, she's got the biggest mouth this side the Mississippi." If that was meant to convince Minna to steer clear of Iris, it made her want to be with her aunt more. She would move in with her, be her daughter if she could.

"You German?" A guy asked Iris out of nowhere. He hadn't been in the bakery before. Stella and Clyde's heads popped up over the tables. "Not another one," Stella said under her breath.

Stalin had a saying about the Germans. They were like willow trees. You could plant them anywhere, and they would thrive. There were still pockets of German colonies in the United States that spoke the mother language. Lila and Iris were grandchildren of Germans from Russia. They'd grown up in a German-speaking community on the South Dakota prairie.

It was news to them when they found out that Nazis were scouring the world in search of Germans who had migrated, some who had been gone for centuries.

"Hitler is the friend of Germans everywhere," recruiters touted. Summer youth camps, like the one in Wisconsin called Camp Hindenburg, dressed the kiddies in Nazi uniforms, drilled them military style, and taught them to deify Hitler.

"I think we should be careful," Lila advised Iris. "It's best we don't try to talk too much with the customers," fearful their accents would single them out. "And let's not speak German around Minna." She thought for a moment and added, "Or to each other."

"No more German, Willy," Lila repeated to him.

"I don't know no love words in English, Lila. You're gonna

have to teach me some now, I guess. Darn good thing," he added with a grin. "I wanna learn. I'll be your best pupil."

"You would say that," she retorted and raised her eyebrows, wanting him to be serious.

"We should know what Hitler's talking about firsthand," Lila advised Willy. "Better to know the devil we're facing." Out of earshot from Minna, they listened to the radio. To one trained in the language, Hitler was mesmerizing. He didn't seem the thug he was at the cinema when his mustache marched submissively on his upper lip. Willy was right. Intimate words from their first language did not have an equal substitute in English.

Hitler was titillating over the airwaves. Lila and Willy understood his words and his convictions. They heard the crowds swelling in the background. When they shut the radio off, the room felt eerie, like a ghost had raged through in a temper, leaving things upended and in turmoil. Lila sighed. "I'm glad I'm not in Berlin. He's too dangerous. People adore him."

The German filmmaker Leni Riefenstahl revealed her rapture. "Can you just imagine what it would be like in those crowds?" Lila shuddered to Iris. "People pushing and shoving each other just to get close to him. They just want to have him to look at them."

"Did you hear that?" a disgruntled newspaper reporter bellowed at the bakery counter on a busy morning. He smacked his hand against the article, and then put it front of Iris to read. "The American Bund played the *Star Spangled Banner*," the fresh-as-a-newborn anthem recently endorsed by Herbert Hoover. "They put a picture of George Washington on the same stage as Hitler with the American flag and the swastika, too. Can you beat that?"

"What boils my blood," the reporter from the *Missoulian* continued, talking with his mouth half-full of cinnamon roll, "is them sons of guns playing the German national anthem, too. They have some nerve saying they're good Americans." He bit down so hard he took a chunk out of his cheek. Lila and Iris hid their fear behind blank faces and kept busy.

"Yeah. And the Ku Klux Klan endorsed the German American Bund," a new guy sitting at a table with Clyde informed the reporter, who had a wadded napkin in his mouth to stop the blood. Iris scrubbed the counter, and her back prickled. She wondered if they were watching her and grabbed the coffeepot heading over to the guy sitting next to Clyde.

"Who needs a fill-up here?"

The guy with the napkin in his mouth tried to get his tongue around it. "There's a bunch called the Christian Enforcers. They've endorsed the bund, too." A day didn't go by it seemed before another organization came out in support of the German American Bund.

"We share common ground," the anti-Semitic supremacists cheered. At rallies in the larger cities, riots broke out that turned into brawls.

Franz had encouraged Lila to change the bakery's name two years earlier. "You don't know how bad it can get," he told her. "People don't dare speak the German no more." He meant during the Great War. "They wouldn't let us play German songs then." Franz eyes were mellow with longing for his German folk tunes. The American government grew an overactive paranoia gland fearful that the 25 percent of the population in the United States that was German might turn traitor on their new homeland.

Franz had been watched. He felt singled out, so he quit his job and volunteered for the army. He decided he'd rather be shot at than accused by a neighbor who was riled up by the government against German Americans. For once the Irish immigrants were not on the receiving end. "Dose guys I went to work with every day." He winced as he told Lila and couldn't finish his sentence. It choked him up. "They started to treat me like I was a spy." One of his German friends who played a tuba in an oom-pah-pah band was told he could no longer perform at the city's bandstand. "If they spotted us eating German sausage at a picnic, they reported us."

People he had called neighbors chastised themselves for having placed trust in any *damn Kraut*. "We thought they were our friends!" they said, shocked at having been duped. It was one short step to get to blame. "They've been lying to us all along. We've been made fools of!"

The government encouraged the mania. People who risked eating sauerkraut were suspect unless they were willing to call it "liberty cabbage."

"Oh yeah," Franz warned Lila about the name Schneider plastered over the bakery window. "You could call it Lila's," he suggested. "No one would know, then." He tried to convince her. He hadn't run to the lawyer on some whim. German American shopkeepers during the Great War were dragged out into the streets and forced to kiss the American flag. If this happened to Lila because *Schneider* was blazoned on Higgins Avenue, well he couldn't bear to think of it. Pet owners who babied their overlong wiener dogs, dressing them in green plaid coats when it was chilly, fussing over them as if they were children, naming them Fritz or Otto or Gertrude, had not been able to take them out on walks because they were dachshunds. They would get murdered on the street.

There was the occasional new customer in the bakery who didn't know Iris or Lila. If one asked where they were from because they heard the remnants of an accent in their speech, the women bristled internally, then smiled.

"Where do *you* come from?" Iris would shoot back. She wasn't going to get cornered. She had that look, the one Paulie knew so well. He envied that fierceness; he wished he had it when he was threatened.

Stella and Clyde smiled to themselves and continued drinking their coffee when that happened.

Thirteen

"You should be locked up with them other Eye-talians at the fort. Nazi lover!" Paulie was ashamed to tell Iris what they had said, but she coaxed it out of him. He didn't want to be diminished in her eyes. If it happened to Iris, she wouldn't back down.

Minna heard a boy in high school algebra say how he wanted to go out to the fort and kill him a bunch of wops. Spray them with bullets. America had gotten stuck in the middle of the war, and the fort was busting with its captured enemies.

Paulie was luckier than many in the forties. He was an Italian on the free side of Fort Missoula's barbed wire.

"Those poor boys," he moaned of the men cooped up behind ten-foot fencing in Montana. "They just kids." Except for fate, it could be him had he stayed in the old country and been conscripted into the army of that fascist Mussolini. "That bastard who is in the bed with that Hitler." He wondered if Italians his age were confined at the fort.

"In bed, not in the bed," Iris corrected him. He stayed away from the fort. He didn't want to be locked up, too, chased with a bayonet at the end of a rifle. "Otherwise—" he started, and this made Iris giggle.

"Say it again, Paulie. Say the word 'otherwise.'" When she finished laughing, he continued as if he hadn't noticed he'd been interrupted. The word sounded sophisticated, not the way Paulie normally talked. That's why she had him repeat it.

"Otherwise, I would talk to them," meaning the thousand seamen arrested and held far away from their Italian mamas.

"But what could you say to them, Paulie, that would help them, anyway?" She had stopped laughing.

"I dunno. I could talk to them about home." He missed the rocky slopes above his village.

"I am getting so mad, Iris," he complained after Pearl Harbor and the Americans went to war. Some ruffians had singled him out on his way home from work.

"You stinkin' no-good Nazi. Jap lover," they cried. They pelted him in the back with rocks. The stones didn't hurt him physically, but he was mortified. He loved America. He loved Iris and all her family, but he was being made to feel he was separate. There was an invisible but definite line he could not cross, for he was marked as an outsider.

"How can people be dis ignorant? I am American citizen. They don't know the difference between them Germans and Italians. If they say *fascista*, at least they talking about my country." He tapped his chest with leftover pride. Sometime after he had migrated, his country had turned to Fascism, but for him Italy was an arid village where his mama was buried. A cousin sent a photo of the grave with Papa's and Mama's names written in the cement. He longed to place flowers over their grave, and clean up the weeds. "I have lived here for twenty years—twenty years, Iris."

She nodded. What else could she do?

"I am married man, to American woman, and I been good citizen all that time. Haven't I?" If he weren't so upset, he'd have remembered to say his *bella* American wife. *Oh, she is bella.*

"I...I..." He couldn't get the words out. "Them—"

"Imbeciles," Iris contributed.

"About my gladiolas." He wanted the name-callers to know. His blossoms were almost as precious as his Iris, and every year they won best of show at the Missoula County Fair.

"Bullies," Iris again. The war had them all on edge. She didn't know what to say to Paulie. She hugged him and lit a cigarette. She wanted to tell him about Lila, but he had enough on his mind already. She wished she had someone to talk to. "Stop the world," she wanted to joke about the fact that Lila, for once, was actually saying out loud what was on her mind. And it was about Minna.

"The way she looks through me," Lila confided to Iris, whose mouth dropped open in disbelief. They were cleaning out the shelves under the counter.

"Rare as hens' teeth," she wanted to tell Paulie. "Lila talking to me. Huh!"

"I don't know," Lila went on. "Like I'm a window. What's on the other side, I ask myself? Because she isn't seeing me, that's for sure."

Wow, Iris thought. *That girl must really be getting to her.*

"I'm not going to shout at her," Lila said softly. Minna was cleaning tables. She had the urge to slap her in the face to wake her up.

"Look at the way she acts." Minna was tossing dirty dishes into a metal basin as if they were enemies. She broke a handle off a coffee cup.

"See what I mean? She's careless. She has no idea how hard I've worked to keep the bakery going," Lila whispered. At the same time Lila made a mental calculation of the cost of the damage. When Minna went into the back, Lila asked, "How did she get to be such a stubborn mule?"

That's exactly what Mama called you, Iris thought. She decided not to say, "Take a good look, Lila. The apple didn't fall far from that tree."

"Why doesn't she see that she needs to cut that girl some slack." Iris relented about keeping mum to Paulie about Lila. He had his worries, but so did she.

"You know what I think?" he responded.

"No, Paulie," she shook her head. "How could I know what's cookin' in that brain of yours?"

"She don't want Minna to end up like she did. You know, marrying Fischer." Paulie felt sorry for Lila, and for Minna, but he didn't see how to resolve it. Iris stared at him. Sometimes, that husband of hers amazed her.

೪

"What about this Archie?" Lila interrogated Minna. It was a mistake to bring it up. Five years earlier Tante had asked this very question about Willy while Lila made dough in her aunt's kitchen.

"Nothin'." Minna shrugged like she was wiggling out of a sweater. Lila wasn't Tante, and she wasn't Iris. She didn't like to sniff around in other people's business, not like her aunt and sister, both of whom were detectives the way they dragged out answers to questions that people didn't intend to reveal.

Even with opaque sight, Tante had seen the future and reckoned it would not go easy for Lila or Minna. Growing up, Lila always had a plan. She organized her days around her chores. This was useful later in the bakery for her yeast doughs that had to be timed at each stage from start to finish. She was at her most comfortable with her ingredients. They were her ancient, consoling friends, and she added new ones to expand her circle, to make her life more interesting, and to bring new flavors to the mix. She was on intimate terms with her recipes, and didn't require or want much human companionship, although people were attracted to her and sought out her company.

"Winchester Bay," she heard Iris tell a stranger. Iris knew the most peculiar things. She wouldn't dream of going deep-sea fishing, you could bet on that, but she'd tell Paulie, "Can you imagine spending a whole day on a boat turning pea green and puking over the side? Talk

71

about feeding the fish!" But after one informative conversation, in which she scoured a person's brain like it was an encyclopedia and she was researching the facts, she could tell any interested customers where to find the best chartered boat service in Oregon. She was the bakery's reference guide and atlas rolled into one. She could answer questions faster than she refilled a cup of coffee, and, in the process, spice it up with an inoffensive sarcastic comment that made her laugh.

"Why do you talk to people that way?" It bordered on the disrespectful, but Lila seemed to be the only one who felt uneasy. Iris slept late when she wasn't working at the bakery. She smoked, she swore, she cooked at random.

"I open a can of Campbell's better than anyone." She smirked, and Minna laughed. But she did not joke about her designs or if someone derided her Paulie. She would not lower herself to accept criticism—if there was any—for her work or her personality. "Take it or leave it," she counseled Minna, who could say whatever came to her mind around Iris. Sometimes they were silly and girlish together, and they laughed like teenagers, but other times it could be a meaty bone they chewed on. When that happened, Iris sat still, listened, and nodded.

Lila wondered how Tante had endured the year Iris lived with them, wishing she were wise as her old aunt. But even Tante changed course once in a while. Onkel Jacob wrote about her eye surgery, the one she was not going to have. *What did Onkel Jacob say to finally convince her?*

Letters were coming again in Tante's flowery handwriting, and the words didn't run off the bottom of the page as they once did. When Iris had lived with them, Tante must have tried to encourage her in conversation. Tante was right. Iris, being a detective herself, would have resisted, dug deep to find her self-control. Mama would have fried her if there had been reports of Iris acting rude to them.

For Lila and Tante the kitchen was a mutual meeting place. Iris viewed it as the room in the house where she could find the can opener and the coffeepot and leave up her ironing board.

Fourteen

"Don't shrug at me," Lila barked, hating herself for letting the girl rile her. They'd finished cleaning the floors, and Minna was putting the chairs in place. Lila thought she saw Franz out of the corner of her eye. It would be just like him, to act the imp, even from the other side. Heaven and hell were nonsense to her, but she couldn't imagine Franz and Martha being anywhere but heaven. It was distracting. Oh yes, it would be just like him to show up to counsel her if it had anything to do with Minna.

She was trying to concentrate, to decide what to say next because Minna's arms were arms crossed and there was fire in her eyes. "Aren't you in the least bit concerned about what you're doing?" There was Franz, at the top of the stairs, trying to get a peek at the baby. Lila hadn't even named her yet. His baker's hat hung, like an extra set of white eyebrows, over his eyes as he peered around the door jamb, his aprons strings askew.

"Go easy, Lila, wit her." He had his bear paw on her shoulder as she debated what to say next to her willful daughter, and he gave her a forlorn smile. He would have sung to Minna. That wouldn't work for Lila. He'd sing even to the point of irritating her, or he'd surprise her with a pair of ice skates she had to have that he bought on the Swap and Shop program on the radio.

"I hate to tell you this," Willy relayed to Lila after he'd caught Minna in the alley. "She was pretty mouthy. Told me I ain't no saint, so I better keep my mouth shut." Willy rocked the foundation right out from under her. Iris probably had been the same at her age, but she wouldn't have sassed her elder. She'd have gotten a whipping for that. She could not imagine her daughter talking to Willy that way, and then saying she was biding her time. *Biding her time? What did that mean? I'm supposed to be able to sleep after that? What does that girl have on her mind?* Maybe Fischer had been bad-mouthing her, slanting Minna against her more than before. She didn't understand why the man never married again. *Loves his independence too much and being mad at me.* He needed to keep the old wound open and bleeding so he could blame Lila for whatever was bothering him.

"I see what's going on in the alley," Lila said, brushing off the Franz imp, "and Fischer's mad 'cause he caught you smoking. What are you up to?"

"No good!" Minna snapped. She grabbed her jacket from the coatrack, almost pulling the stand over because it was caught on a hook. An icy blast rushed in when she opened the door.

"Take your hat, at least," Lila called to her back. "You need your scarf today." She shivered.

"Okay, sister." The back of the door would have smacked her in the face had she been ten feet closer. "You are going to have to ask Iris about Minna," she scolded herself. She couldn't abide Iris knowing more about her daughter than she did. She would rather scrape burnt sugar out of the baking pans than ask for help from Iris. It made her stomach knot up, and she had the prehistoric itch to punch Iris right in the snout for being the winner of a contest she didn't know she was in.

"Well, Lila, I ain't no expert on people." Willy had tried to comfort Lila. "Especially when it comes to Minna.
What do you make of it?" She'd quizzed him about the other thing Minna had said.

"What does she mean about biding her time?"

"Maybe I heard her wrong, but that don't seem the case."

"Was she showing off for that smart-aleck kid?" Lila bristled at the girl's insolence, resented it. "I'm just about fed up with her, Willy. I don't want a spoiled rotten kid around." She wondered if Minna talked to Fischer with the same arrogance. If they had stayed a family, Fischer would have had Minna under the belly of cars at age five or six. He would have propped her up in the mouth of the car, let her get covered in grease, taught her how to change spark plugs and oil.

Minna would have learned the names of all the parts and where they were attached and what they did. Lila imagined Minna would have loved it. The pair may have believed their accidental meetings throughout the years were secret, but Lila often caught sight of Minna lugging her bread and Fischer pursuing her on Higgins, his jacket lapels flying up in front of him. He'd be talking to Minna and suddenly become animated, wave his hands around, a cigarette hanging on for dear life between his fingers because he just spotted an interesting vehicle. He and Willy used to spend hours talking about why one car was better than another, and what the manufacturers improved on with their latest models.

"I gotta problem with the car, now." Paulie moaned on a Saturday morning. He leaned over the bakery counter speaking to Iris in a low voice. She could not bear his long face and furrowed brow.

"What do I know about cars?" she asked ruefully. "Nothing, and that's as much as I want to know. I don't see your point, Paulie, coming to tell me. You're just gonna have to figure out what to do about it."

"What kind of noise is it making, Uncle Paulie?" Minna asked. She was putting out green-speckled sugar cookies.

"It's gotta rumble, like maybe it's gotta bellyache." He squinted at her, as if he had a similar pain in his own gut.

She and Iris laughed at his perplexed face and the implication that the car had a digestive tract.

"I think you need to feed it some of your delicious spaghetti and meatballs," Minna teased. Paulie wouldn't go near Fischer if he could help it.

"Oh, you girls." He grimaced. He was going to get no help for his car problem in the bakery.

"Take it to Uncle Willy," Minna told him. "I think it's a spark plug misfiring."

"She does have a mouth on her these days. No doubt about that," Willy said, trying to console her. "She's a good kid, though. Always done what you wanted her to do. She still does, don't she?"

"Are you saying it's my fault?"

"No, no, no." Jesus, she could go from zero to fifty miles an hour. He tried to back up, start again, but there was no going back with Lila if she already had decided what she'd heard, no matter what he really did say.

"I don't think it's so much what you're doin', sweetheart." She waited for him to dig himself out. "It's partly Minna. Okay?"

"And the other part?"

"Well, it's partly you. It's both of you being who you are."

"And what does that mean?" She put her hand on her hip the way Iris used to do when she was looking to spar. She lowered her head. She was a bull pawing the ground, waiting and watching. Willy had just waved the red cape.

"Oh boy," he said, so quietly she almost missed it. "Am I talkin' myself into a mess here, Lila?" He knew the answer.

"You tell me."

"I'll listen to whatever you have to say till the damn cows come home, if you wanna get it out of your system." He shrugged.

"Out of my system? And watch your language." She was heated up. Her eyes turned the same color as her hair. He meant it. He'd wait around until she started crying and the worst was over. That's when she'd let him kiss her. She'd climb into his lap and kiss him hard, and he'd return the kiss but let her be in charge. He let her decide if they would go further, and maybe it was a way to prove to her he wasn't going to behave like Fischer, no matter that he wanted to lift her up and carry her upstairs and take them to a place of ecstasy. Those times were the center of the jelly roll.

"Sorry. Didn't watch my mouth. Talk to Iris," he said carefully. "Find out what Minna's told her."

"Why is Iris always the one who knows, and not me?" She had a black look. "Why does Minna talk to her and not me?" Willy did know a bit about human nature. He'd grown up with Fischer, and nearly a dozen brothers and sisters crammed into two bedrooms. But he wasn't dumb enough to think she would settle for a logical answer, or that she would even listen to one. He hated seeing her so upset.

"Two's better than one," he wanted to tell her. If they put their heads together they could figure it out. He knew it wasn't the right moment to ask her to marry him—again—but maybe after she got Minna worked out.

He missed that target by about a mile. "Maybe you need to move out." She glared. "Find a place of your own. Away from us."

"What? Where in the world did that come from?" This had the look of Fischer to it. *Dammit. Is Fischer getting in the lead again?* He'd done it in the Dakotas. Swept Lila up and married her, and then took her off to Montana. Willy only heard about it three weeks later.

"I think you'd better move out. Soon." She could have smacked him in the head with a two by four. He would have preferred that.

"You just said that." He was reeling. Hell, there were five or six places he could move into if he had to. He had been thinking that way for a while. He earned enough and had saved plenty to buy a house, and he would have done so already except that he enjoyed waking up to Lila, bustling below him and making her dough. He loved it, too, when he came back early from the garage and found her cleaning. He enjoyed working hard as much as she did and all the little things they did together, even if it was taking the garbage out to the alley.

"It has to be Fischer puttin' that idea in your head."

"Maybe he did. You don't know what it's like having him come around here and saying it's because of you and me about Minna. You think he hasn't told Minna the same? What if he's right? What if it is about us?"

"Lila. It ain't about us, and you know it."

"Besides. What if just one time he gets mad enough and says that in front of the customers? You know what that could do to the bakery." If the bakery went to hell because of Fischer throwing his mouth around, she knew he would support her and Minna. But she'd only get madder if he said that. Why couldn't she see him as a way out? "What am I supposed to do, Willy? I've got to raise the girl. Keep her out of trouble, if I can."

"You could marry me. That's what you could do." God, he could have kicked himself. He couldn't believe he said it. As soon as it left his mouth he knew he was making things worse. She'd shocked him, and so he said a stupid thing. *Stupid, stupid.*

"And just what would that solve? Minna's got it in her head that Fischer and I still would be together if it wasn't for you."

He had a bitter smile. "Well, it's too bad she don't know the truth."

Fifteen

"Okay, Lila, let's have it." Iris had to keep stepping back to stay out of Lila's way because she wouldn't stop cleaning. She wiped the counter tops down like they were infected with the measles or diphtheria. She hummed, too, even while serving customers. Lila only hummed when her temper was on the hot burner.

"What do you mean?" Lila snapped.

Oh boy. Here it comes. It looked like it was going to be a doozy. *God help us.* The air was already thick with mood when Iris hurried in at ten minutes past eight. Three customers were lined up at the cash register. Okay, she was a few minutes late, and Lila would get sulky if someone had to wait to get served. Iris really did her best. It was that last cigarette that had slowed her down. Lila didn't let her smoke out back if Minna was around, or even if she was already gone to school. Iris had to stock up on nicotine before she got to work in the morning. As much as was possible. Some days got really bad, and if she had a free minute she'd holler back into the kitchen, "Lila I need to run to the drugstore for a minute." If she only got three or four puffs in around the corner, it was enough to help her get through the next few hours.

"I'm not taking any chances," Lila had cautioned Iris, "having Minna see you light up. You can go to your own funeral, but leave Minna out of it."

The tense atmosphere was not about being late or about smoking. Those sins were treated to long pauses and short quips to questions Iris asked. "You gonna make muffins today?"

Long pause. Then a maybe that landed like a brick. Iris might try again, and if it fell hard a second time, she kept her mouth shut and watched the second hand on the clock groan from one minute to the next.

Let me guess, Iris mused. *Bet it's got somethin' to do with Minna. Now what'd I do to made her mad?*

They got along most days, not like the old times when they deliberately tried to provoke each other. Iris actually liked her sister.

She'd spend a whole day assembling a fashionable red jacket for Lila to wear home in the evenings when the east winds were brisk.

Even when Lila said, "It doesn't go with my hair," which was a ridiculous statement, Iris refused to take it personally. "Rules are meant to be broken," she advised. "Whoever said that redheads shouldn't wear red, anyway?" The fashion world might be a monarchy, but Iris wasn't its serf.

The broken Iris, mangled and crushed by Papa in the barn, still haunted Lila. In an odd moment, if the sunlight landed on her facial scar, Lila cringed and wanted to nurse her all over again. But Iris smoked. She was careless the way she took care of herself, like time was running out so she was going to do whatever she wanted. She ate stuff out of cans, sometimes not even heating up their cold contents on the stove. She spoke out loud the opinions that others choked back. She couldn't keep to a schedule yet believed her own futile promises about doing so. Iris made Lila feel limp inside.

"Is this about Minna?" Iris had her feet planted when Lila tried to wipe the counter by the cash register.

Lila checked herself, not wanting to react. "How did you know?" she nearly blurted out. She wouldn't let Iris set the pace. She would say what she had to say, in her own way.

She breathed deeply. "Okay, this *is* about Minna." She hated saying it. Hated it! She squeezed the rag, and the water dripped down the front of the counter.

"Is it about that boy, Archie? The cute one?" That was it! That was just like Iris! Lila looked to the future and drew the boundaries for Minna so she wouldn't make the same mistakes she had. Iris, however, saw a boy with charm and good looks who was fun to be with. She threw the future right out the door like she was tossing out dirty water. That was the dividing line between them. Iris would roll her eyes in disbelief if Lila told her she'd sent Will packing.

"Is he? Cute?" The ridiculous word barely got off her tongue. "I didn't notice." Her throat tightened, and they had hardly begun. "So you've seen him, then." She wasn't asking. Of course Iris had seen him. He'd been hanging around the bakery. "What do you think of him?"

"He's a sweet boy, don't you think?" If somebody shook Iris, her brain would rattle around in her thick skull. After all her trauma, it didn't seem possible she could be so gullible. In some ways, she acted pretty normal, but maybe she really had lost some of her marbles the same way Johnny did.

"What I think is that I caught him with his hand up Minna's sweater. That's what I think." Lila glared at her.

"Oh. You're not worried about that." She laughed. "Are you?" She wrinkled her nose.

"You're not?" Lila could not fathom how they could possibly be sisters.

"They're kids, Lila. Of course he's gonna have his hand up her you know what. Weren't we the same?" So that's what Iris did on the farm while Lila took care of the house and kids and fixed the meals.

"Well, maybe you were, Iris. I sure wasn't." Iris flirted with the boys in the fields and behind the barn. The sisters were rivals then, too competitive to share secrets. *How could we be so different?*

"You weren't?" Iris looked at her sister like she could be Stella or some other bookworm who stopped by the shop.

"No. But has Minna said anything to you? About him or the smoking?"

"Honest to God, Lila. I do not smoke around her, if that's what you're thinkin'. Honest to God." She held her fingers up Boy Scout style.

"I don't know what to think anymore. She won't talk to me. Then I caught her with that boy." She made a face. "Then Fischer charged in here Saturday and told me *he'd* caught her smoking. I need to know what she's told you."

"About that boy, you mean?"

"About *anything!* The *boy*, the *smoking*. Anything. You know what she told Willy?" She stopped to get her words around it. "She told him she's 'biding her time.'"

"That little stinker!" Iris squeezed her eyebrows. "Are you sure that's what she said?"

"That's what Willy told me. You know Willy. He wouldn't make anything like that up." She'd made him pack his bags and get out because of it, a fact that Iris hadn't noticed—yet. Lila had already posted ads for a renter. Sooner or later Iris would figure it out. If she didn't see the notices, it would dawn on her that Willy hadn't come around on his coffee break.

"Oh boy." *That little stinker!* Iris thought. Minna had been a little off, it seemed. She wasn't laughing at jokes, or being goofy.

Minna balked when Iris tried to get her up to dance around the kitchen. "I don't feel like it right now."

"I don't know how you could sit still when it's Benny Goodman," Iris mocked her, but she backed off. She recognized moody as the old friend who came to visit and sat at the kitchen table far too long and drank five or six cups of bitter, sweet coffee. It could stay for days or until after dark before it moved on.

Iris could be looking in her own mirror. Minna held steady usually for three weeks in a row. The fourth week was a roller coaster. The weeping began when Minna couldn't get a waistband right on a skirt, or she had to tear out a zipper two or three times. She'd get mad, throw the cloth up in the air, and shout, "I've had it, Auntie. I'm not sewing ever again!"

"Let me see it." And Iris would tell her, "Oh, that's easy, sweetheart."

"Maybe for you it is. Not for me." Minna would storm out and a week later show up to finish what she'd started. But that pattern had changed recently. Minna still showed up to sew. She was getting quite good these days. She'd begun designing her outfits, and surprised Iris with a dress she made her for her birthday.

It hadn't been difficult to hide the dress from her aunt. Iris had stacks of fabric folded and stored in a cabinet. She put notes on fabrics she had plans for but gave Minna permission to choose from whatever else was there. Unless Minna asked for a suggestion or needed help, Iris left her on her own. Paulie had set up a second worktable for Minna, and he'd bought her a used machine on Swap and Shop. He loved coming home from work and finding the two with their machines whirring. It was like a little factory. They would be bowed over their machines and not hear him come in. He'd stand in the doorway, smiling.

Iris had been astonished by the birthday dress with its design and unusual pairing of fabrics and color. Bold golds and aqua, pitted against a black-and-white checkerboard, were new, not conjured by Iris in her imagination. It was like walking into an art museum and discovering a new room, and Iris was thrilled that it was Minna who took her to this place.

"So what *do* you know, Iris? What is Minna up to?" Lila persisted. It was worse than a trip to the dentist to have to ask her sister to tell her what was going on with her own daughter.

Iris was dying for a cigarette. She could not abide anyone interrogating her. Paulie gave her plenty of space. He left her alone to sort her things out and waited for her to ask him when she needed something. Lila didn't ask for much from her, but not because she understood how difficult it was for Iris. She saw her as obstinate, uncooperative, and withholding. There had been one sister too many in the farm kitchen.

"Can I just go have a smoke? Give me a minute to think about it?"

"Iris"—she was practically pleading—"do you know what's

going on?" Lila imagined Iris and Minna bobbing over their sewing machines. "Surely something has slipped out. She must have mentioned something." She imagined Minna saying things that couldn't be said face-to-face, looking into someone's eyes.

"Honest to Pete, Lila. I don't know about the smoking. If she does that, she isn't doing it in front of me."

"But she knows you smoke."

"Yeah, sure. She caught me at it when I was making her birthday cake. Dang it, Lila. I've been about as close to a saint as you can get." That almost drew a smile, but if Iris didn't smoke, she wouldn't have to go out of her way to hide it.

"I think she's nuts about this Archie. But I figured it best to just let it run its course."

"Run its course? What in the world does that mean?"

"Hey, he's shipping out as soon as he gets his orders."

"How do you know that?" Lila took a breath. Maybe it wasn't as dire as she thought.

"I don't know." Iris was baffled. "I thought she was talking to herself when she said it. I asked her, 'cause I wasn't sure I'd heard right." Iris squeezed her eyebrows. "I asked Minna, 'What'd you say?'"

Minna told Iris that Archie, the pretty-boy soldier, was just biding his time at the fort, waiting for a letter telling him to report to some airfield. "He's going to be an aviation cadet," Minna said with some pride.

"Did you know he came to Missoula from Georgia 'cause he'd heard about those two firefighters jumping out of planes to put out forest fires?" Iris asked.

"How would I know that, Iris? Nobody tells me anything."

"Well, he came up here thinking he'd get hired on, but that didn't happen. It didn't stop him from hanging around like a puppy at Hale Field long enough to decide he wanted to learn how to fly."

"How do you know all this?"

"Minna told me. She said his mama sent him money for lessons, and he racked up hours on a Taylorcraft BL 65 and Waco F2. I had to laugh. Leave it to Minna to remember the name."

"Leave it to you to repeat it. That's what she told you?"

"Yeah. Archie told his mama that if the US Army did not order him into the Pilot Training Program he would go to Canada and join the RAF." In the meantime, he was guarding Italian and Japanese prisoners and flirting with Minna.

Sixteen

"*L*et's leave it till tomorrow. I'll clean it all up," Paulie coaxed Iris.

"I vote for that," Iris croaked. If it was just dirty dishes in the sink, not the counters, too, the table, the floor, and even the walls, they would have stayed up to clean them. They headed up to bed. It was late, although Iris hadn't been able to sleep of late. She stared up at the ceiling until she felt like she was lying in her coffin. If she did fall sleep, she would wake up not knowing where she was, and she'd panic. It felt like eternity in the dark to figure out she was next to Paulie. She heard his steady breathing in and out, him whistling the air, and touched his hand to reassure herself that she was where she wanted to be.

"I'm gonna be awake, anyway," she told Paulie on the nights he awoke and went looking for her. He fussed if she missed her beauty sleep. "I might as well accomplish something useful." The light in her workroom glowed at three o'clock many nights. She had orders stacked up to finish but was savvy about taking any jobs that might put her under pressure to get them done in a rush.

"All things work together for good to those who love the Lord," she recited to any client who got pushy with her.

"What?" Most customers did not understand Iris even when she was talking straight. She didn't like them to get too close, didn't want to be asked special favors. She put them off balance reciting pat memorized phrases, things she remembered from her catechism days.

"Making that dang cake 'bout wore me out, Paulie." She was ahead of him on the stairs. They were both beat by the time the party broke up. She looked grim, and the yellow cast from the light fixtures didn't help. Her efforts on the culinary front looked like she'd gone ten rounds by the time she'd finished baking.

"You sure did a nice party for Minna's birthday. She won't forget it, neither."

Paulie woke every day in wonder over his good luck. Sure, there were the disappointments; the worst one was not having any children.

Each of them had grown up with more than their fair share of brothers and sisters. Too many, in fact. They were used to noise and commotion, and the bungalow could feel orphaned at times. Without Minna, they would have a big hole to try and fill. Sometimes Paulie had to chase back the fear that God might wake up one day and realize he'd handed out too much happiness.

Iris had her design work, Paulie the gladiolas, and he was grateful. Iris could get so deep into her work she wouldn't hear Paulie come home. He wouldn't disturb her concentration, just stand at the door briefly, and if she looked up, they'd smile and talk for a few minutes.

"That is beautiful," he'd compliment whatever she was working on. "I'm gonna make us some supper." He'd nod, and disappear to the kitchen. He'd bring her a snack, donning a fancy apron tied around his middle.

"What'd you eat today?" he'd ask as he handed her a plate of celery and cheese. He'd stand over her until she ate the first stalk.

"Can't remember," she'd say dismissively, which meant, he knew, she hadn't eaten anything. He might find a half-empty can of soup left on the counter, the tablespoon still in it. He'd coax her to the table when the pasta was ready. Some evenings when he went to fetch her, he found her sleeping, using the sewing machine for a pillow.

"You are working too hard." Really, it worried him.

"I'm not napping," she countered if he insisted she was asleep. "Just resting, Paulie, just resting for a minute." She laughed at his furrowed brow and pacified him. "I close my eyes, all right, when I'm trying to figure something out. That's all I'm doing."

"I don't want that you should work so hard all the time."

"Now don't you go being an old woman on me, you hear me? I think I took on too many orders this time. What'd you make me for supper?" All she had to do was ask about his gladiolas or what he'd dreamed up for supper, and his face turned on like a light bulb. "Are we having meatballs?" She looked thinner, he fretted, although she had always been trim. She encouraged him to make soup but didn't tell him it stayed down better than meat.

"Listen, Lila." Iris filled a platter with an assortment of pastries for a catered lunch downtown a few weeks before Minna's birthday. Banquet requests deluged the bakery, running in cycles, depending on the time of year.

"Feast or famine." Lila exhaled. The hours were long but she appreciated the extra cash.

"I've been thinking since you're so busy right now I'd pitch in and make Minna's party," Iris continued. "How's that sound to you?"

"What you'd say?" She lost count of the number of chocolate drop cookies she'd put on. The customer had asked for ten dozen of three varieties, one of which had to be the chocolate. They'd be gobbled up before the gingersnaps and peanut butter. "Drats."

"And I'm gonna make the cake, too. Give you a break." It would be worth suffering in the kitchen for one day if it helped Lila warm up toward her. It was icy in the bakery between them, although Iris smiled and acted cheerful. "Just running to the drugstore for something," she'd call to the back when there was a break in business. She hadn't been on Lila's good side since the conversation about Minna. Lila had apparently decided Iris was in part responsible for how Minna was acting.

"If that's what you want to do, go ahead," Lila told her the second time Iris asked. "But really, it's not much for me to throw another cake together," which could have been a put-down. It was no big secret that Iris had a tough time figuring out the ingredients and the sequences. Although Iris did a notable job behind the counter at the bakery, mostly because she was entertaining and would prattle about whatever was coming to her mind, Lila didn't ask for assistance making pastries.

"No. I wanna do it," she insisted. She was going to bake the cake and throw the party at her house. Since Lila had enough on her plate without thinking of Minna's seventeenth birthday, she accepted the offer. Anyway, Minna wouldn't be grateful if she did put in the effort. Let Iris bungle her way through.

"I'm gonna invite Fischer, too."

"Oh, no you're not!" Lila nearly squealed.

"Don't you see, if you don't, Minna will resent you more?" Iris talked like a gentle mother reasoning with her truculent child. It was so unlike Iris it surprised Lila, and she stopped counting to listen. She made Lila see the sense in it. *Imagine Iris being the one going to bat for Fischer.*

"I see what you're saying."

"Besides, Lila. Maybe he will behave himself better. Not bust in the bakery again."

"Better the devil you know," Lila agreed. It was probably smart about keeping him close. Maybe he would go a little easier on her, not act so self-righteous all the time. Still, it was odd for Iris to suggest, and Lila was puzzled about this change of heart.

"Of course, I'll invite Willy," Iris chattered.

"No! What kind of party are you planning? You going to invite the governor, too?"

"No, I'm not." Iris smiled sweetly, pleased that Lila was being agreeable, almost friendly again. "Well, maybe I'll do it just this once since you suggest it," she joked.

Lila groaned. "You would, too."

"What's Willy done that's so bad?" Iris squinted. Lila made a face. The last time she'd seen Willy, he'd given her his goofy bow on his way out the door. What could the guy have done to warrant being pushed out of the upstairs apartment? Lila's mouth was shut tighter than a lid stuck on a jar. She and Willy hadn't seen each other since he left.

"Two weeks," Iris complained to Paulie. That's how long it had been before Iris figured out that Willy hadn't been around. Some guy came into the bakery complaining his car wouldn't start and did they know of a good garage in town? Iris watched the car steaming and belching out front. "Take it to Willy," she'd said. She realized she hadn't seen him for a while. He hadn't been in for his coffee.

"Where's Willy been keepin' himself?" She knew it wasn't an innocent question, and Lila gave her a sour glare in return.

"Don't ask about him. He's moved out."

"Moved out?" Iris stood there with her mouth open like she couldn't get it closed again. "What in the world is going on, Lila?"

"Don't ask," Lila repeated. "Leave it alone."

She did until she rattled his name off about Minna's party. "He's her uncle, for goodness sake." Iris was ready for the argument and the objections. She'd just tackled what she thought was the bigger problem—Fischer. "You wanna break that poor man's heart? He's watched out for that kid since forever. If you wanna tell me a good reason why not, I'll listen. Otherwise, he's coming."

"Okay, okay." Lila pouted. "But if this wasn't Minna's party, I wouldn't come." She'd had it with just about everybody. She was exhausted from arguing and wanted to be rolling out pie dough and stirring cherries bubbling in a sugar mixture on the stove. Instead it felt like she was the dough being rolled over, and her brains were a jellied mess.

"I supposed you've invited that knucklehead, too." It wasn't a question. Minna probably wouldn't come if he wasn't invited. She was struck by a devilish idea. Maybe Iris was wiser than she realized putting

Fischer and Archie together in the same place. She felt the slightest twinge of satisfaction. She had only seen Archie two more times, once in the alley with Minna, the other when he picked her up at the house. If Minna was seeing him otherwise, Lila didn't know about it.

"He's got his orders anyway. Didn't you know?" Lila would be the last to know.

"When did you find this out?" She made her voice stay calm.

"Yesterday. He told me, Lila. I didn't hear it from Minna. I said I needed a favor. I wanted him to get her to the party without letting on it was going to be a surprise. That's when he told me."

"Oh." Lila's shoulders sagged. "When's he going?"

"Shipping out. That's what they call it. It's a few days after her party. He's going to flight school somewhere out east."

"That's the best news I've heard in a while."

"Yeah, but I don't know how Minna's gonna take it, Lila. You've seen how she's been lately." Was Iris colluding now with Lila?

"She's that way around you, too?" Lila *was* surprised. "I thought she was doing it to get back at me."

"For what?"

"I don't know for what. That's what I can't figure out. But she is so touchy I can't ask her to pass the butter without getting a snarl."

"She doesn't snarl at me, but she's so mopey. I thought the party might give her a boost. You know, if everybody's together and getting along."

"It'll be something, you having those three guys in the same room. It's your house. I guess you'll find out if it works." Lila almost chuckled, thinking of Fischer with Willy and Archie, three snorting bulls on the sofa.

Seventeen

"Ohh!" Paulie gasped with pride when Iris came down the stairs. It never failed; when she got dolled up, he gushed. During the evening his eyes would travel to her often; she was his spot, the place he used like dancers do to keep their equilibrium when they spin. She wore the dress Minna had made for her, and except for being a bit pale, she was vibrant. Her shoulders were determined.

"You got that look," he said. The one with her jaw set. The one that wouldn't give an inch but would be downright friendly about not doing so.

"I hate this," she had grumbled as she prepared for the party. She had taken up most of the kitchen for her cake making, and Paulie squeezed around her to roll out his ravioli. He made both cheese and meat, and then his special sauce, and Iris suffered with flour and sugar and butter, much of which she wore on her apron. Paulie patted her on the shoulder.

"You're doin' a good thing, bella." He swore her heart had seventeen karat gold in it, but he was glad to escape to his greenhouse and leave her floured kitchen.

"See this mess?" She bawled him out as though he was responsible.

"Go get dressed," he said when she had the cake in the oven— finally. It had sucked any good mood out of her. He would put out the table linens and the dishware. "You'll feel better once you put on a pretty dress." She gave him a weary smile. Baking was a lot harder than working in the garden.

"I'd rather haul rocks," she said as she went up the stairs.

"We're gonna have a smashing good time tonight." She patted Paulie's cheek. He'd transformed the house into a merry floral shop.

"It's always a good time when you are here." He smiled.

"Let me relieve you of that hat," she told Fischer at the door, waiting for the gray fedora he wore like Humphrey Bogart, the right rim pulled down and the left turned up. He handed it to her like it was a raw egg that might break. He was the first to arrive, both surprising and impressing Iris. She had expected he would show up only after the party was in full swing and then he would make a grand entrance. He walked over to Paulie who was standing at the end of the hallway and shook hands with him.

"Thank you for inviting me," he said in the most considerate way. Iris's eyes went big. The two men had spoken at best ten words to each other over the years.

"We're glad to have you with us," Paulie replied. *My, my, what a husband I've got.*

Lila dashed through the door a few minutes later like she'd missed a deadline. She wore a red dress Iris had given her for Christmas the year before. "Now just look at that"—Iris touched her on the arm—"and you thinking you can't wear that color." Iris knew the men would stare with their mouths open. They'd wonder where they should put their eyes so it didn't appear they were staring. Lila—without an apron, dressed up and not aware of what a stir she made—might not notice the attention. *If only she had any idea what kind of impression she makes. But she probably wouldn't care if she did.*

Lila started to head for the kitchen. "Oh no you don't," Iris commanded. "You're not doing any kitchen work tonight." She took her sister by the hand and led her into the living room. Sure enough, just as Iris expected, Fischer's jaw dropped.

"Hi, Lila." Fischer looked at her and then quickly down to the floor. He spoke so quietly she wasn't even sure he had spoken.

"Hello." She waited, expecting some half-humorous or biting comment. Paulie walked in behind Iris and Lila, and the four stood in the room in an eternity of silence until Paulie had the presence of mind to say, "Sit. Sit down, please. Make yourselves comfortable. I bring you somethin' to drink."

"I'll help you carry." Iris bustled out behind him. She didn't want to stay in the room. The kids burst through the door, Archie in the lead, pulling Minna along.

"Iris wanted me to pick somethin' up for you." Archie had deceived Minna when he picked her up for their date.

"What? That doesn't make any sense." It sounded fishy. Probably Aunt Iris was going to make a to-do about Archie leaving.

"Dunno but let's get it over with before we go to dinner." Archie shrugged. He had promised to take her to see *Casablanca* later.

"There you are. At long last." Paulie pulled them into the living room.

"We're not staying," she said crisply. It sounded more urgent than she wanted, but she had planned—needed—to talk to Archie that evening. She hadn't expected to be waylaid.

"What's going on?" Her parents were sitting on the same sofa in the living room. Lila floored her. She was the stunning but unfamiliar mother.

"Happy birthday!" they said at the same time.

"My birthday isn't for two more days," she cried. She was so angry her stomach clenched. She hadn't even remembered her birthday because she had something much bigger to tackle. They were supposed to go to the restaurant. They *had* to go. She had been rehearsing even before Archie received his orders and was still biding his time at the fort.

"Happy Birthday, Minna!" Iris hugged her.

She stared through her aunt. She didn't say anything. Then, "I thought we were going…" she said to Archie, and stopped. He was surprised, too, by her disappointment. He gave her an awkward smile and was grateful for the knock at the door.

Willy grinned, handing her a tidy bunch of miniature mums. "I know, bad thinking to bring flowers to the greenhouse." Iris took his Gatsby hat and put it on the hook next to Fischer's. He realized how homely and inconspicuous his was beside it.

"Hi, Lila," he said, walking into the room, seeing only her, as if she were the only one there. He took in the dress, too, and held back a whistle.

"And here's our birthday girl!" Iris smiled at Minna, hoping for a smile in return.

"Hello, sir." Archie stepped up to him, addressing Will as though he were an officer. Archie extended his hand and then went over to Fischer to shake his.

"That's a mighty pretty dress, ma'am," he said softly to Lila.

"Hi, Uncle Will." Minna strained to be polite. He was reminded of when he first met her. She was a toddler at the table, eating mashed potatoes and peas and smearing the bulk of them on her face and the table and then on him when he leaned over and whispered, "Hello, little one."

As if she had been submerged, Minna came to life. Iris expected her to make a wisecrack, as she herself would do. "Thank you for remembering my birthday." She was polite and formal, and Lila looked at her with a sudden glimmer of hope.

"So how do you like the dress Minna made for me?" Iris turned full circle to show off the accomplishment that she had saved for the occasion. She thought it would please Minna and, at the same time, make the point that while the others had been singing in monotone about her faults, they were missing the importance of who the girl was. Fischer couldn't abide her smoking, Lila was angry because she couldn't get her to behave, and Willy wanted her to show respect and consideration for Lila. If she could fix their complaints, Iris would. Showing off the dress was a way to be Minna's personal ambassador. But Minna was not smiling. Paulie saw Iris go gray and then quickly recover.

"I need two strong men to make the ice cream," Iris announced. She was coy. Fischer and Archie jumped up to help. "Look at those muscles," she teased, squeezing a hand around each of their biceps before Paulie led them into the kitchen. That left Willy, Lila, and Minna alone in the room. "Come on, birthday girl." She took Minna by the hand, leaving Lila and Willy to attend to their business. She wouldn't let Minna give in to the sulk that hung between the girl's eyebrows. "Help me get the strawberries ready for them."

"Thanks for inviting me," Willy whispered to Lila when they were alone. She was always beautiful. When she was up to the elbows in flour, or scrubbing the floors and windows with that ridiculous bandanna wrapped like a black mammy's over her hair. But tonight he had no words. He looked at her from the corner of his eyes. Otherwise, he thought he would cry.

"Thank Iris. It wasn't me." She sounded regretful.

"Hey, cut it out," Archie yelled from the kitchen. Fischer had slipped some ice down his back. Minna laughed and started chasing him around the table with a handful of ice. Willy came in, and he and Paulie grabbed ice and joined the chase.

"Take it out back!" Iris yelled at the back door and pushed them out over the slippery linoleum.

"Oh heck, Lila, I wish I wasn't wearing this dress." Their hooting and hollering was contagious, and if she had on slacks she would be shoving ice, too. "Come on. Let's watch them," and she went as far as the back porch while Lila took a cloth and mopped up the puddles in the kitchen.

Paulie straightened the dining table after the ice cream antics and then had them sit down to gigantic platters of his ravioli. There was enough for an extended Italian family, but one lone cheese ravioli remained on the last platter. Afterward, in the living room, Iris served her cake, and Paulie came behind her with coffee. During a quiet moment someone chuckled. "Hey, Iris, that was the best ice cream I ever had," and the room broke out in laughter.

"Your cake was delicious," Lila complimented her.

"Delicious? Come on," Iris said. "Now I know you're joking."

"It was light and not too sweet. Just the way I like my cakes to be." Iris was too surprised to let that sink in.

"Course it would'a been nice if we'd had some strawberry ice cream to go with it." Iris smiled and nodded.

"Hey, Lila, let's beat Archie and Minna at hearts," Iris goaded her after Paulie set up a card table. Fischer brought out the accordion, and Willy had his harmonica. They hadn't played together in almost twenty years, yet they started on the same note and with the same tune. They sounded as if they had played a gig together a week earlier.

"Off to Minneapolis, then," Fischer stated to Archie when he and Minna stood up to leave. "Well, good luck over there." He pointed his thumb toward Europe. "Give 'em the business." The others joined in wishing him well.

"I'll do my best, sir. We're gonna win this thing."

"I'm sure Minna will let us know how you're doing." Iris patted him on the shoulder. "Here, take a piece of Minna's cake." She had wrapped a slice for him already.

Lila and Willy started to go back to the kitchen. "Oh no, you two. I'm not letting you clean up tonight." Iris stood with folded arms in the hallway. Lila saw the dark circles under her eyes.

"Okay," Lila agreed. "I'll come back and help tomorrow."

"Hey, Willy, why don't you take Lila home, and I'll help out here," Fischer offered. "I ain't tired yet." Fischer would be surprised to know that Willy now rented an apartment near Saint Francis Xavier. It was on the second floor with large bay windows that faced onto the street.

"I'll see her home," Willy agreed but wasn't sure how sincere Fischer was. It was odd to hear him suggest he take Lila home.

"Go," Fischer added, walking toward the living room to retrieve the dessert plates. Iris walked the pair out to Willy's car.

Paulie took the plates from Fischer and put them into water.

"Thanks again for inviting me," Fischer told him. "You know, I been thinkin' about it long enough. I sure as hell regret slugging you that time before you got married. You been real good for Iris." Paulie handed him a towel to wipe his hands and gave him a sad smile.

"It's okay. I got more happiness than I ever thought." He laughed a little. "Maybe 'cause you knocked me out that night. It's all in the past, anyhow." Fischer looked puzzled.

"She proposed to me that night, you know." Paulie had a faraway look.

"She did?"

Paulie nodded and sighed. "Don't worry about this mess. I'll do it tomorrow."

"What a night, wasn't it?" Iris came in just as Fischer pulled his hat off the hook. "Good to hear you and Willy playing together."

"Hey, Iris." Fischer touched her on the arm so lightly she wasn't sure he had done so. It was very late. He had his accordion strapped over his shoulder. "It was a doozy of a party!" For a second, she thought he was going to lean over and give her a kiss on the cheek. "Thanks for everything."

Minna

Part II

Eighteen

"*L*et me help you with that." The conductor leered as Minna hefted the suitcase to her knee determined to get it to the overhead rack. The merciless eyes behind the smile, and the way he looked through her jacket to her breasts, gave her the willies. He'd eyed her legs when he helped her up the steps to the coach, and she wished she could have pulled her skirt down so he couldn't see above her knees, but these days, with the shortage of fabric, women scrimped on hemlines.

"I've got it," she said firmly and hoisted the case upward. She wouldn't have the protection of the bakery counter, or Aunt Iris, to keep her from middle-aged men who didn't get enough exercise and who thought they could touch and talk to teenage girls in unpleasant ways when no one was there to make them behave. No doubt his breath smelled sour from stomach acid.

"Whatever you say." He put his palms up, acting as if she'd insulted him. They were flabby and pasty, and she hated them for going places they had no right to be. He moved away, and she watched his official-looking hat bob down the aisle. She wondered if she was the only unattached girl on the train.

She would have liked to close her eyes because she hadn't slept that night. She'd waited in her bedroom and then sneaked down the staircase with her suitcase at three o'clock. In the hallway, she heard Lila's steady breathing before she slipped out.

"Don't pick your nose," a frazzled mother across the aisle said to her little boy. The dawn wouldn't arrive for another hour. Passengers straggled on board, and the train hissed and spouted like a hot teakettle, impatient but not to the boiling point. Minna flattened her back into the tweed fabric of the seat, staying as still as a snow hare hiding from a telescopic hawk. She leaned into the headrest's white napkin that concealed the stale smoke and pungent perfumes of recent passengers.

The metal handle of her suitcase had felt brittle when she'd rushed to the station, lugging it in the dark. It kept slipping from her grip because of her gloves. The night sky had been heavy and thick, and the sidewalks were slimy. She'd slipped on a bit of gravel, nearly going down onto the case when she stepped off a curb. She had been sensible about her choice of shoes, though. She hated leaving behind the red sling-back shoes that would add to the weight. "Where will I ever wear them in Seattle?" she scowled. From now on it was black pumps, at least until she found a place to stay; until then she would be toting everything she owned.

Lila had put Minna on the payroll when she turned fifteen. "I'll pay you twenty-five cents an hour." She figured if the girl earned her own money, she would work harder and be more meticulous, take pride and ownership in the business.

"It should improve her attitude," Lila confided to Iris, who regretted she hadn't been given such an opportunity at that age. Iris caught herself, or she would have blurted, "Don't count on it."

"She likes to earn money," Lila continued, pleased how deliberate Minna was, and careful about her purchases. She'd inherited Lila's quick math skills.

"Two-thirds for savings," Minna directed herself in the mirror, "And a third for whatever you want to buy yourself." She giggled. Sometimes on Fridays, she didn't come directly to the bakery from school. She made up an excuse about having to talk to a teacher and then went to the drugstore counter and let boys buy her hamburgers and cokes. She wouldn't dream of spending her own money.

"Lookit," Fischer bragged when he heard how well Minna managed her money. "She's just like me."

Lila found out that Minna was buying lipstick and chided, "Only fools paint their faces." She didn't notice that Minna also penciled her eyebrows.

She purchased the train ticket after Archie's train pulled out of the depot for Minneapolis and flight school and subtracted the amount from her $800 savings. She calculated the remainder and automatically subtracted another forty dollars for the first month's rent in Seattle. She must look for a job as soon as she found a place to live.

"Round trip or one way?" the beleaguered lady behind the ticket counter had croaked when Minna said she was going to Seattle.

"One way." Minna stuck her chin out. "You smoke too much," she said under her breath. Lila would say. "Filthy habit." The woman didn't even look up.

Minna hadn't smoked in the past week, not since Archie had left. The smell made her want to throw up. She'd loved the sensation until recently, especially lighting the tip and taking the first puff, and she had quit, but not because she was scared she would turn fifty years old and wheeze like that woman. The depot had reeked of cleaning liquid, cigarette smoke, and body odors. The spacious room had bustled, voices bouncing off its wood-paneled walls before Archie's train pulled out. Then the room was vacant, and each sound echoed, and it felt ghostly and abandoned.

"What'd you say?" the croaky woman asked. Either she was hard of hearing, or else Minna had spoken too softly.

"One way," Minna repeated, glancing behind to see if anyone saw her, but she was the only customer at the ticket window. She had planned it out. She would leave when Lila was meeting her catering deadline, absorbed in the order. Lila would look in Minna's bedroom before she left for the bakery and see the lump of pillows and think Minna was sleeping. She'd expect Minna to help out later that morning. Minna didn't feel sorry that she wouldn't be there. She hated working at the bakery. Besides, Aunt Iris would fill in. She loved to be useful to her family.

"Chin up," Aunt Iris had advised Minna a few days earlier, as if she had read her mind and knew what she was planning. Poor Aunt Iris had looked so worn out the week of that surprise birthday.

"I'm fine," Minna said too quickly over the mop she was running along the floor. "Why are you here so late today, anyway?" She had been surprised to find her in the shop after she got back from school.

"Helping out, you know, with that catering order comin' up." Aunt Iris seemed fragile as tissue paper. Her disappointment at Minna's party was transparent.

"Thank you so much, Aunt Iris," Minna must have said at least five times to cover for her lack of enthusiasm that evening. But her heart was not in it, and Aunt Iris knew it. Minna complimented her on the cake, and all the work she'd done decorating and planning. She really did try. But she could not shake the gloom that hung over her.

I had other things to take care of then, she mused looking beyond the exhausted mother in the opposite seat and out of the coach window. She and Archie had been the first to leave the party. Minna had made up a lame excuse after a game of hearts.

She frowned. "I think I left the iron plugged in." That excuse might fool the others, but not Iris. Minna didn't miss the tearful clown smile.

"Careless girl," Archie said as a joke, and Lila knitted her brows.

"Lila's going to be boiling mad at me." Minna lifted her head off the back of the seat. "Can't we get this thing moving?" Every moment the train hesitated seemed endless, and it was as if it was doing it out of spite. It began to rain, and it was difficult to see who was boarding the train or waving good-bye from the platform. She scooted back down in her seat. If Lila discovered her missing, she might come searching for her at the depot. It didn't seem likely, though. Her mind would be on the dough for rolls when she peeked into Minna's room before she left the house.

Lila expected Minna to assemble the trays with freshly baked potato rolls and corn bread and carry them to the banquet hall two blocks down Higgins. She hoped Lila would be angry instead of worried when she didn't show up. If she was miffed, she'd say, "Fine. I'll do it all myself." Iris might whisper, "She's on her high horse again," warning her to stay out of her way. Minna hoped she would be mad. Her anger would bring out her stubbornness, and she wouldn't think of the possible reasons Minna hadn't shown up.

The week since the surprise birthday had been unendurable. Minna commanded the train to get moving. She pushed her heels into the floor and gripped the seat. Looking through the rivulets of rain, she felt sick to her stomach about the last few days. The air in the coach stank from the damp wool clothing of the passengers who had gotten caught in the rain.

Archie had shipped out from Fort Missoula the Monday after the birthday party. "I can't believe my luck," he had chirped jumping up and down when he got the news. After months of wondering, he'd finally gotten the go-ahead to become a fighter pilot. "I'm takin' you to a restaurant and a movie to celebrate!"

"Do you mean it?"

"Sure do. Just my generous Southern hospitality." She hadn't seen a Humphrey Bogart film, but Fischer tipped his fedora just like Bogart in the *Casablanca* posters. She was proud of how Fischer stayed up with the new styles. Although he imitated, he had his own style.

"I wonder," she said to Archie, "what it would be like if my parents had stayed married."

"Who knows." He shrugged, eyeing a pretty blonde walking past.

"I just wonder if she'd be running the bakery." She couldn't imagine Lila staying home and cleaning house every day, setting out meals for the three of them. Lila didn't care what she wore or how she looked "as long as it is decent and clean." But she would become as perturbed as Iris struggling over a new dress design if a new recipe didn't work out well.

With the rationing, she had to become even more creative.

"Do you think they were ever in love?" Minna puzzled.

"Heck, how would I know?" Archie sucked on his finger where he nursed a sliver, disappointed that Minna wasn't acting excited about his news. "It don't make no difference, does it?"

Iris measured Minna's disposition as carefully as she fitted dresses after Archie had gone. That first afternoon after she'd seen him off, Minna could feel her aunt's eyes following her while she cleaned the shelves in the pie window. She feared if her aunt Iris didn't already know about the train ticket, she would ask just the right question, and Minna would confess.

"So. You think you and that cute boy might get hitched?"

"Aunt Iris!"

"Somethin's not right," she confided to Paulie.

"She's upset because Archie is probably going for good, the way the war is going," Paulie suggested.

"Yeah. I know that. But there's somethin' else."

"She'll tell you sooner or later. You know she can't keep things a secret from you." *Who can?* He laughed to himself.

"Maybe I'm turning over a new leaf, Paulie. I'll let her come to me when she's ready. Geez, you think I'm growing up, too?"

"Growing up?" He laughed. "You're everything rolled into one." He smiled in adoration.

Nineteen

"*Finally*! she said under her breath when the train jerked backward and then lurched forward, howling as if it had been taken off its leash. The depot's dark brick wall disappeared at glacial speed as the tracks wiggled the coaches by the courthouse and over the Orange Street viaduct. It wormed near the outline of Saint Francis Xavier's spire.

Come on, you lazy beast," she whispered. Not too far from the church sat the squat, smug, and uninspiring Saint Patrick's Hospital.

There was a pelting rain. Lila already would have looked in on Minna, been satisfied with the lump in the bed, and run off, forgetting her umbrella. Her hair would dry quickly once the ovens were hot.

Minna put her head back when the wheels found their momentum and began to sprint. The train's almost incessant bleating made her jump. They seemed to be coming from her own throat, and she was shouting a shrill parting cry to her past.

"I'm hungry," the little boy across the aisle whimpered.

"Go to sleep," his mother scolded. She put her bony wrist around his waist. "We'll eat later."

"But I'm hungry," he whined.

"Shhh." She pulled his head into the crook of her arm.

The train slinked and slithered past the Missoula County Cemetery. The deciduous trees that sheltered gravestones and were shameless in their abundance during the summer, stood pathetic in their skeletons. She had a knot in her stomach. The place felt haunted, as though its invisible fingers reached out to grab her by the hair and pull her back. She'd ridden along with Archie and his friends there one night, one of the times Lila had to wait up for her. They'd crept down Marigold Lane to the intersection with Yew Lane, waiting to get spooked. From the train windows, she imagined herself standing under the canopy of protective trees, over an indifferent, dull headstone, stroking the grainy cement on its top edge as though it was the arm of someone she wanted to soothe.

"Taking reservations for the dining car," the starchy conductor bellowed through their car. Minna looked at the little boy, but he was sound asleep. His mother stared silently ahead at the seat in front of her.

Maybe I'm hungry. Lately, she couldn't tell what was going on with her body, or what to expect. She'd eaten supper the evening before because Lila made her sit down, and she suffered through it. She kept rearranging the blue-checkered cloth napkin in her lap to make it behave. Lila had a navy bean soup, and the ham knuckle floated to the top of the tureen. It was tasty, Minna was sure, but she'd gagged trying to choke the opaque liquid down.

"Are you sick?" Lila looked worried, which surprised Minna.

"No. I'm fine." Minna tried to deflect her mother's stare. But she wondered if she could manage to swallow one thing more without it coming back up on the table or the floor beside her chair. The corn bread felt grainy and thick and got stuck in her throat and she jumped up for a glass of water. She liked corn bread, and she knew Lila made it just for her, because Lila wasn't that fond of it.

Lila looked up but didn't ask her a second time. She held her soup spoon in the air between her bowl and her mouth and waited until Minna sat back down.

"Don't you like the soup?" she asked because Minna was eating so little of it.

"No, no," Minna mumbled. "It's really good. I shouldn't have eaten a blachinda so close to supper," she lied.

"You're not just being finicky, are you?" Lila did not like her food to go unappreciated. Minna glared at her. Lila had stopped asking questions or trying to have a conversation with her daughter since Archie came along. Minna only grunted out a yeah or no *if* she responded at all. Silence dangled between them like smelly wool socks drying on a line in a monastery where vows of silence were cherished.

"Anybody home?" Willy hollered from the back door. Minna ran to open it for him, grateful for once that her uncle had interfered.

"Hello, Minna." Uncle Willy smiled and took off his cap, plopping it on the rack. He had always been gentle with her. She didn't remember a time he was not genuinely glad to see her in spite of how she acted. He was much more handsome than his brother, but Fischer had the pizazz.

"Hello, Uncle Willy." She returned his smile, which caught him off guard, and he grinned at her again. If she behaved as they wanted, she could fade into the background. She needed to pack and was grateful Uncle Willy had shown up. Aunt Iris had explained how to assemble a practical wardrobe using basic pieces that worked together.

"More is not necessarily better," her aunt cautioned. "The more you add, the more you have to consider. Simple basic pieces or else you end up looking like a...well, never mind. You know what I mean." Minna folded skirts, blouses, and some slacks as Aunt Iris taught her so they would not wrinkle. She didn't know when she would have access to an iron.

She included the bronze brush-and-comb set, a gift from Fischer from an earlier birthday. It had turned color and was heavy, but she wouldn't leave it behind. She slipped a photo of her parents' wedding between folds of a skirt. Her parent's marriage had gone sour, and yet Lila's bridal gown was safely wrapped in the back of her mother's closet. Minna stowed some remnants from the fabric of the dress she had made for Iris for her birthday. She worked quickly, mindful that Lila could appear at the top of the stairs and walk in to surprise her.

Lots of women were getting war jobs in Seattle. Maybe she couldn't fly planes, but she could help build them, and she'd do it better than anyone else. She'd overheard people in the bakery talking about how the government was looking for more help; in fact, they were recruiting.

I'm going get a secondhand sewing machine, she decided, *once I get set up in an apartment in Seattle and I'm making money.* In her spare time, she would keep up with her sewing and try to find a few customers. With the government rationing everything from gasoline to rubber, it would be difficult to find new, good-quality fabric, but she would scour secondhand stores and rummage through used clothing for durable fabrics to make new outfits.

"What brings you here, tonight?" Lila asked Willy in a pleasant tone. Uncle Willy and Lila didn't notice when Minna backed out of the kitchen. Lila was still sitting at the table with her soup spoon once more in the air. Willy strode toward her. "I was wonderin' if you might need some help with that catering job tomorrow."

"Sit down and have some supper. You look like you haven't eaten in a while," she teased. "A bit on the lean side, I'd say," examining his backside.

"Now, aren't you the fresh one," he joked. "You know I won't refuse *your* cookin'." He grinned and went to the cupboard for a bowl. They'd made up from their spat, but Willy hadn't moved back into the bakery apartment. Lila had walked around with her lips pinched together after their argument until the night of Minna's party. No one knew what the argument was about since Willy wasn't one to say an unkind word, and it was impossible to get anything out of Lila. However, Iris did her best at speculating. They stared at each other at Minna's party, the first time they'd seen each other in several weeks, like they'd never seen each other before. "I swear," Iris told Paulie later at night, "I don't know why Lila doesn't just get on with it and marry the guy. I can't figure her out."

"People have to get it right for themselves, bella. They'll get it figured out sooner or later, and you don't have to help them."

"Well, how many years of later does she need?"

"Not everyone's as smart as you," he teased. "Especially when it comes to people." Some people squirmed when Iris looked at them as if she could see clear into their souls. Paulie would not say that to her. She'd just brush it off anyway, like a stray thread. "Too bad for those people if they don't want me to see what they are like. Better straighten up and fly right," she'd probably say, right along with Nat King Cole who sang in her kitchen. It didn't matter to her if people understood her like Paulie did. He knew that her heart was loaded with good intentions. She didn't see herself as critical but that didn't stop her from speaking her mind if she was so inclined, like the philanderer she gave a good talking to when he eyeballed her niece as she went to refill his coffee at the bakery.

"Keep your eyes to yourself, old boy," she said to one fellow. She would have said "geezer" if Lila hadn't been in earshot. "She's not even seventeen yet, and lord knows you've got a faithful wife waiting for you somewhere." Iris didn't whisper either. She let her gritty words carry over the counter to the guy's table, and he pulled up the newspaper to hide his shifting eyes. "Though lord knows why."

Lila was of two minds about how Iris treated some customers. On the one hand, she was glad when her sister stepped on toes of people who got out of line. She herself was not direct if someone was rude. Many times Minna saw men try to flirt with her mother. Lila turned deaf and mute to shut down their intrusions, but she didn't want to lose any business if she could help it.

"Your mother's savvy," Iris advised her. "Watch the way she doesn't let the buggers get under her skin, 'Cause then they know they've got you."

"But you do that, Auntie," Minna told her.

"Yeah. I do it when I see them going after you, doll. I'm not letting them treat you that way. And they aren't gonna mess with me. They know it, too. I'll embarrass them outa the place if they don't stop."

"Lila ignores them."

"Yeah. Your mom keeps her distance, doesn't let anyone close enough to get her riled up. You see how she is. Not a smart-mouth like me." Iris laughed.

Twenty

"How much is that one?" Minna asked two days after Archie left, pointing to a silver ring with a small blue stone. She hadn't been in the pawnshop since Franz could still walk without holding onto her arm. After he ended up in the wheelchair, he didn't go into a secondhand store again.

Martha even coaxed him. "I saw Mr. Stevens haul in maybe ten boxes of collections to his shop, odd ends of handles and lids poking out the tops." She was certain Franz would be curious, she wasn't interested herself, never had been, nor did she understand her husband's attraction to digging through and inspecting dusty, grimy objects like he was searching for gold.

"Would you please use your common sense and not bring it up again," he told her.

She was only in grade school when Minna hurried to the bakery where a glass of milk and three still-warm cookies awaited her. Some days, Franz would stand there and watch her take one bite after the other, opening his mouth each time she did. She knew what he was thinking. As soon as she reached the bottom of her milk glass, he'd dash to the coatrack and grab her red wool coat. He'd bend down to put it around her and try to close it, but the black buttons were a trial for his thick fingers, and Minna, as impatient as he, would tell him, "I'll do it myself, Boppy."

During the day he put the dark ryes and wheat and white loaves out on the shelves, and then did the other chores Martha had to remind him to do every day. "Let's go look for da bargains, Minna," he'd chirp, plunking her white-and-red stocking cap over the golden white curls that Lila rolled up for her before bed each evening. Off they went, toddling down Higgins, the unlikely pair, one meaty mitt engulfing a handful of pudgy fingers. They'd quickly vanish into a side street and disappear into the dim doorway of a crammed store, where mysterious treasures waited for them.

When she was very small, her fingers had to touch everything.

She'd walk down the aisles with her hand trailing over flower-painted bowls and paper-thin cups with roses on their handles. She'd stand before the shiny mirrors and stick her tongue out. Once, Franz lifted her hand off a shiny gold ashtray that had enticed and tantalized her. "Let's you and me go find da prize," he whispered. That day she "discovered" the doll that she packed in her suitcase for Seattle. Franz taught her how to let glitz fall quickly through her fingers. It was easy as sifting powdery flour through your hands as he did when he shaped loaves that turned golden in the hot ovens. But Minna beheld the crimson glass plates and azure vases resting on shelves that glistened even though the sun had to bushwhack to beam on them through the filthy window panes. The jewel tones glinted red and green and blue, dancing across dreary hand-cranked meat grinders and aluminum kettles.

Martha addressed their backs as they slipped out through the alley entrance. "Don't bring back stuff to clutter up the place," she commanded. But she could not depend on Franz to obey. For the life of him, he could not help becoming sentimental about a pair of earrings for Martha or a piece of jewelry for Minna. Minna never took the agate pendant from her neck, the one that Franz had given her when she turned ten. He'd told her, "Dis will sure enough bring you good luck." She fingered it as she scrutinized the rings and wondered if Mr. Stevens recognized either the necklace or her.

"You're asking too much," she criticized the owner, after she had opted for the ring she wanted with the azure stone. She locked eyes with him and challenged him, "How much will you really take?"

If Franz stood next to her, he would complain, "Now, Tommy, you know dat is plain highway robbery." She set her feet apart, the way Franz had, like he was facing a cougar on a trail. Franz told her that it had nothing to do with how old you are. "It's how you stand, Minna. You look dem fellows straight in the eyes. Good and solid-like. Don't let nobody pull da wool over your eyes."

She bought the wedding ring for a fair price after she bought her train ticket on that last Monday, the day she walked to the railway station with Archie. He flung his duffel bag over his right shoulder as if it was filled with turkey feathers. He swaggered, grabbed her around the waist with his free arm while they waited for a car to pass by at a street corner, and swung her around until her skirt swirled.

"Wanna dance, sweetheart?" he teased, and she tried to smile at his fooling around. He couldn't wait to get on that train. He had his ticket out before they got to the platform and almost ran off without remembering to say good-bye or giving her one last quick kiss.

"Will you write to me?" It was a foolish question. She already knew the answer. The last thing she needed was to sound like she was pleading. She couldn't stand girls who pretended they were helpless around boys.

"Sure. I'll send you my address as soon as I get it. Course, I'll be movin' around a lot. Here and there." He laughed and shifted back and forth from one hip to the other. At the coach he jumped up the steps to put his bag on board and then turned and looked down at her. "Wanna come on board for a minute?" He was still standing there, looking down at her, but he was already gone.

"No," she pushed a long piece of hair away from her face with her white glove. "You go ahead. Good luck"—she motioned with her head in the direction of Europe—"over there."

"We're gonna beat 'em, Min, wait and see! We'll give 'em what's comin' to 'em." She nodded. Probably he would win the war, and while he was doing it, he would collect the hearts of a few foreign girls. As the train inched away from the platform, she turned and headed into the depot to buy her ticket for Seattle.

"Archie?" He'd been a real gentleman when they left her party that night, offering his elbow on the walk back, wrapping his hand over hers protectively. "I've got something to tell you." She'd practiced saying it. She was going to handle it like Lila would—not show her true feelings. Lila's voice would be so cool, she probably wouldn't blink if someone held a gun to her head.

Minna rehearsed in front of the mirror, mimicking Lila's steady tones, not hanging on any one word longer than another. Lila spoke in crisp and even syllables, precise and uniform like the vegetables she chopped for a sweet-and-sour salad with onions. Minna would use Archie's two words, honor and duty, his answer for becoming a fighter pilot. *Honor and duty, honor and duty*, she repeated. She had planned to bring it up when they went to dinner, before the movie.

"Wanna do it up right," he'd bragged about taking her to a restaurant. Like that would somehow even things up between them. She spent two hours getting dressed. She tried on and took off three dresses, and finally settled on a persimmon-colored rayon with a flared skirt and thick black belt. The red sling-back heels she'd splurged on, took money out of her savings for, emphasized her ankles and legs. Like Iris, she enjoyed violating the fashion color code, flaunting orange beside red. She snubbed the dictators of the fashion industry, who scorned Mother

Nature's own gardens and those very colors that bloomed side by side in brilliant glory.

"Cherry red," the lipstick that Archie said suited her best, "and a touch of rouge," she explained to the mirror.

Lila despised the makeup. "No young girl should wear something that spoils a perfectly good complexion."

Minna would have painted her nails cherry red, too, but chances were that Lila would have seen it and made her remove it. "I wouldn't hire someone with red claws."

Minna would be sent back to her room.

"Like a lobster," Lila huffed of customers whose hands crossed her counter and resembled pincers with garish nail varnish.

"She's such a dope," Minna said to the mirror of her old-fashioned mother. "She doesn't get it, and she never will," fuming because her mother wouldn't budge and even seemed appeased at thwarting her.

"Lila, you would look stunning with some bright lipstick. I've got just the thing." Iris hounded her, envisioning how pleasing her sister could look if she would consent.

"And why would I want to do that?" Lila retorted. If something affected her baking, and she already was improvising with food shortages and finding smart ways to keep her customers coming, she would be avid about making a change.

"Well, now." Archie whistled when he picked her up. He didn't let on about the birthday party. "That's worth lookin' at tonight."

"Glad you like it," she said very casually. She was going to encourage him to do most of the talking at the restaurant, expecting he wouldn't notice. She'd be surprised if he asked why she was restrained, but she prepared an answer, just in case.

"I want to hear all about what you are going to do when you fly those planes." He'd been talking about them from the first time they met. She knew what all the controls did, and how to operate them. She even knew what to do if you had to get out of a plane in a hurry. She thought she could fly a plane herself if she wanted. There were girls heading to Canada to learn to fly warplanes. She would wait until he lit a cigarette for her and one for himself, and had taken a sip of his coffee. That's when she would tell him.

Twenty-One

"Surprise!" Aunt Iris bubbled. She'd ruined Minna's plan with the birthday party. Everyone was so jolly in her aunt's living room.

"Happy Birthday! Happy Birthday!" They flooded her ears with it, and the smiles in her face. She was flabbergasted and disoriented, and she still believed Archie was going to take her to a restaurant.

"But, I thought—"

"That Archie was going to take you to dinner. We know," Iris finished. "That's what we wanted you to think, sweetheart." Her excitement bubbled over with an enormous grin that squished her purple scar into a thin red line. Minna's plan got torpedoed by her biggest ally.

"Come on, honey," Iris said with some disappointment. "It can't be that big a shock, can it?"

Minna tried to find a smile, to dig it up from inside her.

"You ain't an old woman yet," she teased.

"I just didn't expect it, I guess." She joined the frolic when Fischer and Archie got to chasing around and dumping ice down each other's backs, and she doused Archie with a whole pan of ice on his head, and he never did catch up to get back at her. She laughed then, momentarily forgetting her plans. During dinner, she felt the glances at the table, everyone squeezed in knee to knee, and platter after platter of Paulie's ravioli went around. She toyed with the squares on her plate, not able to try one.

"Maybe I put too much oregano in them?" Pauli leaned over and whispered in her ear.

"No, no. I'm just not hungry, I guess," she whispered back and made herself eat one to satisfy him.

Even Fischer watched her. He couldn't believe she liked that fathead Archie enough to be morose at his leaving. He didn't think she could, not his daughter.

She played Hearts because Iris insisted they get a game going then wrinkled her brow and stared at her hand as if she didn't understand the rules. Then, abruptly that changed, and the light came back into her eyes. *The bridge! That's where I'll tell him.* For the first time that evening, she looked like she was enjoying her party. She knew Aunt Iris wouldn't begin to believe the story about the iron, but trusted her to not make much of it.

The sky was murky black when they left the party, walking down the deserted streets toward Pine Street.

"It'd take a million years to get used to livin' in this place. No way I could stand the pitch black nights," although he'd been in Missoula for over a year. "Not like back home in Georgia," he drawled, sounding nostalgic.

There were a few streetlights at the larger intersections. The lamps showered flecks of light on them, and the pair glowed briefly, like shooting stars in the manufactured spotlights, before they dissolved into the deep shadows.

"I want to tell you something," she squeaked when they got to the ramp going up the Higgins Bridge. The words came out awkwardly, not as she had practiced. Not the way Lila would have said them.

He gave her a peculiar smile, one she hadn't seen before. He stopped abruptly and stood so still she almost squirmed. The breath streamed from his nostrils in the cold air. It reminded her of a horse snorting. Suddenly he punched her on the arm, not enough to shift her, but enough to make her wince.

"You ain't gonna tell me you love me now, are ya?" He spoke rapidly.

She sucked in her breath, feeling the cold air freeze all the way down her throat. "I would never say anything that silly." She matched his smile and punched him back lightly.

"Well, that's a relief, then." He grinned. "I mean, we been havin' a lotta fun, ain't we?" Archie squeezed her hand. When they got to the middle of the bridge, he stopped again and looked toward the Wilma Building. "I sure ain't sorry to leave this place," he said quietly. Then realizing what he'd said, "Except for you, I mean. You've been great, Min."

"I..." She didn't finish it. Should she say yes, like he did, they'd had a lotta fun? Their elbows touched on the cold metal railings, and they watched the indigo water swirling below, the edges spouting white lace against the boulders. "You, too," she answered to the river.

"I'm gonna miss this spot." He laughed then. "We shoulda come here before."

She'd been at this very place a day earlier, after she figured out why she was getting sick every morning. At first she'd thought it was the bacon Lila put in front of her and insisted she eat. She couldn't believe it the when the greasy smell turned her stomach. The strong aroma from her coffee with cream helped, though, and Lila didn't catch on. It only took a whiff of coffee to stop her heaving in front of her mother.

After he dropped her off, she sat paralyzed on her bed until her legs tingled and started to go numb. He'd kissed her hard on the lips good night. "For good luck," he whispered in her ear, but it sounded like he was wishing that for himself, not her. Maybe it all had been for laughs, or maybe she'd just been a stupid girl, like all the rest of them who think the guy is going to stand by you. She could see her image in the mirror. A dim figure stared back, couched in shadow from the scant light in the room. She wanted to run to Aunt Iris who would take her side. She knew she would. She'd try to fix it for her. Iris knew a lot about patching up wounded people. She was one of them herself.

When Minna realized she was going to have a baby, she had gone to the bridge. She asked the water rushing below for an answer, but the roiling stream held onto its secrets below its angry surface, and she would have to dive to find what they revealed. Her hands were on the rail, and one foot was already on the lower rung. She pulled her shoulders back. She fought back the tears and the anger. The waves below slammed against the boulders. She was stupid, stupid, stupid. She willed the sky to open up and wash her away. She lifted her face, wanting cold droplets to hit her eyes and mouth. There were clouds, but it did not rain. She threw her insults over the bridge to chase the water downstream. A few people passed by her.

"You all right?" one stopped to ask.

"Right as rain." She tittered.

He touched her on the shoulder and said, "Good girl," before moving on. He turned back, glancing in her direction from the far end of the bridge. Then he shrugged and proceeded up Higgins.

One of the rich girls at the high school had been sent to California to stay with an "aunt" for an extended period in the middle of the year. Minna wondered if Lila would, if she had the money, send her away. It didn't matter. She couldn't tell Lila. Her mother had her own worries with the war on and people learning how to be frugal. With the rationing, she was continually finding ways to provide food for hungry, poor customers. No, she couldn't tell Lila. She wouldn't show her fury, but it would be palpable and unbearable.

Minna stared at the roiling liquid. "Either he marries you, or he doesn't." If he said yes, they could get married before he shipped out. Lila would be furious. She'd bite her lip, but she wouldn't say, "You're throwing your life away." Minna wouldn't tell her she was pregnant. She'd be peeved no matter what, feeling Minna had let her down.

If he wouldn't marry her, she would leave Missoula. She made up her mind. The government was hard up and looking for workers. She'd buy a wedding ring, purport to be married to a pilot, and go to Seattle to build warplanes. She had money to buy a train ticket to Seattle and rent an apartment, and she would be all right as long as she got a job. Maybe Archie would do the right thing by her.

She was seventeen years old—just—on the day Archie left, the day she bought her train ticket, the day she chose her wedding ring with the blue stone.

When she told him the news, she hoped Archie would give her the kind of tender look Uncle Willy reserved for Lila. Maybe he would put his arm around her when she said she had something to tell him. Even a touch on her arm or him sticking his arm through the crook of hers would work.

Her fingertips were icy that night on the bridge, even inside the gloves. She remembered gripping the metal railing and how, when she pulled her hands back, the cloth stuck to the steel. A sharp wind whipped out of the west, and their words floated in the chilly air like balloons.

He was cocky, always had been, from the first time she met him. His brash yet courtly manner had been what attracted her. She shouldn't have been surprised by his response, and in retrospect, she wasn't. He had peered down at her like she was a naughty girl and then asked the fateful question about falling in love with him. She had made her face stay neutral. That's what Lila would do. His frown was like a nightmare, the one about failing an exam because she had studied the wrong material.

"Do you want me to be in love with you?" she'd asked, in part to deflect her feelings, and to hold out a fleeting hope. She squeezed her eyebrows together. She shivered, wished she hadn't, and pulled her coat tighter around her neck. The sky had cleared because of the sharp breeze, and the stars sparkled. Venus twinkled at them above Lolo Peak. She laughed finally, to break the long silence. She didn't want to be a fool, so she acted merry, and he relaxed. He kissed her long and hard, raised his shoulders, smiled a mock grin, and lifted his eyebrows.

"Ha!" He ran his fingers through his sandy hair. "I thought for a second there you had gone and got all serious on me. You knowed all along I'd be shipping out. Right, babe? It was for laughs, wasn't it?"

Twenty-Two

"Good night, Minna. Happy Birthday," Lila whispered outside Minna's door. Willy's truck had purred up to the house after the party, and he and Lila whispered and giggled in the living room for an hour before Minna heard the front door squeak.

"See ya tomorrow," he said softly, sounding hopeful and happy.

Minna didn't respond to her mother. She'd break down if Lila came into her room and asked how she liked the green wool coat. She had hired Iris to make it.

"I don't want your stinkin' money to make a coat for Minna," Iris snapped. "I'll do it for nothin'. She's my goddamn niece, Lila."

"But you know what she likes, and it would help me." Lila twitched. She hated the language that came out of her sister's mouth sometimes. They agreed on a price.

"It's lovely!" Lila smiled when Iris delivered it one morning at the bakery. Lila wrapped it up in butcher paper, tied it with green string and gave it to Minna at the party.

"It'll keep me warm when I get to Seattle." Minna cried into her pillow. She cried throughout the night.

The house seemed dead when she got up. Her face was blotchy, and her eyes hurt. "That's it," she chided herself and set her mind to not cry anymore. "Enough is enough." The tears didn't help. They weren't going to make her problem go away. She was glad it was a Sunday, and Lila would sleep for another hour.

She decided she would go to her aunt and tell her. She slipped out the door and ran for three blocks before she realized Aunt Iris never got up early if she didn't have to, and after all the effort for the party, that meant it would probably be noon—or later. Uncle Paulie would be up, however. He'd fix her a cup of coffee that she would nurse until she heard Iris's slippers flopping on the stairs. While she waited, he'd fry up eggs with onions and homemade stewed tomatoes and garlic, and insist she eat. "Just a bit of oregano for you," he would promise, knowing she didn't like the herb.

"Oh no!" she said out loud when she realized what time it was and how long she'd have to have to wait before her aunt was up. The chilly wind had died down, but frost covered the grass, and it was slippery at the park on Orange Street. She sat on a swing, but the cold came right through her slacks, and she jumped up.

"I'll just tell her straight out," she vowed. "She won't want to hear the rest of it, anyway."

"Don't dilly-dally around," was how Iris counseled customers who could not make up their minds after she'd already given them her best advice. Iris just wanted the plain facts. Once she understood a problem, she could lay it out step by step.

"I won't tell her about Archie borrowing another soldier's car." The park was empty. It was too early and too chilly for anyone to hear her talking to herself. Someone was a few blocks away, walking a very large black dog.

The car he borrowed was a 1939 Pontiac, a fact that Fischer would find interesting. They'd gone up on Waterworks Hill where all the couples went to make out.

"One time, only one time!" She couldn't believe her bad luck. The other girls went up there regularly, and only one had gotten pregnant. Minna told Lila they were going to see Greer Garson in *Mrs. Miniver* that evening.

"She's a real lady." Lila had approved. "Be back by midnight."

Aunt Iris wouldn't get angry when Minna showed up and said she needed to tell her something. She would understand.

"Just one of those dang things," she'd say and shoo Paulie off on an errand. "Don't you need to see a man about a horse?" That was an expression that still puzzled him. The first time she'd said it to him, she'd raised her eyebrows, but he looked at her quizzically.

"I don't know no man with a horse," he'd responded. She shook her head, not quite entirely exasperated.

"These Eye-talians." She shrugged. "Don't you get it, Paulie?" Well, he didn't get it. It took a too-long explanation before it made the least bit of sense.

The second time she said it, Lila was still married to Fischer, and she had just had the miscarriage. Paulie couldn't help it that he was born a helper. He wanted the world to be a pleasant place for everyone. It didn't matter to him that Lila had a "woman's problem." He wasn't afraid of blood like Fischer was. He'd offered to scrub Fischer's car out after Fischer got Lila to the hospital.

"That damn Eye-talian ain't comin' near my car," Fischer growled at Iris. Iris gave Fischer one of her very best "don't cross me, buddy," looks and then said evenly to Paulie, "Why don't you go see a man about a horse." She wasn't afraid of Fischer. If he wanted to go at it, she was more than willing. She just didn't want Paulie to get into the middle of it this time and be smacked in the nose a second time by Fischer and get knocked out again. His pride was still bruised from the other time that happened.

Paulie had squinted at her. "I can't believe it" she glowered at him. "Go!" she commanded.him. "Just go!" Fischer's hands were in fists. She had words to say to Fischer, but not with Paulie there.

"Man…about…a horse. Remember?"

"Oh, I got it." He still looked puzzled but acted like he was about to apologize for not remembering the American lingo. The words made sense to everyone but him, it seemed. The slang was so confusing. It took him precious seconds to engage once he understood. Fischer looked like he was about to blow. Iris wiggled her brows and shook her head, and finally he mouthed, "Oh."

"In the nick of time," she said under her breath before she had it out with Fischer. He cringed, she stood a whole foot shorter, and in retrospect he could have sworn she was eye level. He didn't smack her, although she was ready for him if he did.

The black lab was chasing an equally black bird at the far end of the park. He slipped on the hoary grass when he got close enough to leap for it and then skidded a few feet. Minna would have laughed but she was thinking of Paulie and how he would be when he heard she was going to have a baby.

"You gotta have some spaghetti." The very thought of which made her throat constrict. "First eat. Then think," he'd advise. "You know you can't make no good decisions before your stomach is full." And he'd pat his own.

She didn't think she could stand to see him looking like a puppy. He'd hover over her while he pushed food at her. "Eat, eat." He'd put his arm around her shoulder and whisper that everything was going to be fine. "Just fine," he'd promise. "A bump in the road. That's all." At which Iris would roll her eyes. "How in the hell did you pull that one out?" she would refrain from saying.

"Well, Min. Looks like we've got a problem here, don't we?" she'd say. All problems to Iris, unless they had to do with cooking and housework, had solutions. "Get a piece of paper and let's get started." She'd handle an unwanted pregnancy like a complicated dress pattern that required shifting parts around to arrive at a sensible and satisfactory outcome.

The black lab ran over to Minna when he spotted her. Rubbed his nose against her leg. "He's friendly," the owner promised. Minna wanted to push the dog away but rubbed his ears instead. "He likes that," the owner said and added, "You're up early."

"Yeah. He's a nice dog." The lab saw a bird scratching in the grass and ran toward it. His owner ran after him.

Aunt Iris wouldn't even ask how she got into this fix. She didn't need to ask. She was clearheaded. Lila would ask, like she didn't know how it could happen. She'd mask the fury and coolly lay out the future like it was made of bricks being stacked one on top of the other. "He'll have to marry you." She'd silently gnaw on her disgust when she discovered Minna hadn't told him he was going to be a father.

"Do you love him?" Iris would ask that. "'Cause if you do, sweetheart, you must be hurtin' bad that he's gone off and left you like this."

Minna didn't love him. If he'd asked her to marry him before she found out about the baby, she would have told him no. If it had been his idea. If he'd said to her, "Hey listen, Min, I don't want to leave you." She'd have told him no.

Archie thought it was for laughs. It wasn't that, though. That wasn't the reason she'd gone up to the waterworks with him. She wanted to know what the other girls knew, the ones who giggled in the gym showers. She wanted to be bold, like they were, and free, and to do something Lila didn't get to be a part of, something her mother couldn't decide for her.

The first time he had kissed her, it was outside the drugstore. She had been looking at lipstick shades when he came up to her and said, "The cherry-red one would look the best on you." Perhaps that should have been her clue, before he offered her a Coca-Cola with cherry-flavored syrup at the fountain. She had twirled on the stool until the order came up, then she drank it quickly and asked for a second.

He laughed. "You're kinda goofy," he told her.

She had arched an eyebrow but then replied, "Well, so are you."

The black dog slid again. He hadn't learned his lesson the first time. Its owner waved at her at the far end of the park. She stayed until her toes started aching from the cold. "I can't do it," she said suddenly. It would be a mistake to go to Aunt Iris.

Twenty-Three

"Is that place free, dear?" the woman asked of the vacant seat.

Minna had fallen asleep after the train pulled out of Sandpoint, Idaho. Earlier, when they'd reached the pass above Superior, Montana, the sky was a soupy mix of downy snow feathers. The trunks of straggly pines, pitch black, tucked into the crevasses of massive cliffs, silent as sentinels wearing fresh white blankets on their boughs. The frosty world got devoured each time the train entered the mouth of a dark tunnel, as though the giant mountain ogre waiting around each of its curves opened his jaws, swallowed them up, and spit them back out into the blinding white.

"Would you like some?" Minna had offered some blachinda to the scrawny boy across the aisle who had watched her take the wax paper off her food, almost drooling. He nodded vigorously. His mother mouthed a thank-you.

"Tell the nice young lady thank you, Benny." He had stuffed most of it in his mouth before she had a chance to remind him, and he nodded again.

"Would you like some, too?" Minna asked the mother. "I've got plenty." Her coat hung on her, but she said she wasn't one bit hungry.

"I ate earlier. Thank you, anyway."

The engine had pulled them along, crawling and coiling up the Montana side of Lookout Pass. She wished she could relax, hoped that eating something would stop her from fidgeting. She had crossed and crossed her legs for two hours, tapped her toes, and wrapped and unwrapped her arms about a hundred times, she thought.

After it reached the summit, the train crawled into Idaho. It acted sluggish as if it suffered from the strain of getting uphill, or because it didn't want to leave Montana. The blachinda was savory, and the aroma from the spices smelled good, and her mouth watered. She had not eaten since she'd trifled with Lila's bean soup and corn bread the evening before.

She couldn't fight off the sleep once her tummy was satisfied.

She had watched the clock all night long at the Pine Street house, pinched herself when she got drowsy, made herself get out from under her quilt to go to the bathroom three times. The floor had felt so icy cold that night. She didn't put her slippers on, either, because if her feet were cold, she couldn't fall asleep.

"Where are we?" she asked when a woman propped her umbrella with its crystal crook between them. Only a few lamps shone from the depot. Minna had fallen asleep sometime in the afternoon and had no idea for how long. In the coach's hazy light, the woman seemed an apparition. The light behind her encircled her hat like a halo. Her hands, on her hips, formed triangles on each side like she had sprouted wings.

The boy and his mother were gone. They were replaced by an older couple. The other seats were occupied, and the coach clattered from the shuffling of suitcases being stowed, and everyone adjusting and settling down.

"Spokane," the lady pointed out the window to the sign above the station. "How far are you going, dear? Oh, I'm sorry," she apologized because rain droplets from her Chinaman hat had dripped onto Minna's sleeve. She wiped them off, and her hand was smooth as a young child's. The woman angled the hat on the rack above her then laughed again when droplets plopped onto her own Brillo-gray hair. "The elements, you know," pointing toward the ceiling of the coach.

The woman's wardrobe was an assortment of disparate parts that appeared to have no end. It seemed she wore her closet on her back. Minna counted layers of sweaters—the topmost a sage green, and then a pale blue—under the houndstooth men's overcoat. The bottom was pink and longer by four inches than the other two. Her Levi's were prehistoric and maybe rescued from a miner or logger. Some of the rivets on the pockets were missing, and there were small holes on the thighs and blotches and pinholes where something had eaten away the material.

"I'm Mrs. Erma Shepherd." She extended her hand while examining Minna through no-nonsense lenses, "but I don't hold with the notion of titles, do you?" She paused, giving Minna the chance to reply. When she didn't, the woman continued. "I mean about ownership. What do you think?" as if this was a question all young girls had at the forefront of their minds. "What is a Mrs., anyway, I'd like to know. It's a just a title by default." This time she didn't pause. "Erma will do just fine, dear."

"I'm Minna." She was studying the intriguing assortment of clothes. It was so astonishing she felt dull-headed, like she'd slept too hard and was still in dreamland. She thought she had awakened on another planet. It was a nudge Erma gave her, the first brush with her preconceived notions, and she was baffled.

Erma and her clothing made a single organism that could not to be separated without altering the parts. The entire entity appeared to be neither man nor woman, but a startling combination of both. Erma should have looked masculine with the broad cut of the cloth that neglected curves and dips, and the rough hairy texture that declared its maleness, but instead, the boxy shape and coarse threads gave the opposite effect. It was striking how the female, buried like a ruby glowing inside the clothing, claimed her presence. Her clothing, like Erma, did not belabor categories, for there was no appropriate classification. Everything spoke for itself and had its own voice, like the members of a choir, from the deepest of basses to the shrillest of sopranos.

Minna wanted to stroke the cheeks of the energetic figure. They were like Lila's ripe peaches Minna sorted through each summer for canning. Only hobos seemed oblivious to their clothing, and they fretted because they never had enough layers when the river's edges started to ice over. Now there was Erma.

Erma wasn't like some of the bakery customers who made her so impatient she had to pinch her fingernails into the meaty part of her palms so she wouldn't say, "Did you happen to notice there are three customers behind you who have been waiting for five minutes while you finally make up your mind?" Erma wasn't a thoughtless woman, as Minna first suspected when she parked the umbrella between them. She noticed the water dripping on Minna's arm and made the effort to rectify it. She had put the umbrella between them, that's true, but made sure it was not in Minna's way. She confounded Minna. Who was she really?

"And does Minna have a last name?" Erma lifted her left brow.

"Uh...uh, yes. Benoit. Yes, Benoit." She had hesitated. She didn't have a marriage license to prove it, but what were the chances Archie would find out she had taken his last name? Since he didn't know he was going to be a father, she figured he didn't need to know he had gotten a wife, either.

"That's all right, dear." Erma touched her on the arm. "It's a nice name. That's French, isn't it? I like to guess where people come from."

"It's...it's my husband's name." It was the first time she had said it out loud—Archie's last name—to another person.

"Oh, so he's French?"

"He's from the South. from Georgia."

"But you're not, are you, dear?" Erma's breathing was even and slow. It offered up forgiveness, and it drew Minna. She released a deep sigh.

"No." She worried she might leave a trail for someone to trace if she mentioned Missoula. It would be hard enough for her family to accept her disappearance. She didn't want to leave clues that might make them think they could find her and keep them hoping.

The lights dimmed, and the coach fell quiet. A baby cried out, and a mother whispered to soothe the little one. They heard someone humming "Rock-a-bye Baby in the Tree Top," and then the baby's lips smacking. Minna's and Erma's heads rested against the seat cushions. The train whistled occasionally, bleating like a crabby nanny goat at her offspring. Minna pulled out some blachinda and offered one to Erma.

"No dear, you go ahead. You must be very hungry. You need the nourishment, and I had a substantial meal today," Erma patted her stomach contentedly. "When is the baby due?"

"What?" Minna cried.

"It's all right, dear," Erma whispered. "Everything is fine. Just fine." She patted her on the arm. Minna thought she was going to start crying and politely excused herself to get past the woman.

Minna wouldn't come out of the toilet when someone tried the door. The handle rattled again and again.

"Hey, you almost done in there?" the sleazy conductor barked. She didn't answer, took a deep breath, and waited a second longer before opening the door.

"You gotta problem?" he sneered, standing in her face. She glared and ducked around him.

"How did you know?" Minna whispered when she got back to her seat.

"Little clues, dear. Little clues. I keep my eyes and heart open for signs."

"But what clues?" She'd hidden it from everyone else, she thought, but now she doubted herself.

"I'm pretty observant." Erma chuckled. "It's the freckles on your cheeks and nose. Not the kind you see on a seventeen-year-old girl unless...I would guess you are seventeen, aren't you?"

Minna nodded. Mrs. Shepherd whispered quietly, "Don't worry, dear. You will be able to hide it for two more months. You have enough time." She touched her arm. Her touch felt warm and strangely familiar. Suddenly Minna got very tired. Before they reached Yakima, Minna's head was on Erma's shoulder resting. Minna dreamed about Franz. He was walking with her, had her by the hand, and they were going down a long wooden dock. They were hurrying, and she looked up at him. She was upset and told him he was going too fast for her little legs. "Where are we going, Boppy?" she demanded. "Why, liebling. We go to da shipyards." In front of them, massive boats towered like black menacing monsters. She was frightened and cried, "But I don't want to go there, Boppy. Why do we have to go?" She pulled away from him and put her hands on her hips. He stopped, too, and looked down at her with great tenderness.

"*Ach*, Minna. We go to get your agate necklace," he said, and then she woke up with a start. Erma was looking straight ahead. Minna had drooled on one of Erma's sweaters and tried to wipe the spit off without being too obvious.

"You were dreaming," Erma said.

"Yes. Where are we?" She saw a few lights in the distance, separate beings that seemed suspended by an imaginary wire from the sky.

"We just left Yakima," Erma told her. "It was a good dream."

"How do you know?"

"A little bit frightening, though," Erma continued.

"Yes. Yes, it was. I was walking with—"

"Someone who loves you very much?"

"Yes. Did I say his name out loud?" She turned red. Her face felt warm.

"No, you didn't but this person watches out for you, I think, and I suspect is always with you…no matter what."

"No. Boppy's dead. He died when I was twelve."

"I see. Was he the one who gave you that lovely agate?" Erma nodded toward the pendant. "You seemed to be protecting it in your dream."

"Yes. Before he died." Minna clutched the stone again. "I did talk in my sleep, then."

"No, Minna, you didn't. You haven't revealed anything, and you are safe." Erma looked out the window. "It will be dawn in a few hours. Don't you think you should try to get some more rest? You needn't worry about any more dreams, and I'll keep a watch over you." Although the dream had startled her awake, Erma spoke to her in a voice softer than burgundy velvet. Minna struggled to keep her eyes from closing. She yawned but had one more question to ask Erma before she gave in to the fatigue.

"How did you know I was dreaming about the agate?" Minna fingered the pendant.

"You seemed to be in some kind of a struggle as if someone was trying to take it from you, and you were fighting to keep it."

"Boppy was taking me to get it, but I was frightened. We were in a shipyard."

"And did you get it?"

"I don't know. I got scared and woke up when he told me we were going to go get it."

"It's a blue lace agate, you know, and quite rare. Your Boppy must have been following his nose when he bought it for you."

"You don't mean it's magic, do you?" Franz would laugh so hard his belly would ripple if he heard that. Lila would sniff, "Honestly, the lengths some people will go to make something out of nothing. Superstitious fools!" Iris would not be so sure. "Could happen, you know. Never say never, is my motto."

Erma handed Minna an apple from a mysterious satchel that seemed to have suddenly appeared. Minna hadn't noticed it before. Where the bag ended and Erma began was unclear. They appeared as one solid piece, eternally attached.

"I don't know if it's magic. Maybe your Boppy was telling you he is watching out for you. That you are going to be all right. Dreams are funny that way, but I wouldn't ignore it."

"What do you think he is telling me?" Minna said when she got to the apple's core. She hadn't felt hungry before eating it. She'd been sleepy when Erma handed it to her. She must have been craving one. But how would Erma have known that?

"I don't know, but I do know a little about agates."

"You do? You mean they really are special? I thought Boppy gave it to me because it was pretty. He said it was to make my eyes happy."

"I like that. Yes, they are special. Some people believe if you wear them over the heart—just like you're doing—they will give you strength."

Minna suddenly felt so tired. She wanted to sleep. She whispered before her eyes closed, "Did Boppy send you?"

When she awoke, she didn't know if she had been awake for Erma's answer. She thought Erma had answered, but maybe she imagined it.

"Perhaps he did." Erma's answer rang in Minna's memory. Minna had fallen into a deep sleep. Did Erma also tell her something about the baby? Her brain wasn't clear yet, although the dull morning light was enough to rouse the other passengers who had slept curled up like balls of fuzzy cats on their upright seats. They stood in the aisles now to shake out the sleep from their legs and arms and necks. They yawned with their mouths uncovered.

Minna could swear Erma had also told her, in the blue twilight, "Before your baby girl is delivered, put the agate over your stomach."

"Does Boppy know why the agate is so important?" Minna was getting her dreams confused. Boppy had been in the dream at the shipyard. Was Erma in a dream, too, or was she real?

"Oh yes," she had heard Erma answer. "Your Boppy knows."

Twenty-Four

"Put Minna on the phone, Iris," Lila ordered.

"What do you mean? She's not here. I don't think so, anyway. Hang on. Let me go find Paulie." She was sucking on a cigarette, and her throat sounded scratchy. She checked the sewing room first. Lila heard her yell, "Paulie." He must have been in the greenhouse because it took her a while to pick up the phone again. She sounded breathy. "Nope. He says he hasn't seen her all day. He thought she was doing the job with us."

"Well, she wasn't, was she? Where is she, then?" It sounded like she was accusing Iris.

"She wasn't there when you got back home?" The catering job had run until two o'clock. "You checked her room?"

"Yes. Where do you think she'd go?" Lila loathed asking, but Iris knew Minna's whims. Iris would be the one to know where Minna would be.

"I haven't got a clue, Lila." Iris was agitated. "You're not gonna yell at her when she gets back, are you?"

"I never yell at her."

"No, but doggone it, Lila, we both know you can get pretty tight-lipped when you've got your dander up. Send her over to me when she gets back. I'll give her a good talkin' to. She shouldn't be actin' this way."

"To say the very least," Lila muttered.

"What has gotten into that girl?" Iris was perturbed. "She hasn't done this before, so my suggestion is don't make too much of it. I wouldn't go huntin' for her, either. That'll just make her mad. She'll come home, wagging her tail behind her." She clucked.

"I'll handle it, Iris." She couldn't abide her sister giving parenting advice. "Just call me if she shows up at your first place first."

"Iris don't know where she is, either?" Willy asked. She bristled when he touched her shoulder, and he backed up four feet. "What'd she say?"

"You know Iris. She has to say something ridiculous. A day couldn't go by." Lila was seething when she hung up.

ॐ

"Long-winded bags," Iris whispered to Willy earlier at the catering event. They stood at a side table in the banquet room. He'd had to run back to the bakery for more cookies.

"They got their tanks full. Bet they ain't spent their days workin' in any kitchen," he said under his breath. He laughed.

"I'm all in favor of that!" The less time she had to spend in the kitchen the better. A few women glared at her. She had on one of the fancy aprons she'd made for Lila, looking smart, but she acted a bit sassy. Lila had on the stiffest and whitest linens. She'd ironed them the evening before while Willy finished his soup and corn bread.

"You could wear one of my pretty handmade aprons," Iris had teased Willy when they loaded up the bakery goods into his truck. "You'd look good in the butterfly one."

"Think I'll stick with one of them ones Franz used to wear." He was dignified enough to model in a garage mechanic catalog. He wrapped the apron strings around his waist twice to get it to fit. When Franz was still living, it didn't go all the way around him even one time.

"Tell ya what," Willy said when the catering was done and he and Lila were back at the bakery putting things away. Iris had bucked when they told her to go home and leave the cleaning to them.

"What? You two gonna play around, are you?" She'd used up most of her sass by then.

"Honestly, Iris. Would you stop it?" Lila wrapped up some leftover brownies for Paulie.

"Don't you eat 'em all on the way home," Willy teased. "Save some for Paulie."

"I wouldn't dream of it." She cackled.

"It's four o'clock now." Willy looked at the wall clock over the door as Iris left. "What do you say I drive you home, we pick up Minna, and I take you two out for a bite to eat?"

"That's a good waste of money."

"Aw, come on, Lila. We've been on our feet all day. What time did you get up, anyway? Bet it was no later than four o'clock this morning. Am I right?"

"Yes." She laughed. "What are you now, the night watchman?"

"Hey, I got a better idea. Nobody's up in my old apartment, are they?" He hadn't considered that Lila would rent it to someone else.

"A guy from the railroad moved in last week," Lila felt a twinge of guilt, but she wouldn't pass up the chance to get rent from it.

"What the heck, Lila," he muttered. He didn't want to be upset with her. They'd gotten along since Minna's party, and he didn't want to ruin it. "Who is he?"

"He's new. Came from Alberton I think."

"He up there now?" Willy walked to the bottom of the stairs and looked up as though he would see the guy.

"I don't know. His things are up there. He said he'd be here part time. I guess he's going to come and go during the week."

"Don't like that much. Does he live somewhere else too?" He felt resentful that some strange guy would be the first to see Lila in the mornings.

"I don't think so. He might sleep on the train. Or else they put him up somewhere." It wasn't important where he slept as long as he paid his rent on time.

"Good-looker, is he?" He forced a smile.

"I don't know. I can't tell you what a good-looker is. You jealous?"

He worked to keep the envy out of his voice. "Damn right I am. What's his name?" he asked without inflection.

"Roland. Roland Johnson."

"How old is the son of a gun?" He looked at the wall.

"You are jealous." She giggled a bit. "Oh, I'll be happy to put my feet up tonight."

"I'll rub your feet," he promised. "But come on, Lila. Let me spoil you for once. It'd be good for Minna, too. Her chin's been on her chest since Archie left."

"You think that's what's going on?" She sounded surprised. "You want to take her out after what she'd done today?" Lila was putting the last of the equipment away. She wouldn't leave anything undone and have to catch up on Monday morning.

"Hey. If she'd showed up, I wouldn't had a job today. I got to see you. In my book, she done a good thing." He wanted to kiss her, but she moved back.

"Well, not in my book. I can't have it. I've been thinking all afternoon what I'm going to say to her." She pulled her eyebrows together and by accident dropped a large aluminum tray. It made an awful clatter.

"Here, let me do that." Willy was already picking it up. "I been thinkin' about it, too. I know it ain't right. Sure ain't the way you raised her. She got some funny ideas in her head bein' around that fly-boy.

Good thing he's gone."

"You don't think she'd go after him, do you?" She hadn't been able to get a decent word out of Minna to know how she felt.

"Naah. She's got a head on her shoulders. She's like you. She wouldn't lower herself to go after a guy. Unless…" He tilted his head back considering.

"Unless what?"

"Unless them two were plannin' somethin' all along. You know, like gettin' hitched."

She looked incredulous. "She's too young for that. Impossible! You don't think she'd do that, do you?" She put her shoulders back and looked him square in the face.

"Not without tellin' you and Iris first. Nope, I don't think so." He hesitated.

"I don't think he was serious about her. Do you?" Lila was trying to absorb the possibility. "It didn't seem like it when we were at the party. He was biding his time. Besides, she'd just be in his way." She'd watched Archie playing with Fischer. She watched him at dinner too, the way his leg kept jerking under the table like he was going to bolt at any moment.

"She talk to you about it after he left? How she felt about it?" He was uncertain how much he should ask.

"Not a word. But like you say, she seemed so quiet this week. You saw her last night, though. She was almost friendly. Didn't you think?"

"Yeah. I thought she was comin' around. That's why I think we should take her with us tonight. We won't say nothin' about her not showin' up today. Let her do the talkin' on that score, and if she don't say nothin' the whole time, then you can work it out with her later." He smiled because it sounded like a good approach.

"I don't know. She knows me too well. She'll know I'm mad. Maybe she wants me to get mad at her." She furrowed her brow.

"Well, just don't do it. I bet if we treat her nice, she's gonna feel bad about what she done. She might even surprise you and apologize. Right there, tonight."

"I'll try it your way"—she sounded reluctant—"and if doesn't work, I can say I told you so."

"Good girl. We'll have a good time, and I will rub your feet later." He elbowed her. "By the way, you never did say how old that Roland Johnson is."

Twenty-Five

"King Street Station. Fifteen minutes. Seattle. King Street Station," the sallow conductor barked three times, stamping through the coach. Minna bolted awake and caught the tail end of him before the steel door slammed behind him. She'd been dreaming about traipsing through a massive field with orange poppies. She could still sense the sunlight warming her back.

Her left hand had fallen asleep, and it felt like needles poking into her, but she ignored it and concentrated on her first glimpses of Seattle. The train slowed down gradually, whistling almost nonstop, which agitated the butterflies in her stomach.

The sky was so sad, like it was in mourning but not quite weeping. It was an abrupt contrast after her poppy dream. She'd heard that the city didn't get enough sunshine, but that didn't concern her. She needed to find a place to live and then get a job.

"What time is it?" she asked Erma, only to find she wasn't there. A nubby, passive seat stared back at her, not the comforting lady who had softened the night and listened to her dream about Boppy. Since the purple umbrella was still there, it was likely Erma was in the restroom freshening up. The tips of Minna's fingers felt icy cold, and she pulled her coat down from the overhead rack. The best way to keep track of gloves was to put the left one in the same side pocket of the coat, and the right on the other side. She would need them before the train stopped.

"Did you see the lady who was sitting here?" she asked the conductor when Erma hadn't returned. He grabbed hold of the top of each seat as he lumbered down the aisle like a drunkard. He ignored her. He shouted again, "King Station coming up! Ten minutes."

Minna thought she was going to get sick and jumped up to sprint past elbows, knees, and shoes poking out into the aisle for the restroom. If Erma was in there, she would open it. But the restroom was unlocked, and the nausea passed. She steadied herself to get back to her seat from the train's lurching and swerving around buildings. They were

127

close enough to reach out and touch. Every intersection got its squeal from the train's horn. Each time the door opened, she swiveled to see if Erma was on her way back to their seat. She would come back to collect her umbrella.

The passengers grew animated. They stuffed their books and magazines into their bags, along with half-eaten sandwiches and empty thermoses.

"Excuse me," someone said.

"Can I get that down for you?" a young man asked an elderly lady.

"You are such a nice young gentleman," she heard the woman say. "Thank you."

Minna waited for Erma to return. The umbrella with the crystal handle sparkled in the light. Since the conductor was snubbing her, she made a decision to take it and leave it at the lost and found with Erma's name on it. By the looks of the sky, she would need one herself, but Minna didn't want to take something that did not belong to her.

The umbrella seemed to want to get her attention. It made her feel odd and uneasy, and she looked away and out the window. "Ridiculous," she said to the glass. She glanced back at it thinking she must be imagining it, but it was grinning at her. She was sure of it. She'd have said, "Stop it," if people hadn't started clustering near the door.

She decided to wait until the train came to a complete stop before she picked up the umbrella. Maybe Erma would come back at the last moment before they got to the depot. She kept her back to the umbrella but imagined its fingers tapping her on the shoulder. "Okay," she said to herself. "I give up." She picked it up. Just as quickly, she put it back down. Nothing happened, and she picked it up again.

The train slithered past dingy warehouses and faded-blue factories with broken windows. It blew its agitated whistle again and again. If something got too near the tracks, or crossed its path, it leaped into a fierce tantrum. Minna wanted to yell, "Shut up," at its screeching.

She was about to put the umbrella back where Erma had left it, having changed her mind again. The best idea would be to leave it and let the railroad deal with it, but then she noticed a piece of paper pinned on the back side. The umbrella must have shifted during the night, and if Minna hadn't picked it up she would have missed seeing it.

Minna, I think you should take the umbrella to this address at 517 29th South. I think something will be waiting for you there. Oh, and for some reason, gladiolas seem important. I don't know why. Do you? Erma Shepherd.

Erma hadn't forgotten the umbrella! Minna felt like crying.

She'd assumed she and Erma would get off the train together in Seattle. She had let herself fall asleep because she was safe and watched over. She had wanted to ask Erma for tips about how to get set up in the city, and if she knew where to find a good but cheap room to rent.

When had she written the note? And when had she gotten off the train? The conductor would know this, but he wouldn't tell her. Erma was gone. She had left without telling Minna she was going, but she had left something of herself.

Erma Shepherd could have been a phantom who had appeared in a daydream. It didn't seem real that she had sat next to Minna and had been so reassuring. Perhaps Minna had imagined the woman and her indescribable dress. But that would not explain the purple umbrella and the note. Erma had to have been real!

Erma had touched her on the arm wiping away the droplets that had fallen from her Chinese hat. They had talked, and there was that business of Erma recognizing that she was pregnant. Minna had been embarrassed after drooling on Erma's shoulder while she slept.

Even when it happened it felt dreamy, and if it wasn't for the umbrella, she wouldn't believe it at all. She'd had the dream about Boppy, too, and the agate. The way Erma acted made Minna want to tilt her head and adjust the universe. Her appearance alone was reason enough for Minna's seventeen years of learning to tumble right out of her brain and fall upon a sign that read, ONE WAY, do not turn around!

"Oh well," she whispered as the train slid down the last hundred yards of track. She had taken her gloves off and now wiggled them back over her knuckles. It was a good thing they were black and wouldn't show the dirt. "Here we go," pulling her shoulders back and tugging down the bottom of her skirt to discourage the conductor. She would search out a kind-looking woman at the station and ask for directions, but first she needed to find a bathroom and then have some breakfast.

The conductor turned his back as she pulled her suitcase down, but the same young man who had helped the elderly lady said, "Here, let me help you with that. Hey, it's not too heavy." He laughed.

"Thanks." She smiled but wondered why he wasn't in uniform. His wool scarf was elegant and expensive, as was his tan cashmere overcoat.

"I can help you get it off the train," he offered.

"Thanks anyway. I've got it now," she told him. "Like you said, it's not that heavy." On the way through the door, she knocked one of the metal edges against her knee. It hit hard enough to create a bruise.

The conductor helped the older woman, who was having trouble getting out of her seat. He pretended he had to sneeze and turned his back when Minna got to the platform and started down the metal steps.

"Good riddance," she said loud enough for him to hear. That was the way Iris would handle it and then puff herself up, feeling justified. Minna didn't like the man, but it was the first time she said what she was thinking to someone she didn't know. She wasn't sure that it fit her. It was like going outside in a snowstorm without a coat.

A blast of air so thick and wet hit her in the face, and it made her stomach turn. She felt green. People were running past her, some knocking against her because she was going against the current and because the concrete was slimy. Her heart pounded in her stomach.

"I need some fresh air," she said. What she inhaled felt like cold soup, and she broke out in a sweat. It wasn't raining, but then it wasn't not raining. The air stuck to her. She felt it on her tongue and wanted to gag. It was in her nostrils and on her face.

Shades of brown and blue and an occasional red tone flashed past her in a flurry of commotion. She couldn't breathe in the middle of the swarm. She saw the station platform, and it could have been a mile away, but it was elevated. If she could just get out of this pit of people where everyone had to share a limited amount of oxygen, she'd be all right.

She pushed and got pushed. Someone ran into her suitcase, and she lost her grip. Before she could get a firm hold on it, she got knocked hard between the shoulder blades. It felt like a rock, and she was going to throw up on shoes and suitcases, and it didn't matter. She doubled over and put out her free arm trying to find something steady on the other end while she waited for the sickness to come up.

"Oh no," she cried. Cold sweat popped out on her forehead. She felt light-headed like she was going to pass out. Her hand found something to hold onto so she wouldn't be trampled in the crowd. No one was paying attention to her. A pair of red shoes went by, more pumps, and black shoes with laces, but no one stopped to ask if she was all right.

The nausea eased quickly, and she took in some deep breaths and wiped her forehead with her glove. She had managed not to throw up at the Seattle train station.

Twenty-Six

"She hasn't come home," Lila cried into the phone.

"Give me a cigarette, Paulie." Lila heard her take a deep breath and then exhale. "Hold on a sec, Lila. Give me a minute to think."

"Maybe she's at the movies," Paulie said into the receiver. Iris rubbed her forehead with the cigarette in her hand.

"No, she's not. Willy went over there already and checked. They ran the last movie at ten." Lila's voice quivered.

"What time is it?" Paulie squinted at the kitchen clock. "Oh. Twelve thirty," he answered his own question.

"Is Willy there?" Iris asked.

"Yes. He's right here, why?"

"Tell him to stay there. We're comin' over soon as Paulie gets the car out." She signaled with the cigarette for him to go to the garage. "Jeezus, it's cold," she complained into the phone when he opened the back door. She was wearing a fleecy, tangerine bathrobe. "I gotta get dressed, and we'll be over. Don't worry. We'll find her, Lila. She'll probably get there before we do. She's not gonna like it that we're all waitin' for her, either."

"Where do you really think she could be?" Iris implored Paulie. His hands were gripping the steering wheel, the black sky his immediate antagonist.

"Maybe she's at a friend's house?" He made it sound hopeful.

"As far as I can tell, I'm her best friend," she carped. "You know that as well as me." He didn't want to sound worried, and that worried Iris.

"I'm gonna give that kid a piece of my mind, I can tell you." She stared out the windshield at the objects the headlights illuminated.

"Don't you think Lila should do that?" A car's headlights blinded him briefly. He pumped the brakes, and the car jerked. Missoula didn't have the strict blackouts of the larger, seacoast cities.

"Watch out!" Iris shouted. He was a much better cook than a

driver. "You know Lila. She'll pout for a week and keep her damn mouth closed tighter than a turtle."

"You mean a clam, I think." He was treading on rocky ground.

"Whatever, Paulie. Don't you get it?" He could be so exasperating, entirely missing the point as if he deliberately wanted to do so. "You know how Lila gets if she decides someone's let her down."

"I sure wouldn't wanna be that kid tonight." He sighed. He wiped the inside of the windshield with his sleeve. He and Willy were smart enough to keep their mouths shut when there was trouble. They would get the blame if they said anything, as if they were the root cause of the trouble.

Lila was pacing at the front window when she saw their headlights come into view. Paulie scraped the curb before he came to a complete stop. "What a surprise," Iris grumbled. He couldn't handle a car and his worries in the same instant.

Lila ran out without her jacket. She hadn't changed out of her white linens. She thought for sure it was Minna driving up. "Oh, it's you." She was crestfallen. She'd forgotten about Iris and Paulie.

"Still no sign of her?" Iris couldn't make up her mind whether to take her coat off once inside the door. Willy had a substantial fire going in the living room. "It's so dang cold tonight," she said to him as he helped her out of it.

"Yeah. I think it's going to drop below ten degrees yet."

"My car didn't wanna get out of bed." Paulie chuckled. Iris gave him a sour look.

"So," Iris asked, "I guess you haven't heard anything from her?" Lila shook her head.

"Not even a phone call?" Iris made a face.

"Nothing." The tiny lines around Lila's eyes stood out.

"Did you look around to see if she mighta left a note, or somethin'?" Iris asked.

Lila was stunned. The idea didn't make sense at first. "Oh my gosh. Why didn't I think of that?" she said like it was too bright a light shining in her face.

"You checked her room?" That's the first thing Iris would have done, but she didn't say that.

"No. I called up there. She didn't answer."

"Well, she wouldn't if she wasn't up there, would she?" Iris looked at her sister, dumbfounded.

"I don't go poking around in her room," Lila said flatly.

"Well, there's one way to find out what's goin' on. Let's go take a look."

Willy and Paulie waited at the bottom of the stairs. "Women's business," Paulie confided. Willy concurred.

"A shot of whiskey sounds pretty good right now," Willy said.

"Or Chianti." Paulie grinned.

"Not in this house." Willy chuckled.

"I wonder where she went," Paulie mused.

"Hard to tell. Lila's in a stir, that's for sure. It ain't right, that girl puttin' her through hell this way."

"It ain't like her, though," Paulie reminded him.

"Yeah, I know. She ain't never caused no trouble till this summer."

"Her suitcase is gone," Iris announced at the top of the stairs.

"What?" both men lifted their heads. Lila looked down at them from behind Iris. She didn't say anything. She just stood up there looking down at them.

"You all right?" Willy asked Lila.

"She didn't even leave a note."

Iris added, "Far as we can tell."

"She left her red shoes," Lila said quietly. The men nodded as if they understood.

"Should we call the police?" Paulie said as the reality set in.

"We don't even know when she left," Iris declared. "Was she in bed when you left this morning?"

"I thought so. But you saw the pillows stuffed under her quilt. She was trying to fool me, wasn't she?" She was red in the face from being stupid and being deceived.

"So," Willy offered, "the last time we saw her was at supper last night. Is that right?"

"Yes, I guess that's right." Lila sighed.

"Okay," Willy said. "Let's make a plan. Paulie, would you make us some coffee? If we put our heads together we can figure out what to do next. We'll find her."

"You're right," Iris agreed. "Let's sit down and see what needs to happen first." She and Willy preferred working from plans, following steps.

"Then we will decide if we call the police," Willy acceded to Paulie.

"I don't want to call the police," Lila declared. "Minna's not a criminal."

"Of course not, honey," Iris consoled her. "The only reason

Paulie said that is because we want to know she's all right. Isn't that so, Paulie?" she glared at him again.

"Fischer can find her," Lila declared. The three heads swiveled to look at her. "He can. I know he can."

"Oh boy," Iris said under her breath. "Lila, why don't we lay it out first, you know, like we just said. Think about what we should do first. Then we can decide about Fischer."

"She's his daughter," Lila insisted.

"Yes, she is," Willy said gently. "If that's what Lila wants to do, then we should do it." He smiled, but his eyes were sad.

"Okay," Iris said, "but you know how he can be, Lila. He'll blow his stack at you. You know that. Blame you for it. I just wonder if it's worth it, right now. We got enough on our plates, don't we?" Fischer's drama would only add to their anxiety, and she didn't relish putting up with him.

"It's up to you, Lila," Willy spoke quietly. "We can talk about it first, the four of us, and then go to Fischer. Probably no point callin' him in the middle of the night, don't ya think? How 'bout first thing in the morning?"

Twenty-Seven

"You okay?" someone asked as she undoubled herself. The pillar that had supported her was a solider dressed in olive drab. She hadn't been in a state to observe his sparkling boots among the other shoes stamping past.

"Oh! I didn't know…" Her face felt sweaty cold. "You're a…a soldier," she stammered.

"Yes ma'am. It's okay." His smile emphasized the freckles on his cheeks and nose. "Let's find a seat inside. You look awfully pale." Without asking, he took the suitcase she'd dropped when the sickness overcame her. No one had taken it, thank goodness.

It was pandemonium inside the station. People were yelling to be heard over one another. The voices reverberated off the walls of the grand room and bounced up from the terrazzo tile littered with cigarette butts. A stooped, bald-headed man leaned over a giant broom, striving to collect the stragglers into one pile. Suitcases parked next to men's dark-brown, to-be-taken-seriously Oxfords, stood near ladies' practical navy-blue pumps, and there wasn't an empty square foot of tiled space to take a breath without doing so in someone's face. Minna's head was spinning in the swirl. The soldier rushed ahead with her suitcase looking for an empty seat. When he turned around and saw she had gone gray, he rushed back. "Let's go outside." He checked the time on the west wall clock, took her arm, and pulled her out the front doors to a dilapidated wooden bench by the station's entrance.

There was a snarl of taxis and cars stopping to let passengers out at the curb. Seattle was in perpetual motion, people and machines lurching from one location to the next. Car engines groaned as if complaining they had been dragged into the confusion. The air tasted salty and was saturated with diesel stink, but there was a slight cool breeze that helped Minna's color return.

"When was the last time you ate?" the soldier asked. He put his hat back on, and she liked the way it tilted. He didn't wait for her to answer. "I'll be back in a few minutes. Don't move, understand?" He grinned. He didn't look old enough to be a soldier. There wasn't enough muscle under the uniform. He could be fourteen, he looked so young. He might have been puny, but when he smiled it was infectious, and even with an unsteady stomach, she felt better.

"Okay." She was grateful. Besides, she was in no shape to argue or to wander off, although soon she needed to find a place to rest.

The commotion of cars and people with suitcases and raincoats didn't stop. On the opposite side of the street she grabbed sight of a naked maple tree. It was the only stationary thing in this shifting world, and she possessed it with her eyes to hold herself steady. The army boy with sandy hair returned almost before he had left.

"Here you go." He handed her a small bottle of milk he'd opened. He handed her a hard-boiled egg and an apple. If he had returned with a salami sandwich, she would have thrown up for sure.

She looked up at him. Did he know, too?

"Thank you." She sipped the thick milk. It tasted sweet and creamy, and she smacked her lips and drank the entire contents in a few swallows. She licked her lips like a cat.

"You're getting your color back now." He was pleased. "Eat the egg next. That'll steady those nerves. I know. There are too many people here. It's crazier than I've ever seen it." She nodded.

"You must have a train to catch." She said realizing she might be the cause for him to miss it. He was working on the egg. He banged it against the bench to crack the shell, peeled it, and examined it to see if he had missed any tiny pieces. When he was satisfied, he handed it to her. She preferred them soft-boiled, but this one was delicious, as she discovered from the first bite. She stuffed the remainder down in two bites. "Mmm," she said, wiping her glove on her skirt. He laughed.

"I've got a few hours yet. Sorry I couldn't get you any salt." He was shipping out for Alaska, he said, from Fort Lewis, where he was stationed with the Third Division. "Hey, I'm sorry," he continued, "I'm John Welles. I should have said so sooner. I didn't mean to be rude, but it didn't seem important, with you not looking so good back there. Besides, the end of that purple umbrella was pinned to my boot," he teased.

"I'm Minna," she answered not giving a last name. "Oh, I'm sorry about your boot."

"I was just teasing," he said, "It wasn't a bother." She didn't want to say her last name, stutter over it like she had with Erma. Besides, John Welles would be gone in a few minutes, anyway, and she needed to find a place to stay. The food did help. The sickness had passed.

"And I haven't properly thanked you." She returned his smile. Her insides confused her all the time lately. When she was nauseated, she couldn't stand the thought of eating anything, but if she didn't eat, she got sick. The last thing she had eaten was the apple from Erma.

"You're looking good, now. You just needed some solid food in you." She noticed tiny blond hairs on his upper lip. She wondered if he was the runt of the litter, which made her want to giggle, or if had been neglected by his family, which made her feel sad. Then she thought of the soups, breads, and pies Lila made. Minna had never known what it was like to go to bed hungry and had never spent a night without a solid roof over her head. She wondered if this night was going to be different.

"Where are you headed?" he asked as if he'd read her mind.

"I'm..." She didn't know what to tell him.

"Say! Do you have a place to stay?"

"I..." What should she say, pretend she knew where she was going next?

"Oh boy," John Welles declared. "You don't have a place, do you?" She looked at the passengers running past lugging heavy cases. Then she looked toward the maple tree.

"Come on," he grabbed her by the hand. He picked up her suitcase and tugged her off the bench. "You're lucky you found me." He spoke over his shoulder.

"Where are we going?" She was startled but not afraid. They hurried, and her legs moved like stiff logs from having been so many hours on the train.

"Sorry," he apologized, half turning around because she was having trouble keeping up. "We have to hurry." John Welles was swift. He might not have weighed much, but he moved like a racehorse, and she was sure he was not going to do her harm.

Twenty-Eight

"I coulda called it," Iris sniffed. The table was cluttered with coffee cups and a few pieces of coffee cake. Lila was on the phone to Fischer. They'd decided to wait until daylight before calling him.

"Calm down," they heard Lila say. "I don't know." Her voice was rising. "We've been up all night trying to figure it out."

"I'll make us some eggs," Paulie jumped up while she was on the phone. They were worn out from no sleep, and breakfast seemed a sensible choice.

"Don't you go messin' up Lila's kitchen now, Paulie," Iris warned.

"I'm as neat as a pin." He grinned. She got up from the table and put on her coat.

"Don't say nothin' important till I get back," she told the men and went outside for a smoke.

"Fischer's coming over in a few minutes." Lila peeked around the door to the backyard. "How can you stand it out here? It's so cold."

"I'd be inside if you'd let me smoke," Iris snapped. They were all edgy. Through the night they'd held out a hope that diminished more as the hours passed.

"If you stopped smoking, you wouldn't have to go outside," Lila retorted and shut the door forcefully.

"Dig in," Paulie commanded. They didn't feel hungry but ate every bit of it. Lila made homemade toast and buttered it to the edges, and another pot of coffee.

"Want some breakfast?" Lila asked Fischer. He'd rung the doorbell nonstop until Paulie let him in.

"How can you guys eat when she's taken off?" he demanded.

"Well she's gone whether our bellies are full or empty." Iris was snippy. "It wouldn't do you any harm, either. Would it? To eat something?" She was still stinging from Lila's comment.

"She's right," Lila chimed in. "It's going to be a long day either way." She and Iris shared glances. You could have pinched Iris, who wondered if her sister was apologizing.

"I'll have some coffee then." Paulie made some more eggs and put them in front of Fischer with toast.

"So. Her suitcase is gone, and she's gone. What'd she take with her?" Fischer sounded like an expert.

"Sensible clothes," Iris said.

"Not her red shoes." They looked at Lila, who was stuck on Minna leaving the red shoes.

"Who cares?" Fischer snarled.

"I care," Lila said simply. Willy felt so sorry for her, he wished he could put his arm around her, but she'd push him away.

"What's so goddamn important about them red shoes?" Fischer barked.

"What's important, Fischer, is *why* she didn't take them," Iris scolded.

"Maybe we should go to the police?" Paulie asked again. Iris would get mad at him if he told Fischer to behave toward his wife.

"Forget the damn police." Fischer hated the police. "They don't solve problems. They make 'em."

"The clothes are the important clue." Iris now was the one to sound like a detective.

"How so?" Willy asked.

"Yeah. Who made you the expert, Iris?" Fischer said dismissively.

"I know my niece," Iris raised an eyebrow. "I'm goin' out for a smoke if you don't want to hear what I think." She started toward the door.

Fischer backpedaled. "Okay, okay. Wait a minute. Just hold on." He nearly choked asking her to explain.

"Number one, and we talked about this all night, didn't we?" Iris said, and heads nodded. "She didn't go off on a lark."

"What's that mean?" Fischer didn't get how that was important.

Willy jumped in. "It means that she's been plannin' it for a while."

"How in the wide world would you know that?" Fischer snickered.

"Because," Iris offered, "she took the things she needed to get herself set up somewhere.

"And since you know that much, Iris, maybe you can tell us where she is setting herself up."

"Wish I could. But then I'd be a genius, wouldn't I? Or a mind reader." She fingered the cigarette she was holding as she stood next to the door.

"It don't take a genius to figure out she went after that knucklehead." Fischer didn't like him any better than the others.

"I guess we all agreed on that, ain't we?" Paulie felt skittish when Iris and Fischer stood up to each other. Iris was masterful, but she had to win, and Fischer was exactly the same. It never came to any good between them.

"You think she's gonna marry that little shit?" Fischer was about to the boiling point.

Iris spoke for all of them. "I wouldn't bet on it. We think he'd have asked her to marry him while he was here if

they were gonna do it." They were quiet for a time. Lila had not spoken at all except about the red shoes.

"What do you think, Lila?" Fischer prodded. She acted the same way in every crisis. She got silent. He hated it, never knowing what she was thinking. "You think she went after him?"

Lila shrugged.

"I don't care what you say, Iris. She just can't be that stupid. What would it get her, anyway? You think he's gonna marry her just 'cause she shows up in Minnesota?" Fischer didn't believe it.

"You got a better answer?" Iris challenged him. They were probably right.

"Okay. Say she did go to Minnesota. How'd she get there?" Willy felt his chin. He liked a clean face.

"Well, there's the train," Paulie said, stating the obvious. Iris shook her head. He made great omelets. She wished he would leave it at that.

"Or the bus," Willy added. "Either way, she had to buy a ticket, right?" They nodded. They'd thought the same.

"So, we go to the train depot and the bus station, and we show 'em a picture of Minna. You got one of them, Lila?" Fischer asked and nodded. "Then we find out how she went. We just need to find out where she got a ticket to, don't we?"

"Then, Willy you and me should go out to the fort when we find out for sure that's what she did."

"Okay. You mean to see where he's at." Willy was thinking the same.

"I know some of those guys out there. You prob'ly do, too. You work on any of their cars?"

"Yeah, I know a few of them guys." Most of them were decent

men. They might find one who would help.

"We just gotta find one who'll tell us where that stinkin' Archie went." Fischer spit out the name.

"Then what?" Iris had her hands on her hips.

"We get his commander on the phone, see, and we tell him the story." Fischer expected Iris to have it figured out.

"What if she didn't follow him?" Lila sounded like she was inside a well.

"We'll cross that bridge when we come to it." Fischer paused. "If we have to." Then spoke in a reassuring way that surprised the others. "Paulie, you come with me and Willy to the train station. You know the ins and outs over there."

"I'm ready." Paulie jumped up.

"We'll go the bus station if we don't get anything there. Lila, you keep your chin up, honey. We'll find her. I promise," Fischer gave her a confident smile.

"I'll watch her," Iris said. Lila was exhausted. "Try to get her to sleep a little. Let me know what you hear, okay?" She smiled at Fischer. "And thanks," she whispered.

Twenty-Nine

"Well, hello, John Welles," the dark-skinned woman welcomed them at the landing of her faded-red front door three steps up from the street. The woman was a Negro!

John Welles hadn't spoken one word about where he was dragging Minna off to from the train station. She was out of breath from running up a hill to keep up. He'd helped her when she was sick. He'd even gone to get food. But she didn't know what he was thinking to bring her here.

"What're you up to these days, young man?" The woman looked him up and down and then chuckled. She brought them into a distracting front room. It was like a dollhouse, scented with nutmeg and pepper. It was snug and happy with blue-and-yellow gingham pillows that disguised a sagging brown sofa and a pair of mismatched side chairs. A twin pair of windows faced onto the street, watching outside the home through sheer curtains.

"Mrs. Chaplain," John started, but she raised her palm to stop him.

"Now, John Welles, you know you s'posed to call me Divine. But who's this you got with you here?" Divine extended her hand.

Minna took the black hand into her own. She'd never shaken hands with a person that color before. She hadn't stood this close to one, let alone been inside her house. The skin next to her own surprised her, it was soft like Lila's flour, and the color on the palm was the same as stone-ground whole wheat.

"I'm Minna," she replied, not waiting for John to introduce her. Divine didn't look anything like Aunt Jemima except for the bandanna which she could have taken right off the box of pancake mix. The woman was taller than Minna by an inch and a half, and the same size around the waist as Lila. Her brown eyes bulged behind the metal-rimmed glasses that matched the few gray strands of hair peeking out over her forehead. Her face looked as smooth as her hand. John was watching out for her, and that Divine was warm as a doughnut just pulled from the cooker.

"Um, Divine," John said, "I've got a train to catch in two hours, but I'm wondering if you have room for Minna. Just for a few days, right, Minna? Until she gets settled here."

"Well, we just 'bout gonna have us a full house here." Divine tittered. "My brother's comin' in from Memphis to work in the shipyards early as tomorrow."

"Just a few days, Divine?" John pressed. He used the same smile he had when he told Minna to wait and not move while he went off to get her something to eat. She'd not wanted to disappoint him, so she didn't tell him she was feeling all right, and he could be on his way. He seemed so eager to help.

"Where you off to then in them spiffy-lookin' clothes?" Divine looked him straight in the eye, putting her face close to his. It was like looking through a microscope at those big brown eyes through a microscope. "They not sendin' you off to fight that nasty war over there, is they?" She pointed behind her in the direction of Iowa or Minnesota.

"I'm afraid so. That's what we're trained for, you know." He sounded proud yet uneasy.

"What you got to eat on that train trip of yours? No, don't tell me. I'm gettin' some things together for you right this instant. You just stay here and talk to that pretty young girl of yours, and don't go runnin' off 'fore I get you fixed up. You hear?"

They were nervous after she left, and John suddenly jumped up from the sofa and apologized because Divine had assumed they were sweethearts.

"But who is she?" Minna whispered when he sat back down.

"It's a long story, and there's no time now. I gotta go in a few minutes." John looked at his watch and then wiped his palm on his pants.

"Are they really sending you to fight?" Of course they were. It was naïve to ask, but she could not picture this young kid, who couldn't be any older than she, going off to kill people and probably get killed himself.

"Yep."

"Where are you going?"

"They don't tell us that." He shrugged. If he knew, he'd only wonder how bad it was going to be there anyway. If he didn't think about it, and he could put it out of his mind for short periods of time, he was content. They heard Divine in the other room close a cupboard, then the sound of paper rustling. She was singing softly, and it sounded like a lullaby, slow and a bit melancholy, like a mother ruing the parting from her child. Minna made out the melody. "You must remember this. A kiss is just a kiss…"

"This probably isn't right"—his voice jarred against the kitchen melody—"but I'm wondering if it'd be wrong to ask you to write to me." She saw his hands were clenched against his pant legs, and the knuckles were white. "I mean, I expect you already have someone, am I right? Or maybe you're even married."

Because she hesitated, he said, "Forget it. Please forget it. I shouldn't have asked." He rubbed his fists down his legs then stretched his feet out.

"No!" she answered emphatically but then became calmer. "No, I mean, I'm not married." She thought he had recognized her condition at the station because he had brought her food she could tolerate, like he knew what she needed, but apparently not. He'd not asked her where she'd come from. There hadn't been time. She studied the yellow gingham on the chair opposite her.

"Here you go, John." Divine came in swinging a sack almost half the size of Minna's suitcase. He laughed. "Thanks, Divine, but where am I supposed to put all this?"

"Right there," she said, peering through her glasses and pointing to his stomach. "That don't take much figurin' out. You a smart boy, ain't you?" He took the sack from her and found it wasn't any lighter than it looked.

"What'd you put in here, rocks? I'm gonna break an arm getting all this and my other stuff on that train," he said.

"And I don't want no reports that you leave somethin' on your plate, neither," she commanded. "You knows there's plenty people goin' hungry these days." She smiled at Minna. "Now, you two get all your talkin' in? I done my best to make plenty noise in that kitchen," she teased.

"I gotta go," he said ripping a piece off the top of the sack. He dug into his trouser pocket and brought out a stub of a pencil and scribbled on the paper. "Here," he said, handing it to Minna. "Just in case you do decide to write." He looked at her with doubt.

"Course she'll write," Divine responded. "And I'll keep an eye on her till that brother of mine gets here. Hey, you lookin' for work by chance?" The bug eyes dominated Divine's face at her question.

"Yes, yes, I am," Minna nearly squealed. She almost clapped her hands.

"We'll jus' talk 'bout that very thing when this mister get on his way." Her brown eyes looked big open or closed, and right now they were almost shut as she studied John like she was reading a book. A car revved an engine going by the open red door, another laid on a horn, then brakes squealed, and it was almost impossible to hear each other. John and Divine were eye level until he went down a step. Minna thought Divine might cry.

"Now you listen here, young man," Divine barked to make sure John heard her. "Plenty young men be comin' back after this thing over." She pointed a two-toned forefinger at him. "You don't disappoint me now. I 'spect you be one of 'em. You hear me? I don't mean to say it two times neither. Never did like repeatin' myself."

He smiled broadly, but there was a flicker of sorrow in the grin. "You bet, Divine. I'll keep my head down," he teased, trying to keep it light. "'Course, with all that food you fixed for me, I'm gonna be too fat to run if they start chasing me."

"Don't you give me no business 'bout that lunch there. You need that for them muscles of yours. We won't even recognize him none, Minna, when he come home, will we? He'll be that big."

Minna nodded. She hadn't spoken since they came to the door. "John, thanks for what you did for me today. I don't know what I would've done without your help."

"Someone else would have helped if I didn't. They just didn't want to get their shoes dirty." He grinned at her.

She smiled back at him. "No, John. I won't forget it. Thank you. And like Divine says, you come back safe."

"Well, with you two telling me, I guess I'd better." He put his cap on again, and there was something about the way he did it that thrilled Minna inside. She wanted to ask him to do it one more time so she could feel that charge again.

He backed down the last two steps and waved up at them, smiling, then walked away and did not turn around again. Minna and Divine stood together on the tiny landing and watched him trot down the hill toward the station until he was only a black speck among many other specks, scurrying ants moving with purpose.

"Let's go get you set up, Minna." Divine's voice was hoarse. "Then we goin' make you a fine meal. You hasta try my chicken and biscuits. You ain't had 'em, yet, has you?" Divine squinted down at Minna. "No, course you hasn't. Did John Welles tell you 'bout them, though?" Her voice rose hopefully.

"No, Divine. I just met John at the railroad station. I don't know anything about him."

"Oh, go on," Divine whispered. "There's always the first time

145

to try my cookin'." The idea of preparing food brought back her cheerful mood. "You ain't tasted nothin' like it in you life. You has my personal guarantee. Personal!" She shook her head and laughed a hearty roar.

Thirty

The scent of cinnamon and nutmeg woke her, and she wondered what her mother was preparing. Then she heard rambunctious laughter coming from the kitchen, and realized she was not at home. She sat up at the banter between Divine and a booming male voice and remembered she had gone to sleep in an unfamiliar house. The discrepancy was upsetting, the strange voices interwoven with the familiar spices. She looked at the lavender ceiling and wished for the peach walls of her own room, the maple dresser and mirror, the tiny desk opposite, and her closet with the clothes she'd left behind.

Divine was giggling and the man guffawing. They were talking at the same time, trying to outdo each other, and neither of them stopped. Their voices got higher and higher until they burst out laughing. It was rice pudding. That was the aroma wafting upstairs.

Customers would be lining up at the bakery counter by this time, and Iris would be passing out sass as fast as she served the pastries. On cold mornings, Lila made rice pudding for Minna and left it warming on the stove for her. A skin would stretch over it. She hated the raisins and always chose a piece of toast with lots of butter and homemade raspberry jelly, and then a big glass of milk from the bottle delivered in the green van by George, the milkman, from Frenchtown. She loved the thick cream that floated to the top and tried to capture that in her glass when she poured it out.

"Hello, young Minna," the enormous colored man shouted when she went down into the kitchen. She hadn't felt nauseated. She had dressed quickly, in a practical suit. Her hands were sweating, though.

"Dee-vine told me all 'bout you." He grinned. He was careful, watching out for her knees against the chrome table legs when he pulled out her chair. "Don't wanna bang you'self." His voice softened. She wondered if Divine who, like Erma Shepherd, had guessed about the baby, had told him about it.

"Meet Cosmo," he thrust out his huge hand for her to shake.

It swallowed up her whole hand. "I'm Minna." She gulped,

147

forgetting he'd already called her that. His massive frame was incongruous in that dollhouse kitchen. It was nothing short of a miracle the way he folded himself in at the table. He had to duck to pass through Divine's doorways.

"I'm headin" for the shipyards in a bit. You wanna come with me, and we gets you a job there?"

"Oh yes," Minna replied.

"You got one of them heads for figures?"

"Yes, I do." She had learned how and when to order supplies at the bakery. It was tricky to maintain the stock but she got a sense of what was used up most quickly and what she didn't need to order very often. Lila didn't want anything in storage for too long.

"You can use that money for more immediate purchases," Lila taught her.

"You talk business after this girl be done eatin', you hear?" Divine complained, dishing up a bowl of pudding with a tablespoon in front of Minna. Apricots replaced the predictable raisins, and after Minna took a first bite, she shoveled the remainder down. "You could stand a few more pounds." Divine tsked and laughed. "Want some more?" Minna would have liked a piece of toast but thought it rude to ask. She was bewildered by Divine's generosity, and now her brother Cosmo.

"I hear they need people with that kind o' thinkin'." Cosmo grinned. He seemed younger than Divine, but maybe she was gray prematurely. They were in their forties, a little older than Lila and Iris.

"We goin' to that Todd-Pacific and gets you a job. You and me goin' make sure them boys over there"—he pointed to the Midwest— "gets the best ships to fight them enemies o' ours." He was proud to be a part of the war effort. If she got the job she would do her best to help the fight. She'd buy war bonds, too.

"You got yourself one o' them umbrellas?" Cosmo asked, like a judge evaluating her prospects.

"Yes, I do," Minna said proudly, as if she, not Erma Shepherd, had used common sense.

"Well, that's good then, 'cause look like we goin' have us a rare spot of Seattle rain this day." His eyes twinkled.

Divine was quiet while Minna ate her breakfast. There was a look of regret, like the one she had when she said good-bye to John Welles.

"That all well and good," Divine said after an interval, "But this girl don't have no place to stay with you takin' up so much space now, Cosmo."

"That what botherin' you, Dee-vine? We goin' get it worked out, ain't we, Minna?" He gave her a confident wink.

"I know these hills up and down," he assured Minna. He'd stayed with Divine two years before. His mind was like a city map when it came to figuring out where to catch a trolleybus, and finding a place to live.

Divine knew better. The last time Cosmo had stayed with her, apartments were sitting vacant for weeks and months, and homeowners searched for boarders for their spare rooms. That was past history. Each day now, when Divine read the want ads, a space would come available and then disappear within the next two days. If she had any extra room, she would have advertised for a boarder herself. They were even building barracks in an attempt to keep up with all the people coming to Seattle for the war jobs. The edges of the city were busting open like the pants of a fat man bending over to tie his shoelace.

"Oh," Minna said, suddenly remembering the note Erma had left on the umbrella. Cosmo and Divine waited for her to say more. She waved. "Never mind, I just thought of something I need to do later." This was her first chance to explore Seattle. She would ask Cosmo about the address after they'd finished at the shipyard.

"Set to go then, sugar?" Cosmo asked. "Sure enough, it rainin' now." He laughed when he saw her open the purple umbrella. "Don't s'pose I'll lose you in no crowd." His tiny black one would not cover much more than his head, certainly not his shoulders.

"A very nice lady on the train gave it to me," Minna said, defending its remarkable appearance. Until she met Erma, she would not have chosen or used one like it.

"We goin' go get us a job." He waved to Divine on the other side of the open door. She hadn't shaken that worried look she'd been wearing since breakfast.

When Cosmo got to the last step, he looked up at his sister and jumped back up on the landing. He leaned inside the door, tipping his umbrella over his back and whispered to her, "Don't you be worryin'. I find her someplace." Divine didn't bother to look relieved.

"We could put her up on the sofa till Starr get back, I s'pose," Divine said.

"Yeah, but lord know how we gets on when you daughter is here." He chuckled.

"She ain't that bad." Divine laughed now. She expected the girl to arrive soon.

"She bad enough when she spread out like she be the queen herself," Cosmo reminded her.

Divine brightened at that. "True enough."

Minna waited on the sidewalk, too near the speeding cars that didn't slow down for the water pooling near the curb. She thought about Higgins Avenue and wondered if it was raining in Missoula. At fifteen she had begun dreaming of getting out of there, sure she would not miss it. She had fantasized about a cottage in Hawaii with a white picket fence around it, fell asleep thinking about it. But Pearl Harbor ruined that idea.

She waited for Cosmo under her purple umbrella, and pictured herself peering into the bakery window. Aunt Iris was behind the counter, handing a guy a cinnamon roll after making a smart-alecky remark, and him looking puzzled because he didn't know if she was teasing. Lila rolled her eyes. Minna almost smelled the sharp smell of warm yeast.

"Now we headin' for the Todd shipyards over there on Harbor Island. I goin' show you how we gets there from here so you finds you way back if we gets separated." Cosmo had jumped down the three steps in one movement. Minna looked at him like he had just orphaned her.

He laughed. "We ain't goin' lose you, in case you worried about that. Just in case, we goin' cover the bases. That all right with you?" He squinted at her.

The stinking smell of diesel burned at her mouth and nose, and there was so much noise, she thought she would get sick. "Is it always like this?"

"Like what, sugar?" Cosmo lived in Chicago before the war. He'd moved back to Memphis to help his mama who, when she got so crippled from the rheumatism, had to be carried from the bed to the bathroom to the sofa. Then she died, and he came to Seattle looking for work. He'd stayed with Divine, who had a job working at a switchboard. He made some friends and got a good welding job, but he couldn't get out of his mind a sweetheart he had left behind in Tennessee. He quit the job, then took a bus back across the country determined to marry the woman and settle down in Memphis. But it was for nothing. That lady had taken off with a soldier. "She couldn't resist no uniform," Cosmo had told Divine.

"He's had his fair share of sorrow." Divine said while she fixed Minna her fried chicken. "He's been promised a job when he comes back." She looked pleased.

"Now you listen, sister," he cautioned. Minna burst out laughing.

"What so funny?" He crossed his eyes at her.

"I don't have a brother. That's all."

It took him a second to figure it out. "Oh, that just a expression, don't you know?"

"No, I didn't know." But she liked it. She wouldn't mind having Cosmo as a brother, she decided. He reminded her a bit of Boppy, who had been so solid she could lean up against him and not worry about falling over. That was when he was well enough to be tramping around the back alleys in Missoula looking for undiscovered treasure. Now that the war was in full gear and the government was rationing, Boppy would find less junk to sort through. "Not much luck here," he'd sigh and rue the war.

Cosmo and Minna headed for the bus stop. People stared sourly at them from under the edges of their umbrellas, at least the ones who didn't have a fire to go to. Minna caught their glares, which were aimed at Cosmo. A man wearing soft brown brogues was trying to keep dry jumping over puddles. He wore a dark-gray suit with wide pants legs, a gentleman from the looks of him, but he muttered, "Why don't you go back where you belong?" He tipped his umbrella so the rain splattered on Cosmo.

"Don't pay any attention to him." A sturdy woman with a purple umbrella not unlike Minna's cautioned, coming up from behind them before she overtook them. "Nasty bugger," she added. She had hair like Erma Shepherd's.

"Why was he so rude?" Minna was stunned.

Cosmo shrugged and then laughed out loud. "Some people don't like their colors mixed, you know. Bet he don't put no cream in his coffee, neither." He laughed again. He was too casual about the bully. The man was maybe six inches shorter than Cosmo, too.

Minna refused to join in Cosmo's banter. If he wasn't upset, she was going to be angry for him. She wanted to run back to that man and do what her aunt would. She'd get wound up, Iris would, stick her nose up in the air, push it up with her finger! Then she'd swagger with her hands on her hips as she did with snooty guests from the Florence Hotel who thought they were too important to have to stand in a line and wait their turn. Lila hated Iris doing it. She didn't say anything, but she'd raise a critical eyebrow toward her sister and shake her head, but it was barely noticeable.

"Now listen, sister," Cosmo teased again, seeing her outrage. "Best let it be. Nothin' is gained if you gets yourself all worked up."

"But how can you stand it? Let yourself be treated like that?"

He gave a doleful smile. Then his eyes twinkled again, and he

151

grinned. "Practice. I been practicin' for years. You look at me, sister. I be practiced!" He laughed out loud. "Now, you and me has serious business we need to tend to, ain't we? We ain't goin' let no fancy man slow us down none."

"Yeah. We gotta get us a job," she relented, teasing him back.

"Now you has it right, sister. Were goin' get us that trolleybus next corner. What you do is you get on after me, see, and sit up there right in the front. When I get off, you get off, too."

"Where are you going to sit?"

"I got me a special place all picked out. I need lots of room to spread out. See, this big man, I can't have no dolly like you squeezin' me out." He winked and then told her to watch for him when it was time to get off the bus. When he stood up, that's when she would know it was the right time.

"And you start memorizin' the stops before we get off. You got a head for that, too, ain't you?" He poked her again.

Thirty-One

"That's a fine how-do-you-do." Fischer sat at Lila's table rubbing his hands through his hair. She didn't tell him it was unappetizing. She and Iris had been going through Minna's closet searching for clues while Willy, Fischer, and Paulie had gone to check the ticket counters at the stations.

"No luck?" Iris was puckering her mouth. She hadn't had a cigarette since before breakfast.

"Regular people aren't back on shift till tomorrow. We gonna have to wait till then. Probably the same thing out at the fort." He whistled through his teeth. "You got any more coffee?"

"They don't keep some kind of record?" Iris asked, moving toward the back door. "Hey, listen. I'll just be a sec, okay?"

Lila had started a pot of coffee. She stared out the kitchen window. "It looks like it's going to snow." The men looked at one another and shrugged.

"You think she's got enough to stay warm?" Willy ventured.

"She has the coat I gave her for her birthday. It's wool." Lila had gone with Iris to the Merc to choose the color.

"You find a note or anything?" Fischer paced by the table.

"Nothing." Lila worried that the coat might not be long enough.

"I'm back." Iris shivered. "I think it's gonna snow, don't you?"

"The problem is it's Sunday. You don't think she planned it like that, do you?" Fischer took a sip of coffee and winced because it was too hot.

"Minnesota gets very cold in the winter," Lila said, sounding like she'd been there.

"Not colder than Montana," Paulie said, doubtfully. "I don't think no place gets colder than here."

Fischer smirked. "Hell, Paulie, you ain't lived in the Dakotas, have ya? Out there the wind blows a hundert miles a hour. You can't even tell whether you're livin' or dead by the time you get inside to get warmed up."

"It sure does get mighty chilly." Willy chuckled.

"She took the comb and brush set you gave her," Lila said to Fischer as though she was accusing him.

"Jeezus, Lila. Did you have to go and tell me that?" He slapped the back of a chair. Lila put a plate piled high with blachinda on the table.

"Facts is facts, Fischer." Iris sniffed, passing the plate to Paulie.

"What's that supposed to mean?" Fischer growled. He had his mouth full.

"What it means is that she's apparently not plannin' on comin' back anytime soon." Iris raised one eyebrow like she couldn't believe he was that stupid.

"How do you know that, Iris?" Fischer put his elbows down hard on the table. Paulie got up from his chair, leaving half a blachinda on his plate.

"Maybe we should call the police." He didn't want to confront Fischer, but he would if he got huffy with Iris.

"Paulie!" Iris and Willy and Fischer barked in unison.

"What else we gonna do? We gonna sit around and wait?" The longer they were together, the more likely Fischer and Iris were going to get into it. "We might as well go home if we ain't gonna do nothin' else today." He felt their eyes on him. "Get some rest. We been up all night."

"He's got a point there," Willy agreed again. "All we can do today is wait. Maybe she'll call and tell us where she is. Or, heck, Lila, maybe she'll show up yet." Willy gave her a hopeful look. It wasn't likely, but it made him feel easier.

"I wonder if she's had anything for breakfast." Lila toyed with her fork, pulling the meaty pieces from the center of the pastry.

"Listen, Lila. I could come in early tomorrow and help with the baking." Iris practically choked saying it. Willy smiled, and Paulie looked bug-eyed at her.

"Why would you do that? I think I can manage my own bakery, for goodness' sake." Iris would be more a nuisance than a help.

"I thought maybe you'd like to get a little rest, is all." Iris had offered but was glad Lila wouldn't take her up on it. The mood was funereal around the table. The only things missing were flower sprays and wreaths, and a coffin.

"She coulda told us what was on her mind." Iris opened her eyes wide. "If it was that bad." She hadn't asked Minna, but she'd known there was something. She thought she was doing the right thing—that's what she'd told Paulie—giving Minna the space to talk when she was ready. Sure Minna had been prickly and even snotty these past months. With her missing and them not knowing if she was safe and warm, all that seemed petty and downright thoughtless. Aside from Fischer, they had had no rest. The long hours ahead appeared grim, and they were afraid of what lay in store.

"Do you think the coat will keep her warm enough?" Lila asked Iris like she was interrogating her.

"The coat? Oh, the coat. Yeah. It's wool, Lila. Remember?"

"How cold does it get there?" Lila asked to no one, referring to Minnesota.

"I think they get a lot of snow," Willy said gently. "I don't know about the cold."

"I had a friend once who moved to Minneapolis. She was going to be a nurse. I wonder if she did." Lila had not thought about her for many years.

"Oh yeah. I forgot about her," Iris said. "Katarina."

"She wrote me letters. Not about the cold. She wrote about her curtains." It was the curtains that stayed in Lila's memory.

"Huh?" Fischer looked at her. "What are you talkin' about, Lila?"

"You know what I'm thinking?" Lila answered.

"No. What are you thinking, Lila?" She could be so dumbfounding, Fischer brooded.

"Fischer, when you go out to the fort tomorrow, find out where that boy's mother lives. She's in Georgia."

"What for?" He was not a detective. It was going to be hard enough to find out where Archie had gone.

"Oh, I get it, Lila." Iris jumped on it. "I get it!"

"Do we even know the kid's last name?" Willy asked. That stopped them cold. They looked at each other stunned.

"Damn it. I didn't think of that," Fischer cursed. "How we gonna find out where he is if we don't have no last name?"

"Well, there can't be that many of them guys goin' off to fly airplanes can there?" Willy asked.

"Guess we'll find out tomorrow." Fischer seemed stumped.

Thirty-Two

"Pardon me." A woman with thick black heels stepped on Minna's foot inside the bus. It was more an accusation than an apology, as if it was Minna's fault for having feet. The top of her foot ached. Cosmo was behind her, but he wouldn't make eye contact. He stared out the window. He sat next to a dark-skinned woman wearing a sensible hat with a preposterous orange plastic tropical flower.

"Now, they're goin' give you a test," Cosmo explained before they got to the bus stop. The rain pelted their umbrellas like hail hitting a tin roof, and he talked loudly over the rattle. "You see that number on that there bus?" he prompted her when it came into view. "You got that in you head?" She said she did.

"What kind of a test?" she asked before he climbed up the steps ahead of her. She wasn't afraid of taking a test.

"They're goin' ask you about numbers, I 'spect," he said. He disappeared between passengers toward the rear.

"Well, I'm good with numbers. I've had lots of practice." Two people ahead in the queue turned to see who she was talking to. Lila, who was a whiz at accounting, had turned the bookkeeping over to Minna when she was sixteen.

The bus passed a jewelry shop. A large clockface was mounted on a pillar out front. Minna noted the time and thought of Lila's loaves, golden and plump, cooling on racks, and for the second time could smell the yeasty bread. She nodded to her reflection in the window reminding herself she'd protected her mother from shame by leaving.

"Excuse me," the lady sitting next to her knocked Minna in the ribs with her elbow as she dived into her oversized carpet bag to retrieve an item. Her fussing spilled over. Minna knew bakery customers who didn't see where they ended and others began. This woman was built like a chunk of wood. She huffed as if she'd run to catch the bus and stirred like a dog circling and looking for the perfect spot to curl up and take a nap.

The bus reeked of wet wool. The sun didn't seem to win any

battles in Seattle. Minna was a stranger in a damp world, alone and surrounded by crowds that elbowed and stepped on her. She looked around at Cosmo but he wouldn't look her way.

The bus lurched from stop to stop. People grunted up and down the steps, snapping umbrellas open or shaking them off before they closed them. Coins clacked into the metal container as people paid their fares. She waited at each stop for Cosmo to get off. She wished she could jump off and run. He watched what was happening beyond the bus and avoided looking at the lady with the orange flower.

The aisle of the bus had become more slippery although the rain had stopped. The sun didn't seem to notice the change. The gloom was a dark umbrella covering the city. A workman in blue coveralls heading to the back of the bus fell into her shoulder when the bus jerked forward.

"Oh, I'm sorry." He frowned.

"It's okay. You didn't hurt me."

Lila would go over the accounts once the pastries were out. She would read Minna's clear hand and accurate figures, the only tracks Minna had left behind. Uncle Willy would help Lila now that they had things patched up between them. She could almost hear Aunt Iris cackle about some screwy thing at the counter. Some goofball giving her a reason for living. Maybe she'd head to the Merc after work and give Eunice a hard time. Minna grinned, imagining it, and then sighed.

"What that frown doin' on your face?" Cosmo poked her with his elbow. "Don't you worry none. You gonna be number one on that test," he said once they got off at the Harbor Island stop and walked toward a massive building that felt oddly familiar.

"How do you know?" She poked him back, wondering if this was what it was like to have a brother. Her homesickness lifted. She liked how it was between them, as if they had always known each other.

"'Cause you're a smart girl, that how I know." He poked her again. "I'm goin' talk to the man who be my boss and tell him to find you a job. You wait on that bench over there," he directed her once inside. She followed his instructions and watched him walk away. She decided she loved Cosmo and Divine, but they would disapprove if they knew her story. They thought she was married, so it was all right she was going to have a baby. Her husband was being trained to fly planes so he could be a hero. That's what she'd told them, and they believed her. She was a liar. She grabbed the edges of the bench so she wouldn't bolt.

"What did I tell you?" Cosmo announced for all the world to hear coming toward her a few minutes later. His voice ricocheted off the tinny walls. "They been waitin' for you all 'long. They don't even need to give you no test, they say. They believes me." He sounded boastful.

She wrote her new name for the first time on her employment papers: Minna Benoit, in graceful letters. The capital "B" had a special flourish, and it was surprising how easy it was to write. Cosmo elbowed her when he saw her script.

"See, I knowed you was smart. Lookit all them pretty letters." He disappeared after whispering, "You tell 'em you livin' over at Divine's place."

She sat back and sighed. She had solved one of her problems in less than two days. She hoped her good luck would continue. She still had to find a place to live since Divine had made it clear there was no room for her. Would she just toss Minna out in the street? That didn't seem likely, but Minna was apprehensive. Divine had hinted how hard it was to find even a room in the brimming city. Her worry loomed like the building cranes that bowed and curtsied through the window of the office. She squeezed the agate as she waited for her instructions.

"Minna Benoit?" A woman materialized before her. Minna hadn't noticed her arrive. She could have sworn the door had not opened.

"Yes?" Minna jumped up and pulled the back of her jacket down.

"I'm Mary Evans," the woman said decisively, eyeing her from head to toe. "I'll show you where to report for work. I think they said you're coming on Monday morning." Mary flipped through the paper work. She had on a dark-brown suit, the skirt just a hint below the knees, and matching serious shoes. The hairnet was black and was fixed so that no stray hairs had the chance to liberate themselves.

"Yes." Minna felt like she should salute.

"According to Cosmo you are bright and just what we are looking for. Is that true?" Mary peered at her hard.

"I hope so." Minna laughed, but Mary didn't find this funny.

"Well, either he's right or he's wrong. We lost our last employee who eloped over the weekend and didn't come back. You're not going to do that, are you?" Mary scowled at her like she was already guilty and considering it.

"Oh no!" Minna declared, and then felt a rush of guilt. That's what she'd done to Lila. Left her in the lurch.

"Your husband is a flier," Mary Evans said precisely. Minna couldn't tell if she was asking or stating. "So you're married." She'd put that on the form because of the baby. "You're not going to get it into your head to go where you husband is stationed, are you?"

"No! No, I'm staying in Seattle." She feared she would get fired when they found out she was having a baby. She'd have to work hard, harder than the person who came before her. Be invaluable. There wasn't a chance in the world that Archie would come looking for her. He'd made that clear on Higgins Bridge.

"You'll need to get a hairnet."

"I will?" she touched her hair and didn't mean to make a face. The cooks in the cafeteria at high school wore them, and their heads bobbed around like dull balls when they handed out trays.

"You can consider yourself lucky you're not down there in the yard with the other women."

"I've never worn one before," she said sadly. Lila hadn't made her—or Iris—wear them in the bakery. "Couldn't I just wear a tight chignon?" That had satisfied her mother.

"What's that?" Mary asked, like she was bringing some depravity to work.

"The hair is wrapped up in the back so it's out of your face. I can show you how it works." She started to pull her hair back.

"Don't bother. The other women wouldn't like it. Can't say as I would, either."

"Okay."

"No point having people grumble at the get-go about you getting special treatment."

"No. I wouldn't want that."

"That's right. You wouldn't." She sounded bitter. "You be here on time Monday morning. I won't put up with you're being late. Even the first day."

"I'll be on time," Minna promised. "You can count on me."

"We'll see." Mary Evans turned on her heel, and Minna was alone in the office.

Thirty-Three

"You be lookin' like the canary." Cosmo was waiting for her outside the building.

"What do you mean?" Minna spied him on a metal bench that pined for a shade tree. "Oh, I get it. You mean that got the worm." Mary Evans had seemed severe. She was efficient and businesslike, even the way she dressed and talked. Something seemed out of order, though. Mary had looked her over thoroughly. Minna would dress conservatively. Even after Mary Evans had left the room, it felt like her eyes were boring into her back like an icy breeze blowing under her shirttail.

The salty air prickled and made her cheeks tingle and turn rosy. It had stopped raining again. An odor of decay hung in the air from sea life surrendered and piled up on the shoreline. It was invigorating. She took some deep breaths and swallowed the moist air into her lungs. For the first time ever, she was doing something that was completely hers, not Lila's or Aunt Iris's. She was going to help win the war. She'd gotten a job, and she belonged! Just like all the other people scurrying through the city, in a hurry to beat the Japanese and Germans.

Cosmo laughed. "You goin' swallow up that whole big ocean?"

She let him tease her and tossed back her shoulders. She had a job! She wanted to yell it. She had done it on her own. Except for Cosmo, and Divine, and John Welles. Still, she had started out on her own, and she was determined she would do better work than Mary Evans could imagine. She would give the austere woman no excuse to hang over her or watch her out of the corner of her eye. The woman had given her the jitters the way she'd suddenly come into the room. Minna would be on guard. Mary might come up behind her, breathe hot breath down her neck, on the pretext of reviewing supply orders. The idea sent chills up her spine.

Her head was full of plans when Cosmo caught sight of her outside the building. She had gone over her wardrobe already, matching pieces to satisfy her new boss. On Monday she planned to wear a dark-gray skirt with a navy-blue jacket.

"And add that off-white rayon blouse to take the edge off," Iris would recommend. "It won't be enough to draw attention and upset some temperamental person (harrumph!), but you don't have to look dour just because you're going to a funeral. Ha!" She could recite Iris word for word. She didn't realize she was smiling until Cosmo teased her.

"We is goin' and get us lunch. Then, I goin' show you 'round this little city." So far, everything was working out as she had planned. She had gotten an important job and she had been in Seattle for twenty-four hours.

Mary Evans had outlined the job description, emphasizing that it was critical. It would affect the entire shipyard. It sounded important, but Mary didn't frighten her. In fact, she was ignited to be doing something important and critical to the war effort! Maybe she was riding on luck. She hoped it would continue. She still had to find a place to live and then figure out what to do about the baby. Her heart nearly stopped when that crossed her mind. It happened every time she thought about having a baby.

She went over the Waterworks Hill scenario a thousand times. It went round and round in her mind and wouldn't stop nagging at her. She'd dreamed about it, even. If only she hadn't gone. If she'd just said no! She acted it out sometimes, made up imaginary dialogues with Archie and him badgering her. In her fantasy, she always refused to go with him.

"No sense closing the gate after the horse is out," Lila would say. Unfortunately, the horse was well out of the barn.

Minna, with Cosmo's help, had become an enlisted person who would line up, follow orders, and behave like a soldier, one who was separated from the shrill ring of mortars exploding, and tanks that chewed up everything in their paths. She didn't have to worry about dying, as John Welles did. Everyone had a job to do to fight the enemy, but some of them did it in the factories and shipyards. Seattle had felt frenetic when she arrived, the air thick with the stink of fuel and overburdened with mist, and she had gotten queasy. She'd wanted to yell, "Stop!" and get right back on that train.

She had become a part of the huge patriotic machine with millions of jobs and people like herself. She would break the new job down into pieces, and take it bit by bit, as Aunt Iris had taught her, evaluating each part individually and determining how it fit in the whole scheme. All the parts, big and small, had to fit precisely. Pieces that didn't seem significant, that languished and appeared unattached, were necessary to complete the project.

"Let's go make some seams, just for the fun of it," Aunt Iris had encouraged her when Minna was just learning to sew. They raced to cut pieces from matching fabric, and Minna had hers done up in a matter of minutes.

"What are we making, anyway?" She waited impatiently, proud that she finished ahead of Iris.

"We're making history." Aunt Iris laughed when she had closed her last seam. "Okay, let's have a game of tug-a-war."

Uncle Paulie was in the backyard, his glasses resting halfway off his nose, sweat dripping off his forehead. He watched his two girls through rows of yellow and orange gladiolas while they yelped and laughed, trying to pull their seams apart. Minna argued in the end, once her piece had frayed, that no one would put that much pressure on a dress in the first place. "Maybe not, except that one time when it happens; you want to die you are so embarrassed," Iris told her. Afterward, they stretched out in the grass in the sun, barefoot and giggling, and Uncle Paulie brought them sweet, homemade lemonade and fancy macaroons.

"I've joined the war effort." Minna grinned like she was a girl on an advertisement for a propaganda poster.

"You sure has." Cosmo let out a hearty laugh. Okay, she wasn't fighting in the regular army or navy like the men, or those SPARS in the coast guard who wanted to pitch in and fight right beside the men. She had goose pimples just thinking about being a part of something big, something noble. She needed to find a place to live, and then she would be set. The one thing she couldn't fix was the baby.

"Hey, you still has that grin on your face."

"I have to buy a hairnet"—it changed to a scowl—"Mary Evans says they'll resent me if I don't. They're not making me wear a bandanna, thank goodness."

Cosmo got serious. "You don't have to wear no helmet like those women welders," he reminded her. He was right. She shouldn't complain. That would ruin a hairdo for sure.

"We can get that at the five-and-dime. It ain't goin' spoil you hair, blondie," he teased. The sky had brightened, and the sun was elbowing through the hulky clouds.

"Goin' be one fine day, sister, and I ain't gotta work till tomorrow."

"Oh. I start on Monday." When they got to the bus stop, Cosmo told her he'd get on first again and that she should watch when he stood up, their signal to get off.

"You ever eat fish an' chips?' he asked, walking away from the bus toward pier 54. "We could go see that aquarium," pointing to the building next door. "Naah. The sun's out, and we gotta see us the rest o' Seattle today."

"What are fish and chips?"

"Sister, they is a experience you missed out on so far. But I be rescuin' you from you ignorance in 'bout a minute." He gave her a knowing smile. The idea of watching her taste it was almost as good as trying it again himself for the first time.

The greasy smell made her stomach turn, and she nearly gagged when Cosmo put the deep-fried fish wrapped in oily paper into her hands. He saw her face turn green. "Uh-oh. Bad choice, sister?" It passed quickly. So far, the only inconvenience about the baby, other than changing her life completely, was getting sick. She imagined taking a club to smash store windows sometimes, she got so upset. Archie, too, and him telling her, promising her, that she couldn't get pregnant the first time. Some girls were out on Waterworks Hill every weekend. Sometimes she didn't think about the baby for an hour or so, and she was just an ordinary girl again, and things were normal. It helped with Cosmo keeping her busy with new adventures. She didn't have to make any decisions right away.

"No. I'm fine." She took her first bite, and he was right, she'd never tasted anything like it. It wasn't like the savory lake trout Fischer brought or the smoked whitefish from his winter outings up the Blackfoot River. He'd show up without warning, outside the bakery window beaming and holding his catch up on a string, wiggling them— customers or no. Lila would signal for him to come around back and send him away with a dozen blachinda. Iris said he was unloading them because he couldn't stop pulling them out of the water when he had his limit, and he didn't know what to do with all of them.

The fish were hungry during the Arctic winters, and he'd be at the edge of the river, the end of his nose dripping from the cold. He didn't even notice. When he hiked back to his car, he'd sink up to his hips in snowdrifts. Minna loved the smoked fish. She and Lila ate them for supper with saltines and canned green beans.

Lila twisted their heads off with one quick jerk, then handed one to Minna who pulled the skin back and tugged the meat away from the skeleton in chunks. Minna's first taste of fresh fish from the ocean made her decide she was going to like Seattle after all, even if there wasn't much to speak about if you wanted sunshine.

"You ever had the clam chowder?"

She made a face. "Ugh! And I don't want to either." She could not imagine anyone liking or calling it food.

"You goin' love it when you tries it," Cosmo declared.

"Am not," she countered.

"You is," he insisted.

Thirty-Four

"Keep your gol dang shirt on, Clyde," Iris barked. He was waving his coffee cup like a flag on the Fourth of July.

"I'm on empty, Iris," he shouted back.

"That'll be the day." Fischer had just walked in. "Where's Lila? She in the back?"

"It don't take a genius to figure that one out," she said. He ignored her sarcasm and went back to the kitchen. She tagged along right behind him.

"Iris!" Clyde cried when he saw she was heading to the kitchen.

"In a minute, Clyde. I got important business to attend to."

"But my cup is empty," he whined.

"Amazing, ain't it." She peeked back over the double swinging doors.

"What did you find out?" Lila didn't say hello to Fischer. She was taking a pan sizzling hot with sugar and butter out of the oven.

Fischer pushed his fedora back but didn't take it off. He huffed into his hands and rubbed them together near the warm ovens. "No luck so far."

"Where'd you go?" Iris pumped him.

"I been to the train station and the bus depot." He shrugged, looking at Lila. "I swear they only hire idiots to work there."

"Iris," Clyde bellowed on the other side of the wall.

"Would you listen to that guy? He needs a babysitter, not another cup of coffee." She stamped her foot and urged Fischer to go on. "What happened?"

"I showed the croaky lady at the train station Minna's picture. Know what she told me?"

"What?" Lila walked over next to him and automatically handed him a butterhorn. He took a bite, which left him only half.

"She don't look at her customers, she said. 'I just sell 'em tickets,' she said. Can you believe that?"

"But surely she would know if she sold a ticket to a young girl." Lila looked stunned.

"That's exactly what I told her. You know what she said?"

"What?" Iris fidgeted. Clyde was going to raise a storm if she didn't get him his third cup of coffee.

"She said, 'Do you know how many young girls are riding the trains these days?' She wouldn't even look at the picture."

"You shoulda called her boss." Iris wanted a cigarette.

"Yeah? And who would that be, anyway, Iris? And how would it help?" Fischer squinted at her.

"Was it the same at the bus station?" Lila handed him another butterhorn.

"Yep. 'People comin' and goin' all the time,' a scrawny little guy said. 'We don't have time to see who's who.'"

"What are ya gonna do now?" Iris listened near the swinging doors for Clyde to complain. She'd give him one more chance.

"Well, I'm headin' out to the fort next. Don't know what I'll get from them since I don't have Archie's last name."

"You going to take Will with you? Like you said?" Lila was uneasy about them riding together. But they were going for the same purpose, so maybe they'd be all right.

"Yeah. I'm stoppin' by the garage when I leave here. See if they'll let him go for a couple of hours. We should get some kind of action by then."

"You don't need Paulie's help?" Iris sounded like she was making a joke.

Fischer laughed. "Not unless we wanna call the police, Iris. And we ain't gonna do that, are we?"

"Well, he'd like to help, Fischer. You know he would." She smiled again. Paulie was a great help for ravioli and gladiolas.

"I don't need no fussy ole lady like him tagging along. Besides, he wouldn't be much good out there with the rest of them Eye-talians, would he? They probably put him behind the wire along with the rest of them."

"I don't like that, Fischer." Iris pouted.

"Hey, I'm just tryin' to protect the little wop." He grinned.

"It's too bad we don't have a picture of Archie," Lila interjected.

"Yeah. That'd be the ticket. Well, we'll just see what we can get from those clowns out there. Willy knows a couple of those guys. I know some, too. We just need to find the right ones. But you know how it is tryin' to get into the place. You got to be God almighty for them to

166

open the gates."

"Can't you say it's an emergency?" Iris asked.

"There's a war goin' on, Iris. In case you haven't noticed." He gobbled the last bite. "You got any more of them before I go?"

"I've got some coming out of the oven if you wait a few minutes. They'll be hot, though. I can't put icing on them till they've cooled down."

"I don't need no icing. I'll hang around till you pull 'em out."

"I paid for the coffee, Iris," Clyde yelled.

"I got to get back to his royal highness." Iris motioned toward the front. "If you hear somethin', Fischer, I'd like to know." She sounded pleading.

"Lila will call you, won't you?" he asked, looking at her tenderly. She caught her breath. She looked drained, like she had when she had the miscarriage. He suddenly felt terribly sad. He would like to take her in his arms and just hold her.

"You okay, sweetheart?" He was as surprised as she. Iris shot him a look.

"I'm all right. You think she's had a decent meal today?" Lila would will it if she could.

"The girl ain't a dumbbell, you know. You did a swell job raising her."

Lila sobbed and wiped her eyes with her oven mitt.

"That's for sure. It's the other guy who'd better look out," Iris affirmed. "Speakin' of other guys, I'm headin' back to the coffee whiner. Good luck, Fischer." She almost reached out to touch him.

"I'm gonna find her. I swear I am." He pulled his fedora back in place and stuffed a hot butterhorn in his mouth.

Thirty-Five

"Not so fast, Cosmo," Minna cried, trying to keep up with his pace. Some of the hills were as steep as Mount Sentinel, and a blister was developing on the back of her left heel. The curvy streets confounded her, and Cosmo moved like an eel around the corners. "Where are we going?"

They walked for many blocks, and the sun came out and warmed their faces. They got to the New London Meat Market, but the line ran clean out the door. "Nope," Cosmo murmured, "We is not goin' inside that particular place today."

The hush of solemn people was unnerving for Minna. Their moods seemed contrite, like children standing in line waiting to be reprimanded for naughty behavior. Their ration books were their Bibles. The recipients examined the contents, shifted a few feet forward, examined the books again front to back and back to front. The flimsy pages were falling apart, and people were calculating figures in their heads. It felt eerie, as if everyone was lined up at church to receive dispensation for some sin. They whispered their special requests, hoping a compassionate ear would listen.

"Would you look at that?" she stopped Cosmo at Pike Street Market at a sign above a store. "They are selling horsemeat! Ugh!" It read, MONTANA HORSE MEAT—NOT RATIONED.

"Eating horses from Montana," she blurted out. Cosmo, Divine, and John Welles didn't know she'd only arrived from that part of the world. Crowds pressed in like they had at the railroad station. "There are too many people here," she cried.

"You shoulda seen it before the war." Cosmo frowned. "These blocks was full of them Japanese farmers sellin' their stuff." All those business had shut down when those people shipped off to the camps.

"Well, I'm not eating any of that horsemeat, I can tell you that," she scowled.

"What say? You don't like horse?" Cosmo mocked, put his hand on his chest acting shocked. "Maybe you'll think again 'bout them clams I been tellin' you about." She made another face and then started laughing.

"Come on. We gots to find us the ration board if we goin' eat this next week."

"You get a ration card, you hear?" Divine had warned when they left her place. "Put it at the top of you list after the shipyard." Divine had squeezed a victory garden into her postage-stamp backyard, but nothing would grow in the cold, and she needed the blue coupons for canned vegetables, and an occasional pear. The produce she had canned during the summer wouldn't see them through winter. She had used up the last of her apricots adding them in the rice pudding for Cosmo and Minna.

The first rationing book, War Book One, had come out months earlier. Lila had fussed, "How in the world am I supposed to run a bakery without sugar and coffee?"

Meat and oils and butter required coupons soon after. The sugar pinch allowed each person one half pound a week. Lila adapted to keep her business alive, although concessions were made for businesses like hers. She introduced cheese buttons and made fewer blachinda. She got enough dairy from George the milkman to make her own cottage cheese.

Long before the propaganda about victory gardens, Lila used her backyard to grow produce. Willy hoed between rows of corn and cabbage and tomatoes, and weeded and thinned carrots and beets. Minna picked peas and green beans, and shucked the sweet corn, which didn't require either butter or salt. Summer evenings in the Pine Street kitchen were stifling. Lila boiled water for the prepared jars that were bathed in hot baths. She wiped the sweat off her forehead, and her bandanna hugged her head. "You see," she reminded Minna, "how important it is to wear it when you're working over the stove like this." She meant to convince her teenage daughter of its practical purpose.

"I'm not going to wear one," Minna asserted.

Cheese buttons were filled with cottage cheese, and a perpetual bag of cheesecloth hung off Lila's clothes line drying. The government encouraged the switch from meats to cheeses. Lila made half the quantity of blachinda and wished the railroad men liked pumpkin. Cottage cheese buttons were the best she could offer them.

She used her ingenuity to meet her customer demands, putting together incongruous ingredients. She was smart and savvy. While college coeds idled at her tables lingering and watching men pass by, she improvised. She had missed out on her high school diploma because her mama died, and if she had had the chance, she would have become a teacher. She mixed flour with cornmeal to make muffins filled with strawberries in season, and green beans from her garden with cheese for corn bread. During the cold months, she spiced up the corn bread with cayenne and bell peppers and onions. On Saturday mornings she fried cornmeal mush and topped it with homemade cherry syrup.

The moratorium on coffee was another matter. Without it, she would lose her regular customers. She read a story out of Canada written in the eighteen hundreds about using dried dandelion root ground and boiled as a substitute. To compensate for the strong flavor, she added enough coffee to disguise the taste. A war poster behind the counter next to the coffeepot showed a friendly soldier holding a coffee cup that read, DO WITH LESS SO THEY'LL HAVE ENOUGH.

"Just as I figured," Cosmo said, spotting the line that coiled around the corner outside the rationing board building. "War Books One and Two" was posted over the office. "Goin' have us a wait, sister." The line moved quickly, however, despite being managed by volunteers. Minna filled out a form with her name, her age, sex, weight, and height.

"They're lookin' for cheaters," Cosmo told her outside. The line had grown longer while they were there. Women carried small children on their hips, holding the hands of the older ones.

"When is this war going to end?" Minna asked. She saw herself holding a baby, looking worried and frazzled like these mothers.

"Let's us head back to Dee-vine," he said.

"Cosmo, could you tell me how to get to this address?" Minna pulled out the note from Erma Shepherd. He looked at it for a long minute moving it in and out like he needed glasses. He found places by memorizing which building sat on what corner, not by reading street signs.

"Hmm," he said, scrunching his face up. "Not sure, 'bout this, sister. Who you know there?"

"I don't know anyone there. A very nice lady on the train, the one who gave me this purple umbrella, left this note and told me to go there. Can you help me?"

"Naah." He looked disappointed. He elbowed her and laughed. "You sure you trust someone that gives you that purple umbrella? S'pose you ask someone 'round here, like that lady over there wearin' that green hat." They started laughing and couldn't stop because the hat was wider than she was, and she looked like a leprechaun. "She needs one of them four-leaf clover things."

"I don't think so." Minna poked him the rib.

Then a woman bumped into her. "I'm so sorry," the woman apologized.

"Oh," Minna said quickly. "Could you help me? I don't know how to get to this address." The woman must have been the only person in Seattle who didn't have some place to be in the next five minutes.

"Why, I knowed where that is," Cosmo brightened with the woman's directions. "That ain't so far from here. We can get that hairnet of yours on the way. You ain't forgot 'bout that, has you?"

She made a face back at him. "I wish I could." She had forgotten about it. "How do you know John Welles, Cosmo?"

"I don't know him, sister. That Dee-vine knows him."

"But how does she know him?"

"Well, you has to ask Dee-vine that's for sure, but she was walkin' home from work and falls on the sidewalk 'cause it was wet and slippery. You know, like it was this mornin'. And she can't get herself up till that boy helps her. That all I know 'bout that."

"He must like helping people," Minna mused.

"Don't know 'bout that neither, except for Dee-vine." He paused for moment and added, "And you."

"I guess they don't see each other then. Divine was surprised when he showed up at her place with me."

"Reckon not, him in the army and all." He didn't say that he could think of no reason a white boy would come to see his sister, anyway.

"She sure seemed to like him," Minna added. "She made him a big lunch to take on the train."

"Well, Dee-vine just can't find 'nough people to be feedin'." He laughed. "She'd cook for the whole United State Army, they let her." He stopped. "See, there's that five-and-dime. Right in front of us. Bet you didn't even notice that. You need to wake up, girl. Go get your hair thing, and I wait here at the corner."

Thirty-Six

"How many times I gotta tell you people the same thing?" Iris chided the customers waiting in line. "We ain't no magicians, you know." She put the back of hand to her forehead in mock despair.

"Well, dang it, Iris. I'm sick of corn bread. What's it take to fry a doughnut?" He was a friend of Clyde's. "Tell Lila I want a chocolate one next Saturday."

"Well, stop the world, Walter. I guess you ain't heard about rationing. Livin' in a cave, like a big ole grizzly." He shook his head. He liked to needle her. The others tittered.

"That fried corn bread of Lila's ain't so bad," a guy spoke behind Walter. "With that syrup on it. You can put jelly on it, too." Walter shook his head and frowned.

"And she makes that fake coffee taste like it's the real thing," the clerk from the pharmacy added.

"I miss her rhubarb dumplings." Eunice sighed.

"Well, look what the cat drug in," Iris huffed. Eunice frowned, but it was anybody's guess where she was actually looking. "They let you out of that prison over there?" She nodded in the direction of the Mercantile.

"Hello, Iris"—Eunice pretended she didn't hear the insult—"I hope you're having a good day."

Then Fischer walked in. He nodded to Iris and tapped the counter as he went by. A knowing look passed between them. "See ya in the back when ya get a break." His thoughtful manner threw her. He had his arm over Lila's shoulder when she went into the back. Lila was wiping her eyes.

"So, what's the latest?" She read their looks and dreaded hearing what he had to report. "How bad is it?"

"No luck," Fischer said regretfully. Willy came through the back door.

"Dang cold out there this mornin'." He took his cap off and shook it out. Then he saw Fischer's arm around Lila.

"What's up?" He made his voice stay calm.

"You mean you haven't found out where she's gone, right?" Iris feared worse but willed herself not to ask.

"Yeah. You know that colonel or whatever he is," he asked Willy. "I saw him finally." It had taken a whole week to get through to him. He and Willy had gone to the fort every day, and they'd lost too much time. They didn't say it to each other, but they feared Minna's trail would be cold by now.

"He said he was doin' me a big favor. Maybe he was, but I'll do the same when his car breaks down. Make him wait a week," Fischer growled.

"What'd he mean by that?" Iris asked.

"Said he's 'not at liberty,' that's what he said. Not at liberty to divulge the whereabouts of soldiers."

"But you told him we already knew where Archie was headed, didn't you?" Iris demanded.

"Yep. He said if we knew where he was headed how come we didn't know his last name."

"Whew!" Willy whistled. "He's got us there, ain't he?" He wished Fischer would remove his arm from Lila. He spoke toward Iris so he didn't have to look at them.

"Did you tell him it had to do with our daughter who is missing?" Lila said in a low voice. She knew how devoted men were to their cars and their mechanics and trusted that would loosen the man's tongue.

"Yeah. He said, 'Do you know how many parents come out here trying to find out what happened to their kid?' I told him I didn't have no idea about that but none of them was my daughter."

"What'd he say to that?" Willy still wouldn't look toward Lila. She hadn't even attempted to move away from Fischer.

"He said he'd do what he could. Told me to come back next Monday."

"Monday!" Iris wailed. "Did he at least tell you what Archie's last name is?"

"Nope. We ain't gonna get to talk to Archie, either. Not ever. The best we're gonna get is his commanding officer. If we're lucky."

"If we knew his last name we could get ahold of his mother, at least," Iris lamented.

"Where is everybody?" Clyde yelled. He peeked over the swinging doors.

"Clyde, I swear. Were you born in a barn? We're havin' a private

173

conversation here."

"Well, geez, Iris. A fellow can't even get his coffee around here no more. You been havin' a lot of them conversations. You got customers to take care of. What you say to that, Lila?"

"She'll be out shortly," Lila said evenly. She spoke too softly for him to hear.

"What'd you say?"

Iris moaned. "Never mind, Clyde. God bless us and save us. Didn't your mama teach you no manners at all? You don't go bustin' into private talks like that."

"I don't get it."

"Ain't that a surprise. It don't matter. Go out to your table. I'll bring your coffee in less than three minutes." She stamped her foot. "And because I love you, Clyde, I'm gonna give you free milk for your coffee."

"Wise guy," he grunted, walking away from the doors.

"Honestly, Lila. Do we have to put up with these nincompoops?"

Lila didn't answer. Fischer still had his arm around her.

"Hey, Willy. What say I give you a couple of cheese buttons? You look like you need somethin' with your coffee this morning." She hated seeing Fischer and Lila cozy, too, but she couldn't stand to see Willy's downturned face.

"We done here, then?" Willy turned to Fischer. "Till Monday?"

"Looks like it," Fischer said.

"Listen. I'll go out to the fort with you Monday. We can pester some of them other characters. Between us, we oughta be able to get somethin' more out of 'em." He glanced at Lila, hoped she understood how much he wanted to help her. "Try the ones we ain't been able to get to before. Who knows? Maybe one of 'em will crack."

"Yeah. Okay. Not much we can do now but wait." Willy regretted he didn't have an excuse to hang around the kitchen. He wished Fischer would leave. He could console Lila, although she might not let him do so.

"Those cheese buttons ready?" Iris barked over the swinging doors.

"Five minutes," Lila said, walking to the ovens.

"I'll talk to you later," Willy said, intending it for Lila. Iris had a mug of coffee waiting for him on the counter.

"I could come over tonight," Willy heard Fischer say. "Who knows? Maybe she'll walk back in the door with her suitcase." Lila banged the oven door, and Willy couldn't understand what she said when she answered.

"It'll pass," Iris whispered when she refilled Willy's cup. She wished he'd look up at her. She'd wink at him, but he stared into the dark liquid as though he was going to sink into it and drown.

"How do you know?" he said under his breath. "I ain't seen this before."

"Her daughter hasn't gone missin' before," Iris reminded him. "They got somethin' in common just now, but that don't change who they are in real life."

"Do you think she'll go back to him?" He hunched over the counter like his back was aching.

"Not a chance. She's not thinkin' about how it was between 'em before. She's so worried about Minna, she'll eat crumbs right now. Don't you worry, Mr. Handsome. You're still the one for her," she promised.

"You some kind of expert, Iris?" He hoped what she said was certain.

"Honey, I'm the expert of the world. Know what I think?"

"What?"

"I think our little Minna decided to spread her wings. That's what I think. And I think she's gonna be just fine. She's gonna be gone for a while, I figure, but she's not gonna marry that dope flier, either."

"How can you be so sure?"

"I just know. That's all. Feel it in my bones."

"You not worried about her, then?"

"Of course I'm worried. But she's got a head on her shoulders. She's gonna have troubles. No doubt about that. Who doesn't? But she's gonna come out all right. She'll walk in this door someday, dollars to doughnuts, and she's gonna have some handsome fellow with her. Good lookin' like you," she teased, hoping for a smile, "and we're gonna drop our jaws. You wait and see, Willy. You hear?"

"I hear." He was mentally taking Fischer's arm from Lila's shoulders.

"You havin' another one of them private conversations?" Clyde yelled across the room, "I'd like to have my second cup of coffee if it ain't no skin off your nose, Iris."

She smirked. "Well, Clyde, I'd be happy to refill your cup. I just been waitin' for you to ask. What took you so long?"

Thirty-Seven

"Cosmo?" Minna called. He wasn't at the corner, and two men were loitering where she'd left him. One had a fresh bruise blossoming on his right cheek. The other was wiping blood from his mouth with his sleeve. They made fists and snickered when she walked by.

"Hey, honey."

She stared straight ahead. She'd sifted through the stack of hairnets, most of which she would dread wearing. "Cosmo?" she called after she'd turned the corner. A few people stared. The two men cackled behind her. She had refrained from poking through the lipsticks in the five-and-dime, heading straight toward the hair products, and then debated between the spider web choices of steel gray and black. When she discovered one lacy black net that was actually a snood, at the bottom of the pile, she was consoled. It had been stashed probably by a person who wanted a way around regulations. She decided she'd sport a chignon despite Mary's displeasure. She would wrap it in the snood, and it would look quite smart. Even Mary Evans couldn't object.

She glanced at the magazines at the cash register but hurried on so Cosmo wouldn't have to wait.

She spied a sign on the side street, *BUY*SELL*TRADE*, deciding that was where Cosmo would have gone to wait for her. She peered through the window but could see nothing beyond the musical instruments, silver chafing dishes, and watches with leather wristbands.

"Cosmo?" she called. A bell on the knob tinkled, but the door squawked with misery, and the chime was superfluous. The stored smelled musty and felt suffocating, crammed full of odds and ends, and she tucked in her elbows to avoid knocking anything off. Sunlight would give the place an unrecoverable shock. "Cosmo?" she repeated to the meat grinders and chipped plates, gemstone necklaces, gold rings, and guitars. A pregnant woman about the same age as Minna was the only person in the store. Minna wondered if she was buying or selling, or pawning her wedding ring. She didn't wait to find out.

It was shift change for the factories, and back outside, the sidewalks were packed. The day shift flooded toward home, the swing shift crossed their paths, hustling to be on time, and it was impossible to search for Cosmo in the crush. The two thugs were gone. Minna headed back into the five-and-dime. She went up and down the aisles, past shampoos and soaps, kitchen hardware, and men's T-shirts, peering around displays and wishing Cosmo to be there. Maybe he'd come to find her. She ached to run from one end of the store to the other, yelling, "COSMO!" to manufacture him from an aisle.

She was overcome and feeling utterly alone for the second time. On the bus the woman had stamped on her foot, and the lady next to her had banged against her, either not recognizing what she did or not caring enough to apologize. Minna looked at faces expecting a smile, or nod. She'd been raised to make eye contact, to say hello, to show respect. She felt like she was an obstacle in the way of indifferent strangers, and longed for her familiar upbringing. There was a public phone twenty feet from her. If only she could call long distance and hear Lila say hello on the other end. She felt sick to her stomach. It wasn't nausea from the baby, but worse. It was a gnawing inside her, like a meat grinder in the pit of her stomach. She felt alien and abandoned in the dusky evening, and she was frightened.

Her tongue moved around like it was cotton. She had drunk nothing since the fish and chips, and her throat was scratchy. Her hands sweated inside her gloves, and her heart pounded. Outside the store every loud noise jangled her. She wanted to be in her own bed with the heavy quilt pulled over her head. She got bumped and poked. A rib from an umbrella barely missed stabbing her in the eye. That made her angry, and she pushed right back. She was appalled at how rude people could be until she realized she stood in the middle of the traffic flow. People negotiated around her.

"Look out," a man snapped.

"Look out yourself," she cried, but he had melted into the crowd.

"Watch where you're goin'," someone in overalls growled when she took a step backward. She bit her lip but didn't say, "Shut up."

She was in the center of the fast-paced crush, and aimed for the wall of a red-brick building ten feet away. That distance seemed like a mile before she could weave through a sea of elbows and feet.

"Watch out," a boy her age said, and she still had a yard to go. She couldn't keep the tears back. She kept her eyes on the wall because the swirling commotion made her dizzy. The rain was coming down harder.

With her back firmly against the wall she grew calmer, and motionless as a marble sculpture. The crowd began to thin out, and the rain slowed down. If she could only manufacture Cosmo out of the dwindling crowd, but more than an hour had passed since he had inexplicably disappeared, like a ghost. She didn't move, held out the possibility of finding him, stood against the wall, and waited. It was foolish. She had trusted Cosmo, spent the day teasing, him, acting like she had discovered a long lost brother, one who abandoned her to Seattle. She was distressed, and her hurt grew until anger took charge; she didn't consider Cosmo might be in trouble.

The dependable agate rested at the hollow of her neck. Absently, she fingered its edges, the constant and familiar appendage, enclosing it in her gloved hand, comforting it as she would be comforted. Her breathing slowed down. Her ears had felt on fire, like she'd had them too close to a campfire. She rested a bit and felt Cosmo was directing her, telling to move on.

"You're a real lout," Minna would accuse Cosmo when she got back to Divine's. She pictured him at the kitchen table scraping his soup bowl clean with a piece of bread. "What kind of lout leaves a person all alone and lost in downtown Seattle?" That would pierce him and go out the other side.

He wasn't a lout, but it felt better to think that while she stood alone on the strange city's street. He had shown her how to get around, as though he was prescient and knew she would require it. He had guided her, making it lighthearted and gay. While he teased, she was deciding he was her brother. His jokes, near landmarks, made them memorable. They tied her back to the locations they had visited. Pike Street Market was not far from where she stood, she could find her way there or to the horsemeat market without a bit of trouble. She could get to the ration board office, to the pier where he had introduced her to fish and chips, where he'd egged her on about clam chowder. He'd badgered her about learning which buses would take her where, and back to Divine's. She laughed about the oversized green hat and then thought of the address Erma Shepherd had given her.

It was a few blocks away, closer than Divine's, and she quickly made up her mind to go there. She brightened with that and clapped her hands, proud of her initiative. Afterward, she would take the bus to Divine's. It made sense to go to the address now; it was nearby, and she wouldn't have much free time after she started work on Monday. She'd be looking for a place to live. She felt a burst of confidence, although she resented Cosmo playing this trick on her.

She was going to let him have it when she got back to Divine's. He deserved a scolding. If he wasn't eating in the kitchen, he would be lounging with his long legs folded around Divine's sofa resting his curly dark mop on her gingham pillow. She wouldn't tell him how scared she'd been, but she hoped he wouldn't pretend it had been a joke and tease her. If he acted sorry as she expected, enough so that he would get up from the sofa, she would thank him for all his help. She'd put out her hand, and they would shake on it, and she would tell him he'd better never leave her again because she had gotten worried about *him*. That's what someone would say to a real brother, if she ever had one. It was funny to think of Cosmo as a brother or as a teacher, but he was.

Probably it was a waste of time, traipsing after an address, but Erma Shepherd hadn't steered her wrong up till now. She opened her umbrella, but the fickle rain stopped. One minute it was dribbling, the next it wasn't but acting like it wished it could.

Happily, she left the wall behind. The damp weather intensified odors, and on the busier streets, fried food mingled with gasoline fumes. Her stomach was unsettled again, and on a side street, she covered her nose from a sharp whiff of urine. She took a perfumed hanky from her coat pocket and then noticed a man on the opposite side of the street, watching her. She couldn't really make him out, but he reminded her of one of the two hoods on the corner outside the five-and-dime. He turned abruptly and entered a small café.

She wouldn't let her imagination frighten her. She was nervous, she told herself, because she hadn't been able to find Cosmo. It was his fault for putting her on edge, disappearing as he had.

She kept a good pace, although the blister was talking to her. She squinted at street numbers on doorways and occupied herself between them with ideas for how to wear the hairnet. She'd practice when she got back to Divine's that evening. She dismissed the lukewarm notion of waiting until the next morning, figuring it would take several tries to get it just the way she imagined. She needed to polish her shoes, too, from the wet weather. Mary Evans would scrutinize her skirt and jacket. She would ask to borrow Divine's iron.

The guts of Seattle, its lights, its clamor, and smells began to fade at the top of a block that sloped downhill. She pushed her heels into the sidewalk to slow down her pace, clacking with each step. By the middle of the block, the banging made her cringe for it was the only sound she heard. The city noises had been reassuring, and with them mostly silent, the night felt eerie.

By the next block she was certain something wasn't right. The street leveled off at the intersection, and she waited for a single car to drive past before stepping off the curb. Judging from the street numbers she was near her destination, but the back of her neck prickled. The street lamps were dark, but she felt like an insect under a microscope.

She picked up the pace in spite of her blister. The dusky sky had dissolved into gunmetal gray. Images that in daylight were solid and defined were melting together and becoming ambiguous. She regretted her earlier feeling of confidence, being pleased that she'd been resourceful. The positive attitude slipped away, but she tried not to conjure shadows in doorways of shuttered businesses she passed. She didn't want to imagine things that weren't there. She told herself it was because she was tired and hungry and because she was upset with Cosmo. She blamed him for making her wait around. She wished Uncle Willy was walking with her. She'd be safe with him, and he'd never go off and leave her alone.

Before she reached the next corner, any reassurances evaporated. A thickness, sticky and ominous, pressed itself against her. She wanted to run, but didn't know where to go. She clutched her agate, and weighed going back to Divine's instead of going forward with this fanciful fishing expedition. She felt a pair of eyes boring into her shoulder blades. She shrugged to get them off and refused to turn around for fear of seeing someone behind her. She thought of the man who had ducked into the café.

She needed to push the panic back. She turned a corner and continued toward the address Erma had given her. If someone was following her, it would be too risky to try to go to Divine's. According to the directions the woman had given them, she was almost there. There were fewer storefronts, some abandoned, and others down on their luck, but she could see the outline of houses in the next block. It wouldn't be long. She was nearly there.

She reviewed the last few days; she made herself think about the lecherous train conductor and then Erma Shepherd and the purple umbrella. John Welles had propped her up when she got sick and peeled a hard-boiled egg for her. Divine and Cosmo, and oh yes, strange Mary Evans and the darn hairnet. And what about the horsemeat! She wanted to make herself laugh but couldn't. She was too scared.

One more block to go, judging by the street numbers. Her family didn't know where she was, or that she'd gotten a job, but they didn't have to bear the shame or disappointment either. She walked faster, ignored the blister completely. She had held her arms snug at her sides, but swung them to increase her stride. Just ahead of her, in the next block, she could make out a row of houses. The night sky was impenetrable without stars.

She drew even with a deserted storefront, the second to last building on the block, before the footsteps appeared at her heels. Someone grabbed her arm. Then a hand went over her mouth, and she was pulled into the doorway. She could see ugly orange paint peeling from the ceiling and despised its shabbiness.

She couldn't breathe, and the stench of foul breath felt violent in her guts. She managed to get her teeth around a piece of fleshy palm and bit down until her jaw popped. The man jerked his hand back and yelped, "You fuckin' bitch," slapping her hard across the face. She screamed and screamed before he could cover her mouth again.

"Shut up, you fuckin' whore," a second man hissed. She'd thought there was only one. This could be the one from the café, the one drilling his eyes into her shoulder blades before. The first one pinned her arms with such force she almost passed out. When she started panting he covered her mouth again.

The second man pushed her legs apart and snarled in her face, "This is what we do to nigger-lovin' whores." She fought for breath, but the first man had her nose covered, too. She twisted madly trying to get air and at the same time to push away the second man. She kicked wildly, and he couldn't hold onto her legs. The heel from her shoe connected with his face, and she felt the impact that knocked him back against the peeling wall next to the doorframe. Although the first man held her head back, she saw the blood spurting from the other man.

"Oh God," he moaned, holding his broken nose. She could make out his face. He had been at the five-and-dime, leering at her while she looked for Cosmo.

The other one was pinning her arms and covering her face. The first one, enraged and seeing his blood, rushed at her. He stuck his face into hers, an inch from her eyes, and grinned fiendishly. Then he punched her hard in the stomach before he ripped off her panties. She vomited from the excruciating pain into the hand held over her mouth.

"Jeezus, you bitch," the one from behind snarled, wiping his hand over the front of her blouse. "She puked all over me, Louie," he grunted. Nothing mattered now. Everything went black.

Thirty-Eight

"What're you doin' in here with the lights off?" Iris was in the sewing room, and it was five o'clock in the morning. The tip of her cigarette glowed, and the place reeked of smoke. She didn't respond, which didn't deter Paulie. "How long you been sittin' down here, bella?" Sometimes, when he called her by his pet name, she softened. He hated waking up without her beside him. Whenever he got restless during the night, he'd reach across to feel her warm body. Only then could he go back to sleep.

"Iris?" She didn't say anything.

"You okay, bella?" There was a start in his voice.

"Something's wrong," she whispered.

"What?" She spoke so softly he couldn't make out her words. She wouldn't say it again, so he waited. "Should I turn on the light?" he asked after a long pause.

"No. I wanna be in the dark." It wouldn't be daylight for a few hours.

"You feelin' sick?" He dreaded those times her body took over and laid her low. Her energy sagged like a spoiled pumpkin, which happened when something upset her badly. She hated it, saw it as a failure, a weakness that she couldn't cajole or boss around. She tried to, though, throwing acidic accusations at the deficiency. It never worked. Her body won the battle every time.

"Maybe if you stopped smoking?" Paulie gently suggested early in their relationship. It was physically painful for him to find her curled up on the sofa under an enormous blanket. When that happened it could go on for weeks. Then, one morning she'd be back up, smoking and getting dressed for work, like it never happened.

"You goin' to work today?" he asked timidly. He wouldn't be pacified either way. If she was ill, he didn't want her to go. If she did go, he'd just worry about her the entire day.

"Of course I'm goin' to work," she snapped as if he was being ludicrous.

"I'll make an omelet, then." A good meal was the answer to life's dilemmas. Once he got Iris to the table, and she sampled his eggs with three kinds of cheeses, she'd be all right.

"I'm not hungry. I don't want nothin' to eat," she complained.

"A nice cup of strong, hot coffee, then." He wasn't about to give in. "You can't go to work like this." He turned to go the kitchen.

"Somethin's wrong, Paulie." She said it loud enough for him to hear. He turned around and moved closer to her. She was in the rocker he'd bought for the children they didn't have. He wanted in the worst way to turn the light on, to see how ill she looked.

"Can I turn on the light?" he pleaded.

"In a minute. Give me a minute." She sounded like she'd run out of air.

"Where you feelin' sick?"

"I'm not sick."

"Oh." That gave him a second's relief. "What's wrong, then?" Maybe her sewing machine was on the fritz. His shoulders relaxed. He could take care of that. If it couldn't be fixed he'd buy her a new one immediately. It would cost some money, but what was money for if not to be used?

"I dunno," she eked out. That confounded him. Iris always knew what was wrong when something was wrong. She might not be able to make it right, especially if it had to do with her health, but it wasn't like her to not jump in and have a solution. Her ideas didn't always work, but he had to give her credit for getting the ball rolling. It wasn't like her to stay mired in a boggy problem.

"C'mon, Iris. Just tell me what it is."

"It's Minna," she finally admitted.

"Huh? Minna? You heard from her? Where is she?" He couldn't figure it out, her sitting in the dark and smoking, instead of announcing to the world that she'd heard from Minna. You'd think she'd have the phone line humming. She'd still be smoking, though.

"That's just it," she said as if she'd answered his questions.

"What's it?" He squinted at her. He was really confused, as if he'd come in on the tail end of her explanation.

"I don't know where she is." Her voice cracked.

"Then…" He waited. "Then how do ya know somethin's wrong?" He was trying hard as he could to make sense of what she said, but she hadn't given much to go on. She might lose her temper if he asked too many questions, if she felt he pushed her too hard. He waited and hoped she'd say something concrete.

"Did she call you?" He couldn't wait. He needed an answer.

"Not in so many words," Iris mouthed. She was infuriating.

Paulie slapped his hand to his forehead. "Iris, please, please. Tell me what's goin' on." He waited for her to explode, but when she didn't, he added, "I don't wanna upset you more, but would you give me some more to go on?"

"Call Willy," she said finally. He cocked his eye at her.

"Huh? Why Willy?"

"Just call him," she commanded. She was sounding stronger now that she'd made up her mind.

"You gonna come to the kitchen to talk to him?" He wished he could read her face. The glow from the embers of the cigarette didn't make adequate light.

"Unless you know where there's another phone, I guess so." She was getting her sarcasm back.

"Okay. He's on the phone," Paulie hollered a minute later.

"Spare me, dear lord," she grunted at the intense light from the kitchen fixture. She shielded her eyes with the hand that held the cigarette, using the other to hold the phone.

"Must be somethin' big. You outta bed so early," Willy teased. He was too cheerful. He inhaled deeply. "So what's up?"

"It's Minna." Her voice was raspy. Too many cigarettes, Willy surmised.

"You heard from her?" Dang girl. Why wouldn't she call Lila instead? He didn't want to be the bearer of that news.

"No," Iris said but seemed unsure.

"No?" Paulie had been baffled, and now it was Willy's turn. "What do ya mean, no?"

"I mean…" Iris took a drag on another cigarette. There was another one lit and hanging off the edge of the ashtray on the counter by the phone. "I woke up and knew she was in trouble."

"What kinda trouble?" He sounded aggravated.

"You don't need to get on your high horse," Iris barked. "I don't know what kind of trouble."

"Iris. Did you hear from her or not?"

"I told you I didn't."

"Then how the hell do you know she's in trouble?"

"Because," Iris started to shout, "I woke up. Didn't I just tell you that? I was sleepin' like a log, and boom. Just like that. I'm sittin' up, and I know as sure as anything, Minna's in trouble. I could practically make her out in the dark."

"Oh boy," Willy whispered. Paulie shook his head. He never doubted Iris, but this was a stretch.

"Remember when I told you she was gonna have some trouble?" Willy remembered, but he'd had his mind on Lila at the time. Her letting Fischer keep his arm on her and not moving away from him like he hoped she would.

"Any idea where she is?" Willy hated to ask.

"I'm no fortune-teller, Willy."

"What do ya want me to do?" He sure didn't want to go to Lila with this.

"Nothin'!"

"Huh?" Why would she call him at this early hour if she didn't want him to do something.

"I am tellin' you for the record," Iris said. Her voice was high-pitched. "You wait and see."

"You think she's gonna be all right?" he asked almost timidly.

"I think so, but I'll let you know. Go back to sleep, Willy. We'll keep this to ourselves. No sense upsettin' the apple cart."

He was relieved. "I was gettin' ready for work, anyhow. I'll keep it under my hat."

"You do that. Some day you gonna say, 'Iris was right.'"

"Okay, Iris. Guess we'll see 'bout that."

"Yeah. Guess we will."

Paulie started melting better in the pan. "Eggs'll be ready in ten minutes." He smiled at her and handed her a mug of coffee.

Thirty-Nine

"C'mon, sister," Cosmo sobbed. His tears pooled with blood collecting from a gash below his left eye. "You got to help me, now. You hear? Wake up!" He propped her up on her feet. His arm supported her under her arms, but her legs were rubber. She moaned steadily but was indifferent to his pleading. He lifted her up and dragged her across the two unconscious bodies sprawled in the doorway. One of them groaned.

"Minna. Wake up," he urged. "We got to go now." He tapped her gently on the cheek with his palm and then wiped the vomit clinging to her face with the cuff of his shirt. "Minna, we goin' walk now. Okay? Come on. Walk with me, baby. Take a step. Take jus' one step."

She heard him, but just like he was talking to her from under a pile of mattresses. "Cosmo?" she asked flatly.

"Yeah. It Cosmo, sister," he cried. "Yeah, it Cosmo." The streetlight and storefront lamps were turned off, and the sky was murky. If there were shadows, they were indistinguishable.

He heard footsteps behind them by the next storefront and whipped his head around. He half hauled Minna, pleading for her to engage her legs.

"Lila. I want Lila." She mumbled.

"What are you sayin'? Who's Lila? Don't talk just now, sister. Okay?"

At the far edge of the skyline, clouds tumbled like giant balls of cotton saturated in ink. Minna's legs would not move on their own, and Cosmo turned to face the attackers once more in an attempt to fend them off. He waited silently. One hand was frozen into a fist, the other hand around Minna. He would ease her down to the sidewalk and quickly move away from her the instant the perpetrators emerged from the dark. He prayed that Minna would not moan and uncover their location so he could surprise them, get the first swing in before they could double-team him. The footsteps faded off to the right somewhere into the wet evening. He waited for more footsteps, but there were none, and they moved on.

"Jus' lean on me, sister." He tried to hurry her along. She started to become alert, and the feeling was coming back into her legs, but she was unsteady, and her chin banged against his shoulder with each step. Cosmo winced and ignored the sharp pain in his gut but could not avoid dragging his left leg. Until he was able to get Minna safe, he would try to disregard it. But it was all he could think about as it slowed them down. He kept jerking his head over his shoulder. Minna shivered in the chilly dampness. It was like a cold cloth pressed against her face, but it was enough to revive her. He put his jacket, which was mostly in tatters, around her shoulders.

"Where are we? I want Lila." Her voice sounded hollow.

"We goin' that address you asked 'bout today. You 'member the green-hat lady?" He forced a laugh. Her eyes weren't focusing, and she missed the fact that two of his front teeth were missing. "We goin' see if they helps us."

"Cosmo?" she whispered.

"Yeah little sister?" She lifted her head slightly off his shoulder, and although it was dark, she saw the slash under his eye. He slurred his words like the drunks in Missoula who got confused and wandered into the bakery insisting they be served a shot of whiskey.

"This isn't a saloon." Lila didn't say she was irked. It was the way she held her shoulders and her mouth.

Minna needed to tell Cosmo something, but she couldn't figure out what that was. "I'm all right." He saw her terror. "You jus' keep helpin' me now, you hear?" He hoped her memory remained cloudy. She needed a doctor. He wished Divine was there. It was a race with time. Minna was going to get hit hard when she remembered sooner or later. "That's a girl," Cosmo said each time she took two steps on her own. "One foot front of t' other." He spurred her forward.

"We is almost there." She'd take a step, then she'd stop. "Almost there," he said each time she took a step.

"Look!" he exclaimed. "That's the number you asked 'bout, ain't it? On you piece of paper?" He pointed toward a house where the numbers jumped out insisting they take notice. She turned to look and then nodded.

"You go get my mother."

"Huh? Where's you mama?"

She was walking because Cosmo kept urging her, but he was becoming more annoying with each step. He added length to each of her strides propelling her forward, and she wanted him to stop it and let her go to sleep. Why did he keep pushing her around? Why wouldn't he let go of her? She wanted to tell him, "Put me down. I want to go to bed."

But he kept talking and talking. He just wouldn't stop spouting. She wished she could cover her ears because of the stupid comments, one of them about a green hat, and him looking at her and laughing like he was making fun of her. He was making her mad, and he was holding her around her ribs, and it hurt! She tried to ask him why they were wandering around in the dark and why he wouldn't let go of her. She got so exasperated she shouted at him, "Won't you please just shut up." Or she thought she did.

"I want Lila." He kept urging her to walk.

The fog swallowed the distinguishing features of all the houses. Cosmo had gotten them to the address, and he wouldn't let Minna relax until he had her safely inside, although she was sure she had told him to put her down. He did not stop talking even after she told him to do so. Cosmo examined the house's exterior, which seemed peculiar in some way, but it was probably the night moisture making it mysterious. He brushed aside his misgivings because of Minna. The numbness was easing in her legs, and she felt the tingles, like pinpricks, when the blood flooded into them.

The sudden pain ripped through her whole body, and she screamed loud enough to shatter the thick air. It sent a chill up Cosmo's spine. Her groin felt like it was on fire.

She moaned. Then she shrieked, "Oh, make it stop. *Please* make it stop!"

"You hang on, sister," Cosmo commanded. He was gruff, rattled by her scream, and shaken up. "Hang on, Minna," he urged. He still had his arm under her arms, and he felt her going limp.

"Minna. You stay with me, you hear?" he demanded. "Don't you go nowhere."

She moaned. "It hurts too much. Where's Auntie? I want my aunt."

"We goin' get you inside and get us some help." He jerked his head around because he heard the noise from metal clanging in the next street over. He waited and held his breath, but there was only the one bang, and then it was quiet. He breathed again.

Cosmo wouldn't stop his inane yakking. She hated him. She needed him to listen to her! To quit dragging her and spouting and leave her alone. She couldn't think, and she had to concentrate on the pain that was coming in waves.

"We goin' up those steps right there," he said with icy calm and aimed her toward the clapboard house with the wide porch.

"No!" she screamed but had no will to prevent him from

moving her.

Her legs went numb again, and she fell back into his arm. Her head bobbed against him as he half hauled her up the first of the five concrete steps. The living room window opened onto a wide porch but was opaque from the blackout curtains. Stray cracks of light escaped at its edges. Everyone was diligent about not leaving windows unconcealed that could be targets for enemy Japanese fighter planes.

Except for the threads of light peeking out, the house appeared to be empty. Cosmo prayed that was not so but he didn't hear any noise coming from inside. It was too quiet. In the sparse light, he could make out the odd color of the door. It was the same color as the flowers on Divine's twin lilac bushes beside her front door, hugging the sidewalk. Pedestrians who came and went on Divine's street went out of their way to avoid bumping into the blossoms. People hurrying to work in late spring, or in the evenings, stopped to smell them. They inhaled the spicy sweet scent before moving on.

Cosmo was nearly frantic that no one would come to the door. It had been a desperate decision, a blind guess about what they would find. The night was slipping away, and he had more than enough worries. He would lose his job if he wasn't at the shipyards in the morning, even though he was injured.

If he could, he would have gotten Minna back to Divine's, and she would have patched up the worst. She'd done it before and would know what to do for Minna. They'd grown up in Memphis. Nobody who was colored and lived there came away without scars, either of their own or of someone dear to them.

But to get to Divine, they'd have to ride the bus. He cringed at the idea of carrying Minna up the stairs, his arm around her, and her being in the state she was. His face looked like raw meat, and he was dragging his foot, and they hadn't even come to the part about him being a colored man holding a white girl. He would be lucky if they locked him in a jail cell and slammed him around. The other alternative was more likely, and he'd faced that once already on this day. Lord knows where Minna would end up. Besides, he had already called in all his luck to get them this far.

On the second of the last two steps, Minna erupted. It came with a vengeance. She screamed at him, ranting about
a green hat that wanted to go to sleep, her arms flailing at him.

"What you sayin', little sister?" he said very softly to get her to stop yelling and struggling.

"Let go of me," she screamed.

"Oh, Lordy," he whispered. "Minna, what you sayin', girl?" He willed her to get quiet. "Hush up, sister. We gettin' help."

He dreaded the neighbors climbing out of their beds. They'd come charging at him on the stoop. He was at the end of it. There was only so much one person could do, and he had given all he could. That's when she smacked him square in the face, right on the bloody gash. He cringed, then moaned.

"Cosmo!" she cried. The smack and his groaning awakened her. The pain hurt like hell, and he buried his face in his elbow.

She sobbed, "I'm sorry. Oh, I'm sorry." He was shaking, maybe bawling, and she put her hand on his elbow, patting him and crying. She couldn't stop sobbing. "I'm so sorry," she said again and again.

The pain eased, and he took her hand. "It's okay, sister." But he turned his head so she wouldn't see him wincing. She kept patting his face. She tried to pat the back of his head and his neck, although he still had hold of her under the arms.

"What the hell is goin' on out there," someone yelled from a nearby house. Cosmo watched for a light to go on, but nothing happened.

The muscles in Minna's back went rigid. Cosmo felt her body harden like cement had been poured into it. She had slapped him and heard him react in pain. She saw his blood, and it woke her up.

She panted like a black dog on a simmering day. She was going to start wailing, he just knew it. He'd seen it happen in Memphis after a lynching. The boy's mother found her son hanging from a tree limb, his tongue swollen and extended, his bare feet blacker than coal. The mother fell onto the red dirt lane, right below her dead boy's toes, and screamed and wailed and wouldn't be comforted. She kicked at her friends when they tried to come near to console her and get her back on her feet. They were not able to move her until she succumbed, by which time the rivulets of tears on her face were crusted in dirt, and her fingernails were filthy and torn down to the nubs.

Cosmo looked down the street once more, then lifted Minna up the last two steps, dragging his leg behind. She was rigid as an overinflated tire, but she didn't wail. She hummed. She was like a bee that couldn't stop to take a breath. "Goin' be okay, sister," he murmured.

On the porch, he leaned her up against the wall and found the door knocker. White folks just never stopped amazing him with their quirky ideas. This door knocker was more peculiar than most—a bronze, upside-down triangle. He felt around to see how it worked and then banged it three times in double time. It sang out with a most pleasant resonance, a deep bass voice, rich and oddly tuneful. He looked once again out into the dark street, and the dense night air reassured him that the world was slumbering and at rest.

Forty

"Who is it?" an inscrutable blue eye scrutinized him through a peephole. Cosmo jumped back. He had to say something and do it fast, or the eye might disappear and leave them standing outside.

"It's Minna and Cosmo," hoping that answer was sufficient. The eye did not waver, and he glanced back toward the street and waited. What would they do if the door did not open to them?

"Who?" the blue eye bellowed. He shrugged and repeated, "Minna and Cosmo." What else could he say? It was absurd telling that solitary eye their names. Ridiculous as it was, he whispered a quick prayer, like he had uttered before bed to pacify his mama. "Please let it be enough."

The blue eye remained impassive. Cosmo expected the peephole to slam shut in his face. He held a tiny hope because it hadn't yet, and because he had said their names twice. Maybe the eye would show some compassion. Maybe after it consulted with the other eye.

That he was a colored man stood against them. They were strangers coming to the door late at night, which didn't help their chances. There was no reason the eye *would* open the door. It was more likely to disappear and call the police. If that was what was meant to be, he would accept it. Minna was in bad shape, and if there was no other alternative, that would be better than going out to face whatever might be lurking in the fog. He was in no shape himself to come up with another solution.

The door flew open suddenly, and a gnome, almost as thick and solid as the door itself, stood in its frame. She put her hands to her hips as if she was perturbed they had arrived so late while she'd been waiting for them; her nerves were taxed, and she was tired from her effort. If Cosmo hadn't been wearing a shirt, she would have had a ringside-seat view of his belly button. She craned her head back to take in the length of Cosmo, noted the flour sack of a girl hanging under his arm, and commanded, "Put her in there on the sofa." She pointed. Her voice did not match her size. It boomed like a tuba trying, but failing, to play softly with the rest of the band.

"Uh," Cosmo muttered. She limped ahead of him, one leg shorter than the other, and Cosmo hobbled along behind her. They were an awkward match, the white dwarf and the black giant, both owning a gimpy leg. The light in the hallway was dim, which made the glow of the next room inviting, as though they were being drawn into a sanctum. Cosmo didn't have time because everything flowed swiftly, nor was there enough light to sort out the gnome's features. In the hideaway, the walls snuggled around them, and three lamps with red lampshades beamed three matching circles of rose-colored light. Cosmo gaped. At least he'd stopped running at the mouth. The warm air covered them like a cozy blanket. It had the effect on Minna of sleeping medication. She put her head on a pillow and fell asleep instantly.

"That girl's had some trouble tonight," the gnome said as her voice modulated. "And by the way you look, so have you."

Cosmo nodded. He wanted to be polite and not stare but couldn't help himself. He'd encountered innumerable shapes and forms living in cities, particularly Chicago. He knew better than to gawk. He was exhausted, and his leg, his gut, and his eye all throbbed. He must behave the gentleman, not rise above his station with a white woman, even a woman who barely stood as tall as his waist. Her hobble was like his own, except hers was due to a short leg, which was shorter still than her other short leg. One side of her face drooped with so much drama that it looked about to fall into her neck. The weight of the sagging skin pulled down her lower eyelid, and she appeared bug-eyed, but just on the one side. The eye itself floated among red streaks, but the other blue eye remained composed and attentive, in its pool of white, uninfluenced by its distorted partner.

She wasn't normal like everyday people. To Cosmo, what people called normal was some contestable reality. From his point of view, normal was an imaginary standard that no one could measure up to, at least in his world, unless you used Divine as the starting point, for she epitomized what normal should be. At the moment, what seemed normal was the eye looking at him, studying him with tenderness. The other eye lived a life of its own.

He tried to calculate her age, but she seemed to have no age at all, and despite the encumbrance of a shorter leg, she moved with remarkable speed. "I'm bringing another pillow to put under her head," she said as she left the room. "And something for those cuts on your face. I'll take a look at your leg, too. You sit over here and pull up the leg on those pants." She gestured toward a stuffed purple chair that shouted bliss, and he thought he would cry.

The spittle flew, escaping from the droopy side of her mouth. He forced himself to listen to her directions, although the balmy atmosphere was distracting, and he had to concentrate to understand. Some of her words came out slurred, and he was exhausted, and the warmth was invading his body. But pain rushed in along with it. The muscles he had called up to protect himself in the two separate encounters with the thugs insisted on having their misery. When the gnome left, he stood over Minna who was sleeping hard and peacefully. His own urge to sleep was overpowering. He wanted to do what Minna was doing, block out the memory of a lovely day that had turned into a nightmare.

Minna looked so serene he pushed away the image of bending over a coffin. He desired nothing more than to take up the easy chair and follow the gnome's command. It was winning, but he was not ready to abandon Minna. If Divine was in charge, she'd have everyone taking orders. She would know what to do first and last. He felt useless looking down at Minna. The best he had been able to do was haul her away after she'd gone through the worst of things. He leaned down and touched her forehead. It seemed the right and only thing he could do. It was what his mama would have done for someone who was ailing. Minna felt cool. She still had his jacket around her shoulders. He tugged it closer around her and then pulled out the afghan under her feet and covered her with it. The top of her face poked out like the center of a delicate rose tucked up in red petals.

Cosmo snapped awake at the tuba voice, which was trying to speak quietly. She wasn't talking to him, but it yanked him awake. Minna answered her sweetly. He gasped, pulling himself up. "What be the time?" He couldn't see out of the eye with the gash below it, and he panicked, fearing he'd gone blind.

"It's all right," the gnome assured him. "It's almost two o'clock. That's just a poultice." She soothed him, pushing his hand away when he tried to pull it off his eye. "I know you have to be at the shipyard in the morning. By that time, the swelling will be down."

He couldn't stand the poultice on him. How could he know she wasn't lying about him ever being able to see again. But he obeyed her and left it alone. His mama healed people just this way, but it seemed against nature that a white woman would be practicing his mama's methods. He tried to dismiss the suspicion that she was a witch. If she was, what could he do, anyway? Still, he wished he could get the poultice off and test his damaged eye. Maybe she had cast a spell on him. He tried to calm himself.

Minna was watching him. She was propped up by a surfeit of red pillows. This gnome didn't do things halfway, he realized.

"Aha," the gnome said when he turned to look at Minna. "I'm going to bring you a special tea now," and then she scooted out of the room. He imagined he saw a cloud of dust rise behind her. Things were slightly off-kilter, and it was not consoling to see a silver vase on a homey wooden table between himself and Minna in the shape of a test tube with one enormous red rose exploding in size and color.

"How long you been 'wake?" He spoke just above a whisper, hoping they were out of earshot of the gnome. Minna was so tranquil he feared the gnome had put her in a trance, hypnotized her, or cast a spell on her. Minna was sipping something in slow motion, and he watched the vapor rise above the cup. Now the gnome was fixing him hot tea. Was he next?

"Don't worry, Cosmo. Everything is all right." She nodded toward the kitchen. Minna looked at him as though they were old friends with a shared history that went back to their childhoods. In her smile he envisioned a warm day when they had played together in a grassy yard, kicking a big rubber ball to each other. He had inherited his mama's talent for reading people on the inside, and Minna was telling him, without saying a word, that he did not need to be afraid. They were in safe hands.

Her eyes spoke of forgiveness, too. He read in them that she would wait for as long as needed to hear what had happened at the corner of the five-and-dime. Her young eyes seemed seasoned and wise, and as she returned his gaze, he saw something profound. They were not the eyes of the teenager he had met only the previous day.

He had left her stranded. He ached with shame, a pain worse than the one in his gut. He could not stand to look into eyes that forgave him without even demanding an explanation. He had failed her utterly after she had trusted him. She'd gone into that store carrying the promise he would be waiting for when she returned. Did he even dare mention the two guys who had come up to him and wanted to fight him, and how he tried to put them off? The same two that would be her attackers later?

They were provoked wasps. They'd tailed Minna and him since Pike Street Market, gritted their teeth when he elbowed her and got fresh with her, the two laughing. The bullies threatened they'd go after Minna if he refused to go with them.

They shuffled off the main street, one on either side of him, and ducked into a dingy alley, screened from the heavy traffic. He'd been in jams before, but not of his own making. One time three guys jumped him, and he fought them off, sustaining a broken middle finger. These two were salivating for a fight, and he wanted to slow down the momentum so he made each step deliberate, although they pushed at him, and knuckled him in the ribs. He wasn't going to talk his way out, but he might be able to foil their attacks and get back to Minna. He dreaded her finding him missing. She was a sensible girl and smart, and if he could not come back, she would find her way back to Divine's.

They would try to trick him, and he watched for it, wouldn't let them get behind him, knowing that was how it would start. Get an edge on him. They had it worked out ahead of time. Later he analyzed how they had set things up beforehand. It must have been a regular game for them.

He was inconsolable for having failed Minna, for not preventing the thugs from attacking her. He wouldn't find a hole deep enough to hide in. He once had a dog named Jasper who tried to pull a sizzling pork chop off the stove. Cosmo caught him with his paws on the stove top and the meat between his jaws. Jasper shook his head, trying to get rid of the heat on his tongue but would not let go of the pork chop. In the end, he couldn't endure the pain, dropped the meat, and slunk to him with his tail between his legs, ashamed and wanting to hide.

Cosmo should have been watching for hoods. He wasn't in Memphis, but he wasn't a free man in Seattle. He had relaxed his judgment and enjoyed himself. He knew better. He was guilty of walking down the street with Minna at his side, ignoring the barrier between coloreds and whites. He'd foolishly thought the divide had evaporated in Seattle because of the war, where every hand was essential to that effort. He could never leave the South behind.

The gnome materialized in the room. She appeared and disappeared like a spirit. She was holding his tea but it was hot, so she set it beside him. "You start drinking that, young man," she directed, "while it's still good and hot. Just start with a sip at a time, but drink all of it." Minna nodded to encourage him.

He seemed to have missed an essential piece because after he had dropped off to sleep, Minna and the gnome had become acquainted. He didn't know the woman's name and put out his hand. He started to stand up, but his leg went out from under him. He shook his head and said, "Cosmo here."

"I know who you are." She grinned from the side of the mouth that worked dependably. "You told me that at the door."

"Oh," Minna interjected. "I'm sorry. Cosmo, this is Celeste Lehrer." Cosmo couldn't believe Minna's startling recovery. He must have been in a deeper sleep than he realized. Sometime during the night the two had leapfrogged into a friendship.

"Um, how you do, Miss Lehrer." Cosmo tipped his head.

"No Miss. No Miss!" the gnome shook her head. "Just Celeste. Just Celeste."

"Yes, ma'am," Cosmo agreed, but that didn't satisfy her either.

"No ma'ams, either," she demanded. "Just Celeste." She smiled at him. "Honey, you look puzzled, like someone sneaked a biscuit off your plate, and you can't figure out where it went." The gnome belted out a laugh from some deep inside pocket of her being, as if someone had played this trick on her as a child.

"Celeste?"

"Yes, Cosmo?"

"Can I ask a question?" He realized he hadn't felt sharp pain in his eye since he discovered the poultice, which now was hanging precariously because he had tried to stand. His gut was not hurting as much as it had after only one sip of the tea. But it tasted just downright god-awful. He nearly choked and almost spit it back out with the first swallow. He pretended he was clearing his throat so he didn't appear ungrateful. Lord knows, this Celeste woman seemed to possess some miracle powers in patching the two of them back up. Minna was bright-eyed and not in a frenzy. She acted like she was sitting with a group of friends at a tea party. Cosmo just could not figure it.

"You can ask me anything you like." Celeste was composed except for the one side of her that wasn't ever going to look regular. If he knew her better, he'd maybe get around to asking how she'd come to be that way. If they were friends, she'd tell him without him having to ask.

"Well," he started. He wasn't sure if he should ask why Minna was doing so well. It didn't make sense. She'd have this horror with her for the rest of her life. She wouldn't live a day without thinking about it, and he guessed she would never walk a street again without looking behind her. Maybe she would become a hermit, stay holed up in an apartment, opening the door only to receive groceries and newspapers.

He'd seen it before with women of his own kind, mostly young girls, some as young as twelve and thirteen. They wouldn't come near a man if they could help it. They'd turn in their tracks and go the opposite direction. Some of their daddies forced them to get married, like it or not, the others ended up on the streets in Memphis or headed to New Orleans.

He was afraid to ask about Minna's baby, sure she had lost it. He prayed Divine would be fair with him if that was the case, for she had given him the obligation of watching out for the girl. His assignment had been to show her how to get around, find a job, and learn what to do to survive there. John Welles had entrusted Minna to Divine's care, and she would not want to let him down.

"I'm jus' wonderin' why you open your door to us when we was strangers bangin' on it? I guesses it's 'cause of that friend Minna meet on the train."

Forty-One

"You mean Erma Shepherd, who shared the seat with Minna on the train?"

"Yeah, I believe that is the name." He looked to Minna to confirm. "The one who got that crazy purple umbrella." This tickled Minna, and she giggled.

"Well, Minna and I have discussed this, Cosmo, while you were taking that good long snooze of yours. By the way, how are you feeling now?"

He couldn't believe it! He'd forgotten about it. The swelling was nearly gone. There was some dried blood where the gash was. He still had pain in his leg, but his gut ache was gone. "I am feelin'...mighty...good," he declared, stuttering in amazement.

"Yes. Just as I expected. Now, let's fill you in"—Celeste patted Minna—"and prepare yourself, Cosmo. It *is* going to sound strange." Her good eye studied him. He nodded and tensed his shoulders. He *knew* all along something

was amiss. The feeling was strong again, the one he had earlier when Minna told him everything was all right.

"The fact is," Celeste said softly, obliging him to lean forward, "I never heard the name Erma Shepherd before." Her good eye pierced into him. The tuba voice tempered to a near whisper, no longer punching out its syllables.

"Huh?" he wrinkled his brow. "That don't make no sense at all." This news loosened the double knot tied in his stomach since coming into Celeste's home. There was no mystery then, although Celeste seemed to think there was. It was some old lady not remembering another old lady, and he was relieved! Old people were always forgetting things. If Mama had lived much longer, she wouldn't have recollected her own kitchen!

He tried to act stunned. "But how that train lady know for Minna to come here, then? Gives her that address and all? That don't make no sense at all."

Celeste shrugged, but with her short neck it was difficult to tell. Her errant eye stayed stationary, unblinking, on Cosmo, which unnerved him. He squirmed. The other eye seemed benevolent and something else. Accepting, he decided. He realized that she intuited exactly what he was thinking.

"You know how these things are." She rode right over his disbelief, bulldozing it. Simultaneously, she drew him into her thinking, assuming he didn't need to be convinced of strange happenings that have no logical explanation. If he could see into people's souls, and she read that possibility in his eyes, he had met his mate, staring right back.

"That don't add up," he declared. "You musta forgot, ma'am...uh, Celeste, I mean, that's what happened. Maybe it slip your mind. It weren't important to you back then maybe, and that's why you don't remember. Maybe it were a long time ago, on a train or sumptin', but you musta knowed her from somewhere."

The poultice slipped off his injured eye, and when he touched the gash, only a small ridge remained. What was more remarkable, he was feeling no pain at all in fact, he felt energized and restored. Something was very strange about this

house and the gnome. He felt renewed, his anxiety had disappeared, and it felt bewildering but liberating.

And then there was Minna, who looked curious and attentive, even playful. If they tried to explain the terror they'd come through, they'd hear, "Ah, come on. You jus' jokin' 'round with me." The attackers were a bad dream that broke apart as daylight appeared.

"That doesn't *seem* to make sense, Cosmo. I agree," Celeste consoled him, deferring to his logic. She sat next to Minna on a stool, and when she stood up it added very little to her height. "You'll be leaving for work soon, and we need to settle a few things before you go."

How it could be morning was beyond him. He could have sworn he hadn't slept more than twenty minutes in this woman's house. "What things that, Celeste?"

"Well, first off, I need to know where your sister lives. Minna has decided to stay here and board with me. She said Divine doesn't have room for her, and I do, and I am delighted to have her here for as long as she wants to stay. If you tell me where I need to go, I'll get her things today."

"She goin' stay here with you?" Minna nodded to him. "You

mean you got room for her here?" He squeezed his eyebrows at Minna.

"Thanks, Cosmo." Minna felt shy toward him. He was her brother. She had claimed him, but those words remained in her heart.

"Yes, she is," Celeste was resolute. "Usually, I live alone. By choice. But I've got one boarder now. I think you should meet her when you come next time. Right now she's on business down in Portland."

"Hey, I gets it now. See, that how that Mrs. Shepherd knows 'bout this address. When you put an ad in the paper for a boarder, that lady saw it."

"Erma," Minna reminded him. "She doesn't like to be called Mrs. Shepherd." Minna had stayed in the background listening to their discussion about the unusual coincidence. "Her name's Erma," she repeated. "That's what she asked me to call her. She said she doesn't like titles."

Cosmo and Celeste smiled at her. "Okay. *Erma,*" Cosmo agreed. "Erma saw the ad in the newspaper, dollars to doughnuts."

Celeste nodded. "That would seem the logical answer *if* I'd taken an ad out. But I didn't. Sorry, Cosmo. It seems we still have no plausible explanation." Her wayward eye had started winking at him for what reason he could not figure. He looked to the other eye for verification, but it gave him a steady, forthright gaze. "It seems we are not going to get to the bottom of this tonight. Or should I say this morning? But before you leave us, Cosmo, there is one more thing to discuss. Minna says you got her a job at the shipyards yesterday."

"Yeah, that's right. Oh, I get it. I got to go tell that woman who hired her she not goin' make it, right? That Mary Evans woman."

"Mary Evans," Minna repeated.

"We've talked about that, haven't we Minna?" Celeste patted the girl on the shoulder. "You are going to take that job. Right, Minna?"

Minna nodded again. Her youthful color had been restored. "Celeste says if I rest through this weekend, I'll be right as rain. Isn't that right, Celeste?" Minna's skin glowed with the signs of motherhood and the peach freshness of a teenage girl. The afghan was draped over her shoulders and once again it reminded him of a rose, both delicate and imposing.

"Right as rain, Minna." Celeste laughed. "Especially here in Seattle. She just needs a few days to get her strength up."

Cosmo was sure she must have lost the baby, or that she would lose it soon. He hoped he could get Celeste alone to find out. He dreaded the accounting he was going to have to give Divine. Knowing his sister, it better be sooner than later, and it better be the straight truth, or hell would be paid, he was sure. When Celeste showed up at Divine's front door without him preparing her, his sister just might kick him out while he was working his first day at the shipyards.

Minna seemed steady, not unnerved, which he couldn't get his head around. She should be frantic and hysterical or acting loony as a bird. She didn't seem fragile or unable to face up to bad things. Maybe it was a time-out, a chance to get her strength back, and that's why she seemed all happy and sunny, sitting there like a flower. But could the gnome help her, would she even be around, when the aftershock hit? He'd seen it before, among his people who had experienced some terrible event. The more ghastly or gory, the more they were likely to just go on and live their normal lives, smile and greet you when they passed you on the sidewalk like nothing had ever happened, and they'd handled it inside themselves in some private way. They emanated a calm outward attitude. Then, out of nowhere, something erupted, and there was no way the damage was going to be chased away any longer.

Minna might go on for a long time this way. Maybe one day she'd be in the grocery store, looking at the canned meat, and it could hit her like someone knocked her smack on the back of the head. The odd thing was she might not have an inkling that it had anything to do with being attacked by two muggers. She could burst out screaming, fall to her knees, and bawl like a calf in front of all the other shoppers and not even know why she was doing it. Those aftershocks, when they came, look out!

"Minna's told me a bit about your sister, Cosmo. What a big heart she has. Sounds like her brother." The gnome grinned.

"I don't hold no candle when it comes to her." He was busy in his head concocting a story for Divine that he hoped would garner sympathy, not the shame and heaping of guilt he expected.

Celeste brightened. "I'm looking forward to meeting her."

Cosmo figured Celeste already knew he wanted to speak with her alone about Minna, to get some questions answered. "I tell you how you get there," he suggested. "You got paper so's I can write it down?"

"I've got paper and pencil back in the kitchen. You come with me, Cosmo. Minna, I'll be back with some more of my good tea in a minute. I think you're almost on empty, dear. I'll just get the water heated." She nudged Cosmo out into the hallway.

Forty-Two

"What're you so happy 'bout today?" Clyde interrupted Iris, who was humming.

"Ain't the world a beautiful place, Clyde?" She hummed some more and then stopped. "Let me guess what you're having this morning," she said with the bite of sarcasm.

"Looks like you slept well." He was responding to her friendliness. He didn't pick up on the sarcasm.

"If you only knew, Clyde. If you only knew." She had made herself calm down in the car before Paulie dropped her off. The humming helped. She didn't want her psychic hunches to flop over onto Lila. She had to protect her sister from her speculations.

"Back door locked?" Willy walked in the front way and surprised her.

He was prepared for her question. "Wanted a change of scenery," he hoped that would stop her from prodding. It was anybody's guess where he stood with Lila since Fischer was back in the picture. He couldn't read the temperature back by the ovens, nor could he stand the thought of running into Fischer who appeared to be closing the gap with Lila.

"And ain't it beautiful scenery?" Iris concurred.

Clyde sniggered. "What're you talkin' about, Iris? It's stinkin' cold out there."

"Never know it, Clyde, with your long underwears hangin' out again." She laughed.

"So, handsome"—she poured Willy his coffee—"You all right?" She'd probably put him in a tizzy with her early morning phone call.

"Gol dang it, Iris. No it ain't." She could rile Clyde in one sentence, but he did check his shirttail just in case. He took his cup and headed for the table farthest away, hoping she'd take offense.

"I'm fine." Willy tapped his fingers on the counter.

"Like hell," she whispered. "I'm sorry about the phone call. I had to tell someone besides Paulie. You know him. He's ready to go to the police at the drop of a hat."

"Yeah. I get it. We'll just have to wait and see, like you said." He was sure he could hear Fischer back by the bread racks.

"Maybe I got it wrong, anyway." She hoped so. She was going to have a lot of sleepless nights otherwise.

"Hi, Willy," Lila came in with a batch of cheese buttons. "I didn't see you come through."

"He was lookin' for a change of scenery," Iris tittered, answering for him.

"What?" Lila didn't understand the two of them sometimes. They talked in some crazy code, just as Iris and Minna had. "Fischer's in the back. You'll want to hear what he's found out."

"You leavin' again for one of them conversations?" Clyde hollered when Iris and Willy followed Lila to the doors. He was the only customer in the shop, and the vacant space made his legs twitch.

"Yep," Iris said over her shoulder. "Goin' on a long vacation."

"When do I get my second refill?" he spoke to her back, but she didn't answer him.

"Nothin'," Fischer said grimly. "Can't come up with nothin'." He had gone to the fort, and he hadn't taken Willy with him.

"I thought you were gonna stop by and get me." Willy was irked. Fischer was trying to move him out of the picture. He got it. Fischer wanted to be a hero to Lila.

"You were workin' on an engine when I came by earlier," Fischer lied. Willy didn't disagree. He would only come across as resentful.

"So what exactly did you find out?" Iris wasn't blind. Maybe Lila didn't get what was going on, or maybe she didn't want to, but everyone else in the kitchen knew Fischer was finagling.

"That colonel who told us to come back today shipped out over the weekend."

"You mean you didn't get to talk to none of the brass?" Willy couldn't believe it. A whole weekend had gone by. They'd waited around for Monday hoping they'd get the name of Archie's commander.

"I talked to the guy who took his place. Colonel Cornett. He said he didn't know nothin' about it and didn't have the time nor the inclination to hunt down some kid in Minnesota. Said he had just about enough on his hands already."

"Where in the world does that leave us, then?" Lila looked like she was going to cry, and Fischer slipped up to her like butter on hot corn on the cob. "Isn't there anyone else to talk to?"

"I gotta get back out front." Iris was fuming but for once didn't let on. She and Willy exchanged a quick glance.

She heard Fischer speak to Lila as she left. "Honey, I'm not gonna give up. Not ever. She's our girl."

"I'll heat your coffee," Iris told Willy. He had followed her out to the counter. He didn't look at her.

"Come on, Willy," Iris coaxed. She couldn't console him, and Fischer had blown their chance to hunt Minna down, acting like he'd been lied to and duped.

He spoke quietly. "I think I'll head out to the fort later. See what I can dig up for myself." Fischer was still in the back with Lila.

"It's worth another try." She frowned, fearing Fischer had ruined their chances.

"I don't imagine everybody's shipped out." He gripped his cup and took a swallow.

"I'm thinkin' maybe I got so worried last night because I figured somethin' like this was gonna happen."

"I thought you was scared 'bout Minna bein' in trouble."

"I'm rethinkin' that, Willy. Now that Fischer has gone and screwed things up."

"What did you say?" Lila's eyes and nose were red. She had a tray full of muffins.

"Those smell tasty," Iris said to distract Lila. "What are they?"

"Carrot. What'd you say to Willy?"

"I said how the army screwed things up with Fischer. You okay? Want me to close the store up today?"

"Why would I? I still have my arms and legs, don't I?"

"I just thought you might need a break, that's all."

"That's the last thing I need now."

"Hey, Clyde. Better come and get 'em while they're fresh." Iris preferred his company to Lila's, and she wondered how he would like carrot muffins.

"What are they?" he came to the counter and looked them over. She would bet he wasn't a man to appreciate vegetables.

"What do they look like to you, Clyde?" He examined them. They were dark, and he liked the aroma.

"Somethin' with chocolate?" he said hopefully. That didn't quite make sense with the rationing, but Clyde didn't go for in-depth analysis.

"That sounds about right to me," Iris agreed. Willy shook his head and almost smiled into his coffee. "You wanna be the first to try 'em? You can brag to the other customers."

"Yeah. Gimme one of 'em. No. Gimme two." His mouth watered.

"I'm thinkin'," she said to Willy after she served Clyde, and Lila had gone in the back, "that if we can't get anything from the fort, maybe we should take out some ads in the newspapers in Georgia."

"Sayin' what, Iris?"

"Sayin' somethin' like, "If you're related to a boy by the name of Archie who's learnin' to fly airplanes in Minnesota, please contact us at this address.""

"That's an idea all right." He tried to sound encouraging. He'd go to the fort, see what he could find out, and then tackle that idea of hers later.

"Hey, Iris." Clyde was smacking his lips. "You tell Lila these are the best chocolate things I had since the war started. What they called again?"

"Chocolate muffins, Clyde. I told you once already. But you know what? Maybe you and me should call 'em 'special muffins.' Keep it a secret. What d'ya think of that?"

Forty-Three

"Holy smoke!" Cosmo whistled when Celeste led him to a room in the back. He nearly had to pick his lower jaw off the floor.

"You call this a kitchen?" he asked under his breath. It wasn't like any he'd ever seen, but heck, he didn't know about white women's kitchens. Maybe they were all like this one, or maybe he had it wrong. Maybe it wasn't a kitchen at all.

A broad butcher block dominated the center of the room and was cluttered with long-necked glass tubes, a crucible, and a mortar and pestle. Most everything was caked with white residue and looked worn and tired, and neglected—like orphans—until they would be used again. He recognized some of the equipment, but not by name, from a stint as a janitor in a high school on the South Side of Chicago. He did not recognize the tubing at the far end of the table connecting two beakers.

The most peculiar aspect came from above and reminded him of the ceiling in a Catholic cathedral in Chicago where he was pretty sure God lived. He was no expert on churches, much to Divine's disappointment, but he'd sneaked into some he liked the looks of from the outside.

Celeste's overhead fixture glowed a brilliant red. It had the particular shape of a large orb in the shape of a giant eye. He got goose pimples on his forearms, wondering if God was trying to get out.

Celeste watched him take in the features of the room. Cosmo couldn't help himself. He breathed, "Jeezus."

And then Celeste smiled. "Maybe," she said, affirming his comment. "Probably." She nodded. Just as she had surmised, he understood. He wouldn't know the name of her brand of sacredness, but he figured she didn't invite just anybody into the room. They'd be horrified or struck dumb, afraid they were in the presence of a witch who was brewing up trouble there. He was dumbfounded, but Celeste figured that after he recovered his amazement, he would be curious, curious enough to come back as a regular visitor.

Cosmo became an explorer, although he didn't move. He was

207

fixed to the spot where he'd entered the room, and it was from his observation post that he began to absorb the ingredients surrounding him. He was a dieter, consuming small bites.

All the available open wall space supported shelves—there must have been fifty of them in all—holding transparent Mason jars. The jars competed for space and were scrupulously alphabetized. Each letter claimed at least one shelf to itself, and sometimes two or three. The jars bore white labels with some names he recognized and that demanded he take notice. Angelica root leaped off the first shelf; on the second bay leaves and belladonna blustered. Other shelves yielded elder and jasmine. They declared themselves ahead of the marshmallow and passion flower, pining for recognition. Rose brier and yarrow fairly yelled at him. Most of them were old acquaintances, plants his mama had collected. She had studied their properties, using them to cure illness, but didn't write their names down because she couldn't read or write. She identified roots, leaves, and flowers by their colors, shapes, smells, and where they were gathered.

He encountered unusual names. Some seemed bizarre, like deerstongue and dragon bones, blood and teeth, mandrake, and mugwort. It was like a library, browsing the shelves of strange and exotic titles. His logical mind wanted to count the species, to acknowledge them as living things with human personalities, not to overlook or ignore a single one of them.

The room was the marriage of the Chicago chemistry lab, his mama's workroom on the outskirts of Memphis, and the soaring Chicago cathedral. Except for the absence of the rancorous stink of the classroom, some of which should be attributed to adolescent boys, or the pungent incense of the cathedral, the essence in Celeste's kitchen, if it really was a kitchen, spoke of substance and character. If it could be captured in a vial, the first part would be tangy, smelling of the decaying prehistoric forests of the Olympic Peninsula floor. Above it would be a hefty whiff of the Pacific Ocean, and the remainder a mixture of attar and loam. The room did not reek with acrid gaseous vapors made by teenage boys who experimented with chemicals to make theatrical explosions.

Celeste observed Cosmo with her good eye and the other one also. She was a presence, unique as the ingredients in her jars, yet blending with her surroundings, and he didn't separate her from them. He left his post and orbited the room, and without intending, he ended up beside her. He stared down at her, mute. She cranked her neck back to look up at him, and for a brief moment, neither spoke. Cosmo was the first.

"This some outfit you got here, Celeste. What you make in here with all these jars? You some kind a magician, is you?"

She laughed deep from her belly. "Now, Cosmo," she admonished him, "next you'll be accusing me of being a witch."

"No, ma'am. Oops—I means Celeste." He shrugged. In the several hours together, even Celeste could not undo a lifetime of rigorous conditioning in the matter of addressing white women. He had to choke down the "ma'am" each time he said her name. He shied away from any form of address. If she had the power to change that habit, then maybe she was some kind of witch. But he didn't want it changed. When he left her house, the same world that he had shut out when he came inside would be waiting for him out there.

"I seen some of this stuff before." He pointed to the filled jars.

"I thought that might be the case."

"I jus' never seen so many of these things in one room." He was still absorbing the myriad of details. He pointed to the equipment on the worktable. "I used t' see some of these in the high school where I worked."

"And the jars?" she probed.

"My mama had some of them. Not like this, though. But people come to her when they's in bad shape."

"And she helped them?"

"Most times. If she could. Sometimes they ain't no fixin'."

"Yes. To some point that is true. You want to know about Minna, don't you? If *she* can be fixed?"

"Yes, ma'am…Celeste, I mean, 'cause I reckon she can't jus' walk away from what happened to her. And what 'bout that baby? You cast a spell on her. Ain't that right?"

"In fact, Cosmo, I did *not* cast a spell on her. I don't believe in that kind of interference. I would never countenance trying to control someone's spirit."

"Then what? I figure the bad stuff is goin' a hit her someday out o' the blue. Wham! You do some voodoo?" He scrunched his eyes together and peered down at the top of her head.

"No. I don't perform voodoo. That's in the same league as hypnotism." She thought it ironic and almost laughed out loud, not at him, but that he would ally her with the Caribbean tradition more akin to his background than hers. "But there are some things that can be done to ease people through a particularly bad trauma. That tea she's drinking, for one, is a start."

"How that help her? What tea is that? And what 'bout that baby of hers?"

"The baby's fine. You may have noticed that pendant of hers?" He shrugged, though he remembered it because it had a queer look to it, like it came from outer space.

"Well, it's an agate and just exactly what is required to protect a baby from harm before it's born. She has it lying on the baby right now."

"You sure 'bout that?"

"I'm sure." The way she said it, Cosmo had to believe her. She didn't leave a question hanging in the air. "And about the attack, she will have a memory of it. She doesn't have amnesia, like I suspect you think. Am I right about that?"

"I jus' wonder if you gives her somethin' that make her forget."

"No. That's not how it works, you see. You can't play the body for a fool. It knows what has been done to it, even if the brain blocks it out. You would be surprised at the many who believe that you have to force yourself to ignore pain and terrible hurt under the pretext that, given enough time, it eventually will disappear as if it never happened. You and I know that isn't true, don't we? I see that's what you are worried about. That she won't ever be right in the head again."

"Yeah. That's my worry. I seen it before." He didn't add that Divine also would have his hide over it.

"I figured that. What I'm helping her do is to remember, let the horror pass through her, and move it on its way. She's never going to forget it happened. What I am doing is to help her transform something that is evil, something no one wants to have happen to them, into the gift of her life. Something that will make her stronger than she already is. She's a determined, smart girl, and when she's through this, she will be more tenacious than ever. Now, that probably sounds like witchcraft to you, I'd bet." She laughed.

"All I knows is that so far, you been right on target. If you is a witch, I guess you the good kind."

Celeste let out a throaty burst. "Let's give her a few days. You go straighten things out with that Mary Evans. Tell her if she asks, but only if she asks, that Minna will be there on Monday, without doubt. And," she added, for she must have read his mind once again, "don't worry about Divine. She *will* understand."

Forty-Four

Celeste brewed a very lovely tea for Minna on her first day of work. "This is delicious," Minna praised. She was jittery and fumbled with the handle of the delicate cup.

"You are ready. Although you may not feel that way right now," Celeste said.

"I don't know what I'll do if Mary Evans finds out I'm pregnant."

"There's not much for her to go on right now, is there? You haven't been getting sick, and that would be her biggest clue." Celeste had prepared a bland breakfast just in case. "By the time you're showing, they'll see you're an asset."

"You think so?" Minna's voice quivered.

"I know so." Celeste had packed a lunch for her that would be easy to keep down.

"I'm nervous about Mary Evans."

"That makes sense. I suspect she'll be demanding. You are efficient and disciplined, and that will go a long way with her." Celeste had brewed another pot of tea and refilled Minna's cup. "Even if she is stiff and critical and tries to trip you up, to make you fail, you will ride through it. It may be a dog-and-pony show for a while, but you have your goals, and you won't let Mary stop you."

Mary did nitpick. Right from the beginning. She scrutinized each piece of paper, and when she wasn't hanging over Minna, she threw side-long glances at her. She glowered about the snood, but Minna had met the company's requirement.

"I wonder," she said disapprovingly on that first Monday, "what other rules you'll stretch. We'll see. We'll see."

"I won't let you down," Minna vowed, and before two weeks had passed, she had memorized the inventory system.

Mary refused to be impressed. "That's the simple part," she sniffed dismissively.

Minna grew more determined. She studied in the evenings,

211

pored over the reports from the day, swing, and graveyards shifts, trying to understand when and how fast materials were used up. She couldn't solve it. "I'm never going to get this." Minna tore up one worksheet after another and frowned. Fearing she'd be replaced, she drew diagrams and charts to help her untangle the complexity.

She considered Lila. The many details at the bakery must require similar effort to keep the shop running. Celeste's phone rested on a table in the hallway. The urge was intense sometimes. In her mind, Minna traced the fingers on the dial, 7-3-8-0. She imagined her mother picking up the receiver and sounding efficient when she said hello. Would she be angry that Minna was calling? Maybe her mother was relieved she was gone and out of her hair.

Celeste retrieved the torn bits of paper from the wastebasket, Minna's failed attempts to create a workable pattern. "I'll use them for labels."

"I get it!" she said, jumping up one Friday evening. It was nearly midnight, and Celeste had yawned several times but refused to go to bed until Minna did. The mystery was solved. Timing was key, she finally determined. After that it was a matter of creating charts to determine how supplies were expended.

"I thought you were getting close," Celeste cheered.

A month into the job, Minna's waistbands began cutting into her skin and leaving bright red ruts around her tummy. Up until then, because she was tall and slim, she'd been able to wear her regular clothes. She resorted to sucking in her breath at the office, but that didn't help, so she bought secondhand clothing with elastic and added materials to the side seams of her skirts. She added length to her jackets to hide the bulging and divided her evenings between sewing and mastering her personally engineered flowcharts.

"She hasn't said anything yet," Minna confided to Celeste of Mary. Minna examined her profile before she slipped into her fleece pajamas and automatically stuck her tongue out at herself. She didn't want to think about Archie because he made her mad. She was the one paying the price, but when she saw herself from the side, he showed up in her head.

"Perhaps you are ready to let her in on the news," Celeste suggested. "I suspect she's quite satisfied with your work and would regret losing you. You are a remarkable young lady."

Minna was uncomfortable with Celeste's praise. She was always so positive. Maybe she overlooked Minna's faults or didn't know her well enough to see them—yet. "Thank you," she said shyly. "I thought you were going to say you suspected Mary already knew about the baby."

Mary didn't know about the baby. She was trying to figure out how Minna could work through the reports from the graveyard shift in the mornings and have the results checked against available stock before the bell rang for lunch break. While she waited for the day-shift reports to come in, Minna went over in her head how to announce her pregnancy.

The shipyard workers were separated by groups according to their specific function, and each group's leader checked off the materials used that day, and what they would need. The lists of supplies and each form was unique to its group. Minna checked the lists against available stock, and assembled a comprehensive order for requisitioning. This was straightforward, but with the war on, and because of the shortages, the lag time for turnaround was uncertain. Minna handed the orders to Mary, for all requests went through her.

Mary pored over Minna's totals like a lepidopterist classifying a rare butterfly under a magnifying glass. She inspected each line twice and ran the figures on her adding machine, flitting over the digits and expecting them to keep up with her. Then she'd run the numbers again.

From the first day, Minna caught Mary stealing glances. Apparently she thought she was discreet. If Minna looked up, Mary was studying the length and breadth of her like she was trying to uncover a truth or a fatal personal flaw.

"Have I made a mistake?" Minna asked once. In its former life, their office was a closet. With institutional pale-green walls, the room seemed more cramped with the two desks and a hideous gray filing cabinet monopolizing a third of the space. It was stifling. Minna started a habit of inhaling sharply and then holding her breath. A lavender plant, a gift from Celeste, was the only living thing in a room with no windows.

"Not yet," Mary retorted, rifling through the paper work on her sullied brown desk.

Mary ate her lunch at her desk, and Minna decided to do the same. She packed a tin of peaches, a hard-boiled egg and a grainy piece of Celeste's bread that looked suspect but tasted good. The half hour dragged, punctuated by crumbs plopping on their wax-paper wrappers.

One day Mary opened a tin of sardines that sent Minna flying to the bathroom and heaving. "I think I'll go to the lunchroom," she said the next day.

"No law that says you can't." Mary shrugged and tore off another sardine lid. Minna was getting sick less often. She didn't get triggered by most smells, except for Mary's oily fish. She did have a twinge of nausea when Mary stared at her, too.

She returned from the cafeteria one day to a massive woman sprawled at her desk asserting herself like a landlord, making Minna the renter. The woman's lunch stretched over the desk, on top of Minna's reports! She didn't know the woman, or her position at the shipyards, and didn't point out the stains falling on her work.

"Hello," Minna said, avoiding a half-eaten sandwich and the ring from the juicy syrup of canned pears that stained a requisition list. She didn't stare and focused on the puke-green wall. The woman didn't respond or get up to remove herself from Minna's space.

The woman appeared to consider something. She nodded but did not attempt to move. Minna looked to Mary, expecting her to concur about the mess on their mutual work. Minna had a frightening moment wondering if Mary would turn the story around and blame Minna for the stains, and her stomach did a flip.

The woman came to some realization and began to unfold herself from the chair. It appeared to take a profound effort for she moved in slow motion. She stood the same height as Cosmo, and she huffed. Minna cast her eyes on the file cabinet. She held them there while the woman packed up her lunchbox. Saltine crumbs littered her chair. The room reeked of sardines, and Minna pushed down the urge to get to the toilet again.

"See you, Phyllis." That was the first time Minna saw Mary smile.

Mary dressed severely, but Phyllis did her one better. Her legs and feet were giant timbers supporting her six feet and completed by specially made shoes. A specialty shoe store would not carry that size. The sleeves of her dark-gray suit jacket, purchased from a men's department, did not reach her wrists, and her hands dangled like canoe paddles. Her hair was akin to the battleship metal Cosmo welded. The thick glasses kept her eye color a secret as well as disguising her expressions.

Phyllis was the bookend to the monstrous filing cabinet, and on the days she ate lunch in the little office, the stale, rank air oozed out into the hallway. Minna knew before she opened the door that Phyllis was lolling like a sunbather in her chair, and she gritted her teeth. It felt like she and Phyllis were competing for Mary, but she didn't know why.

"You ready yet?" Cosmo waited for Minna at Celeste's door each morning from the first day she started work. He showed up just as Minna finished breakfast, and he thought he'd stepped back into his mama's kitchen. Almost everything on Minna's plate was green. He'd grown up on collard greens with ham and eggs. Cosmo couldn't make out if it that's what it was, but it sure was something like that. He was overjoyed that Celeste was going to see her right.

"What are you doing here, Cosmo?" Minna grinned to cover her relief that first day.

"I wants to make sure you don't make no fool o' me. I get you a job, and you don't show up, how's that make me look, you think?" He winked at her.

He failed to notice the other woman at the table, but that would not happen again. "I'm Terra Fields, Celeste's other boarder." The woman stood up and extended her exquisite hand. Minna thought Cosmo blushed. Cosmo couldn't utter his perfunctory, "Cosmo here." Without words, Cosmo stared and didn't think to blink, despite the fact that he was gaping at a white woman.

"Ah, Cosmo. I see you decided to come back and meet my boarder." Celeste hobbled into the room, beaming. It was no surprise to her that he stood stiff as a stone pillar. Judging from the looks on Terra's and his face, God had smacked them on the foreheads to wake them up.

Cosmo waited each evening for Minna to come off shift. "Now, don't tell me," Minna teased once or twice. "You think I can't find the right bus to get back to Celeste's, I bet."

"You got that right, sister. You end up at ole Divine's place by mistake, and you goin' hafta share a closet with that crazy daughter, Starr. That be pure misery. I couldn't let you suffer that one." He laughed.

"What do you think of Mary Evans?" she'd asked him a few days into the job.

"She a bit strange, you think?" Cosmo laughed. Minna raised her eyebrows. If he were under Mary's lens, it wouldn't seem funny, but Cosmo could make just about anything look humorous. He rode Minna's bus, not the one that would drop him off near Divine's. He parked himself in one of the backseats, tried to get one where Minna could see him. She knew what he was doing and why, and she appreciated what he did. She would be all right once the baby was born, and she would tell him that. She didn't expect him to keep this up forever.

"I'm going to tell her today," Minna announced to Celeste before she left for work one morning. Her regular clothing was not going to hide things much longer. "Good for you!" Celeste ran to one of her shelves. "Mary might enjoy a bite or two of this candy. Just to sweeten things up a bit." She tucked them into Minna's glove.

Forty-Five

"You thinkin' of puttin' up decorations?" Iris wasn't sure she should ask, but Lila was satisfied with her fruitcakes despite the lack of ingredients, so Iris seized the opportunity.

"What's the point?" she sounded distracted.

"For the customers?" Iris asked tentatively.

"If you want to do something, go ahead. I don't have anything to celebrate." Iris echoed her sentiment. Christmas was going to be worse than eating stale bread that got stuck in the back of her throat, but she didn't want to give up stringing popcorn for tree trimming. If she shunned the rituals she cherished, she would be turning her back on life itself. If she went forward, there would be countless pricks to the heart.

"If it's okay with you, I'll just hang a few balls in the windows." She'd assembled oversized red bows too, with pine greenery Paulie had collected for her, and set them out on the tables.

Clyde stumbled in. "Look at that. I was wonderin' if we was gonna ignore Christmas this year"—he took in the festive effort—"what with the war on and all."

"Well, Clyde, ain't you just full of surprises. Who'd a thought you'd notice a thing like that? I coulda sworn you only had eyes for me."

"Are you in one of them moods again?" He squinted at her.

"I don't have a clue what you're talkin' about, Clyde."

"I ain't seen Minna 'round," he said apropos of nothing. "What she up to these days?" He got a smile like suddenly he'd gotten a bright idea. "She gone off with one of them soldiers?" He laughed again.

Stella stood behind him. "Good morning to you, Clyde." She was formal but friendly. He turned to see who she was. As far as he could figure, Stella didn't know his name. He was sure she hadn't spoken to him before, but the way she addressed him, it sounded like he might be sent to the principal if he didn't behave.

"Oh," he stammered. "Uh. Good mornin', Miss." He didn't know her name and was too shy to look her in the eye. Stella shot Iris a knowing look. She knew, Iris realized. Stella had figured out about

Minna's disappearance, although none of them had said anything to the customers. A good schoolteacher didn't miss much, Iris concluded.

"I guess you're still enjoyin' a change of scenery." Iris poked at Willy, who no longer came in through the back door. He'd headed for his stool intending to slip by the other customers.

"Never know who you gonna meet up with in the alley." He looked tired.

"They workin' you too hard over there in the garage?" Iris felt worn out just looking at him, but she'd been feeling that way anyway.

"Draggin' my dang tail," she confided to Paulie. She fell asleep some afternoons in the car after he picked her up from work.

"It's the worry," he counseled. It weighed on all of them. Willy made an attempt to cover his fatigue.

"Naah. I'm up to it." His shoulders sagged over his coffee. Iris figured it wasn't because of work.

He brightened. "I almost got somethin' out of one of them officers, though."

"You went back out there? To the fort? When?" Her eyes grew wide. Maybe they'd have a good Christmas yet. Maybe the best one ever.

"Yesterday. Naah. I didn't go out there. I was fixin' a car for this one."

"What'd you find out?" She was already planning what splendid decorations she could make for the table. They wouldn't make a fuss over Minna being back. They'd act like it never happened. She imagined someone saying, "Hey, Minna, pass the green beans, would ya?" It would be like every year, but Iris would treasure this holiday above all the others.

"Found out his last name, for one thing."

"You did?" She couldn't believe their luck. "Willy, you are downright marvelous!" She gave him a huge grin and handed him a cherry tart. "I'd kiss ya if I wasn't already taken," she joked. "You tell Lila, yet?" Surely, if he had, Lila would have come out and told her. Knowing Lila though, she'd wait until some of her pastry came out of the oven, and then deliver the news along with a tray of cookies.

"Nope," he said like he was putting his brakes on.

"Why not, for goodness sake?" Iris was ready to jump up and down.

"Keep it to ourselves, for now," he said quietly and nodded toward the tables. There were five people at five separate tables. They all had their noses buried in the *Missoulian*, except Stella. She took deliberate

bites of rye and watched passersby on the sidewalk. Some workmen were decorating the lampposts with evergreen boughs.

"Why are we whisperin'?" Iris said aloud.

"Don't wanna get nobody's hopes up too high." He'd never forgive himself if Lila got brokenhearted because he couldn't deliver, and if he did find Minna, it would be without Fischer interfering.

"Would ya just look at that?" Walter was nearly drooling over the special muffins. "When did she start makin' them?"

"Where you been hidin', then?" Iris was elated. "Somehow, Walter, the world's gone on without you, I guess."

"Don't make one of them comments of yours, Iris."

"What comments?"

"'Bout me livin' in a cave. I don't live in no cave."

"Coulda fooled me." She smirked.

"I want one of them things." He pointed to the carrot muffins. "I thought we wasn't gettin' chocolate no more."

"We couldn't live with you complainin' all the time. Lila made 'em just for you." She raised her eyebrows, adding, "And Clyde over there. Ask him about 'em. He's even got a special name for 'em."

"Clyde'll eat anythin'."

"Unlike you," she nodded toward his belly, resting on the counter. The pharmacist waited behind him in line. Iris had a terrible urge to rub cherry juice into his colorless cheeks. She didn't speak to him unless he asked a question. He made her think of the stern Lutheran pastor from her catechism training.

"Gimme two of 'em," Walter commanded.

Iris prompted him. "Please."

"What?"

"You forgot to say please, Walter."

"You ain't my mother, Iris," he retorted.

"Thank the good Lord for small favors," Iris muttered, avoiding a glance at the pharmacist. "You could learn a few manners, Walter."

"I don't have to listen to you," he grumbled.

She put his muffins on a plate, and when he turned to walk away, she said to his back, "You're very welcome."

"I swear, Iris." Willy came close to chuckling. He hadn't done that since Minna vanished. "You gonna teach the whole world manners?"

"Gotta try."

"Probably could find easier subjects, I'd say."

"Probably. But you gotta start where you are. Don't cha?"

"That's about right. You look a little peaked today. You feelin' all right?"

"Don't go gettin' all Paulie, on me, Willy."

He laughed and seemed a little sunnier. He had a lead for Minna that gave him some optimism.

"So what happens next?" She meant about Minna.

"That officer is gonna get back to me. He said he'd find out Archie's whereabouts. It's a start."

"When you gonna let Lila know?"

"When I got somethin' hard and fast. Not before. Can you keep it under your hat?"

"My lips is sealed." She drew a straight line like a zipper across her mouth.

Forty-Six

"It looks like you've got something on your mind." Mary hit Minna first thing when she came to work.

"Do I?" She had made her face look calm. "I was just thinking about the inventory list from yesterday."

"And what was wrong with it?" Mary jumped on the chance that Minna had made a mistake.

"Oh nothing's wrong with it. Just the opposite," Minna said, explaining that it would be useful as a blueprint.

Mary's face fell a bit. "No two days are alike," she countered. "And you see how they're working in the yard, trying to beat their records down there. It's going to get harder and harder." She sounded like she couldn't wait for it to get tougher.

"We'll be ready for them, though," Minna persisted as if Mary was a colleague.

Mary frowned. "I will be. I don't know about you."

Minna pinched the flesh on one hand. Aunt Iris would have a snappy response. She wished she had one. "I thought you'd like some candy." She held her palm out. Mary sniffed at them. "To go with your coffee."

"I'm not crazy about sugar. We shouldn't be eating it with the shortages, anyway."

"But these are made with fruit," Minna replied.

Mary eyed them. When she took them, she acted as if she was doing Minna a favor.

"Oh," Minna added as if she had just remembered, "if you've got time after lunch today, maybe I could go over something with you."

"Another one of your bright ideas?"

"More or less." Minna was guarded. She'd thought she had the right approach to assure Mary that the baby would not interfere with work. She would take a short break, not long enough to create snags in the ordering process. She'd point out, being careful not to boast, that she was efficient, and the work could run without her. She'd emphasize *short time*, just in case Mary got the notion to replace her.

Not one day passed that Mary failed to mention the woman Minna had replaced. She had up and quit without so much as a good-bye. Mary bristled as though it was Minna's fault. Her litany sounded like a warning.

Mary niggled about the woman's departure every morning. It was a fresh, newly hatched egg each time the sun came up. The woman had eloped, and Mary was the jilted lover. Minna completely sympathized with her predecessor for running from Mary's greedy stare.

"Is there anything else I can do?" Minna asked Mary following lunch. Her morning reports were completed, and she was waiting on the day-shift managers and their paper work. Mary looked up from her desk and frowned as if Minna had trespassed.

"Soon enough," Mary quipped. Minna idled, waiting for afternoon report, and sifted through papers. With Mary constantly keeping tabs on her, Minna wasn't about to come up with ideas to manage the workflow. She did that in the evenings, with Celeste nearby, and then memorized everything so she couldn't be criticized for her efforts.

The candy hadn't been eaten. If Celeste had given them with the purpose of sweetening Mary up, it appeared a fruitless effort. Then Phyllis dropped by.

"Well, hello there, Phyllis." Mary was suddenly buoyant. Phyllis apparently believed her arrival equaled a greeting and didn't respond. She looked at Minna as an alien being that had sneaked passed a barrier to get into her universe, but she lit up when she saw the candy.

"Sweets for the sweets." She bit into one without invitation. "Mmmm. Where'd you get these?"

Mary almost choked. "I haven't tasted them myself."

"Well, what are you waiting for, Mary? Life's short, you know." She guffawed and leaned over to put one in Mary's mouth. Minna kept her eyes on her paper work. "See. What'd I tell you?" Phyllis said when Mary uttered, "Oh! That is good." They finished off the remaining pieces.

Minna looked at the clock. Afternoon reports would be coming within the next fifteen minutes. If she was going to raise the issue of her pregnancy, she'd need to do it soon. She willed Phyllis to leave the office.

"What are you working on, Mary?" Phyllis went behind her and peered over her shoulder, giving no indication of leaving. She gave Mary's shoulder two substantial rubs. "You work too hard. Always got your nose in some report or another."

"We can't all be geniuses like you," Mary gushed. Phyllis put her head back and roared. Minna looked at the clock. Ten minutes before the managers would file their paper work in the boxes at the base of the metal staircase. It was Minna's job to retrieve them. If a report wasn't there, she had to hunt the manager down and insist it be completed. The staircase wobbled and clanged. She wasn't afraid of heights, but this staircase had no landing for its twenty-five steps. It was a straight shot from the ground floor to the offices.

"You're doing it all wrong," Phyllis said suddenly. Minna jerked her head up, thinking Phyllis was criticizing her. She wasn't. "Just look at that," Phyllis pointed out to Mary how she had reversed some numbers.

"Oh, my goodness. You're right! What would I do without your eagle eye?" Phyllis liked that and patted Mary on the back. "You'd be just fine." Phyllis was generous. "But, hey, you've got me to check on you. Just in case." Mary gave her a wide smile. In five more minutes, Minna would chase down reports.

"Well, I guess I've done all the damage I can here." She looked at Mary and moved toward the door. "By the way, thanks for the candy. That was brilliant. I'll pop in again and keep my fingers crossed for more." She didn't acknowledge Minna on her way out.

"Well, just look at the time," Mary said. "Reports out in five minutes." She sounded positively gleeful. "You said you had something to discuss, didn't you?" Minna sucked in her breath. It was now or never.

"I'm going to have a baby," she blurted. Not what she'd planned, but she'd watched her chances fade with Phyllis, the minutes yapping at her with each loop around the circle.

"Of course you are," Mary said like she'd known it all along. She wasn't ill-tempered, didn't hurl accusations, and most important, didn't threaten to fire her. "When's it due?" She sounded sober, as if the announcement had only caught up with her.

"Not until this summer," Minna said sweetly. "And I'll be gone just for a short while."

"You mean you're coming back?" Now Mary was sober, but her face relaxed at that. "You aren't going to quit?"

"Oh no." Now it was Minna's turn to gush. "I don't ever plan to leave." She sounded desperate. She had two minutes to convince her boss and solidify her future.

"We'll see about that." Mary reverted all of a sudden to her usual manner. "Time will tell," she muttered. "Only time will tell."

Minna got out of her chair. The reports would be in.

"I don't know why you'd want to stay on when the war's over," Mary continued, oblivious of the clock. "That doesn't make sense. You'll be taking care of a kid and a husband then, won't you?" She had a puzzled expression that made Minna uncomfortable. She wondered if Mary had figured out she didn't have a husband.

"I don't plan on quitting. Even when the war is over. Do you?"

"Who knows what'll happen by then?" Mary seemed to be hinting at something. Maybe she had someone else in mind to take Minna's place. But that didn't make sense because she talked about when the war was over. It could be that she had already made arrangements with a person who was working elsewhere and who would be available only after the war was over.

"I'll just go collect the reports now." Minna motioned toward the door.

"You do that," Mary advised. "When's that baby going to be due?"

"Not till early summer."

"Those candies were pretty good. Phyllis sure liked them. You think you can get ahold of some more?"

"I'll try." Minna smiled.

"What kind of fruit are they, anyway?"

"I think it's blueberry. I'm not sure."

"They didn't taste like blueberries. Anyway, if you can get some more, it'd be good."

"I'll try," Minna said, going out the door.

Forty-Seven

"Try this on for size." Mary baited Minna the following Monday morning. Minna had stumbled into a puddle at the bus stop, and her toes were cold and wet. She wanted to slip her pumps off and rub her feet together.

Mary stood stiff and puffed out, like a general displaying her medals. Very military, very precise, an individual with authority who expected to be saluted. Under Mary's right index finger was office work, and Minna guessed Mary had found an error in her work.

"This is a new responsibility." Mary exhaled for emphasis, waiting for Minna's promise she wouldn't fail. Minna scanned the words not hidden under Mary's hand and found it was an extension of her current work.

"So are you up to this?" Mary tapped the desk and looked immediately at Minna's midsection. So far, Minna had been able to minimize the baby bulge with her usual clothing. She added cloth pieces on the inside seams that weren't visible from the outside. Mary's looks felt proprietary.

"Yes, ma'am," Minna responded, imitating Cosmo, not knowing how to address her. If she called her Mrs. Evans and the woman wasn't married, which is what Minna suspected, chances are she'd be offended and spit out some invective. Minna said, "Pardon me, but…" if she had a question, and she behaved like Lila, who kept people at arm's length, except when she gave Uncle Willy an occasional reprieve.

Minna relished the added responsibility but was soon disappointed when she found it didn't offer much of a challenge. This perturbed Mary, who had planned to spoon-feed Minna new tasks, making each a delectable and treasured morsel. She embarked on a new course, dumping one task right onto the next in the hopes that Minna would capitulate. Mary waited until Mondays when the workload was the greatest to make the most impact.

"How does this look?" Minna asked Celeste and Terra one evening. She'd sewn pouches into her skirts to accommodate for the baby and strengthened the seams again. She couldn't button the suit jackets any longer and fashioned bulky tops from men's sweaters purchased at secondhand stores.

"Adorable," they chimed.

"You are very talented," Terra commented.

Cosmo ate most suppers with them, and he and Terra gave each other bashful smiles over steamed vegetables.

"That Starr drivin' me nuts," he complained. "She think Divine whole house her closet," stretching his legs in Celeste's living room.

"I think you are big enough to handle it," Celeste said.

"You ain't met Starr. Has you?" He squinted, and they all laughed. By then, he and Terra had begun sitting next to each other on the sofa. Celeste and Minna spent more time in the kitchen to give them privacy.

Seeing Terra and Cosmo together made Minna long for home. She was very happy at Celeste's, and that only made it harder. She wished she could tell Aunt Iris about Mary Evans, she'd have a made-to-order response about that, and she missed Lila's steady presence in the background. Like Cosmo, Uncle Willy watched out for her. But, she'd left them all behind without even a note. She wished she had told them she was going away and not to worry. She would be all right. She loved them. Maybe they'd forget her before long. That would be better for them, but she would not forget them.

"You're very quiet tonight," Celeste said after they'd washed and dried the dishes. Minna was redesigning a gray sweater to wear over her navy-blue skirt. "Anything you want to talk about?"

Minna exhaled. She pushed the longing back.

"Is Mary causing problems?"

Minna snickered. "She wouldn't have a good day if she didn't try to mess me up, but I'm getting used to her. I guess she has her reasons."

"I'm very pleased to hear that, Minna. I think Mary will sort herself out. She already recognizes how valuable you are."

"It's the other thing." Minna pointed at her growing belly.

"I see. Are you worried about it?" Celeste looked at the protruding lump.

"I'm scared all the time. I hate looking in the mirror. I don't know who I'm looking at anymore," Minna whimpered. "I don't see me at all. All I see is a huge belly, and I'm never going to be like I was. I'm not going to be normal again."

Celeste listened. She didn't offer empty promises about the future. "I'm sorry, Minna." She heard Minna's grief and honored it.

Minna must find her way to come to terms with this.

At the shipyard, on days when Mary acted too friendly, Minna pulled her oversized woolen sweater around her swelling belly. Minna had devised a mnemonic technique that confounded Mary. She resented Minna's ability for recall and liked to confuse her. Whenever Mary showed a personal interest, asking Minna how she was able to manage with her husband gone and if she had plans ready for the baby, Minna burrowed like a mole into her reports.

"I'm all set," she lied. She wasn't good at lying, she confessed to Celeste.

"But you are set," Celeste affirmed. She wondered how Celeste would know that if she didn't, or that the baby was going to be born no later than early July, but more likely mid-June. Celeste noticed the shadow pass over Minna, gloomy as the Seattle winter sky.

"I'll stay by your side, dear," she promised. "You mustn't worry about that. You are going to do just fine." She refrained from saying more. Minna was facing some big decisions. The baby was growing inside her, and Celeste would labor with her one careful step at a time.

"It's not that, Celeste," Minna asserted to the gnome. Celeste was reviewing the contents of her jars. She waited but said nothing and patted her hand.

"Take your time, Minna. There is no puzzle without its particular solution."

"I don't know what I'm going to do when the baby comes."

Celeste gave a relieved sigh. Because Minna spoke the certainty, touched the dilemma with her words, Celeste trusted Minna was at the starting line, finally, and at last in the race. She would find the way forward!

"How am I going to manage a baby and work?" She'd come home in the fog, and the dampness was chilling. She tugged at her green woolen coat, trying to get it all the way around her on the bus. Celeste's red lamps were glowing in the hallway and a steaming mug of tea waited for her. Her belly was swelling. Every day it grew larger. Her old skirts didn't fit anymore, so she bought skirts that were two sizes bigger and altered them. She moved her chair farther from her desk and ran to the bathroom every hour. At night, she put a pillow under her leg, and went to the bathroom every hour.

"Is it like this for everyone?" she cried to Celeste about the pokes and kicking on her insides that had begun a month after she started at the shipyard. At first it felt creepy, like someone was tickling her belly. She gasped when she realized the alien sensation was coming from the baby. That was only the beginning. She—Celeste and Erma had informed her it was a girl—poked out an appendage, Minna thought it must be a finger, and she pushed back at it. It buried itself in the belly, but then reappeared on the other side. More pokes came more often. The baby was taking over. It began shifting and rolling and growing more assertive.

Minna started to expect that if Mary was standing over her flapping some paper, the baby was going to put up a fuss. It also happened during the night when she needed her sleep. It was the worst when Phyllis was at her desk and Minna had to wait for her to unfold her massive, yet strangely bony body from her chair.

"I'm grateful for my job," she told Celeste that clammy evening. The tea was easing the tension from her shoulders. "But it's gotten harder with Mary." She trusted Celeste's intuition. "She's just waiting for me to make one mistake so she can fire me. Do you think that's what's going on?"

"No, dear. I can see how you might feel that way, though," Celeste answered.

That surprised Minna. "How do you know that?"

"Because it bears the familiar earmarks of envy." She peeked at Minna's cup to see if it was empty. "From the way you describe her, and by how you say she behaves, I gather that she must be middle-aged."

"She's old! Probably forty-five at least. Older than my mom, for sure."

Celeste smiled. "Well, she's not so young, then. I'm going to warm up our tea." She limped back to her kitchen. Her short leg ached from the cold and damp and she rubbed the thigh as she went down the hall. She returned with a steaming teapot a few minutes later.

"Do you think"—Celeste was refilling their cups—"Mary had to work hard to learn what you have come to know in a very short time? What you do is important, which could be unnerving. If she can trick you—as it sounds like she is doing—maybe it makes her feel better about herself."

"So if she embarrasses me, she'll feel better? That's what's she's doing?"

"I think so. But just remember, your good work makes her look good, too. You are doing everything as you should, Minna. Just keep doing it, and if she upsets you, it's best to not let her know that."

"You mean like making a face at her? I don't do it in front of her, but I do when I go to the bathroom."

Celeste laughed. "That's excellent! You shouldn't bury your

feelings and pretend you're not upset. Just keep your own counsel on it."

"You mean it's all right to be upset?"

"Of course. No one wants to be mistreated like that. I think I will make up a special tea for you to give her as a little present. That should help ease things a bit."

It was the way Celeste listened and her belief in Minna that allowed the girl to open up that Friday evening.

"I have a technique," Minna confided. "When Mary gets too close, I blink my eyes like I've got something stuck in one of them."

"What a piece of ingenuity," Celeste said, clapping her stubby hands together.

Forty-Eight

*I*t was nearly midnight when she opened the closet door of her heart. "You probably won't like me anymore when I tell you how I was with my mother." She wrinkled her nose. "I tried to get her goat. Make her mad. I was snotty, and I ignored her."

"Mothers and daughters, dear. You will understand someday that it is no one's fault. What happened between you and your mother was necessary. Don't judge yourself too harshly."

"But why?"

"This is not easy to understand, but take your work as an example. The many evenings you spent figuring it out, wanting to master the unknown. You haven't forgotten that." Celeste certainly hadn't. She'd stayed up late, brought tea, encouraged her. "Mothers do the same thing when they raise their girls." She chuckled. "They want to do it right. They do what you've been doing. Figuring it out as they go along until it becomes second nature."

"Until it doesn't work anymore?"

"Exactly. Even when it doesn't fit any longer."

"You think I was doing the right thing?" Minna was stunned. "Even when I was mean to her?"

"I think you did what you had to do. Sometimes we don't see other choices and feel trapped. It is best not to sum up one's character from that instant."

"But what about Aunt Iris and Uncle Paulie?" Celeste sensed Minna's deep love for them.

"I've disappointed them."

"Most things can be redone, Minna," she said softly. "The people who love you, love you no matter what."

Minna described the bakery down to the stained-glass lamps, the pies in the window, the types of pastries on the racks in the case, the elegant cakes under glass on the counter, and the varieties of breads. She talked of Boppy, of how big he had been, her little hand in his gigantic mitt as they scoured the alleyways for treasure. "He gave this to me when I turned ten." She touched the agate pendant.

"He loved you very much," Celeste assured her.

"That's exactly what Erma Shepherd told me."

Celeste nodded regarding her life in Missoula, patted her on the arm about Aunt Iris. She didn't click her tongue, or worse, say, "Oh no" or "dear me." Even when Minna described how she'd sneaked out with her suitcase and put pillows under the blankets, or how she'd let down Aunt Iris at her birthday party.

"You are fortunate to be loved so well." Minna gasped when Celeste added, "Fischer loves you in his special way. But he has a tight hold on his heart."

"But how can you know that?" Minna demanded. "You've never met him." She didn't trust Celeste's assessment of her dad.

"He blusters, if I'm correct?"

"I guess that's how he is." It sounded accurate.

"It might carry over from childhood when he needed to protect himself."

"I don't know anything about that."

"It will be quite propitious for everyone when Fischer decides to open his heart once more." Celeste used big words, but Minna got the gist. Celeste didn't add that her family missed her. She came to that on her own.

"I don't think I should keep the baby." It was late, after one o'clock, when the crying started. She wanted to believe what Celeste told her, but she'd botched up everything.

Celeste coughed. "That must be very hard to say."

"No," Minna cried. "No. I'm not ready to be a mother. Not a good one. Not now." They sat in the same seats as they had the night Minna and Cosmo invaded Celeste's private world. Celeste held Minna's hand.

"I think we need a bit of dessert. Big choices require a bit of sweetness to help them go down," Celeste said abruptly and stood up. Her knees creaked from arthritis and sitting too long.

It was nearly two o'clock, but back in the kitchen, Terra and Cosmo were frying chicken and hovering like a pair of nannies over the hot stove. They were competing, bantering about who was most qualified to judge the perfectly crisp golden-brown legs and thighs.

"It all about the timing," Cosmo insisted.

"I'm not arguing that," Terra rebutted. "You're just looking at the chicken. I'm looking at the color of the fat." They banged each other's hips and poked with their elbows. "Outta my way, Cosmo," Terra warned, waving the flipper at him.

Celeste listened to their joking from the hallway. She had forgotten they were in the house, thought they'd gone to a movie. They must have come back and slipped inside without making noise, assuming she and Minna were already asleep.

They were hugging and kissing and ignoring the oil spitting from the stove. They'd forgotten about the chicken altogether.

Celeste regretted interrupting their play. She laughed. "Go on, go on. Don't let me stop your fun. I'm just coming after that peach cobbler." Joyful, gentle Cosmo was so handsome and intelligent, much like Shakespeare's Othello, Celeste decided, as if the poet had Cosmo in mind when he penned his role. Terra was the feisty counterpart with skin so pale you could almost see through it. Her fire-red hair and green pools for eyes fueled her spunky spirit and encouraged all her knee-jerk decisions, which were always dead-on right.

"It doesn't matter, Celeste, does it?" Terra surprised her. She'd intended to slip in and out quickly and hurry back to Minna. She liked their gaiety and didn't want to stymie them. Even the walls smiled from their happiness. "I mean about us getting married so soon?"

"Of course not." Celeste's tuba voice punctuated the air. "When a thing is right, it's right no matter what. Who's arguing, anyway?" She squinted, looking up at Cosmo.

He shrugged. "Not me," he answered, but he wasn't smiling.

"What is it then, Cosmo?" Celeste was chasing an orphaned peach around the pan with her spatula. She heard his hesitation and the solemn surrender in his voice.

"You knows already, Celeste. Without me sayin' one word. Plain as it get. I is *colored*. And this lady"—he pointed to Terra—"mighty special. You know that. But they make her life misery." He pointed to the outside, where he conjured people lurking beyond the safety of Celeste's door. "And the love be gone sure 'nough before you shake a stick."

"Well, I won't pretend there won't be troubles, Cosmo. I'm sure there is a fair chance that might happen."

"Exactly what I'm sayin'."

"Add that to the mix of all the everyday struggles you will have," Celeste said, "just like every other couple has to do."

"See. That's what I tell Terra here. But she's not buyin' it. See what she says, Terra?"

"Good for Terra." Celeste continued letting him have his rant.

"You can't run from this because you're afraid of it, Cosmo. It's noble, and just like you, to try to protect Terra, but I would guess you're thinking about what happened to Minna. Aren't you? And *that* wasn't your fault."

"I ain't so sure 'bout that," he almost whispered.

"That memory, horrible as it is, serves you well. I know, I know." She raised her chubby hands in defense. "You don't want it to happen again. But Cosmo, think about this. When someone comes to you as a gift, you must accept it. You should never turn your back on it. That goes against nature. Terra is that gift to you, Cosmo."

"You make it sound easy," he said, barely above a whisper.

"No. That's not what I'm saying. I'm saying even when it gets hard, it will be worth it."

I'll try," he said, relaxing his shoulders. "How's Minna doin' in there? Seems you got somethin' goin', too."

"Ah, yes. Everyone has a story to tell."

A puzzled look crossed Cosmo's face. He wondered when Celeste would share hers.

"She's fine. She's doing very well at work, although she doesn't yet believe they realize it."

"I know. I heard talk 'bout that at the shipyard."

"She worries about her boss. She watches her like a hawk and tries to get her rattled."

"'Tween you and me, she's a bit of a mean one." He chuckled. "But nothin' that girl can't handle. Minna do all right. They like her work."

"That's just what I figured. She doesn't see it. She's too close to it, not sure that she fits in, and if that Mary Evans is hanging over her every move, it's hard for her to feel optimistic."

"Maybe I'll tell her what they say 'bout her at the yard."

"I think that would be good. It might be useful because she has some big decisions to make very soon."

"'Bout the baby, I 'spect."

Celeste nodded and smiled. "The baby that's coming about the same time you two marry."

Forty-Nine

*E*veryone was in a mood at Celeste's. It was an awkward time, with unsettled decisions swirling around like cranky untethered spirits waiting until concrete plans got put in motion. Celeste served up some foul-tasting teas.

"What you put in this time?" Cosmo sniffed and made a face. "You goin' kill us all, I swear," he said reverently. Anxious spirits were most active during the evenings, and the vapors from the teas dissipated them. Celeste measured progress when new resolutions were reached. Short tempers made her smile, affirming her purpose. Her boarders ate their greens at breakfast, sipped teas in the evenings, and accepted her helping hand.

"You been cookin' somethin' up."

"Whatever are you talking about?" He caught the edges of Celeste's grin because her back was turned. "I'm always cooking something up." They were alone in the cookhouse. That's what Cosmo called her kitchen.

"You makin' batches of somethin' in this place. I mean, you got me and Terra this close"—he made an inch between his forefinger and thumb—"to tyin' the knot."

"Yes?" She looked up at him like a disapproving parent. "And if I did, which I am quite sure I did not, are you disappointed? If you and Terra are getting married, you did that all on your own."

He shook his head at her and laughed. "You is a stinker, little Miss Celeste."

"I most certainly am not." She glared, trying to hide the smile from an unruly son. They'd been lucky. Terra had been on her way from work when she discovered a small house, three blocks away, eager to find renters. Many people were pitching tents in unlikely places to go to between shifts at Boeing or the shipyards. As improbable as it was, Cosmo and Terra found a home.

"You comin' with us to that judge who says he marry us this Saturday, ain't that so?"

"We'll be there. Minna and I wouldn't miss it for all teas in my kitchen." She chuckled at her own humor.

"You think Minna be all right?"

"She's as all right as she can be. A bit better now, I think, that she's come close to making up her mind. She's pretty much decided she's making the best choice she can. I believe each of us knows what the right course is if we put our hearts into a decision."

"I ain't goin' argue with that, seein' as I agree." He pretended to study the labels on her jars. "Do that go for me and Terra?"

"Cosmo, you of all people don't need me to answer that. Unless...you are too blind from love."

"I not blind to that particular lady."

"I didn't think so. Terra's right for you, Cosmo. But I see you're gearing up. It's not going to be easy, but you don't need me to tell you that. You will endure more than your share, and you're not going to get much sympathy or compassion along the way. Most likely, you'll get just the opposite. But as long as you stand together, you will survive."

"We got you"—he wanted to pat her head—"to make us some of them teas when things go 'wry. Cook up some potion and cast your spell. Prob'ly you got 'em ready on one of them shelves already."

"Whatever do you make me out to be, Cosmo?" She winked with her wayward eye.

"Well, somethin' been goin' on here. I ain't blind. First they is me and Terra gettin' married. And what you do to Minna? What kind of tea you fix for her?"

"Minna just wasn't ready to make up her mind until now."

"What make her do that?"

"You'd probably say it's magic," she teased. "Your voodoo, maybe. Or witches? You think because I look odd, I'm a hag?"

Cosmo thought he must have gone too far. He'd offended her by implying that, because she was an oddity, she must have supernatural powers. "I'm not meanin' to offend you, ma'am," he replied, slipping into the language of distance and submission.

"What's this?" She raised her good eyebrow at him. "Calling me 'ma'am' again, are you?" She turned serious. "We are different from others, aren't we, Cosmo? I suspect you get mean stares that say you don't belong here, or probably anywhere. And they call you names. People make faces at me as if I'm invisible. They act like I don't have the capacity to be hurt. Sometimes they stick out their tongues at me and drool, or talk like they are retarded, or limp as if they are deformed."

"Yeah," he said quietly. "I get that. I'm sorry, Celeste."

"It's all right, Cosmo. I've made my peace with who I am. It was hard fought, though. I got sorcery in place of my looks. Voodoo," she goaded him with a laugh, "or do you prefer witchcraft? as a trade. It was the bargain the gods made with me, but they didn't ask my approval or my input. If they had, they would have heard a thing or two. They were brutal in one way, and generous to excess in another. Maybe you can't have both, and from my viewpoint, nobody gets everything. Not even the rich, well-proportioned, beautiful white people."

"I know what you sayin'. I so mad bein' born colored that my mama got worried. When I was sixteen, I got so fired up I was goin' a find me a white bastard and kill 'im. I don't care who he was, I goin' a kill me a white man, jus' 'cause he's white, and I'm colored. Mama sees me all worked up. I'm so bad my hands shakin'. She gets me by the hand and takes me to her garden. She shows me this plant, I don't know the name, but it grows in the shade. It big and half as tall as me with them white feather tips on it. I seen it there every day o' my life. She growed lot o' stuff. This day she makes me see it different than before. She says, 'Cosmo, ain't that a pretty plant?'

"I think she's crazy, draggin' me out to her garden to shows me some stupid plant. I get even madder than before, and I tries to pull my hand away, but she's stronger than me. She got clamps for hands. Then she tell me that pretty plant ain't a goin' a grow unless it be in a dark place. It has to be in the dark. She says, 'See how this place shine so happy 'cause o' that plant? Them white feathers 'live 'cause they has the dark. They needs each other.' Then she push my hand into that black dirt. Makes me feel it all warm and wet. I still be feelin' that dirt."

"She was a very wise woman."

"Yeah, she sure was. Divine like her. She smart like Mama was."

"And so are you. Your mother guided you away from harm. That's what it takes. One necessary phrase or word, or even a touch or a look during a time of excruciating pain, can make you start changing how you see things. I didn't wake up one morning transformed and suddenly feel grateful to be born a dwarf in this awkward body with giants all around me. And who would ask to have a face like mine?"

"Then somebody help you, too?" Cosmo squinted down at her.

"Cosmo, I know you mean well, but that's my private story, and I prefer to keep to myself."

"Yes, ma'am."

"Oh, no you don't. Don't start that again."

He laughed that she scolded him.

"I think," she continued, "you've made your peace. Haven't you?"

"Not lots o' choice, is there?"

"Well certainly not if you go the other direction. We're in good company, you and me. You have to be determined, and we are. You know what's worse than being taunted?"

"Yeah I do. Somebody pretendin' we ain't what we is and actin' like what we is ain't important to them, but they thinkin' jus' the opposite."

Celeste clapped her hands together like a gleeful child. "See, I knew you were a kindred spirit. We have to be careful to separate the sincere ones from the rest. The belligerent ones are easier. Black versus white, if you'll excuse the poor example. Yes. Insincerity is so exhausting and never ending. That's one reason my work is so important to me. I've got alchemy coursing in my blood. Not a witch, mind you, but I do like repairing the troubles of the world when I can, if you know what I mean."

"You turns the other cheek?"

"I mean *being able* to turn the other cheek. You can't buy that in a shop, can you? It's can't be manufactured because it's one of a kind, and you're the only one who can create it. But you know all that."

"I knows it means makin' lot 'o mistakes tryin' to stay out of hot water. But you know that if parents be teachin' it at home and all them preachers sayin' it in all them different religions o' the world, it might be fixed. Then maybe we don't need you' potions anymore."

"You trying to put me out of a job?" She elbowed him in his hip. "Turning the other cheek is the crutch you need to let insults roll off. Thank goodness we've got that when we are mocked and mistreated. But you're a mighty handsome fellow, Cosmo. Don't say I haven't noticed, and Terra is one fortunate woman."

"I'm the lucky one. But what 'bout you? Who do you have?" It hit him hard all of a sudden that she was alone. There was no match for her.

"Why, that's simple, and I'm surprised you haven't noticed." She wrinkled her brow, frowning as if this astute man had missed a key ingredient. "Right now I have you, Cosmo. And Terra and Minna. And after Minna moves on, I'm sure someone else will show up to take her place. There is always someone."

"So what 'bout Minna? What happen there?" He had embarrassed her and was glad to shift the topic.

"She's a special one. She doesn't know it quite yet because she's young. Her mind is clouded with a young person's doubts, part of which stem from a lack of experience. Then there's the guilt that confuses her and continues to make her feel ashamed."

"It coulda happened to anybody."

"True enough, but try telling her that. I'm working on that very thing, Cosmo. Now that she's finally begun talking about it, I think we're making some progress. She still has to go through the birth with that child, and I am going to help ease her through that. But what we need is time, my teas, and a huge dose of honesty."

"She not honest?"

"She's as honest as she can be. Sometime after the baby is born, we will find the right time to discuss how she can make amends with her family. I feel so sorry for them not knowing where she is, or how she is, or even that there is this baby."

"I gets it. You can't tell them."

"I would never do that. She will decide how and when to do that. But that's not our current situation. First the baby, then whatever comes after that."

"Is she goin' be all right?"

"That baby has changed her life. In time she will come to appreciate that this had to happen. She would ignore it if that was possible. But the body doesn't let you lie to it or deny its truth for too long. That's what's going on with Minna. Her body has been catching up with her, and she's forced to make a big decision."

"I know you ain't no witch, but that girl act like she ain't havin' no baby till you talked to her."

"Aha! Are you saying we peculiar people have special powers?" She laughed. "Minna has needed time. She's had to wrap her soul around a reality she didn't want. But that baby has a mind of her own."

"Yeah. That baby lookin' huge these days."

"She's going to be a normal healthy girl. Minna's young, too young, but she's going to be all right. She's single, and of course there are lots of mothers raising kids on their own with husbands off fighting this blasted war, or dead even. But Minna will need to put things aright, go back to her family at some point. I don't believe they would have turned her away. I think she is loved, no matter what. In fact, if she did go back, they would be relieved. But she has yet to forgive herself. It will come. It will come."

"I believes it will." He patted the top of her head.

Fifty

"I'm not makin' the same mistake twice," Iris spoke around the straight pins.

"You scare me half to death," Paulie complained.

"What now?" He looked horrified.

"Oh. I thought it was a cigarette," she joked. "Have I ever even once swallowed a cigarette, Paulie?"

"There's always the first time."

"Don't be such a fussbudget."

"They'd have ta operate"—he was matter-of-fact—"at the hospital."

"I'm not gonna swallow them. There, see? I took 'em out." During Christmas Willy had followed the lead from the officer at the fort, but it had gone cold. "Just like that?" Iris demanded while Willy cooled his coffee with a glum face. She acted like it was his fault.

She took down the trimmed Christmas tree and the ornaments. Paulie made pasta. "No duck this year," she muttered. Lila wasn't acknowledging the holiday, and Willy wasn't going to if she didn't. Fischer worked on a truck.

Iris didn't use her table decorations. Paulie bought her a pair of shears, and she wrapped a hoe in tissue paper. She put it next to the pasta.

"I know what that is."

"I don't think so." She fooled with him, but it wasn't her best humor. "Get ready to go fishing, mister." As if Paulie would leave his gardening to chase illusive fish. But he believed her. In their seventeen years together, he still couldn't tell when she was teasing.

"I'm not gonna mention Easter." She was resolute. "Hand me a cigarette, would ya?" She pushed herself away from her sewing machine. She had to have something in her mouth. "I'm not putting myself through more heartache," she reminded Paulie. "Get my hopes up, and for what?" When Lila baked fake brownies and garnished them with dried apricots, Iris couldn't believe it.

"What're these?"

"Resurrection?" Lila didn't make jokes.

"What'd ya mean?"

"I don't know what I mean. It's Easter week." Like Iris didn't know.

"Yeah?"

"I've had this idea bothering me," she said, referring to the notion of the recipe, "and here it is."

"What's in 'em? Do I tell them it's brownies?"

"It's the usual stuff. I had to use carrots again. I wish zucchini was in season. I put in some cocoa powder."

"Then I can say there is chocolate in 'em this time. No foolin'."

"I've been hoarding that powder for three years."

"How 'bout we call 'em Burst of Life? Too corny?"

"It sounds right." Lila almost smiled. "Especially since we have to put up with this late blizzard."

"The apricots sure dress them up." The men would like the chocolate. There hadn't been a complaint over the carrot muffins. They'd leave the fruit on their plates.

"I'll whip up some cream, and you can put a dollop on them." She almost smiled for the second time. "I hate this snow. Things were just starting to turn green. I wish I had spearmint leaves to top them off."

Through the whole winter, Willy and Iris had kept their secret. "We could tell them we know his last name," Iris suggested. They'd put ads in ten papers in Georgia. Willy went to the library to study the atlas.

"I heard of Savannah and Atlanta before. Some of these places got me wonderin'." Iris read the list.

"John's Creek? You sure 'bout that? That sounds 'bout the size of Podunk, USA."

"I'm just goin' by what the atlas says, Iris." They put their heads together to write the ad. Willy got the addresses for the newspapers. He spent money on long-distance calls to find out how much it was per word.

"What are you two doing?" Lila hurried past them with a hot pan. Their heads jerked up like they'd just been caught cheating. "I've got three more pans coming out. Can you make room for them?"

"You expectin' the whole army to show up today?" Iris joked. She hurried over to move the muffins, and Willy discreetly tucked the paper in his back pocket.

"I don't know why we're hidin' it from her anyhow," she said to

Willy.

He shrugged. "Guess I'm worried."

"'Bout what?"

"You know." He nodded. That they would never find Minna. He wouldn't say it. That something awful had happened. None of them would put the worst on it. If they could, they'd find her, and that's what they hoped for, putting it in the want ads, and sending cash through the mail. A phone call could tell them where she was. That's all they needed. If they got that, they could tell Lila.

"Lila'll be on a train in a heartbeat if we find her," Iris agreed. She sounded excited. "What'd we just write?" Willy pulled the paper out of his back pocket.

"Take a look in the back. See if she's gonna come back again." Iris stood on tiptoes over the swinging doors. Fischer was by the ovens, next to her, and they were whispering.

"Looks like it'll be a while. Go ahead. Read what we wrote." They had made it sound friendly.

"You wouldn't answer an ad, would ya?" Willy pressed when Iris insisted it to be straightforward. Get right to the point. "If you was his mother, and it sounded like he was in trouble?"

"Probably not," she had to admit. "What we gonna say then? Make it sound like we gonna send her flowers or somethin'?"

He chuckled. "Naah. Come on, Iris. How 'bout we say somethin' like, 'Important news for Archie Benoit. Please call this number.'" He looked up. "Your's or mine?"

"Are you ever home except to sleep?"

"Kinda lonely at my place."

"That's what I thought. Okay. Put down my number. Lord knows if Paulie answers it, he'll be callin' Lila."

"Hmm. What're we gonna do 'bout that, then?"

"Say to call around suppertime. When I'm back home."

"Do they eat the same time as us in Georgia?"

"You jus' can't get it out of your head that I'm the expert of the world, can you?"

"Guess not." He laughed. "You tell me. When do you want her to call?"

"Just say in the evenings. It gets dark in Georgia, don't it?" She poked him across the counter.

"You're the expert. Okay. I'm gonna write them up tonight. Ten of 'em. Mail 'em in the morning."

Iris frowned. "What if she don't read papers? Maybe she can't even read at all." She screwed her face up.

"Yeah I know. I thought 'bout that, too. If that's so, let's hope somebody she knows reads them."

"What if she don't even live near one of them towns?"

"Yeah. I thought 'bout that one, too. It's a shot in the dark. The whole thing."

"I know. But it's gonna break my heart if we don't hear somethin' back."

"It might take a while, you know. If ever."

"What'd we do in the meantime?"

"Keep doin' what we're doin'. Stay busy. That's all we can do." He put his cap on and headed out the front door. It did not occur to her until after he was gone how much they had talked. She smiled, thinking what a good brother-in-law he would be.

Fifty-One

"Nine minutes apart," Celeste encouraged Minna. "It won't be too long now, dear."

"I hate this!" she screamed. "Hate it! I hate it!"

"Of course you do," Celeste consoled her. "I don't like it very much myself, right now." She wished she had a free hand to wipe the sweat from her own forehead. She was applying all the pressure she could to Minna's backbone, and her hands ached. Between contractions, Celeste adjusted the blue lace agate on Minna's belly and rubbed a special cream over her back. She dashed to the kitchen for warm poultices and tucked them under Minna.

"When's this going to be over?" An enormous contraction felt like it had kicked her spine open. "I want it to be over! I hate her. I hate you, too!" she snarled.

"Of course you hate us." Celeste pushed harder against her back.

Minna was tranquil between contractions. The poultices were working, Celeste observed, and she planned for a speedy delivery.

"It's his fault," she yelled with the next contraction. "Stupid uniform. Stupid airplane."

"Yes, dear."

"It's all Lila's fault," she cried a half hour later.

"I see," Celeste murmured.

"She should have told me. Shouldn't she?" Celeste nodded. Minna got mad at her.

"Go ahead, dear. It's all right."

"I'm sorry," Minna said afterward. "I think I said things I shouldn't have."

Celeste had been subtly preparing for the delivery. It had rained the night before, and the sky was crystal bright as Minna's agate. "You might enjoy sitting in the rocker on the porch," Celeste said.

"Just smell that sweet air," Minna said lazily. She'd cleaned all morning. Celeste had found her just after dawn wiping down the herb jars. She was singing "That Ole Black Magic" and standing on the step stool, swaying her backside.

Celeste said calmly, "Here, let me help you with that," and took her hand to get her down. She knew it was beginning.

Minna rapped her foot against the porch planks to Artie Shaw's "Moonglow" from the radio. "I'll just go make us a nice cup of tea," Celeste said. "Something that will help us relax after working like a pair of woodchoppers." She squeezed Minna's knee. Aunt Iris was probably crooning and smacking her lips over tomato soup. Minna giggled. It was just what Celeste wanted before contractions started.

Hobbling toward the kitchen, she lit juniper twigs and berries in a chafing dish. They'd help purify the air. Minna wouldn't have a seven-hour birth from start to finish. The universe in its wisdom allowed some women to sail through deliveries with a few twinges of discomfort. Minna wouldn't be one of them, but she was young and strong, and Celeste had black cohosh on hand. If that wasn't powerful enough, she would use goldenseal. She had been using beth root for a few weeks.

The recent rain rinsed away grime and stagnant odors. Spirits chattered nonstop in the air before Minna felt a first inkling or faint pang. The prescient Celeste had sensed a heightened pull even before the storm.

"I've put some chewy oatmeal bars in your lunch for work, Minna." That was two weeks earlier. Her wayward eye was starting to act up, as it did with her premonitions. It compounded its usual irritability in a particular fashion. The first day it rustled like a disturbed hibernating bear. She noticed this while she advised Minna, "Do try to eat them during your morning and afternoon breaks, dear. They're full of nutrients." She neglected to add that the bars were sprinkled with beth root. She'd neutralized the bitter herbs with a mixture of honey and marmalade.

On the second day the eye was entirely aroused from its residual drowsiness. The third day, it didn't behave at all. It was a cub playing friskily, ignoring its mama's caution.

"Did you eat *all* the oatmeal bars yesterday?" Celeste asked the following morning. She sounded edgy, as if she expected Minna's answer to be no.

"I did, Celeste," Minna replied obediently. Celeste sounded like Lila when a pastry didn't turn out as she expected.

Celeste had a modicum of control over the wandering eye most of the time. When it started its peculiar twitch at the temple, wriggling like a snake through the eye, migrating into her sinus where it itched and ached, she was helpless against it. She was never on friendly terms with the eye, always kept an uneasy truce with it, but when it mutinied, it was her adversary.

She resorted to teas that pacified the rest of her body, for fear the other parts would join in the revolt. At first, on the defensive, she abandoned her gifts of discernment and sound decision-making. She failed to remember the eye was her beacon, a precursor to a sea change, because of its shenanigans, and steeled herself to its antics, not its message. She lived inside a body that was relentless to remind her of its failings and continually coped with pain and defects.

Her calming teas and bitter herbs produced a pinch of success. Their mediocre results indicated a need for a another solution. In the end, she gave in to the aberrant wanderer and asked it to speak to her. Until then, she hid in a permafrost of avoidance. When she grew weary of resisting—as she always did after battling for control and losing—she submitted to its will. It was then she discovered that there was something greater than her ailments at the root of the agitation.

She began to watch for signs that would confirm the eye was speaking to her. Color was the first indicator. Color when yellows were not just yellow anymore. Orange came alive as if her good eye was starving to devour the juicy fruit. Colors blazed, invited, begged her to reach out and touch them. Across the street, the normally quiet dark-green undergrowth encouraged her to run over to embrace it. She looked to Minna to see if she also was infected by the vivid palette, but Minna's eyes were closed, and she was breathing deeply through her mouth. The azure tiles on a small patio table glistened despite the shadow passing between them and the sky. The prevailing light was so intense it bore straight into Celeste's psyche.

"It smells like perfume," Minna had said just before drifting off. "Everything is so sweet. Like a bouquet." The fragrances were potent and overpowering, as they are before a storm. Celeste tasted the silky breeze from the west. The powdery salt teased her nostrils. She felt it in her mouth. It tickled her skin. Her carmine roses, in concentric circles to the side of the porch, lobbed their perfume with attar-rich grenades over the handrail.

Celeste listened to Minna's labored breathing and waited. Fate was coming for a visit, and as always, would flaunt its two sides.

Sensuous particles bounced about the porch. Celeste acknowledged them, laughed as they banged into each other like a crowd at a party with no elbow room, and surrendered to the flow and its inevitable outcome.

Minna moaned in her dreamy sleep and then stirred and opened her eyes. She smiled.

"I'll make us some more tea." Celeste had turned the radio on before Minna had fallen asleep. She'd just walked past to the hallway when the swing melody was interrupted by a booming male voice barking out numbers. She thought he was announcing a winner of a race. He wasn't. She knew at once, this was what the eye had been preparing her for.

The radio smelled of hot plastic. They'd had it on all afternoon. Celeste felt queasy and off-balance. "Get on with it," she commanded the radio. The announcer's voice rose to a shout, and Celeste turned the volume down so Minna wouldn't hear him. But Minna walked in from the porch.

"I want to hear what's going on," she said. They had missed the announcer's first sentences, the ones that would have told them what was going on. The man was nearly incoherent, and Celeste reached for Minna's hand, remembering December 7, 1941, when the frantic announcement about Pearl Harbor was broadcast—the day the war began in America.

"Over three hundred thousand of them!" the announcer said over and over.

"Three hundred thousand what?" Celeste demanded. Her tricky eye glared at the contraption and then settled down, like a dog closing its eyes after being released from its responsibility.

"Allied troops have landed on the beaches of Normandy," he spoke directly to Celeste. He mentioned other places, places Celeste had visited: Omaha, Utah. Then there was Juno. "Over three hundred thousand of them," he said again.

"That's somewhere over there by France," Celeste interjected when he said Normandy. "But why are troops landing in Utah and Omaha?"

"John Welles was headed to Alaska," Minna murmured.

"Three hundred thousand." He started to sound like a windup toy that needed its crank turned.

"What in the world is he talking about?" Celeste said, parsing his repetitions. Then he was booming again, this time repeating, "At Sword Beach and Gold."

She completely forgot about making tea and headed off to her eclectic library with research articles and heavy books about herbs and alchemy. "I'm going to find my atlas," she declared over her shoulder.

"I wonder where John Welles is now." Minna spoke to her

back. Cosmo had hand delivered a letter, sent to Divine's a few months earlier.

Dear Minna,

I hope you get my letter and you're doing well. I'm just fine. We're waiting to be shipped out but don't know where to yet. I guess we'll find out when we get there. Ha! I couldn't tell you if I did know, anyway. Everybody here hates the waiting. We want to get going and get this war over once and for all. We joke about who is going to make the best soldier. Our commander tells us we are going to win the war. At all costs, he says. Keep your fingers crossed!

I sure hope you'll write to me. If Divine knows where you are, I know she'll get this to you. Maybe you are still at her house. That would be great. When I get back, I'd like to drop by and see you. I'd really like that.

Did you ever get sick again? You sure looked pale that day I saw you at the train station. I hope a good soldier is standing by if you aren't better and gets you a hard-boiled egg and a bottle of milk. But I bet you're over your big-city jitters by now.

Well, I guess that's it for now. I sure do hope you'll write to me.

Your friend (I hope),

John Welles

Fifty-Two

"Holy moly! You hear that, Iris?" Five people in two minutes reported to her about the invasion. The radio played "Over Hill, Over Dale," then "O Beautiful for Spacious Skies," and "From the Halls of Montezuma" for twelve solid hours.

"I got ears. Geez," she huffed. "I ain't deaf, you know."

"Any chance we gonna start gettin' real chocolate and real coffee again?" Clyde was exuberant. Iris had never heard such chattering in the bakery. They were talking about when rationing would end, and they could get as much gasoline as they wanted and buy new tires. People who never sat together crowded around one table and talked about what they were going to do when the war was over.

"Always thinkin' about how you can help the world, ain't you, Clyde?"

"Hey, if I was a young guy, I'd a been first one over there fightin' them Jerries."

"And complainin' 'bout the food."

"I don't know why I keep comin' in here, Iris."

"Because of the food, Clyde," she snorted. She told Lila, "We should make cookies with red, white, and blue frosting."

"It's not the Fourth of July," Lila countered. "And we haven't won the war."

"Well, we're going to," the pharmacist grunted. "It's a matter of time."

Lila looked at him like she'd never seen him before. "What a grouch," she whispered to Iris when he got to his table.

"You just notice that now?" For Lila to express an opinion was about as monumental as the invasion. Iris was stunned to the point of almost letting slip about the woman who claimed to be Archie's mother.

"Five months to the day," she whispered to Willy the morning after the phone call.

"No kiddin'?"

"Well, it was somethin', I guess." When she picked up the

phone and said hello, she knew it was Georgia calling. The drawl was that thick. The evening had not gone well up to that point, as if it was setting the stage.

Paulie had started a pot of minestrone soup when they got home. He sang a tender Italian melody and tampered with the seasoning, adding more parsley, making a face because something wasn't quite right. He sniffed the oregano before he crumbled it into the pot and added a touch more pepper.

Iris had gone directly to the sewing room. She wanted to get the sleeves finished on a rich-blue taffeta gown. Paulie came in when she was at a tricky spot.

"Jus' get a whiff of my delicious soup," he coaxed.

"Not now," she muttered. "Can't you see I'm right in the middle of this?" The fabric was slippery, and she was concentrating.

"It's gonna get cold." Paulie's face dropped.

"Well, just heat it back up then." He was still at the table and sulking when she came out.

"I'm ready now." She was breezy, pretending she didn't know he was upset. "That smells tasty," she lied. She wasn't hungry and would have to eat a big bowl for him to be satisfied enough to pull him out of his mood. She'd managed a few spoonfuls when the phone rang.

"I'll get it," Paulie jumped up. If she left the table, he knew she wouldn't eat more. She'd tell him she was full if he tried to lure her back. His attempt to add a few of the pounds she'd lost since Christmas would be useless. She beat him to the phone and heard the words, "a little place outside Augusta." Iris pictured green viny things crawling up trellises, and snakes.

"Cigarette," she whispered to him. His shoulders sagged. "I think I got one goin' in the sewing room," she held her hand over the receiver and pretended to be worried. She'd have to talk fast while he was out of the room.

"I seen your ad in the paper," the woman stated.

"Just now?" They hadn't run any more ads after January. Willy had warned her at the outset it was just a shot in the dark. They had agreed how much they'd spend, sent the letters out, waited, and then pretty much given up on it.

"I don't get 'round to readin' too much," she quacked. Apparently not, Iris thought. She was a smoker, Iris noted.

"You called 'bout Archie." Iris was careful.

"He's a good boy," the woman replied.

"Yes. Yes, he is." Every mother says that, Iris thought, no

matter what.

"He gonna make somethin' of hisself." She paused. "Sooner or later."

"Sure seems that way, don't it?" Paulie came back to the kitchen.

"Who's that?" he mouthed. "No cigarette," he added smiling with relief.

"Hand me one," she whispered and pointed to the pack at the other end of the counter.

"What'd ya say?"

"I was jus' talkin' to myself there for a sec," Iris answered and whispered to Paulie, "I think I forgot my purse in the car." She shooed him out the back door.

"Yeah. He one fine boy," the woman repeated. "Makes his mama real proud."

"He's sure a handsome fellow," Iris prodded.

"Him and his red hair," the woman laughed. Well, that was it, then. Archie was handsome, but he sure didn't have red hair.

"Would you call that bright-red hair?" Iris pushed.

"'Bout the same as a tomato, I 'spect." The woman roared.

"That's 'bout it, ain't it?" Iris laughed, blowing smoke out of her nostrils.

"So"—the lady was getting to the point—"I'm a wonderin' if there some kinda reward my boy got. That what the ad 'bout, ain't it?" Iris felt sick to her stomach. They'd patted themselves on the back, she and Willy, about their wording for that ad.

"Jus' goes to show ya." Willy hunkered over his coffee. "No tellin' how people are gonna see a thing." He'd started coming through the back door since spring. Fischer was busy with customers who wanted their cars tuned in the hope the war would be over and they could go on long drives. He wasn't hanging around Lila much, so Willy didn't expect him when he walked in and saw them holding each other.

"It's a cryin' shame what some people will do," Iris agreed. She hadn't heard Fischer come in the back. Willy shook his head.

"Gonna head out now." He hadn't drunk his coffee.

"You ain't even touched your coffee. What's wrong with it?" She made a face. "Maybe we are gonna get real coffee again. Soon?"

"Jus' not in the mood." He pulled his cap on and started toward the front door.

"You goin' sight-seein' again?" she said. He wasn't leaving out the back. She wanted him to smile, and he tried his best. It was all he could do.

"I believe summer's gonna come early," she said out loud to everyone to cheer herself up. The dour pharmacist happened to walk past on his way out the door just then.

"Time will tell," he said evenly.

"That's the truth." She didn't want Willy's disappointment or the pharmacist's shilly-shally attitude to pull her down. She hadn't been able asleep after the charlatan's call and spent the night taking the sleeves out of the blue taffeta and putting them back in. It was the wrong thing to do with material that shows every stitch mark.

"I guess you ain't gonna tell me about it." Paulie sighed. He had waited until three and then went looking for her.

"Me and Willy tried a experiment." She pulled her shoulders back. They ached from straining over the sewing machine. "It didn't work."

"'Bout Minna?"

"Course."

"We never did try the police."

"You just don't give up, do you?" The dark circles under her eyes scared him.

Fifty-Three

"Crystal Lace," Minna said for the second time to the pastor of the First African Methodist Episcopal Church. He peered at her over the top of his spectacles, the open Bible between them, and raised his eyebrows. She rocked her hips jiggling the baby and said, "Crystal Lace," nodding to put the period on the end of it. That was the third time.

"She sure be beautiful," Cosmo glowed. Everybody laughed. He had been saying it ever since he and Terra adopted the girl.

Minna wore a soft-pink print dress and a peaked hat of black velvet with black lace that fell below her eyes. The preacher's eyes floated like blobs of bewildered brown through his glasses. She expected him to rebuke her for the baby's odd name.

"She goin' have to live with that the whole rest o' her life."

She waited, but he looked down at his Bible and cleared his throat. He hadn't hidden his surprise that the baby wasn't colored, a fact Cosmo had failed to mention. Cosmo had told him the baby was adopted, and that his wife was a white woman, and he hadn't ask for more details. He was pleased to add to his congregation. He was a massive black slab in his preacher's robe, and the baby wriggling before him the color of Saharan sands.

"He's all right." Cosmo nudged Minna. Terra stood on Minna's other side, and they supported her at the elbows. Minna had scoured the secondhand stores looking for fabric to make Crystal's christening dress, and she looked like a miniature angel.

"Most people get baptized at one point or another, don't they, Celeste?" The ceremony was still a few weeks away. They were making supper. "Did you?" Minna asked.

"They didn't take me out in public if they didn't have to." She stared with her good eye at a pot hanging from a rack above the stove. "It's true. They do it either way, as babies or adults."

"What's the difference? They put water on your head, either way, right?"

"Some get dunked. The adults I mean."

"Where do they do that?"

"I guess it can happen most anyplace. A river, a lake, the ocean even. But I know some churches have big tubs where the minister preaches." Minna imagined standing in front of people and going into the water, hair and all, exposing your body. She shuddered.

"That's not what's going to happen to Crystal Lace is it?"

"No, no. I think that's the Baptists, who do it to emulate what John the Baptist did with Jesus."

Minna remembered a photo of Lila as a young girl. She had on a white dress with a pleated bodice, and she wore white stockings and white pumps. Her hair was loose and flowing. Since it was a black-and-white photo, the red hair didn't stand out. Lila cradled long-stemmed white flowers and looked straight into the camera, but she didn't smile.

"What absolute nonsense," Lila said when Minna wanted her to explain the photo.

"But what was it?" Minna insisted. Lila frowned and got one of her buttoned-up looks.

"Was I ever baptized?"

"Now what would that have accomplished? A one-way ticket to heaven?" Minna didn't ask any more questions.

Minna was propped up on the sofa when Cosmo and Terra came to take the baby home following the birth. She sniffed the baby's feathery scalp, like a mother cat licking her kittens.

"Can you believe she likes 'Begin the Beguine'?" Minna boasted. "She perks right up at that. I think you should keep the radio on for her." They gave her their best smiles and promised they would do that.

Cosmo took down a closet door and created a makeshift alcove with a cot for Minna who often dropped by after work. She liked making baby clothes on Terra's sewing machine, and she discovered she had a knack for pacifying the baby.

"It's easy. Like learning to sew a straight seam. It just takes a little practice and effort." She recognized before Terra when the baby's tummy was in distress and how to relieve it, putting her over her shoulder. "Look, Terra. You just need to keep pressure on her stomach, right here." She pointed to the spot.

"How do you know so much about this?" Terra was learning a lot from the new mother.

"It's just common sense. You'll get it," she assured Terra, sounding like she'd had years of practice. She thought Lila must have done that for her if she had been colicky. "You don't have to worry about her so much. She's tough. Just look at her." Minna smiled, looking over the ruffles and the patchwork quilt Terra had made. "Besides, who knows what Celeste's been brewing." They laughed about the benevolent little woman who continued to ease their lives with her concoctions.

"Then I'd better get some." Terra doted, and fussed, and worried over each whimper and jerk. If the baby slept longer than she thought she should, or woke up minutes before she expected, Minna volunteered to stay with Crystal so Terra could run errands and take a break, but when Terra was away, she fretted about and hurried to get back home.

"You ain't give that baby girl 'nough air, way you hover over her." Cosmo, teasing, pulled Terra out the door to get some alone time with her. "Don't you go mindin' us none," he told Minna. "We goin' get it figured out soon 'nough."

Terra long before had given up hope of having a child. Before they met, both she and Cosmo had resigned themselves to the single life. Available men her age had joined up three years earlier. Then, in one fortuitous stroke, she and Cosmo found mates and gained a baby in the process. Life, with its ruthless and merciful whims of giving, withholding, and taking away, had blessed them. They were as rich as the residents up on Queen Anne Hill and stumbled around in a daze at their good fortune. They started to believe they could trust it was real and that it would last.

"When you come down from the clouds," Celeste noted, "you'll be fine. It's that it's all new and full of surprises." Terra confessed she might not pass the test as a mother, although Minna and Cosmo and Terra had arrived at a suitable and remarkable arrangement. Crystal was to grow up knowing her birth mother.

"She got two mamas fussing over her," Cosmo bragged, and she was a happy child, right from the start.

"Was this your doing?" Minna questioned Celeste.

"No, no. This was not up to me. If it had been, you can be sure I would have seen to it. No, this is what the gods ordered for you."

The baby was teething when Terra got it fixed in her mind that Crystal should be baptized. Cosmo was willing. He knew that Divine would be pleased. Crystal was gumming Minna's finger, and Minna wadded up a damp cloth adding a tincture of cloves for her to chew on. "I've never been to a baptism," Minna revealed when they asked her to stand up for the baby.

"Nothin' to it," Cosmo assured her, beaming. "They jus' put

that water on her head, and you stand there and hold her. And you try to keep her quiet while they do that."

"That's it?"

"Well, not quite it," Terra gave him a skeptical glance. "Do you know what a godmother does?"

"No. I don't know." She felt embarrassed.

"It's a serious and solemn commitment to be the moral guide for the baby, and see she grows up with love and discipline and in a Christian environment."

"What does that mean, Terra?" It was going to be a lot more difficult than holding Crystal and keeping her quiet.

"Capricious," Celeste disclosed to Minna weeks before the baptism. Her eye had taken to misbehaving again. "Something's going on up there." She pointed to the heavens. "They're moving the furniture around. Spring cleaning."

Minna felt it, too. Crystal was doing something new every day. In the beginning, she'd slept and cried. Then she started smiling. After that she was babbling and giggling. Then, with just a fraction of help, Crystal was sitting up.

Minna noticed the changes at the shipyard, too. There was a hopeful hush. The workers had outperformed quotas for many months and were proud, but the war was not won. There were recent rumors, though, that it might be winding down. The latest reports were optimistic.

"The air is swimming in particles," Celeste confided to Minna. "Nearly knocking me over. Don't mind me." She hobbled back to the kitchen to brew a new tea.

The baby was seven months old and soon to be baptized. Minna was flooded with ideas. On her work breaks, she drew sketches for christening gowns, and baby-girl dresses and jackets and bonnets. The lunchroom hummed with its own undercurrent of excitement, and the whispers of a military peace. It wasn't spoken out loud for fear it would be jinxed.

Minna brought treats for Mary Evans, who shared them with Phyllis. Mary had not once asked about Crystal. Minna had returned to work a week after the birth, and it was as if it had not occurred.

People were distracted. Minna watched as women who worked at the shipyards got off a stop early, realized their error, and came after the bus yelling. A manager filed a report in a trash can and blamed Minna when it wasn't where it should be. It was unmistakable. The war was winding down.

Mary and Phyllis moved about in shadows. They lurked like spies with an important secret.

Minna cut up a satin wedding gown for the christening dress. She'd found it at that pawnshop where the door squawked near the five-and-dime she'd been in the day she and Cosmo got separated.

"What do you think, Celeste? Would it be wrong to use this?" Celeste was at her elbow.

"It's a fine choice." It was the only quality satin she had come across in her searches. "Just because someone has sold it doesn't mean it's full of sorrow and pain. That's what you're thinking, aren't you?"

Minna nodded. "I don't want to make a bad choice for Crystal."

"No, dear, you're not. The woman who gave this up has a generous spirit that doesn't need to hold on to old memories for fear there will be nothing to replace them. She already has more than enough."

Minna couldn't imagine how Celeste knew such things. She whisked it off the hanger and haggled with the owner. Boppy stood right behind her tsk-tsking. Being with Celeste made her as happy as if she was with Boppy, but she'd never been able to keep up with Boppy's legs or his enthusiasm. She slowed her pace to match Celeste's gimpy leg, but Celeste was keen and forged ahead and did not let on about the throbbing pain.

People stared as they passed them. They didn't attempt to hide their astonishment at the dwarf with the sagging face and auspicious eye. Considerate people pretended not to be taken aback but then could not resist the pull to give a quick gander. It was a challenge to take in all the disparate parts of Celeste in one swoop. They scrutinized Minna, too, this lovely young woman being friendly with this strange creature.

The people in a hurry didn't pay attention. A young woman dressed like a model in a fashion show stared outright and made no attempt to look the other way. When she was even with them, she said out loud, "Good lord. What next?"

Minna was about to dress her down. "You don't know her, or you wouldn't be this way."

Celeste interceded. "Just look at how the sun makes that purple glass glow." She put her hand on Minna's forearm and pointed to a display in a storefront window. Minna ached to put a protective arm around Celeste to mitigate the harshness. She looked at the glass but could not see the nature in it that Celeste wanted her to see.

Both Minna and Crystal fidgeted at the altar. Minna imagined being a delicate fairy floating above her daughter to help when she was called on. She would wave her wand and take away all the girl's hurts. She promised Crystal, whispering it to her once the minister put the water on her head and she was pronounced, "Crystal Lace," in the First African Methodist Episcopal Church.

"Lovely. Just lovely," Celeste murmured behind them. Divine sat in another pew and said, "Amen. Amen," and wiped away her tears with a dainty white handkerchief. If Minna turned to peek, she thought she would see Lila, Aunt Iris, Uncle Willy and Uncle Paulie in the same pew, smiling. Even Fischer would be there, grinning alongside Bopppy.

Afterward, they went back to Cosmo and Terra's cottage to celebrate.

Fifty-Four

The sun was clambering up the summit of the Cascades on the Tuesday morning President Truman's voice broke over the airwaves from KIRO radio in Seattle. It was going to be a gorgeous day.

"This is a solemn but a glorious hour," he drawled, his nasal twang affirming his Missouri roots, announcing the Allied Victory in Europe, which had happened the day before on May 7. "I only wish that Franklin D. Roosevelt had lived to witness this day." He paused in honor of the former president who had died from a cerebral hemorrhage a month earlier.

"General Eisenhower," he continued, "informs me that the forces of Germany have surrendered to the United Nations. The flags of freedom fly over all Europe." The listening audience stood by their radios while he paused.

"At last," Celeste said afterward, sighing as her eye settled down. She and Minna scooted around each other in the kitchen, one of them scrambling eggs while the other steamed the greens. Unofficially, the news had been reported over the AP wires the previous day. Germany had surrendered, but people wanted to hear it from the president's lips. The mood in Seattle on the seventh was both joyful and sober. People went to work as usual. There were no celebrations in the streets, and the city police made a third fewer arrests than normal for an average Seattle night.

"We're at least halfway there, then," Celeste agreed when the president reminded everyone it was not yet over and to remain determined until the last battle was won.

"Until that day," he directed, "let no man abandon his post or slacken his efforts."

Later in the day, Mayor Devin cautioned the city. "This is not the appropriate time to celebrate. Men are still dying. This is not the time to make revelry. Ships and planes still are needed. This is the time humbly and reverently to give thanks to God for the victory which is ours, and to renew our hope and trust, and to work harder than ever before."

At the shipyard, the workers dug in. Cosmo said, "We pullin' out all the stops now."

"Yeah," Minna agreed. "Even Mary smiled when the orders came in today."

She hadn't answered John Welles's letter. He was the only soldier she knew, the one who had asked her to write him. Some of the girls at the shipyard had stopped writing to their fellows after meeting guys at the USO club, although they had made promises to be faithful to the end. That didn't have anything to do with her and John Welles. Still, when the war ended, if he made it back and he came looking for her, he would find out the truth.

She had let him down. She'd ignored his letter in case he got his hopes up. She would have had to tell him about the baby, and she didn't have the courage to do that after he'd helped her get started. He'd looked at her with his soft brown eyes in such a sweet way when he asked her to write. He wasn't tough enough to survive the fighting, and that made her feel even worse, for she might have brightened a few of his last minutes if she had answered him.

Did Archie ever get his plane? He might have been among the twenty-four thousand planes over Normandy when Crystal was born. He'd bragged about doing loop-de-loops over Germany, like it was a game he couldn't wait to play. John Welles wouldn't get through, but Archie was sure to find his way back, probably without a scratch. He'd strut and find more girls to entertain with heroic war stories.

She'd listened to the snippets of phrases from the women in the lunchroom who had sons overseas and got an occasional letter that didn't tell them much. They'd guess to fill the void of not knowing. Wherever the fighting was fiercest, they prayed their boys were not there. Some of the war wives carried lucky charms in the pockets of their overalls and gently held them while they ate their sandwiches or when one of them got a telegram.

People could nearly smell coffee brewing and began to envision thick chunks of juicy beef, followed by sugary desserts—the ones like the missus served after Sunday dinners before the war.

They were coming to the end. The final assault was near, and victory would taste as sweet as the sugar they craved. Welders, electricians, the riveters, and the janitors dug in to muscle it through. When Japan was defeated—and they held their breath that it wouldn't be very much longer—they would celebrate whether the mayor closed the taverns or not!

Mary walked past Minna's desk, dropped a package on it and kept on walking. She said, addressing the wall ahead of her, "Here's a toy for the baby."

It was wrapped with used string and no tape. Everyone did that, hoarded pieces of string, and then used and reused them until they finally snapped from one too many uses. Rosie the Riveter's muscle bulged off the oversized calendar from the wall opposite Minna who checked to see if she'd missed an important date. Not that Mary celebrated occasions. She had not offered even a whisper of curiosity or congratulations when Minna returned after Crystal Lace was born.

Minna blamed herself; Mary had carried the brunt of the workload during a critical time. Minna didn't speak of the baby. Mary had ignored Minna's pregnancy, even when Minna was rushing out of the office like clockwork to get to the bathroom.

The gift was confounding. It didn't seem connected to anything. Mary hadn't asked who was taking care of the baby, or how Minna managed now that she was a mother. She hadn't even asked what the girl's name was, although she seemed to know it was a girl. There was a positive side to Mary's detachment. It eliminated having to answer questions Mary could be asking.

"Here, let me show you a little shortcut," Mary said after the VE announcement. Minna could have choked on her own saliva. Mary held onto the minutest bits of knowledge that could simplify the process, portioning it like it was rationed meat.

"I suppose your husband will be coming back, then," Mary said after President Truman reminded the nation to hold firm till the end. "Where's he stationed, by the way?" She hadn't asked after Minna's husband all the while they had faced each other across their desks in the puke-green closet. Minna hadn't been required to guard her personal information without creating offense.

"You know they aren't allowed to tell us much." The old fear of losing her job came up again.

"Well, I guess it all will become clear before very long." Even with the help of Celeste's teas, Mary could sting her. If Mary threw out a barb, she probably wasn't drinking it, Minna suspected, especially when she and Phyllis disappeared for extended minutes to get sodas.

Mary's supervisor, Mr. Bieber, had kept Minna under observation because of a report she put together. Mary handed it to Mr. Bieber telling him Minna was responsible. Mary hadn't wanted her name attached to it as it seemed overly complicated and time-consuming. Mr. Bieber recognized its value and recently had begun assigning some of

Mary's work to Minna. It was awkward for Minna who liked the supervisor, but feared Mary would take it out on her. Mary did not suffer slights well.

"I've been watching your work," he said in front of Mary. "You have a knack for this." Minna peeked at Mary and felt squeezed from both sides, but Mary didn't appear at all perturbed. She was even smiling! That was Mary. When you thought she was going to behave one way, she acted the opposite. She was a perpetual mystery.

Crystal turned one year old, and the country was celebrating one victory. Celeste decided to make a special event. "For the parents," she said, adding, "I think I'm a parent, too."

"You certainly are," Terra, the blooming new mother, agreed. Celeste had engineered the trepidation right out of Terra. It didn't matter to any of them what mystifying brews that involved.

"Stage right," Celeste told her, "that's all it is. Plugging up your nurturing qualities." There were also the earaches and fevers and teething. Not to mention that Terra carried around the insupportable notion that in order to raise a loving child, she needed to be an ideal parent.

"We won't make too much fuss over Crystal," Celeste pronounced. "She is the crowning achievement, of course. Without her, we wouldn't be together," and then appeared to forget all about a party. They were baffled but embarrassed to ask if she'd changed her mind.

She was dilly-dallying. Her eye was going awry, and she was limping more. The others decided, without asking, that in her gigantic heart, generous as she was, Celeste was no longer capable of such an undertaking. They did not want to hurt her feelings so Terra baked Crystal's first cake, Minna sewed a dress for her, and Cosmo built a wooden rocking horse that Crystal would be big enough to play on in two years.

They had a quiet party, just the three of them with Crystal Lace. It had rained all that day, and the ground was soggy, so Cosmo kept the rocking horse in the living room.

"Guess I'm bein' premature." He chuckled sadly when he gave it to Crystal and she wasn't interested. He put her on it and held her in place and gently rocked the horse. Crystal pushed him away and slid off it. She'd started walking at nine months, which convinced her parents and Minna of her genius.

When they put her in her crib, the three peeked over the railing like the three wise men. Then, they sat around the tiny living room and toyed with the cake on their plates. Cosmo balanced his plate on the horse's back and attempted a bite. No one had an appetite for cake. Terra had written the numeral "1" in green frosting across the white icing. The dress Minna made was soft and pink. Without Celeste, it felt like they were cheating.

"Don't feel right," Cosmo grumbled. Terra and Minna nodded.

Fifty-Five

"One becomes two," Celeste mumbled. Minna was washing up dishes. The sun hung in the sky late these days. The window over the sink was open, letting in a soft, perfumed breeze.

"I'm sorry," Minna said. "I must have been daydreaming." Celeste was making less and less sense. Either that, or she was measuring proportions for her herbs. It was disconcerting. Celeste was the model of clarity. She had her peculiarities, but they had all but evaporated in Minna's eyes as time went on.

"One becomes two. Two becomes three, and out of the third comes the one as the fourth." Minna couldn't believe what she heard. She had her back to her, but Celeste spoke like no one else was in the room. Minna held her breath until she thought she would explode. Celeste repeated the garble, and Minna said it to herself for recall until she could write it down. She'd report to Cosmo and Terra and ask what they should do to help Celeste.

Celeste spoke again, apparently aware all along that Minna was present. "It is of the utmost importance that we have the celebration on Midsummer's Eve."

"What?" Minna dropped a plate into the dishwater, and the water splashed into her face. The plate didn't break, and to cover her surprise Minna said, "I'm sorry. I think I must have been daydreaming. What did you say?"

"No need, my dear, to be embarrassed about me."

Minna blushed. "You said something I didn't understand," Minna confessed. "Were you talking to me?"

"No, no, dear. I was reciting the axiom of Maria. You probably don't know what that is"—she waved her hand, dismissing the remark—"and it's not necessary that you should, but when I remembered it just now, I knew why I've been dragging my feet about Crystal's birthday."

"Oh," Minna gasped. "We thought you'd forgotten about it."

"Forgotten about it? Not at all. Poor dears, you must have thought me off my rocker."

"Well, kind of. We were worried."

"It's always best to say something if you are, Minna. Don't let unnecessary questions hang like dreary clouds." She laughed. "We have enough of them in Seattle already to make us more than melancholy."

"We didn't want to embarrass or worry you."

"Embarrass me? Worry me? Far from it, my dear. If you had asked, I would have told you that I was in a muddle about Crystal's birthday."

"We thought you had changed your mind about that. That you regretted saying you'd make a party because it would be too much work. Either that or it had slipped your mind. We didn't want to upset you."

"But you were worried, I see. Of course you were, but I can promise you that I still have at least half my faculties, if that relieves you any, but I doubt you are quite convinced yet."

"What are you doing, then?" Minna now was curious. "What was that you said a bit ago, about one becomes two?"

"Ah yes. Well, let's just say that comes from a lifetime's work. But now that you mention it, you can all help me prepare for our Midsummer Eve's celebration." She stood next to Minna and drew a picture. "This is a maypole. Do you know it?" Minna shook her head.

"No? Well, never mind about that. Now Cosmo can get the material and put it together, like this." She didn't doubt that he could manufacture what she needed. She drew a straight vertical line for the pole and wrote ten feet next to it. Then she drew a horizontal line, for a cross arm, one third from the top, and from each end of that, she hung a circle. Then she made a triangle by attaching the ends of the pole pieces. "Those rings are wreaths," she tapped the paper with the pencil.

"I have a much bigger yard than Terra and Cosmo. He can dig a hole out back for the pole. But before he buries it, you and Terra will decorate it with greens and flowers. Every inch of it should be covered. You can get the peonies and daisies from Terra's yard. Use my sweet peas and spiraea. Make sure there are lots of greens." The spittle flew out with her words, and Minna felt the excitement in her stomach.

"Oh, and tell Cosmo he will need to get enough wood to build a bonfire. Well, not a huge fire. Don't want the firemen knocking down the door. Just a small bonfire." She giggled.

Minna watched Celeste write a list on another piece of paper, not the one she would take to Cosmo with the precise instructions that he would follow to the letter.

"Rosemary, lemon verbena, St. John's wort, foxglove, and

elder," Celeste scribbled. While writing, she spoke aloud, but not to

Minna.

Spirits were jovial at the shipyard. The latest output had beaten every previous outstanding record. In the early days of the war, someone in management put together a contest to boost morale and to help meet quotas. The rivalry between departments grew fierce after it caught on, but mostly it was convivial, although there were weeks when the competitors grew bad tempered, especially if someone in one of the groups received a telegram from the War Department. That was worse than shutting down an engine.

With the war in Germany over and the workers egged on for a final victory, effort was at an all-time high. Since VE Day, the teasing and the flirting was more overt. Sometimes it could be crass. The women welders adored Cosmo. They'd worked next to him for nearly two years, and he charmed them with his jokes and his unexpected assistance when they needed help. A few of the women, too long without men in their personal lives, indicated they would like to take him home.

"Hey, Cosmo. How'd you like to try my victory stew this Saturday night?" one queried and wiggled her backside at him. "You'd eat it up."

"Oh, forget her stew," another remarked and winked. "I'll put sugar in your hot chocolate and sweeten you up."

"That sure is a tempting offer." He'd smile politely and tell them again, as he had to do every Friday afternoon, that he already was taken by a beautiful wife and an even prettier baby girl "by the name of Crystal. Crystal," he'd repeat.

"Can't you forget them for even one single night?" glamorous, redheaded Lois coaxed.

They were intoxicated about winning the war in Europe. They walked the corridors with heads held high because, they crowed, "We put them Jerries in their place." They waited for news about the ships they had a part in building, and if one had success, they hollered and hooted, convinced it was because of their outstanding work. They were pulling together, putting out the maximum effort to see the rest of the fighting finished with Japan.

"Look at that, will you?" Mary shoved a letter of commendation from the Department of the Navy under Minna's nose. But she pulled it back before Minna could touch it and held it at arm's length for her to read. Not wanting the edges to be damaged, she briskly whisked it away. It had that official look to it, embossed with gold lettering.

"When's that husband of yours coming home again?" Mary

pressed the next day. She'd put the official letter in a black picture frame and was looking for the most visible place to hang it behind her desk.

"Soon enough, I expect," Minna tossed back. "Any day now." She wondered how she would explain, if Mary kept asking, that he was never coming back since he didn't exist. And why the sudden interest in a husband?

Fifty-Six

Midsummer's Eve arrived on Friday. The weekend before, Cosmo dug the hole for the pole in Celeste's good-size backyard. Two days earlier, they'd had a downpour, and the loamy dirt smelled of rich humus. Celeste had told him exactly where she wanted him to dig.

"Yes. Exactly," she said. "Abundant"—she spoke of the soil—"and fertile." He had dug down four feet.

"Now listen, Celeste." Sweat was dripping off his forehead. "I don't want it to topple over and be knockin' someone silly."

"You digging to China?" She ignored his consternation. The size of the pole seemed ridiculous to him.

"Why, dear Lord, does it have to be so tall?" he asked. "How much that green stuff you puttin' on it, anyways?" Terra and Minna had accumulated a sizable pile of sturdy flowers and greens, and Cosmo feared the pole would fall under the weight. He noted to everyone, although it didn't appear that they were listening, "Seem I be the only one worried about this pole."

Minna and Terra sat on the damp grass several feet away from Cosmo, choosing the vines for the first wrapping. The stems needed to be pliant but dense to conceal the naked pole and hold the stems of the flowers they would add afterward.

"Let's attach the peonies after the greens," Terra said. The heavier blossoms would need to be near the bottom. They'd collected a pile of greenery three feet high and heaped it near the reclining pole, and they'd knocked on people's doors, asking to snip some of their creepers.

"Nobody goin' turn down two beautiful ladies," Cosmo said when they returned with their arms loaded. The weather was moist, and the collection would not dry out before they festooned Cosmo's creation.

"Too deep, Cosmo," Celeste quibbled about the hole, worried that a good portion would be wasted below ground. When the time came to celebrate, *he* wouldn't fit under it.

"Don't you go fussin', little lady," he told her. "I account for the part that's in the hole. It'll be tall jus' like you want."

Cosmo had used Herculean effort to get the unwieldy pole to Celeste's, and not one of them thought to ask how he'd done it. Celeste expected him to do as she wanted and didn't ask how he would manage it. He didn't offer up that he scrounged the scrap wood from a demolished building site. She knew he had his way of getting things accomplished.

"What that little woman up to?" he had asked when Minna brought the dimensions and directions for the pole and the bonfire pit. They saw her hands busy, her mind weighing and discarding ideas, and her gimpy leg trotting along trying to keep up with the rest of her. Cosmo shook his head in wonder and followed her lead.

"It's not big enough," Celeste nagged after he had dug the fire pit.

"Now you listen"—Cosmo shook a finger at her—"I don't know what you need that big fire for anyways, but seein' as we live in the city, Celeste, we got neighbors here who don' want they houses goin' up in flames jus' so's you can have your party."

"There's not going to be a tragedy," she argued. "For goodness sake, Cosmo, let's not be overly dramatic." She bustled around her workroom, talking to herself or to her herbs, tying them together in bunches. "Rosemary here…and where have you been keeping yourself?" she chided the St. John's wort as though it had been in hiding during roll call.

By Saturday morning, everyone was talking to either themselves or each other. Cosmo was outside Celeste's back door, speaking to the hole he was digging. Terra and Minna were two robins gabbling, and Crystal was playing in their pile of greenery. They would wait until the following Friday to add the flowers. On Thursday evening, they twisted and wrapped and tied vines to make long garlands around the pole. Their fingers turned green, and their hands were cold. They didn't stop until they met Celeste's satisfaction and had covered every inch of the pole. It was nearly midnight before they were satisfied.

"Whatever happened to your hands?" Mary sniffed and

wrinkled her nose on Friday morning. "They're green!" she informed Minna as she handed her some paper work.

"We were decorating for a Midsummer's Eve party we're having for Crystal," Minna told her.

"Who's Crystal?"

"My daughter." Minna nearly choked.

"Your husband going to be there for that?"

Here we go again. Why this preoccupation about a husband, shoving it in her face each chance she got? "I doubt it. We still don't know when he's coming back."

"What kind of a party is that? Midsummer's Eve?" Minna didn't know herself, to tell the truth. It all had been Celeste's idea. None of them knew much beyond that. The way Celeste raced around and talked to herself and everyone else in rapid-fire commands, coming and going in jerks and starts, she certainly had some specific notion of what should happen. Like she always did. Minna didn't mention to Mary about the preparations, the pole, or the bonfire pit, or about Celeste, who had been in her workroom tying bunches of herbs together.

"It's just that summer is starting, and it's Crystal's first birthday. We're going to celebrate them at the same time."

"Lye soap." Mary sniffed at her fingers. "For those green stains. They've got plenty of bars of that down in the welders' bathroom. Ugh." She started back to her desk but then turned. "Oh, by the way. I almost forgot"—she tapped her forehead and chuckled—"Mr. Bieber wants you to come by his office before you leave today."

"Did he say what he wanted?"

"Well, don't ask me. I don't have my *crystal* ball with me at this exact minute." She cackled.

"Meanie," Minna whispered under her breath. She said the same thing out loud after work when she was leaving the supervisor's office. He hadn't asked to see her.

"What was Mary thinking?" he wondered, as if Minna knew. "I told Mary to pass on a compliment to you, that's all. You did a darned good job on the orders this week. It goes a long way in helping us as we wind things up."

"But, since you're here, I'll say it again. You've been doing a great job. I think you're going to find there will be work here once this goddamn war is finally licked." Minna didn't mind his swearing at all. In fact, she liked that he was so direct with her. He was near Fischer's age and was a kind man, and she liked working with him. There was never guessing with him about what he wanted, not like with Mary, when you had to play her game but didn't know which game she was using. He liked his projects expedited with precision, and he appreciated Minna's logical and efficient approach.

"When the soldiers come back after that fighting's over, they'll get first crack at all the jobs here." Her first thought was for Cosmo. But knowing Cosmo, she figured he'd land on his feet somewhere.

"Mostly it'll be the women," he continued. "Husbands will want 'em back home 'cause they think that's where they belong. And because the men will need the work and will be banging the doors down looking for jobs. He poked his thumb to his chest. "I myself am damn impressed with those women down there in the yard doing all that heavy construction. Not an easy job, that's for sure. I'd keep 'em all on if I could. But how many ships we gonna be building once it's all over in the Pacific?"

"I guess you're right," she told him not knowing what else to say. The women building the ships, some of them rode her bus every day. The one with pepper-streaked hair wore a navy-blue trench coat, buttoned to the neck, even during the hottest months. It went down to her ankles, which were red and swollen. She shuffled like a clown from the bus stop to the shipyard in oversize boots, always the last to reach the building. What would she do? The sassy blonde teased the bus driver when she boarded. She pulled her skirt up three inches above her knees to give him a good view. If she wasn't in the queue when he pulled up to their stop, he waited for her. She knew he would. She'd make him wait, too, keeping the bus idling like a purring cat until he could wait no longer. Then she'd dash out of the building. She had it timed to the second. Her bright-yellow, unbuttoned coat flew behind her. As soon as he saw her coming, he'd put the bus in gear and crank open the door.

After she found a seat, she turned to seek out and flirt with Cosmo, who had his pick of women at the yard if he was of a mind. She stared until he was forced to acknowledge her, and he was polite. She was loud so she could be heard over the engine. She'd say something, laugh, and turn around to see if the bus driver was watching in his rearview mirror. Of course, she knew he would be. When she saw he was, she'd turn around again and make a joke, and Cosmo smiled politely, but his shoulders released after she got off.

What would happen to the women who lost their jobs? The blonde could find a husband anytime, someone to support her. But what about the trench coat? Was she married? Had she ever been married? Did she have a family to go home to? Could she be happy making meals, raising the kids? How many of the women were widows by now and needed the income to raise their children?

Minna barely caught the last bus because of Mary's deception. Mr. Bieber had been kind, but she grew anxious the longer he talked. He'd invited her to sit down, and then she got the picture. He needed someone to talk to. He was lonely. That's why Mary steered her into his office—so she wouldn't have to stay and listen to him.

Minna wondered if he was married and had children. There were no photos on his desk. Quotas for the week had been met, inventory was ordered, and he wanted to talk.

Minna smiled and nodded at the appropriate pauses and wondered how to release herself from his monologue. Terra at this moment was beginning to arrange the flowers. Minna's fingers turned in her lap as if she was twisting peony stems and late blooming azaleas into the garlands.

She jumped up suddenly. "My bus! Look at the time!" She pointed to the industrial clock on the sickly green wall. "I'll miss the last one if I don't go now." She shook his hand before he understood she had to leave.

"Oh," he said. "I didn't watch the time. I'm glad you stopped by." He was still in his postwar reverie as she scooted out the door.

A different bus driver picked up the last group of Friday evening stragglers. Minna ran out of the building just as he was about to pull away. Unlike the other blonde, she had to scream and wave for him to wait. He hesitated but then opened the door. Then he took off so fast that she fell backward and would have fallen in his lap if it hadn't been for Cosmo.

"Hey, I been lookin' for you." Cosmo had jumped on board right behind her. He had watched three buses come and go, and there still was no sign of her. He sat on their bench outside the building. Then he went back inside and climbed the long flights of metal stairs to her office, but the lights were off. She hadn't seen him waiting outside the building.

"I think Mr. Bieber is lonely," she whispered to him. "Does he have any family at all?" He shrugged. Now that she was safely on the way home, she felt sorry for him. He had apologized for keeping her as she flew out the door.

"Oh no." Cosmo frowned as if he had failed her again. "He behave himself?" He squinted down at her.

"It's nothing like that, Cosmo. Don't worry. He just needed to talk is all. He wanted to be listened to." She planted herself in a seat near the middle of the bus although there was plenty of room at the front. She didn't think she was going to like this bus driver and hoped he wouldn't be on her regular shift.

"Well, they is not payin' you to listen to his talk." Cosmo poked her, relieved he had found her. "Unless it be 'bout work."

He headed to the back where he could see Minna. The bus was half-empty, and he caught the driver studying Minna in his mirror. The sun stood high overhead, refusing to give up its place in the sky, making its full claim for its day. It was going to be a lovely evening, like the early summer days in Montana when the air was so sweet she could taste it on her tongue.

The bus lurched and stammered from one stop to the next. The driver couldn't get the gears to shift smoothly until he was halfway into the sprint before the next stop. They passed familiar landmarks and bounteous maples. She couldn't wait to start decorating. She peeked at Cosmo, who was watching her and the bus driver.

They had thrown themselves into Celeste's projects. They were like excited children at Christmas. They followed Celeste's directions to the letter and suspended their need to know what was in store. Cosmo argued with her about the size of the pole, and the hole, and the bonfire pit, and she and Terra laughed at their good-humored imbroglios.

Minna wished she could tuck a nectar-tinted rose behind Aunt Iris's ear. She put one in Terra's instead and hugged Crystal.

"I is still not certain about that bonfire of Celeste," he said on the walk from the bus stop. "And, lord knows if that maypole stay up." He had been bossy with Celeste, and despite his truculence, remained calm. Terra was full of joyful optimism, and Crystal glowed with the light that sparkles with blue lace agates.

Fifty-Seven

"You go ahead, Cosmo. Get that fire started now. We won't wait for Divine to get here." The maypole towered over the yard like the disrobed mast of a square rigger. It sprouted lavish blossoms, with the wreaths dangling lifesavers at its two ends. Late-evening shadows elongated the upraised post and magnified the dark circles upon the grass.

"Divine won't be long," Celeste promised. "She had to see to something first, she said. Or somebody. That sister of yours, Cosmo, thinks of everyone but herself."

"Yes, I know that for a fact, Celeste." He leaned over to ignite the pile of kindling.

"Oh, but what am I thinking? Goodness me. We didn't make a toast yet," Celeste backtracked.

"All right then." Cosmo grinned and stood up from the pit. Celeste had greeted them at the front door from work.

"There you are," she shouted, bounding out the door. "At last." She handed them beakers with her special wine. "Time is marching on," she reminded them. She had decorated each of the doorframes with hanging bunches of herbs. The whole house was permeated with peculiar scents.

"Now make up you mind," he bantered. "Is I suppos'd drink wine or make you fire?" He could have sworn he saw a ten-year-old girl hiding in that defective body, at once impish and animated, who couldn't decide what she wanted first.

While Minna squirmed in Mr. Bieber's office, Terra was adding the final round of flowers. They each took one of Crystal's hands and walked to the pole. Then they circled round it. Crystal stretched her head back to see the flowers float above them. "Ring around the rosie," they sang to her, and she giggled when they dropped to the ground at "all fall down." Crystal stood up immediately and squealed with delight. "Again." The moist twilight air was saturated with the perfume of roses and sweet peas.

"Cosmo." Celeste's tone was serious. He expected her to complain one last time about the size of the bonfire and didn't look at her.

"This is an auspicious night, and we must adhere to the protocol required for Midsummer's Eve."

"What in the world does you mean?" The years had evaporated from her face. She was an eager maiden in the golden evening light. He wondered if Celeste had ever held wide-eyed, romantic notions or fallen in love. He hoped so.

"I think we here to have a birthday party for Crystal, who turns one year old. Ain't that so?"

"Of course that's so. You must not have noticed the desirable cake I spent half the afternoon baking. But Cosmo, my dear, let us not forget tonight is also Midsummer's Eve."

"That why we gots that giant pole stickin' up so's all the neighbors get to see we be nuts. Ain't that right?"

"Tonight," she said, ignoring his exaggeration, "is to acknowledge the mysteries of the universe. It's a powerful moment when the sun reminds us who is in charge. We are—I wanted to say 'silly,' but that's not the right word—we believe we control our destiny and pay no heed to the sun's rhythm and potency. How many people will observe what is happening in the heavens tonight, this special night?"

"Jus' us, I guess."

"I believe you are right. But that's not true in other parts of the world. Did you know that?"

"My mama knowed 'bout the stars and they business."

"Did you think she was crazy?"

"No. I jus' figure she was doin' black magic."

"Well, I trust there is magic to be had tonight. We'll listen and watch and suspend ordinary belief and see what happens."

"Oh. You mean then that this more than Crystal havin' her birthday party, and I should be watchin' for the other stuff. You ole witchcraft, or ain't it that voodoo? Good thing I don't sneak a piece of cake when I come here. Prob'ly gets the evil eye if I does it." He poked her.

"You watch yourself, Cosmo. There is a time and place, this evening, for all things. Surprising things happen that come as no surprise on Midsummer's Eve."

"I don't get what you mean at all." Cosmo looked at her but with a smile.

She chuckled at his goading and winked with her good eye.

"Let's take care of business and see what happens. The rest will get done by itself."

Everyone had dressed in white as Celeste requested. "Just humor me, will you? It's only one night in the whole year."

"I don't have a white dress." Terra smiled, thinking of her violet two-piece wedding suit.

"Don't worry about that." Minna jumped in. "I'll make the gowns. But what do you want them to look like, Celeste?"

"They just need to be white," Celeste told her, "and it would be lovely if they were flowing." She looked in the distance as if the scene stood before her.

Celeste looked like a Renaissance woman, in spite of her height. The gown Minna designed made the gnome appear two inches taller. Celeste acted taller in it, and was certain she could now see above Cosmo's belly button. The gowns had pleated bodices that revealed ample bosom. The bright ribbons fluttering off the sleeves entertained baby Crystal who ran her fingers through them. Since Minna and Terra had small waists, Minna added darts to follow their curves and belted the material with chords. The skirts were full, to the floor, and fluid.

Minna's shirt for Cosmo opened halfway to his waist. Terra sucked in her breath. "You look like a Greek god."

"A dark one, that's for sure, and you *is* the goddess." He laughed, pointing to the garland of daisies and ribbons on the crown of her head. Even before Celeste's party had gotten underway, a dreamy spell had fallen over them.

"Now you stand back," Cosmo warned Terra and Crystal who moved a safe distance when he lit a stick to the tinder. Terra squeezed Crystal's hand, afraid the girl would dash toward the curious fire because Papa Cosmo was there. "Fire," Crystal repeated after Terra. "Fire, fire."

Minna rested on the grass, leaning on her elbow, watching the fire come to life. The flames made her drowsy. Celeste's planning, and all their preparations had brought them together in a happy way. She still didn't understand, her feet warming near the fire, why Celeste put so much emphasis on a single day.

The air was cool, not chilly, and Minna felt warm near the pungent fire. Crystal looked adorable in her white dress and the flowers in her hair, and kept asking why when Terra explained why she should not pull them out. Celeste and Cosmo had fussed about the pole and the bonfire, which, if Celeste had her way, he was certain would brighten downtown Seattle. The sachets, the white dresses, and the garlands all seemed right and purposeful, although Minna didn't know why.

"Looky, looky, Miwah," Crystal yelled to her when the sprouts of flames leaped over the rocks Cosmo used to enclose the pit. Terra and Crystal clapped their hands and giggled.

"You be careful, you hear?" Cosmo warned, still concerned about the will of the fire. He grew friendlier and more relaxed once he saw he had done enough to contain it. Celeste had been right all along.

Minna beamed at her Cosmo who lived the Golden Rule. His love was boundless, as was his concern, but he never was mundane or banal. Like the flames in his carefully tended fire, he leaped to life with his humor. He had the gift of seeing below the surface of skin or color or personality, and he was truly her brother.

Minna watched Terra mothering Crystal. They had inched closer to the fire, and Terra showed Crystal how to warm one side and then turn around to warm the other side. Cosmo gently reminded her, "Watch out for them skirts. Don't get too close."

Terra was the ideal parent. The best one for the child she had waited for many years to call her own. "Wait for me," Terra called after Crystal, who grew tired of the fire and went off to explore the backyard. Terra stayed watchful in the background and let her daughter search and research her world, one step away if she needed to close in quickly.

"Ain't they jus' beautiful." Cosmo was overcome, close to crying. His Terra was transparent, as gossamer as her skin. She was as beautiful and vulnerable as she was loving and faithful. Crystal was secure and happy.

"I made a good decision," Minna whispered to herself, and to Lila, as the sun edged toward the Pacific.

"Flowah," Crystal attempted. Her vocabulary was growing. She ran to Minna with a pink peony that had fallen from the maypole.

"Yes, it is a flower. That's a peony, Crystal." Minna hugged her and set her free to run back to her parents. "Mama," Crystal shouted, running to Terra with the blossom she had shared with Minna.

Minna leaned back on both elbows, watching the three of them move from the fire to the Maypole. They held Crystal's hands and danced around it, and they sang and laughed. Crystal's giggle filled the dewy night air that was crawling in. As they danced Minna felt life had come full circle. These loved ones before her whirling around were a complete and closed unit of three. Perhaps it was Celeste's wizardry that helped open her eyes. The circle was about things coming together to make something complete, to put things in their rightful place, and to create an end without a seam. She sensed a profound finality, as though she had accomplished what she had needed to do, and she was not astonished. Celeste had prepared her for Midsummer's Eve.

"It's a night to expect the unexpected." She wasn't afraid that she had come to the end, but she was sad and regretted she had not said good-bye to her mother and Aunt Iris—and Fischer. They were a lifetime ago and a world away, yet near as the sweet peas on the verdant pole.

"Ah, here you are," Celeste announced in a foreign squeaky high tone, her manufactured height appearing to have raised her voice. Celeste was the picture of a nature sprite bedecked with her garland and leaning over her in the dim light.

"Yes, here I am," Minna responded, but she felt faraway. She looked up at Celeste, who sounded like a fairy from a distant planet speaking above her.

"Now see who has come to our party," Celeste crowed. Divine was standing just behind Celeste. Minna came to her senses and jumped up to give her a hug.

"Hello, Divine," she said happily, "and happy Midsummer's Eve to you."

Divine laughed. "And to you, too, Minna. My, don't you look jus' special tonight. Midsummer suits you fine. But looks at my bad manners, now. See who I brung with me." She shifted, and there was John Welles right behind her with a huge grin.

"Hello again," he shuffled up to her as if he was coming back with a hardboiled egg and milk. He couldn't be here! He'd died in the war on some bloody field in France like so many others. She was so sure of that she had stopped thinking about him. She hadn't written to him, to protect him if he had any notion about her, yet here he was. He leaned on a gnarled wooden cane.

"These are for you." He limped a few steps to hand her a bouquet of red and white gladiolas.

"Erma Shepherd," she whispered.

"He knows 'bout everything," Divine whispered.

Her mouth was moving—she could feel it working, but no words came out. She felt the tears rushing down her face. He looked at her with those soft eyes. She remembered those brown eyes. That's why she couldn't write to him. It was his eyes!

"She's a beautiful little girl," he said. Crystal was dancing with Cosmo. "Like her mother," he added. She was still silent.

"Maybe I shouldn't have said that?" he asked. He didn't hide his disappointment.

The fairy Celeste, in diaphanous gown, stepped up to them. "Why is everyone standing around? Let's get started with the dancing.

Come on everyone. Get to the maypole!" She looked across the grass toward Cosmo and flashed her widest smile. "Oh, and thank you to Cosmo the Magnificent for tonight's entertainment!"

He howled and pointed a finger. "You is one sneaky little gal, ain't you?"

"I have no idea what you are talking about, Cosmo," she huffed, walking toward him. "Now, we must all join hands, you understand, in a circle," she declared. They gathered under the maypole, following her direction.

The bonfire glowed, and its heat cut most of the evening's chill. It didn't light up Seattle, but its bewitching flames cast shadows about the yard. *And its magic!*

They joined hands. Terra and Cosmo held their daughter's hands between them. Celeste tucked herself between Cosmo and Minna. John Welles dropped his cane, tentatively reaching for Minna's other hand, and Divine moved in to complete the circle.

They were shy, hesitant, and in their uneasiness looked at Crystal's bright face. "Pole," she shouted. "Pole, pole, pole."

"That's right." They laughed and timidly began to move around the pole. John's hand felt warm in Minna's. Divine's swallowed her other hand. They circled the pole four times and then Cosmo started teasing, which got them laughing. Somewhere after that, they weren't moving as individuals. Their rhythms became one single rhythm.

That Midsummer's Eve, they twirled and danced beneath the flowers, under the stars that punched holes into the black sky. They swayed and sang.

Celeste would remind them in later years that it was the most magical of Midsummer's Eves. The night *was* bewitching them. *She be a witch for sure.* Cosmo laughed to himself. Crystal giggled until she was so tired she started to cry, and their songs changed to lullabies. Terra slipped from the circle, wrapped Crystal in a warm blanket, and rocked her to asleep.

They danced and sang until they wore down and simply held on to one another and swayed in place, hands still holding hands. In that quiet night, Celeste began to chant. John Welles leaned across the circle and kissed Celeste just below her errant eye.

"Yes, sweet boy." She smiled from another plane.

Her incantation, at the beginning, was a string of words. Words that didn't fit together. Minna had heard them before and knew Celeste would make it clear. They heard the gnome sing. It was unearthly yet beautiful. She was singing to no one, but to everyone, to Midsummer, to the solar system, to the universe, and to whatever lay beyond.

"To her voodoo friends," Cosmo would say.

She smiled from her distant planet. The pink morning light was just peeking over the Cascades, and it glowed on her face as she chanted, "Join the male and the female, and you will find what is sought."

Minna

Part III

Fifty-Eight

*L*ila was flirting with the man idling at the corner table of the bakery. This was the tenth day in a row—skipping Sunday, the day the store was closed—that he'd come in. He sat with his back to the wall and with a clear view to the door.

When he made his initial purchase after eyeing the pastries, he didn't ask, like most new customers who hemmed and hawed, pointing to one object after another in the case, "What's that one filled with?"

He caught her off guard. He asked smoothly, "What do you recommend to fix a broken heart?" Men questioned her often enough about how to get rid of a hangover or calm an angry stomach. No one had ever asked about a heart.

She felt it right in the middle of her stomach before she even lifted her head to see what he looked like. He seemed pitiful. Men had tried all kinds of starters with her over the years. This one, if that's what he was doing, got a response. Mainly, she avoided making eye contact, particularly with men. Martha had warned her early on that they would clamor to get her attention. "They'll pester the daylights out of you if you let 'em."

She couldn't read this one's face. Was it sad, or was he teasing her? Willy sat at the far end of the counter, tinkering with his midmorning coffee. He performed his daily ritual there at ten o'clock, unless he was stuck in the shop with a broken-down car. He poured the top quarter of his cup of coffee into the saucer, blew on it, and then drank it from the saucer if Lila wasn't watching, or put it back into the cup if she was. He'd cooled it that way since he was a boy and was reluctant to break the habit. She hated it. "Why don't you let it sit for a minute, for goodness' sake, and read your paper?"

"Doesn't taste the same that way, Lila." He heard the stranger and mumbled under his breath, "Find a mechanic to replace the engine."

Lila heard Willy. She knew before he even thought about things, how he would respond. She gave him a vague look. That guy was up to something. Willy felt it in the back of his neck. He fixed cars for guys like him. He had an eye for the kind who would get away without paying.

"Hmm. A slice of sour cherry pie, maybe?" Her lips curved almost to a smile. Willy winced and looked down at his cooling drink when she took the bait.

"Well, that makes perfect sense." His grin revealed a stunning white set of perfect teeth. "It's darn near the same color as your hair." For more than twenty years, customers had been commenting on her hair as if they had discovered it on their own and were telling her something she didn't know. She was adept at ignoring the attention when they pointed it out to get her to take an interest in them. That didn't stop them from trying. Sometimes it happened over and over with the persistent ones. The first timers proceeded to check out her left hand for a sign of a ring. This guy sneaked behind her defenses with the first sentence.

Willy groaned quietly when she giggled at another comment the guy made that he couldn't hear. Lila was tittering like she was a teenager. The guy saw Lila dig her eyes into Willy's back. He had the relationship figured out by the time Willy asked, "Hey, Lila, could I get a refill?" calling down the counter, hoping to pry her away. He would never have asked otherwise. He wouldn't let her wait on him. He'd jump off the stool when he saw her heading toward the coffeepot and refill his own cup because he hated to see her work so hard. He would be damned if he would ask her to do something for him.

It was four years since Minna had disappeared, and Willy and Iris had been nudging Lila for the past three to find a replacement. She promised she would. "Soon," she told them, but she didn't advertise the job. At the end of the workday, after she'd put up the CLOSED sign, she'd give the counters and shelves a thorough scrubbing until they shone and she could see herself in reflection. With her bucket and mop she'd get started on the speckled linoleum at the time when Minna should be returning from school. A tug pulled her every afternoon to the pie window. Lila peered between the empty glass shelves, her mop in hand, wearing her bandanna, imagining Minna among the girls in their bright sweaters and scarves passing the bakery on their ways home.

Iris worked the counter on the mornings she was able, when she wasn't feeling too sick. Their brother Johnny had come to live with Lila after Tante Catherine died, and he did all the heavy work, stoked the ovens, hauled the bags of flour and sugar, and by late afternoons had all the pots and pans sparkling. He even made some deliveries for her after

she walked him to any unfamiliar locations. Willy helped with the catering on Saturday afternoons and in the evenings.

"Hey, Lila," Willy called again, asking for a refill. She shot him a glare that irked him. He frowned back at her.

"In a minute, Willy!" she snapped in a manner she disapproved of when it was uttered by someone else. It reminded her of Fischer and their years of past arguments. While she still lived on the farm, Iris made her so mad that Lila pulled her hair and dug her fingernails into her arms. Back then she vowed she would not let her anger show itself. She was careful and controlled, and she managed her temper—until Minna vanished.

She kept grinning at the guy. He'd already bought the cherry pie, paid her for it, praised it, and said, "Oh, I'll take a cup of that coffee. It sure smells like a bit of heaven. I bet it is, too." His face had a warm smoothness to it, like soft dough that invited stroking. And when he put his head down to peer into the lower shelf of the case and she could see the crown of his head, there was a mass of short brown curls, sprinkled with bits of gray. He spied the two remaining blachinda. "What are those? They look tasty. I'll have one of them, too," not waiting for Lila to describe what was in them.

She had a reputation for being an astute businesswoman, and on occasion they featured her and the bakery in the newspaper. She didn't go looking for advertising because she had put her trust in what Franz and Martha had taught her—that a business grows because people like what you do and want to share their enthusiasm. Still, every now and then the *Missoulian* ran a short article about the bakery. The editors and reporters all stopped by during the week for a doughnut or two, and coffee. Lila treated them all the same. She fed congressmen, mayors, even one or two governors, and they were just customers. When the governor came, the newspaper photographer was not two steps behind him, and he wanted Lila in the picture.

"Let me get a shot of you with that," the photographer said as she passed by, carrying a tray of cream-filled crullers. "Next to Governor Bonner."

"Take one of the bakery instead," she advised. She kept the articles and pictures in a tin box near the ovens. Some years there was an outside shot of the store with SCHNEIDER'S BAKERY as the focal point. Once the photographer blew through the door on a blustery cold Saturday morning to discover a cozy and cheerful atmosphere, inspiring him to take pictures of the merry customers. During the war, they showcased her meatless blachinda, praising her efforts for keeping spirits high despite rationing. "Minna would like this, I just know," she murmured on those rare instances she went through the tin box. Willy and Iris were mute. Minna's absence was still agonizing. It was an open wound that Lila dressed with fantasies of Minna's joyful return.

"What the heck is this?" Fischer asked on the Saturday two weeks before Christmas. He'd just established himself at his usual table when the back of his neck started tingling. The sensation arrived before he realized he was disturbed. The annoyance was coming from Lila, of all people! To his credit, he didn't jump up and bark as if his tail had been bitten off, but Stella, another of the regulars, was sitting a few tables away and observed the tremor. If Fischer acted on what he was feeling, he would let Lila have a piece of his mind because he realized what was going on between her and the lout. But he'd have to keep his fists behind his back because Lila became impossible when he blew up at her. Her eyes would turn so cold, they made him freeze up. If he started on her, said, "Have you lost your cotton-pickin' mind, Lila? What in the Sam Hill do you think you're doing?" she'd turn her back on him and walk away. There was no fighting fair with her. He wouldn't even get the chance to bring up Minna, ask Lila if that's what she would want her daughter to see, her sashaying in front of this joker, pulling on the edges of her white apron like she was about to undress herself. Right there in public.

Lila didn't show any signs of leaving the guy's table, either, even after Fischer showed up for his Saturday treat to himself. He'd open his auto shop late in order to get her cinnamon rolls fresh from the oven. He always got his table first. Then he collected the pages of the newspaper the other customers had left. Lila ignored him. She was giggling when he came in and pretended not to notice him. Willy was at his usual place at the end of the counter. He'd been watching Lila for ten minutes. She'd been over by the guy for so long his coffee had cooled down without him thinking about blowing on it.

Stella was the only other customer. There had been the early rush just at opening time, but that had turned into a dribble by the time Fischer arrived. The usual crowd of relaxed customers, the doughnut eaters and coffee drinkers, had come and gone in advance of the Christmas parade scheduled for the afternoon. The day was overcast and dull. The kids riding the floats, even with their earmuffs and scarves tucked around them, would find scant warmth perching on the hay bales, but their excitement would quell the chill.

"Your usual, Stella?" Lila had served her just after the early rush. She and Lila were about the same age. For four years, Stella had been coming to the bakery each Saturday, arriving just ahead of Fischer. She brought her own coffee mug and would be sipping from it when he walked through the door. She loved watching him. He was meticulous about his fedora. He'd stand at the hat rack inside the door for a full minute, deliberating where to put the hat so it wouldn't get nudged or knocked down.

If he considered Stella at all, Fischer would say, "She's a schoolmarm. Plain as the nose on your face." But he didn't. She sat at the same table each week. She gave him the space, saw he was a man who needed plenty of room and would not appreciate feeling closed in. She chose a table an appropriate distance from his to prevent him from someday realizing she watched him and say, "Why are you staring at me? Can't you find another table, or am I just too bea-u-ti-ful?"

Willy sat at his private stool at the counter next to the baked goods. He hadn't missed one day since Minna's disappearance. Fischer claimed his center table by the window. An imaginary line divided the two parts of the bakery, and the brothers wouldn't consider crossing to the other side and sitting together, as if the one might contaminate the other. They did nod to acknowledge the other's arrival. Fischer showed up every Saturday, and like Lila, he scanned the street through the window for much of the morning as though he was waiting for someone.

"Has everyone here tried the best blachinda in the world?" the man questioned no one in particular but obviously included all three of them. He glanced across the room at Willy's back and saw the muscles in it tighten. Stella looked at Fischer, who seemed startled to find there was another female besides Lila in the place. But when Lila started babbling, that's when heads popped up like fledglings in a nest on their mother's return with lunch. Even Stella, who only ever spoke to ask for coffee and rye toast, expected Lila to tell the guy to tone it down, and if he couldn't, he would need to leave.

"Oh, Frank," Lila gushed. That was just too much for Fischer. He shoved his chair out, got up, and walked past Lila to the guy's table. "Are you done readin' the *Missoulian*, yet?" He glared at Lila, who shrugged like an adolescent refusing to bow to a parent's annoyance.

"Go ahead. Take it," Frank said. He caught the exchange between Fischer and Lila. "Hey, Red," he said when Fischer started back to his table. He saw the tendons in Fischer's neck pop out and his face turn red.

"What you starin' at, lady?" Fischer growled at Stella. He had to refrain from turning around and going for the guy's throat.

She looked like she'd been kicked, but she said, "Nothing. I'm not staring at anything."

"Well, just don't, then."

"How 'bout one more of them delicious pork blachindas for the road?" Frank's grin was halfway to a sneer. "Red?"

"Listen." Fischer had sat down again, but he jumped up when he heard the guy. The chair legs screeched on the floor. Fischer traveled the fifteen steps over to Willy, across their dividing line, and he snarled, "Are you blind or what?"

"No, I'm not blind," Willy snapped. "What's botherin' you?" Lila had them both on edge.

"I just plain don't get you," Fischer spoke into his ear. He nearly spit into it. He didn't sit on the stool next to Willy. He stood over him, breathing hard into his ear, and his fists were clenched.

Fifty-Nine

"Now, Minna, be generous when you sprinkle it in." Celeste was pouring hot wax into glass jars.

"It smells so sweet, and Christmasy." Minna inhaled the strong-scented clove and cinnamon mixture into which Celeste had ground the zest of an orange peel. "My mother will be making dozens of pfefferneuse for the bakery this week," Minna said, although this had no connection with the candle making beyond the aroma of the spices. She pictured herself in the bakery, standing beside the pie window, and looking out on a rainy Higgins Avenue while drops of water trickled down the glass, blurring the SCHNEIDER'S BAKERY sign. "She'll have done up her fruitcakes. She wraps them in cheesecloth and stores them in giant crocks in the back of the bakery. She makes them up before Thanksgiving," she added, nodding. "You should taste some, Celeste. Even the people who say they hate fruitcake like hers."

"I see. She sounds like a wonderful baker. I wonder when you will go back to see her."

Minna was stirring the scents into the hot wax but paused. "One day I think I will. The time will have to be right."

"I think so, too. Now hold the wick in the middle. Remember, it's got to be long enough to light with a match."

Cosmo came bouncing in from the backyard. "Okay, I think we got a fire ready to go that'll be big enough for you this time."

"Now, Cosmo, I told you it doesn't have to be a big fire. Not a bonfire. Just a small fire."

He grinned. "I know what you told me. I jus' don't want you to do you complainin'."

"This isn't Midsummer, Cosmo. Completely the opposite, in fact. We're not going to be using it for more than ten minutes. The winter solstice doesn't require a large fire. It isn't a grand gesture to welcome summer. This is about the coming of winter, of quiet, dark days." Celeste spoke softly, as though she was observing winter's arrival at that moment. She concentrated on pouring the hot liquid while counting the number of jars. She had twenty-five small ones on the table, and one large one.

"You goin' ta get you wish on the weather, though, I bet. Mild winter," Cosmo said, overlooking her comment. "S'posed to be fifty degree and no rain," Cosmo caught a whiff of the cloves. "Them candles makin' me hungry. You sure we ain't goin' eat 'em?"

"Help yourself to those cinnamon rolls on the counter, Cosmo." Minna smiled at him. "I made them just for you." Her mother would be delighted to see Minna's pride in what she had baked. Franz would be pleased, too, but often he had counseled Minna, "You can do whatever you want, liebling, when you get growed up. That darn bakery is hard work."

"How's Terra coming along getting that mistletoe together?" Celeste was filling the last jar.

"She say she got as much as you ask for."

"Good. Terra is so good that way, Cosmo. You have a fine wife."

"I guess you 'spects we goin' do a whole lot of kissin', Celeste." He put his arm around her shoulder and bent around as if he was going to give her one just then. "You best watch out. You get smothered with 'em."

"Oh you! Get away from here. You'll get burned." But she smiled. "Now, you do know why we need to have the mistletoe, don't you? And don't go on with that nonsense about the kissing."

"Well, since it be you askin' for it, I 'spect it got more to do than jus' that, though I like that idea a lot."

"You'd be right, too. Do you know what the druids called mistletoe?"

"The who? I ain't heard that one before."

"They were an ancient people, an elite group that lived mostly on the British Isles. Some think they were magicians. They appear to have been well educated, at any rate. Anyway, they had a particular reverence for the winter solstice *and* for mistletoe. They had a name for it. They called it 'all-heal.'"

"See. I know'd this 'bout you, little Celeste. You pretend you ain't no magician, and then what you do? You turn right 'round and talk 'bout magicians, *and* you use they ideas." Celeste didn't bother to comment, since he was joking and knew firsthand of healing powers.

Minna laughed. "You two are so funny when you start teasing." She was putting the last wick in the liquid. She felt relaxed and at home with her odd mix of friends. They were nearly family, but as the holidays neared this year, more than in the other years she had to fight off a sadness that clung like salty air in her hair on clammy days. She missed her home. Every year Uncle Willy and Lila and she had driven out to Blue Mountain to find a tree. If there was enough snow, he packed her sled in the trunk. She couldn't wait for him to stop and tie it to the back of the car and pull her along behind. It didn't matter one bit that her fingers in her red mittens were biting from the cold. When Uncle Willy stopped and it was time to go home, she was never ready for it to end. Her scarf was filled with ice, her cheeks burning red, but it was never enough. The only compensation was that they had the Christmas tree, and they would put it up that evening and decorate. Lila would have divinity and fudge, and they'd drink hot chocolate. She and Minna made popcorn balls while Willy hung the lights.

"Where do you want me to put the candles once they're cooled?" Minna sounded faraway.

"You and I are going to go hunting first, Minna. Before we place the candles in their respective spots. We will go on a search for red berries. Cosmo?"

"Uh-oh"—he rolled his eyes—"I hear 'nother job comin' my way."

"You're right. We need all the branches and berries from juniper bushes that you can rustle up."

"They grow on other side of the Cascades, Celeste." He nearly moaned.

"Yes, I know, and I'm glad you know, too."

"Yeah. I figured you does."

"You'll have them by next weekend, then?" It was more a command than a request.

"Yes, ma'am. How many you want? At you service, ma'am."

"Cosmo?" Celeste frowned.

"Yes, Celeste?" He bit his tongue to not say "ma'am" again to further irritate her. "What that mistletoe heal anyway?" he asked to change the subject.

"Well, all sorts of maladies. It's even an antidote for poison."

"You not plannin' on doin' us in, is you?" he teased.

"You and your folderol, Cosmo. Mistletoe also ensures fertility."

Minna blushed, and Cosmo said, "That what the kissin' 'bout, then," and laughed.

"And you'll love this, Cosmo. It protects against witchcraft."

Cosmo roared. His laughter made the already cozy kitchen, mellow from the aroma of hot wax and spices, even more warmhearted.

"And you two have cleared it at work, right? They know at the shipyard you are taking off Monday, December 22?" It was still over a week away, yet she'd asked them this very thing repeatedly over the last three weeks.

"For personal reasons." Minna smiled at Cosmo. She had told Mr. Bieber she had family business to attend to that would require taking the day off. He didn't press her on it. She rarely asked for anything, and she never skipped work for sickness.

Two years earlier, Minna had replaced Mary Evans who, along with Phyllis, evaporated on August 7, 1945, after the news that Hiroshima, wherever that was, had been destroyed when the Americans dropped an atomic bomb on it. Within two weeks, Mr. Bieber had promoted her to be his assistant. This was a step beyond Mary's position.

It was as if Mary and Phyllis disappeared off the face of the earth. They didn't even provide a forwarding address so their unpaid salary could be sent to them. Minna thought of the young woman employee whom she had replaced, who had run out on Mary to get married, and how Mary couldn't get over the girl being so irresponsible.

When Mary did not show up on the eighth, also—and worse, had not contacted the office to say she would be missing work that day or give a plausible reason for missing the previous day—it seemed to Minna that Mr. Bieber was practically elated by the time five o'clock came around. He bounced in and out of her office five times after four o'clock. She didn't know if he was checking on how she was doing filling in for Mary, which had required her staying late and coming in early, or if he was actually relieved that Mary had failed to contact the office. There would have to be some very convincing reason, if she did return, for him to agree to keep her on.

In the two years since Mary's sudden departure, Mr. Bieber mentioned her only in regard to any document that still had her name attached to it. Minna was impressed that he refrained from saying anything negative concerning her. He seemed to have forgiven her, or at least he appreciated her reasons for leaving and going without giving notice. Minna was moved by his behavior; he seemed not to carry hard feelings toward Mary, nor did he gossip. It was ironic, for Mary had seemed to take being abandoned by her employee as a personal insult, and complained often to Minna about it.

On the morning of that day, President Truman came on the radio when the day shift workers had been on the job for two or more hours already and were glancing at the clock, waiting for the ten o'clock bell to ring for coffee break. It was some time before they heard his exact words. "The force from which the sun draws its power has been loosed against those who brought war to the Far East."

By lunch hour, however, most people wondered if they should go home or get on with what they had been doing. "What is an atomic bomb?" people asked. They hadn't heard of it before. "Is it really any worse than the London Blitz?" They knew about the firepower that had dropped on Dresden and Berlin. This one, they heard, exploded into a mushroom cloud that could be seen hundreds of miles away. Jaws would drop in the following weeks in absolute awe and horror when the cinema newsreels ran the motion pictures revealing the extent of its power.

"If the Japs don't surrender after this…" almost everyone was saying, passing it down the line. "Well, they'll have to, won't they?" They listened to the reports on the radio in the lunchroom and heard that a whole city of 350,000 people had been destroyed, wiped off the map. What was not said but was at the front of many minds, and what they feared more than an all-powerful bomb dropped on the other side of the world, was whether their jobs were in jeopardy once the war was over and the surrender was signed by the Emperor Hirohito.

There was so much commotion that day. The hubbub could have lit up the whole city without turning on a single light bulb. That's why Mary's and Phyllis's absences that day at the shipyard barely registered. It would be a few days before it created some discussion. Oh, there were those who said things like, "It couldn't have happened to a better person," or "It's about time."

Minna returned home the evening of August 7 to Celeste talking to herself. On seeing Minna, she included her in the conversation. "I wondered what was going to happen next. I have felt it since July 10. I hated to think it, but I expected it was going to be much worse than anything we've seen before. As Cosmo would say, this one is a real doozy." She was patting her chest to calm herself. "Those poor people. Think of the children," she cried again and again. "Obliterated. And for what? War is a monster, created by monstrous people."

Minna sat with her and listened. "What about the orphans?" Celeste sobbed. "Who will tend to them?" Celeste was in no shape to find the kind of herb that could calm this catastrophe. Minna gently touched her on the knee and said, "I'll make us some tea," and went to search among the many jars for a mixture to brew that would soothe them.

❧

In July, about the time Celeste's eye started acting up, Minna was privy to a lunchroom conversation about Mary. Some of her odd tics, many of which Minna had regularly endured, were played out in the work areas to the point of malicious gossip. She'd always seemed odd, impenetrable as the "Big Bertha" howitzer, some said, but they hadn't observed her tugging at the imaginary wisps of hair sneaking out from under her hairnet. It made no sense, wearing hairnets in an accounting office, but she insisted on them, as if they were proof of solidarity with the women welders. She yanked the hem of her skirt, too, to pull it down farther than midcalf. "I think she's gotta be half nuts," Minna heard someone say. "The war's gettin' to her," someone else said and laughed, adding, "like the rest of us," and pushed the butt of her cigarette, with a bloodred lipstick smear, into the ashtray.

Mary had always been curt, and the workers expected that—respected it, even. It was appropriate for the job, for everyone to know their place. For Minna, the quirks, the snorts, and the exasperated sighs to be withstood each day were dwarfed and seemed insignificant when new and odder behaviors surfaced. For one thing, Mary chewed the ends of her pencils. Every day. She was like a beaver on the edge of a stream gnawing frantically at the trunks of aspen on her side of the room, like she had to hurry to get a dam built. Each new day she started another pencil like it was a fresh log. She didn't bother to apologize when she ate the eraser on the end of one, chewed and swallowed it, and then choked up the little pieces, launching them clear over onto Minna's desk. Minna ducked to get out of the line of fire and couldn't guess if Mary was aware of what she'd done.

Then Mary began to do a lot of mumbling to herself. She had done some of that in the past, but she would catch herself and react as if a nun was standing over her demanding she get hold of herself. She would shake her head vigorously, wiggle her shoulders, and become quiet again. Then she started doing it all the time, and no imaginary disciplinarian seemed to be in charge any longer. It was more than distracting in the small office. Minna wished she at least had a window to get a different perspective, but there was only the framed letter of commendation behind Mary's head on the ugly green wall. Minna silently sang the songs her Boppy had sung to her to block out the interference. When she couldn't take another minute of it, she went out in the hall to breathe deeply. She was grateful to Mr. Bieber on the days he came in with an assignment that called her away from her desk. The peculiarities reached their peak when Mary began to start her workdays already mumbling while actively picking her nose. Minna had to keep her eyes on her own desk, or she would be sick to her stomach. She avoided touching anything Mary handled. Minna frequented the restroom to wash her hands, and brought a damp washcloth to work with some bar soap rubbed into it. It was as if Mary had developed a serious illness that had begun prior to V-E Day, and it was getting progressively worse.

On the Monday afternoon of the week before she disappeared, she belched five times in the space of three minutes, like a man who doesn't care who hears him. Minna whipped her head up the third time and gave Mary a disbelieving stare. It didn't faze Mary that Minna was pointedly looking at her, or that she was belching like a logger alone in the woods. She seemed oblivious to both. Minna could hardly refrain from asking, "Are you all right?"

Mary hunched over her desk, looking like an eighty-year-old woman who was permanently frozen in the position. She was chewing on a new pencil. Minna absent-mindedly wondered if anyone questioned the increase in the number of pencils their office was using. Not only was Mary gnawing on the end of the pencil, she was chomping away at the fingernails on the other hand.

Sometime before coffee break she said to Minna, "So your husband…" *Here we go.* Minna clenched her jaw.

"Well, you must be so relieved. Knowing he's going to be coming home now for sure. This war is finished." That was before Hiroshima and Nagasaki. Mary must have been psychic. She actually smiled at Minna and looked like she was sincere. Surely Mary Evans wasn't being kind. To her credit, she didn't ask *is* he coming, or *when* is he coming, and that was unusual.

Each time the question of her husband arose, Minna was on alert. She teased John Welles once, asking him, "Hey, if I need to come up with a husband to keep my job, will you pretend for me?" She was serious, though. With all Mary's prying, she was worried she might lose her job if they found out the truth.

"I'd be proud and honored," he replied. "Just let me know. I'll be there!" They only mentioned it that one time. Both of them blushed.

There were other subjects that didn't get mentioned either. He didn't talk about his stint in the war. He got very quiet if someone asked how he'd been wounded in the Pacific. His temper got short, and his tone was almost biting if anyone brought up the topic. It didn't fit with how he behaved at other times, but Minna learned not to ask him any questions about what had happened to him. His refusal to discuss it told her enough. It was more horrific than he could bear to recall.

Sixty

On the eleventh day, December 14, Frank did not show up at the bakery. Lila was in the kitchen making holiday cookies in the shape of miniature bird's nests. She rolled balls of dough, dipped them into egg white, and rolled them in crushed walnuts. After that, she poked a thumb in the middle but instead of a bird's egg, she would add a dollop of homemade raspberry jelly after they came out of the oven. These particular cookies had always been Minna's favorites. Lila hummed "Jingle Bells" along with the radio and carefully separated the cookies by two inches on the baking sheets.

"I've already sold all the gingerbread men," Iris banged the empty tray through the swinging doors. "It's not even ten o'clock. You gonna make more of them today?" She adjusted her handmade crocheted hat, as colorful as a Christmas tree, which she had designed herself while she was recuperating. The tiny gold balls on the crown of her head sparkled under the kitchen lamp.

"Paulie," she'd asked her husband before they left to go the bakery, "do you think I should wear the blue-and-white one with the silver sparkles instead?" They had been in the hallway putting on their coats. He pulled on one boot, holding the wall for support, his glasses sliding off his nose when he looked up at her. She looked bewildered as she showed him the other hat to get his judgment. He'd given her his brightest smile to hide his unbearable sadness.

"Oh, I like the one you've got on just fine. I think this one is perfect for today. It's very happy. Save the blue one for after Christmas, why don't you?"

"You don't think Lila will get huffy and tell me it's too showy?"

"She'll like it, too, Iris. Don't worry about that." He gave her a solemn, protective look and said, "Now, you're not going to stay and clean up today. Understand? Lila can manage. She's got Johnny to help her with the heavy work."

He parked the car directly in front of the bakery. She told him she did not want him to make such a fuss. "It's embarrassing, Paulie," she scolded when he got out and walked around to open the door and then insisted on walking her into the store. Once inside, she got excited because of the laughter and the bustle, and she forgave Paulie his doting. She loved being around real people again, hearing them talking out loud, not whispering behind the doors like the doctors and nurses at the hospital, and seeing customers eagerly bite into fresh pastries and just enjoying themselves. There was no better antidote for the many days she'd languished in Saint Pat's, looking at the white ceiling and wondering if heaven would be this bland.

"I'll be back at three." Paulie gave her a serious look. "I'll come inside and get you," he promised, "if you're not waiting by the door for me."

"I'll be ready." She sighed and then smiled at him so sweetly he didn't know whether to cry from joy or heartbreak. Her smile always got inside his internal parts.

There was a small tree in the corner opposite the door, strung with popcorn and berries, that Willy had set up for Lila. "You're a little early, aren't you?" Lila had asked when he came through the back door, carrying the tree in one hand. She liked to wait until just before Christmas Eve to put up a tree. But she decided she liked how this one brightened the shop after it was decorated. She caught herself taking glances at it when she made her trips from the kitchen.

The scent of holiday spices had smacked Iris in the face when she walked through the door. If she had an appetite, she wouldn't resist the temptation to indulge. As soon as Paulie had helped her out of her coat, she stepped away from feeling tired. It had already been a good day, starting out well because she hadn't been sick. By nine o'clock, she'd brewed three pots of coffee and sold out of apple turnovers. "No more refills for you, mister," she teased the old man at the counter.

When she showed Lila the empty gingerbread man pan, Lila answered, "Not today," sliding the last pan of cookies into the oven. "I'm going to finish these up and make chocolate cookies next. I'll make the batter for the gingerbread before I finish today. How many customers at the tables?"

The back door banged open, and Willy came through before Iris could answer. He shook the snow off his cap and pulled off his leather gloves. He put the cap back on, but when he saw Iris, he tipped it and said, "Hey, Iris, hi, Lila." He didn't want to stare at either of them. "Those look good," and nodded to the bird's nests.

Lila wouldn't look at him. "Ah, come on, Lila," he grimaced.

"You ain't gonna be mad at me today, are you?" He had his cap off again and fingered its edges.

"What did Fischer say to you on Saturday?" She didn't even say hello.

"Not much." Willy dodged her glare.

"You and Fischer were talking in the bakery?" Iris butted in. "Well, that's a new one." Plucky Iris was back, and Willy couldn't smother his smile. He almost laughed out loud, except that Lila was glowering. He'd missed Iris spouting her banter between the pastries in the background of their daily lives. He'd taken her for granted, like most everybody else, he suspected, dismissed her as Iris being Iris—to be taken with a grain of salt. It struck him in an unpleasant way that while she was on her own and battling disease, they'd carried on without a hitch, but it made him realize it had been like eating a meal minus one key ingredient. He hoped that the worst was at last behind her, but he didn't ask, and no one was saying.

Lila didn't appreciate her sister's interjection. It distracted Willy and helped him avoid answering her. Iris pushed her cap back. She'd lost her hair from the nitrogen mustard treatments, and with nothing to hold it in place, the hat had the habit of sliding down onto her forehead.

"He didn't say much." Willy tried to divert Lila's scowl. She was scooping teaspoons of the jam into the centers of the cooled cookies.

"He said something," she snapped. She'd refilled Iris's empty tray with two dozen of the birds' nests. "I saw the way you two were carrying on. Like two old gossips." Then she added, "Not that I care a stick what you two gossip about."

"Will I miss any of the good parts if I leave now?" Iris interrupted because the bell on the bakery door had tinkled, announcing that someone had come in.

"That isn't funny, Iris," Lila muttered. She stopped long enough to take a breath so she wouldn't get heated up at her sister, too, on top of being upset with Willy and Fischer. It tormented her to watch her sister being eaten away bit by bit by the cancer.

Iris saw the pity and pushed it away. "Well, I'm on Willy's side"—Iris started through the doors—"no matter what he's done to get himself into hot water *this* time." She winked at him before the doors banged behind her. It *was* a good day. Iris was feeling spunky and coy. Lila said half to herself, "I wish Paulie could see her right now. I don't know if he'd laugh or cry. With his Latin nature, he'd probably do both." It was a rare glimpse of Iris from the old happy days.

Willy had agonized the whole weekend. He'd gotten mad at Fischer and slapped his cap on and left the bakery without saying a word to Lila. He'd gotten so riled he forgot his gloves, which he realized as soon as he was outside. "Damn cold," he muttered. He never cursed, didn't believe in it. He worked with the guys in the garage and was around it all the time. Lila frowned on it, and he agreed with her. "Better to say nothing at all than say something that demeans you." That was her motto.

On Saturday night he took himself to the movies at the Wilma. They were showing *The Bishop's Wife*. At the beginning, he marveled at how devoted Loretta Young was to David Niven, her bishop husband. But the guy acted like an idiot, he decided, and Willy wondered what she saw in him. He was single-minded and remote with her, dancing to the tune of a sour old lady. He was cold. Downright cold, actually, and rude to Loretta. But what would Willy know? He had enough trouble of his own. He couldn't get it pinned down with Lila. That's what Fischer had said to him, too. Imagine Fischer getting mad at *him* because he couldn't get his former wife to marry him, his own brother. Fischer told him, "There's somethin' real wrong with you, Willy. Otherwise, you'd a tied her down a long time ago." He pointed to the jerk who was carrying on, pumping her up over in the corner of the bakery. "If she was serious about you, this wouldn't be happenin'." He poked his thumb over his shoulder.

Fischer, of all people, who couldn't get over being mad at him, blamed him for Lila leaving nearly twenty years earlier. "What in the hell is the matter with you?" Fischer had whispered in his ear, right there at the counter.

"Nothin'," Willy said. "Nothin' is the matter with me. What's the matter with you?" That's when he got up and stamped out, leaving his gloves on the counter.

Much as Willy did not want to hear what Fischer had to say, he had to admit it was true. He walked down Higgins for a bit after the movie, going over what his brother had made clear. Lila would have married him by now, wouldn't she? Wouldn't she, if the thing with Minna hadn't happened? Well, he thought, they could have gone to the altar a long time ago. It had changed them all, that was for sure. There were a few months not long after Minna disappeared, when it looked like Lila and Fischer might get back together. It didn't last long, though. The funny thing was that in the last three years, Lila had outperformed herself at the bakery. When the rationing was going strong, she had gained more customers than ever. People told her no one could make dull fare taste good except her. They raved over her fake coffee. She couldn't keep the larder full, and it was obvious she was making good money. She only had time for the work.

Cary Grant had been too real to be any kind of angel, Willy decided after he left the theater. It was hard not to like him, though. He was charming. Willy had decided Loretta was going to dump the bishop in the end, with her new hat and all, but she hadn't. He got into his pickup and rode around town. He couldn't face going back to his apartment. Lila had fixed it up a bit for him, but it seemed gloomy. He wanted an ice cream cone, which even to him seemed absurd, as cold as it was. He didn't even have heat in the truck.

He couldn't bring himself to go by Lila's to deliver the wood he was hauling in the back for her, although he'd promised to bring more for her fireplace before her woodpile got too low. She'd need some before Christmas Eve, as cold as it was. He would prefer more than anything to be with Lila to the end of his life if she let him, and if she didn't get hooked up with someone else. The way she was carrying on in the bakery, he wasn't sure where he stood anymore. Not that he really knew for sure at any time. She wasn't one to get affectionate unless it suited her, and she had gotten a lot less warmhearted since Minna wasn't around. He sympathized even when Lila became distant. He'd never had children of his own, but if he did, he was sure he would be in just as bad shape as she was.

When he couldn't stand it any longer, and he'd been driving up and down Higgins—then onto Front Street, over to Broadway, and out toward the Mullan Road—and his legs got so cold he had to smack them, he drove past her place. He regretted it as soon as he made a right onto her street. It was after ten o'clock, and she would be asleep. He should have gone home to bed instead of going down Pine Street, but it felt like his home even if he didn't live there. He was surprised to see the lights on in her upstairs bedroom. It was as bad as a punch in the gut when he recognized the snazzy blue 1947 Cadillac convertible coupe parked out front. He'd fixed an electrical problem on the vehicle earlier in the summer. He tried to remember if the guy had weaseled out of paying.

"You can't corral her, can you?" Fischer's taunting banter from Saturday morning rang in his ears as he turned the corner and headed toward Broadway. He'd scraped the ice off the windshield after the movie, but his breath was fogging it up again, and every few blocks he wiped it off with his old glove. His favorite gloves were at the bakery. Lila probably put them under the counter for him to pick up the following Monday. He couldn't shake his brother's accusation. He parked the truck in front of his apartment, got out, and slammed the door behind him. He probably woke up some neighbors from the banging. "Let her wait on the wood," he growled.

"How many years you had the chance?" Fischer had goaded him that morning. "Now look it she's doin'. You seen that fathead over there hustlin' her, and she's actin' blind as a bat." They had studied her standing by Frank, who looked like a squatter over there at the far table. She saw them looking at her, but turned her back right at them. If a customer hadn't come in, she would probably have stayed that way until they left. As it was, she made the customer wait longer than she should have. Actually Stella, in a quiet but authoritative teacher voice, had said to Lila, "I believe there is a customer waiting to be served."

Sixty-One

"Where are all your books?" Minna teased.

"You were the one who was always hogging the table if I recall," John shot back. They'd carried on this banter for more than two years. "Besides, you should be celebrating that I passed all my exams."

"And why would I do that?" she liked to rile him, and he liked it when she did.

"Hey, look at how many books you have spread out here," he had teased her when they first started studying together. "Let's see, here's one. Here, look at this. Two, three, you've got *four* books out to my one. Four."

"Yeah, but look at the size of yours." She tapped his world history tome.

For the past two years, John and Minna met one evening a week to eat at the Little Bit of Sweden Restaurant and to study. The price was right, and so was the location. John walked the three miles from the university, and she rode the bus from work. They shared the grilled salmon with coleslaw, which came with chicken gumbo, a potato, and another vegetable for ninety cents. Sometimes they splurged and spent a dollar to share the swiss steak with vegetables. Each week, Lottie, their waitress, had cleared the table and brought them thick, dark coffee and a sweet pancake to share afterward. She moved the candle to the next table, and they got out their books. The owner and staff liked the young couple and from the beginning gave them permission to study there if it wasn't crowded. The pair's repartee was entertaining on slow evenings, relieving the boredom of waiting for a customer to walk in.

"But *that's* interesting," John had countered, fondly touching the history book. "Not like your manuals figuring out how to get people to do the work they're supposed to do on the job." Minna, at Mr. Bieber's dictate, was learning how to become a manager, and it wasn't an easy business.

Midsummer's Eve had brought them together three years earlier and thrust them into a relationship of familiarity and affinity that seemed right and natural at that moment, but afterward felt awkward. Neither of them was sure they could trust what they thought had happened on that one particular night, and although they didn't discuss it, they both leaned toward believing it had been a lovely but probably a fantastical experience. They didn't broach the topic to confirm or dismiss what may have occurred, and the event, magnificent as it had been, was disappointing to some because the outcome had not made them into a couple. Celeste didn't mind. "I'll bide my time on that," she said to herself, grinning inside. "No one is going to prevent something from happening if it needs to happen down the road." She repeated, "Down the road. Time is a teaser. It stretches and contracts as it needs. Who are we to think we have some power over it?"

Cosmo hadn't been of a similar mind, however. He wasn't convinced that Minna's future should unfold willy-nilly, in its own time or way, leaving it to chance. He, like Celeste, saw the magic that took place on that special night, and he didn't want to just stand by and let it wither and fade away before it had its chance. "Gotta grab that iron when it's hot."

"Hmm, Cosmo. That sounds a lot like what I said to you when you were hesitating about going forward with Terra."

He shook his head like she'd just stung him. "Ain't this jus' the same? You steered me right. How come you ain't doin' that with Minna?"

"Well that hot iron you mentioned isn't warm enough yet, Cosmo. We're going to have to wait and see if it heats up."

"Sometimes you jus' has to dictate how you wants things to be," he insisted to Terra. "Not like that ole Celeste that plays with the universe, hittin' them balls like she's playin' that funny game croquet."

Terra laughed. "Oh Cosmo, you romantic man," she said, pulling him to her and kissing him full on his mouth, which made him stop worrying about Minna and John for the moment.

"You be comin' to supper at our house from now on," he commanded John two weeks after the Midsummer celebration, wanting to move things along and determining if he didn't do it, it wouldn't happen. He sure wasn't going to leave it up to Celeste. For John's part, he was happy to get a free meal once a week. Divine had him over, too, when she could, between dramatic episodes with Starr who was getting married next week, comma, then the following week she wasn't ever going to get married.

John rented a room above the bookstore where he had a part-time job. It was around the corner from the Swedish restaurant. "Hey," he told Minna when he started at the university, "if it wasn't for the GI Bill, I don't know what I'd do." He was smart, very smart, Minna found out when the first round of grades came out that year. She'd peeked and found the results among his papers.

It had taken a few months for her to learn some elementary things about him. The day he told her he'd been raised in an orphanage, she was shocked. "You haven't mentioned this before. Why is that?"

He shrugged. "Not something you want to boast about." That didn't satisfy her. She was raised in a bakery. Was that anything to boast about? Her mother was never happy, no matter what she did, and her father embarrassed her when he flirted with the women guests who came into the bakery from the Florence Hotel. John seemed ashamed of his past, but he didn't hide it from her when she asked where his parents were, unlike what she did. To be fair, he didn't ask about her family or where she'd come from, and she had appreciated that she hadn't needed to do any explaining. He wasn't like Mary Evans, who had pried to dredge up some horrible secret she was sure was lurking in the background, waiting to come out. Minna didn't talk about Lila or Fischer or any of them. Together, it was as if neither of them possessed a past. It was simple in the beginning between them, an unspoken pact about what they asked each other and what they revealed of themselves.

"Do you know anything about who your parents were?" She couldn't resist prying when she learned about the orphanage. He didn't seem like someone who was raised without parents, but then she hadn't met anyone who didn't have parents.

"Better not to know, I figure." He surprised her. He was inquisitive about most things, how things worked, how people did things, who they were, so why not about his own background? In the weeks and months, as she got to know him better, she found he was open with his feelings, most of the time saying exactly what he thought but in the kindest manner, and then there were the other times when he got downright closemouthed, as Lila would have said. If he had inquired about her circumstances, chances are she would have done the same. She wanted to know more about the orphanage, though. Where it was, what it was like there, and whether it was as unpleasant as in the stories she'd read in high school English.

In the beginning, they saw each other on Saturdays at Cosmo and Terra's. He'd be on the floor playing with Crystal when she arrived. She spent her Saturdays cleaning Celeste's house, down to the hardwood floors. "Now, dear"—Celeste would shake her finger over Minna, who was waxing the wood—"we are not meant to be too fastidious." Celeste regretted that her bad leg prevented her from diving into jobs she wished she could do for herself. *We're all meant to suffer something*, she told herself when she got edgy because her body acted as gatekeeper.

Celeste looked forward to Terra's suppers on Saturday evenings. If she was feeling particularly spry and witty, the evenings could get very lively. Celeste studied Terra when she did tarot readings. They'd have the dishes cleared, and Minna and John would have taken everything into the kitchen to be washed and dried and put away while Cosmo and Terra arranged the dining table. Some evenings they played hearts or gin rummy. When someone had a question about the future, though, Terra was ready. "You look out, Terra," Cosmo warned her. "That Celeste goin' throw in her two cents, and you can trust me on that."

"I will not," Celeste barked at him and then promptly said, "Now, Terra, I see what you're driving at, but look at how the empress is positioned near the magician." Terra was a fluent card reader, but she didn't dismiss Celeste's observations—or any other comments, for that matter—for they made things clear that might be otherwise obscured.

"You go right ahead, Celeste, if you see something I'm missing," Terra declared.

Minna and John didn't see each other except at Cosmo's until he went back to school. After he returned from the war, he spent much of that summer at the Veterans Hospital Outpatient Clinic, learning how to walk without a cane. He'd already had the job at the bookstore before he connected with Minna when he turned up for Midsummer's Eve. He didn't earn much money between his salary and his disability payment, and he was just making ends meet.

Celeste clapped her hands when she answered her door one lovely fall day to find John Welles, standing there with his arms outstretched to show her he was not using a cane. "Look at you. Did you walk all the way over here?"

He laughed. "Yep. They told me I don't get to rely on the crutch anymore. I'm on my own now."

"You always were, John," Celeste reminded him. "You don't need any kind of crutches. You are doing very well and will only get better."

"You reading that in the tarot?" he teased.

"You're talking too much like Cosmo for my taste." She laughed.

Celeste watched but said nothing concerning Minna and John. During the war when the older women at the shipyard had been hostile toward Minna, saying nasty things behind her back about how she had gotten the job, Celeste listened and soothed her feelings. Celeste reminded her how hard the work was physically, and how easy it was for them, with her dressed well and working in a comfortable office, to be resentful. Once the war ended and most of the women disappeared from the yard, the insults started again, but this time it was the men who bore the grudge about an attractive young woman in a job who held some authority over them.

There were some very rough days. She avoided eating in the lunchroom for a time after she walked past a table of five men, and one said, "There's the slut now."

"Just a tart," another piped up. She could go into the ladies' restroom and bawl, which she hadn't been able to do when the women had attacked her.

It didn't help that Mr. Bieber complimented her in front of the workers. He admired her work, but she was uncertain that he was accurate. Was she as good as he said? Was he playing favoritism? She went home edgy and stopped dropping by to see Crystal. Celeste gave her the space to sort it out.

"I don't think I like men very much." Celeste and she had just finished eating a dish of sausage with sweet potatoes, onions, and cabbage. They were clearing the table.

"You know what Cosmo would say," Celeste said lightly.

"Yeah. You mean about men making up half the population?" Minna didn't smile.

"That's not always a comforting thought, though, is it?" Celeste agreed and added, "But they sure come in handy at times, don't they?"

"Not at work, they don't." Minna frowned.

"Is Mr. Bieber giving you troubles?"

"No, no. It's not him. If anything, he's too good to me. I just wish he'd stop praising me in front of everyone."

"I see. Well, I suppose you could tell him that."

"But he's my boss."

"Well, even bosses are human sometimes," Celeste reminded her.

John Welles got the sharper edges of Minna's temper. What she kept bottled up all week would fly out at him on those Saturday evenings at Cosmo's. He joked with her, and she thought he was making fun of or criticizing her. "You men are all alike," she snapped.

Those two could bicker. In the early days, John was having his own battles at the hospital, with the severe pain and miserably slow recovery time from a wound that didn't want to heal. He refused to give in to the doctor's prognosis that he would never have full use of his leg. He remained stubborn, to the point of arguing with the medical staff who told him they had done all they could for him and that he needed to get on with his life. "Just live with it. You're one of the lucky ones. It's only a limp."

"Lucky how? Would you say it's only a limp if it was your leg?" he retorted. He refused all pain medication, too, said it made him feel like he was drunk, staggering around.

"Those two ever goin' be able figure it out?" Cosmo asked Celeste five months after the Midsummer event. He was becoming impatient. He heard them arguing. He believed if they warmed up, got cuddly like he and Terra did when they got exasperated with each other, they could get things going.

Celeste started on him. "Now, Cosmo, what's your stake in what they do?"

"Uh-oh. Here we go again." He groaned. "What I missin' this time?"

"Don't give me that nonsense."

"I know, I know. But I can't help worryin' 'bout that little gal."

"She's not little, Cosmo, and she's plenty able to make her way in this world. With or without John, or any other man, for that matter. And that includes..." She elbowed his thigh. "And right now, they both have some troubles.Give them time, Cosmo, to sort things out. Then we'll see what happens."

Celeste had taken Minna in when she was at her most vulnerable. She'd gotten to see the girl dig down inside to retrieve her spunk as she went through some tough storms. She'd made great progress. She was strong, she was fit. More than that, she was facing difficult people every day, some of whom despised her without plausible justification. She had taken over where Mary left off and then was promptly promoted.

Mr. Bieber was not satisfied. He informed her of this one Friday afternoon when they were in his office. He had spent an hour mulling the repercussions of the Yalta Conference, which happened before Roosevelt died that year. "I've got relatives in Prussia, and things aren't looking very good for them." He chewed his thumb and wrinkled his brow. Minna nodded, wondering where exactly Prussia was. Since it rhymed with Russia, she decided it must be next door, or close by.

"Your work is good, Minna. Very good, in fact," he assured her. "But I see you didn't finish high school."

Minna's stomach knotted. "No, sir." She felt sheepish.

"Now why is that?"

Minna almost choked. She'd had the baby, he knew that. He wasn't like Mary, though, who pried and seemed to need to make it her business to discover whether or not Minna had a husband. She wore the wedding band she'd bought before she left Missoula and hoped Mr. Bieber would conclude that she had become a widow sometime during the war. Because she had cycled this idea repeatedly to herself, it was nearly her truth.

"It didn't work out," she answered.

"But you were almost finished. Weren't you?"

"I didn't do my senior year."

"Well, are you interested in doing that? Finishing it, I mean. I hope you are. It could make quite a difference for you here."

She practically melted into the chair she was so relieved. "But how could I? I have to work."

He'd looked into it, he told her. "The University of Chicago offers correspondence courses that you could work on if you have the time."

She nodded. "Yes, sir," she said then, her voice rising. "I do have the time."

"And don't think I'm going to be satisfied with you getting a high school diploma." He shook his finger at her in mock disapproval. "This will be the beginning. A young lady as sharp as you are. And if you think I'm blind about those tough guys who give you a hard time, I'm not. You're going to be fine. I can see that. Just don't let them have the upper hand. Ever."

Sixty-Two

"What are you looking at?" Iris came from behind the counter to stand beside Lila who was peeking out the pie window between the one pecan and two pumpkin pies still on display. Iris had sold three apple, two cherry and three pecan pies before noon.

Lila shrugged. "Oh nothing." Iris didn't press. They stood shoulder to shoulder. Iris looked about a half inch taller from behind because of the Christmas balls on her hat.

"I wonder if it's really going to snow so hard tonight," Lila said. The jeweler had mumbled some such thing earlier. It sounded like an afterthought coming out of Lila's mouth. Four times that morning she'd gone to the pie window and stood looking out as though she was expecting someone.

Iris was not in the best of shape, but even so, she had figured out while Willy was at the counter blowing on his coffee that there was more than a tiff going on between him and Lila. Lila wasn't staring up at the sky simply because she was preoccupied about the weather.

"Have you been *this* busy these past few months? More people came through that door today than I ever remember. I had to put on another sweater to stay warm." Iris had missed the whole season, all except for the few treetops she stared at for hours, watching them change color from the hospital bed.

Each time the bakery door opened, a draft came through ahead of the shopper. She'd been out of the hospital for a month. Some moments she felt colder than she ever remembered being. It was worse than the Dakotas, where the wind could not be reined in because there was nothing to halt it, let alone slow it down.

"I see we're almost out of pies. Those two should sell before we close," Lila mused. "No, it slowed down after Thanksgiving and picked up again about a week ago. These are mostly holiday customers now. Except our regulars."

"I had two people ask if you were going to make more popcorn balls before Christmas Eve."

Lila laughed. "It always amazes me that someone would spend money for something they can do in half an hour at home."

"But they are not *your* popcorn balls, Lila. You have to admit you fancy them up a bit."

"They wouldn't buy them otherwise, would they?" She raised her eyebrow. "I'll make up about twenty or so later today. I'll probably have to make one more batch after that. We've got a bit more than a week before Christmas." Iris looked so pale and so frail, her elbows stuck out like sticks.

"Why don't you go home for the rest of the day?" Lila was shocked at how gaunt she looked. Even while she was at the hospital, she didn't look so sickly. "I think the rush is behind us, and Johnny will help me." He was in the back banging something around. Probably putting flour in one of her bins, or sugar.

"Hey, cut it out," Iris snapped. "Do I look that bad?"

"Oh, you look like Christmas, Iris, with that great hat. That's not what I mean. It's been so busy, that's all," she said, trying to cover her worry. "It's enough to take the starch out of anyone. Even me, and I've been doing it every day. I don't want you to go overboard and not be able to make it back in tomorrow."

"I'll make it back just fine." Iris was feisty.

Willy had said just about the same to Iris while hanging over his coffee that morning. "Don't you go and try to make up for the time you was away," he cautioned while she was dashing back and forth at the counter. He got up and did the refills for the two other people sitting on stools. "You don't need to be hustlin' like that, or you're gonna run out of steam."

Iris snapped at him, too. "How many mothers are going to boss me around today?" Paulie hadn't bossed her exactly, but she hated being tended to and fussed over. She wanted to do the fussing. She'd had enough of that from the nurses and nuns.

"I'm sorry, Iris. I just care, you know." Willy looked glum.

She made such a huge grin then that her girlish eyes crinkled at the edges. "You want to know a secret, Willy?" she said quietly leaning over next to him. He felt the warmth from her shoulder next to his. Her voice had that husky gravel of a cigarette smoker.

"What's that?"

"Just between you and me and the fencepost, I was pretty crazy over you when we were back in the Dakotas." He blushed, and she laughed. "Don't worry"—she tapped him on the shoulder—"I'm not making a play for you." He didn't say anything, just peered at her with a side glance. "I knew it was Lila for you all along. Hey, what's going on between you two now, anyway? I stay away for a while, and things go south. You two ever going to figure it out?" She didn't imagine the two could be on the outs for very long.

"Not by the way it's lookin'," he stammered. He kept looking toward the door, watching and wondering when Frank would show up. Ever since the first day he made his appearance, he had come in by about this time. He parked himself at that corner table, the spot where Willy and Fischer watched Lila acting goofy over him last Saturday.

"What happened this time?"

"I ain't gonna talk about it. You want to know, ask her." He pointed toward the swinging doors. Lila was banging trays in the kitchen.

Iris sighed. "Willy, you know as well as I do that hell could freeze over before she tells anybody anything."

"True enough."

"Am I going to have to die before you get it figured out between you?"

"Don't say that, Iris." His face was a scowl. "Don't joke about things like that."

"Who says I'm joking, Willy?" She laughed. "I believe I've been the one who has patched it up every time you've gotten into your confounded messes. Maybe I'll just take myself out of the picture and see if you can do it on your own for once."

"It don't seem to be 'bout her and me anymore."

"What's that supposed to mean?"

"Ask her." He pointed to the kitchen again. "Ask her about Frank and her flirtin'."

"Lila? Flirting? You have got to be kidding me. Come on, Willy. You've got the wrong end of the stick about that. My sister is straight as an arrow. And who the hell is Frank?" Her scrawny little arms stuck out from her hips like she was a stick figure in a cartoon.

"I ain't sayin' no more, Iris. But you know I wouldn't make up a story on no account."

"Well, I can't say I believe it, and that's saying something. You sure you're not imagining this?"

"I ain't imaginin' nothin'. Ask Fischer if you don't believe me."

"Do I have to? This is a new wrinkle. I never thought I'd live long enough to hear something like this. Does Paulie know about it? 'Cause he ain't said a word to me."

"Nope. This guy showed up 'bout two weeks ago."

"Who is he?" Iris asked, and just then Lila came through the swinging doors with another tray of her bird's nests.

"What are you two talking about?" She glared at Willy.

Iris, in spite of the amount of time she had spent lying in bed, still had a quick mind. "Paulie hired a guy to build a ramp to the backyard. That silly Italian. He's worried I won't be able to get around on my own come spring, I guess." She rolled her eyes. "I was just asking Willy if he knows who the guy is, 'cause the first I saw him, he was pounding nails outside beneath my bedroom window. Woke me out of a dead sleep."

Lila shrugged. She wasn't going to argue with her ailing sister, despite knowing she was making up a story.

"I thought maybe Willy had told Paulie to hire him. He seemed drier than toast without butter. You know what I mean. The kind that sticks in your throat, and you choke on it. This guy had *no* sense of humor, far as I could tell. Bet I didn't get more than two words out of him." Ordinarily both Willy and Lila would find that funny. Iris could squeeze words out of a dead man. "Maybe he felt sorry for me," Iris added, and Willy and Lila both looked away.

Lila walked over to the pie window, and they followed her with their eyes. She stood there for a full two minutes. There was only one customer at a table, the jeweler from the next block. He was at Saturday Stella's table reading the morning paper. He only came in and sat down if the place was nearly empty. He'd walk down the street from his store, the newspaper under his arm, and if there was a line at the counter, pirouette, and head right back where he came from. He might do this three times in a morning if the bakery was busy. Some days he didn't get his morning coffee until almost noon. If it got to be that late, he'd order something for lunch.

Lila had hung gold holiday swag over the window after Willy's little tree was decorated. "You got me in a Christmas mood." She sounded as though she was bawling him out. The swag framed the pie window. Two days after Frank turned up, Lila added three red dangling balls from it.

Willy was surprised at the addition and told her, "Cheers the place up more than ever." The swag and the tree next to the door drew a lot of comments. Steady customers said, "Hey, Lila. Looks like you're really getting into the spirit this year." They were happy for her because she had ignored all the holidays, except for making the gingerbread and the other holiday baked goods, ever since Minna had gone.

"Might as well go whole hog." Willy beamed, convinced it was because of his doing, bringing in the tree. She and he had spent a whole evening trimming it. She'd made an extra pot of popcorn, and they'd strung it along with the berries. "Needs a star, though," he said, "on the top," and he fashioned one then and there from two paper napkins from a dispenser on the counter.

Lila continued staring out the window into the gray street. Willy and Iris watched as she took down one of her red balls and absently rolled it around her palms like it was dough. It had started to rain, more sleet than rain, like it couldn't make up its mind. Iris and Willy raised their eyebrows at each other. The jeweler spoke to her back. "Looks like we're in for it this Christmas. Five or more inches by this weekend already, they're saying." Iris practically dropped her jaw. As far as she knew, the man had not uttered a single word before beyond asking for "the regular."

Lila moved away from the window without speaking or looking at him. She held the red ball cupped in her palms, still rolling it. The jeweler didn't notice. He had tucked his head back into the paper, trying to ferret out more details for his weather report. She walked past Willy on the stool at the counter, and Iris. She headed toward the kitchen, and Willy almost blurted out, hardly able to contain himself, "Do you want me to deliver the firewood after work?" But she was turning the Christmas ball and seemed dazed as the doors banged behind her.

"What in the world was that?" Iris said in a loud whisper.

"Got me, Iris." Willy put his change on the counter. "Gotta get back to work. No sense hangin' around here anyhow. It's dead quiet at the garage, though. Everybody thinkin' 'bout Christmas, I guess."

"Should I say something to her?" Iris was nonplussed. After Minna had disappeared, Lila got so blue there were days she was back in the kitchen pacing like a penned-up wolf looking for a hole in the fence. She still did all the baking, got up in the middle of the night and went to the bakery, and the food was tastier than before. Willy didn't sleep much then, either. He just knew she wasn't at home in bed, and he'd get in his truck and drive down the alley of the bakery. Most of the time, the light was on. He didn't interrupt her. She would have gotten angry if he had. She was working her grief out on the bread dough.

Before she got really sick, Iris did all the counterwork. She gave up her sewing business to help out because Lila was upsetting customers and didn't even realize she was doing it. Everyone pitched in to help, one way or the other. Paulie made meals, packed them, and had them warming in Lila's oven for her when she got home. Willy learned how to arrange pastries on platters for banquets, and Fischer ran the deliveries. Willy discovered Fischer and Lila in an embrace by the bakery ovens. They were weeping and holding each other and didn't see him come in.

He quietly slipped back out. That was Easter weekend, six months after Minna had disappeared.

It was because of Iris that Lila finally came out of that spell, but not before Iris had ignored the lump in her breast for far too long. She didn't say anything to Lila and didn't pay much attention to it for a few months. When it didn't go away and became annoying, she thought she'd better find out "what the heck this is about," and made an appointment to see the doctor.

She didn't like doctors. That was one reason she stayed away. The other reason was it seemed a stupid, annoying thing to have to give her attention to. But she found it was getting to be harder to work a whole day at the bakery. "I believe, Paulie, your wife is getting old. I'm dog tired these days." She kicked off her shoes as soon as she was inside the hallway. He had supper ready every evening, but some nights she was too tired to lift a fork, she told him.

"Now, you have to eat something," he had coaxed. He taxed his brain to come up with food that would tantalize her. He'd wave a fork full of aromatic pasta heavily laden with garlic in front of her nose. She didn't tell him about the lump, and luckily, she thought, he hadn't noticed it.

Sixty-Three

"Listen, smarty," Minna said. "I don't get to stick my head in a stupid thick book and get a grade on a test. I get tested every day." She had finished her high school courses in six months. Mr. Bieber didn't let her stop once she got started. He handed her a stack of manuals.

"Work through these as you can," he had suggested. "Maybe they'll help you figure out how to win over the tough ones." He shook his head.

"I thought we were getting along better." John hoped that would bring a smile, or at least take the edge off. He didn't shy away from her as some would, those who can't abide a forceful woman who expresses a certain amount of passion, and in order to protect themselves must put her in her place, say she was just a man wearing women's clothes, or worse, a bitch who needed to learn how to keep her mouth shut.

John liked her spirit and her independent thinking. He didn't believe the business about a woman being fashioned from a man's rib sometime in ancient history, which first of all, made her inferior, and, in addition, put her in an indebted position because of his sacrifice, and finally resulted in her being his servant. It seemed mighty convenient for men, but not so much for women. He hadn't known very many women, but he thought they should all be like Divine who was his first real woman friend. Minna pleased him, tickled him in places he hadn't felt before. Even when they argued. There were girls in his classes, some who wore tight pastel sweater sets with pearls and red lipstick and had big curls and seemed interesting for a while. But he was always disappointed when he got to know them better during the school term.

"Better than what?" she had barked. "I don't get As at my work for getting correct answers. That would be a snap." She snapped her fingers to make her point. "I have to figure out what to say every time I open my mouth to the floor managers to get them to do what they *should* be doing. All these books"—she pointed to the four he had teased her about—"can't show me how to get Mr. Griffiths to quit tinkering with the inventories to make me look like I'm not doing my job."

"Still having trouble with that old coot, are you?" John really had been very sympathetic. When he wasn't at the bookstore stocking shelves, or helping at the cash register, he was studying. The orphanage hadn't emphasized education or suggested the children consider going to college, so in order to not simply survive at the university, but to do well so he could achieve his goal of becoming a history professor, he devoted his energies to his books. He, like all the other orphans, had been trained for jobs they could slide into right out of high school, which made sense because the kids then had necessary skills they could rely on to support themselves. They could go into a trade like carpentry, which is what John had begun learning at age twelve. He had taken to it easily. He loved running his hands over wood he had sanded and got good at measuring and cutting lengths of boards, and he enjoyed standing back to view a finished project. As much as he liked the work, though, there was a part of him that felt lonely and rather empty, as though something didn't quite fit into place.

"If all else fails, Minna," he once confided to her, "I can always go back to being a carpenter. It's what I did until I was drafted."

In the army, he was singled out almost before he got settled in. It didn't take long to sift through the new recruits and find out he was one of the smart ones and move him up to corporal a few weeks after he was out of basic training. "Fool I was," he rued. He should have stayed an infantryman instead of having to put up with the kind of antics Minna had to deal with at the yard.

It was folly to think you could get more than the minimum from the people you were in charge of, to hope for more or better work, or helpful attitudes, but Minna did. She wouldn't give in or give up, even when she could see how easy it was for the workers to resent her. In John's case, he had faced that attitude while he was in the army, giving orders. Minna had it tough, though, because many of the men were ten—some twenty—years older than she, and among them were those who had suffered through gruesome scenarios abroad and never talked about how bad it had been. He sympathized with them, too, and supposed there were days they came to work nearly drugged from the nightmares that woke them, screaming, from their sleep. The men got cocky, sometimes downright mean, with their grudges, especially because it meant they had to report to a woman. And it did not help matters that she was barely out of her teens, and looked it.

"Wait 'em out," Cosmo had advised early on. "They'll come 'round when they see you're the best man for the job," he teased. He

313

had been uneasy, too, about how it was for her at work. He hated seeing the girl he loved like a relative being mistreated by the men he worked side by side with, and who were mostly decent men. If he went to her defense it would make it worse for both of them. He had confided to Terra, "But it's hard to bite my lip when I sees that girl gettin' business she don't no how deserve, and them not lettin' up on her. I jus' wish they open they eyes."

The way Mary had left was surprising but perhaps foreseeable if an informed individual had been observing. Because she had been meticulous and exacting, because she was obsessive about each detail, her departure was unexpected. Yet looking back on it, her behaviors grew more erratic and extreme toward the war's end. Close scrutiny would have revealed a major shift was occurring.

Minna got hit hard after she took over for Mary, and it wasn't due to the paper work being more complicated or obscure, nor was it because she had to learn the processes that Mary had guarded for fear of being bested in her position. No, what Minna encountered in those next months helped her to understand what Mary had confronted every day on the job. Mary must have felt she was going into battle each time she entered that building. Minna's scorn for Mary faded once she saw how Mary must have strained to get through her shift. Minna's contempt had been misplaced, and after she was gone, it was replaced with a belated regard and respect.

"Poor Mary," Minna cried to Celeste in the evenings, sitting in their safe living room and drinking a soothing tea. Although Mary was gone, she wanted to protect the strange woman. "How did she manage to work there for as long as she did?"

Mary hadn't shared her stories with Minna about growing up, when her days were seeded and sprinkled with snide comments and jeers long before she was hired at the shipyard. Those messages shaped her, made her turn cold and dismiss and distrust personal contact, Phyllis being the one exception. Mary had trained herself to let remarks and sneers pass by her. She shut down her peripheral vision and tightened her jaws to reduce voices, and she countered the unkindnesses by being precise and thorough and not letting an error slip by her. She made it a point to find the errors of others. Her strategy was to go on the offensive.

While she shared an office and sat across the desk from the woman, Minna didn't consider that Mary was receiving insidious taunts, the kind you can't go to a boss and say, "See, this is what's happening," because they were unobservable, even though you knew they were there.

That is exactly what some women in the work crews did. Some of it came from envy, and some of it came out of having miseries of their own, and using Mary as the target to unload. Mary was a perfect foil because, in spite of thinking she was subtle, nearly invisible, her actions were like a sign on her back that said, "kick me."

Every day Minna stared at a sour middle-aged woman dressed for combat. Minna had to gear up to face the comments that swirled around her, too, and deflect the looks when she went down the stairs to collect reports or eat in the lunchroom. The work was dangerous, and the noise in the yard was deafening, not suited for a well dressed office worker. A girl showing up down in the work area from a clean, quiet office, carrying around paper work, aroused bawdy and rough comments. Minna didn't see why it had to happen, but she needed the job, and she liked her work.

The odd and furtive behaviors, the annoying habits started to make sense only after Mary was gone. Her abrupt manner was a necessary wall of self-protection. Minna had received catty remarks and unfriendly stares while she worked for Mary, but she had attributed them to her youth and inexperience. After she took over, and the war was finished, the men became the troublemakers.

The transition was grueling. Some of the women had been there for five years, and in their remaining weeks on the job were required to train the men coming in, how to operate the equipment. Many of the women cried, especially if a man was sloppy or careless, and some got angry with Mr. Bieber and to his face told him he was unfair. Hadn't they done outstanding work, exceeding quotas, getting ships to sea ahead of schedule? The men couldn't wait to see the backs of them, and frankly, Mr. Bieber felt like a shirt being torn apart piece by piece.

Minna endured the men's comments, and like Mary, she distanced herself. She'd count the steps down from her office to the yard, to make herself get calm when she had to face a difficult manager. "One," she'd think on the first step, "everything is okay. Two, you're not going to die. Three, don't let your face show how you feel. Four, do not let them push you around. Five, be fair but firm." That's what Mr. Bieber counseled her. He really did want her to succeed. But what was she to do if they made excuses for not getting their reports done by day's end?

"Make them stay until they do," Mr. Bieber had told her early on. "Don't threaten, but strongly hint that you will discuss it with me, and that it could lead to decisions that might be detrimental to their position. Do they think I don't know what they're doing already?"

"I'm sure they don't, Mr. Bieber." But her mind was a blur.

How could she make a grown man stay after work because of unfinished reports? She wasn't a schoolteacher, for goodness' sake.

"I don't want to crack the whip over this if I don't have to, Minna. Most of these guys are good employees, and they know it. They need the steady work."

"Yes, sir." Minna was stumped, and she was afraid. Would they push her so hard she would give in, like Mary had done? Just up and quit without a word? Walk away without collecting the final paycheck? Prickly Mary used her clothing like it was battle fatigues, as a way to ward off the enemy. No wonder she left without a word, and no wonder she required Phyllis, the giant pillar, as her backup.

"Teeter-totter," Celeste whispered in the glow of the red living-room lampshades one month after the changeover. If someone other than Celeste had said it, Minna would have thought it peculiar, but Celeste's assertions often started out seeming odd and then ended up being useful and practical. Minna pictured Celeste on a teeter-totter, but it was hard to see how she would have negotiated it with her short legs. Did her parents take her out in public to a park or a schoolyard? She tried to imagine how Celeste, with her gimpy leg, would have landed when she came down. Then, all of sudden, Minna's internal light went on.

"You mean finding the balance," she screeched. The pillows next to her jumped with her enthusiasm. "That place in the middle of the board...what do you call it? Oh, I remember. What is it? It's something from science. Let's see. It's the fulcrum!" She clapped her hands and at the same time pictured one particular shy, freckle-faced, fat girl on the end of the board at the park, and a skinny one with Daddy longlegs stretched over the other. "It's math!" she nearly shouted.

"Yes. That's true," Celeste said, puzzled because she didn't know herself why she had just mentioned teeter-totter. "I guess," she added, not following the direction of Minna's thinking. Minna was excited. She shifted in her chair, uncrossed her legs, and sat quite straight. Her eyes sparkled with a gleam that made Celeste want to laugh out loud, but she didn't, for she saw Minna was serious and invigorated. Minna looked half like a child on the playground who had found the solution to keeping the teeter-totter in midair, and half like a young woman who had landed on an idea about how to handle an annoying problem that had kept her flummoxed.

"It's logical," she exclaimed. Celeste nodded vigorously, trying to keep up with her and as always being thankful for a diverse universe with its limitless possibilities to help humans find solutions. Who would know that Minna required a logical answer derived from science and math to find a way to repair an incongruous people problem that was out of balance? She put the first step in place that evening in Celeste's living room. When something doesn't work in science, one must begin by defining the problem. That was both easy and difficult. She thought she knew why there was a problem, but whom could she ask to verify? *Well*, she determined, *I'll find a way*.

After that, she could find the balancing point and bring it to rights. Mr. Bieber had advised her to be firm and friendly with the managers, and that made sense, but only if it did not have her running in circles looking to find the right words, the right look, the right approach. That seemed false and out of character. She had even gone so far as to consider wearing a severe wardrobe like her former boss. Except for the hairnet, which was an idea she absolutely refused to entertain. Geometry was her old friend, the angles and the theorems, and she laughed that her problem was really simple. Thank you, Pythagoras! She merely had to set the problem up to get to its solution.

Even Mr. Bieber was astounded when she found a way through that strange and unpleasant interlude with the men who had sabotaged her efforts. "Math," she had confided to John on a Wednesday evening over Swedish meatballs when he asked why she seemed happy. She might like meatballs, but they wouldn't have her grinning like she was.

"I hate math," he replied. "What about it?"

"That's what was missing," she exclaimed.

"I don't get how math would get those guys to do what they're supposed to do in the first place."

"Well, you're a carpenter. It's like making a chair, isn't it? You've got to measure it all out. If it's crooked when you get through, you've got to go back and see where you can straighten it out. That's what I did," she told him and then said, "I don't want to talk about this anymore. It would be too hard to explain." That was fine with John, who preferred analyzing people through their history.

Minna continued to calculate and learn. She'd gotten her high school diploma, she learned how to work as a manager, and she asked Mr. Bieber what else she could learn to help him.

"I know how well you do with the figures." He didn't add that she was quicker than he was with numbers. "How would you like to take a course in accounting?"

The war had been over for two years by then. "But you must be thinking about having a family one of these days. Aren't you?" Mr. Bieber asked in a squeaky voice. He'd been concerned for a while that he would lose one of his best employees. The managers knew she was married…well, she wore a ring, didn't she? So she must be married, but she didn't speak of a husband. Some of them had grown protective and on their own decided she was a war widow. No one came straight out and asked her. They were afraid they might make her cry or get upset. Besides, how many buddies had they seen go down, leaving behind dog tags and pictures of the women they loved?

They spoke about Minna's husband but kept it among themselves. Cosmo listened to their conjectures and said nothing, but he smiled. His little Minna had become a bit of a mystery while gaining respect because she had lost a husband in battle. They speculated and decided her husband had been an airman. "Had to be." They wouldn't have it any other way, and that got them closer to the truth than they would ever know.

"Do you think that's quite fair," Terra asked him, "letting those men think Minna lost her husband in the war?"

"Fair or not, I ain't jumpin' in that fray. They don't know, and I'm not goin' change they minds. They got him killed over Germany. One has him shot down in the Atlantic, another says he died a POW after his plane went down. For sure, he flied a plane. They all say that."

"But do you think that is quite honest?"

"Now, Terra. No one come to me and ask what the truth is 'bout Minna. Things fine as they are. She's got 'em practically eatin' out of her hands. She knows the name of ever' one of their kids and asks 'bout 'em. That girl ain't no dumbbell."

"No, she isn't that. I just wonder what happens if the truth ever comes out."

"What you kids gonna study now?" Mr. Peterson, the owner of the Little Swedish Restaurant examined their table, empty of books, on December 16. He and his wife had hung festive gold swags over the windows and there were tall, slender red candles on the sills. Shiny green letters saying "god Jul" hung in one window. Each table in the Little Bit of Sweden Restaurant had a Christmas candle surrounded by three reindeer that twirled when it was lit. The sheer lace curtains, the candles, and holiday garlands swagging along the walls near the ceiling made the atmosphere snug and intimate on a winter's day. The pair were feeling hearty and relaxed.

"It feels so merry in here tonight," Minna jumped in. "I love it here."

"Ja, sure!" he exclaimed. "Make everybody happy."

"I finished my final exams Friday." John smiled at her and told the owner. "Somehow, I made it through the French Revolution."

"Terrible time, terrible time dat was." The old Swedish man shook his head. "You study 'bout the Swedish people, too?"

"Not exactly," John told him. He explained that in one of his courses they had discussed history of the Nordic countries, particularly in regard to the Vikings and how far their influence had been felt. "Clear into Russia."

"What you do with all this knowledge?" The old man crinkled his brow.

"I hope to teach it if I've passed all my exams."

"You be gut at it, too." Mr. Peterson put his hand on John's shoulder. "And dis pretty girl here, she study as hart as you do." Minna nodded. "But she do all these figures. You kids should take a break," he counseled. "Go away on the holiday." He laughed. "And come back and tell me how much you miss my Swedish food."

Sixty-Four

"You feeling okay, Iris?" Lila couldn't miss the beads of sweat on her sister's forehead when she carried in a fresh tray of gingerbread men Wednesday morning.

Iris winced but then smiled. "It's this damn heat wave we're having," she joked. "Just give me a minute, and I'll be fine." It was so cold, the door cracked as though it was breaking off the hinges when the customers opened it. "What you doing out in this kind of weather?" Iris gritted her teeth, put on a smile, and then teased each of the patrons who were hardy and wouldn't let the cold stand in the way. "Shouldn't you be home with your feet propped up by the fire, sipping coffee with brandy in it? I sure wish I was." She laughed. The customers didn't notice when she wiped her brow, she was that quick about it.

"Oh Iris," her regulars said. "Leave it to you to make a joke out of this blasted cold."

"What would we do without you to brighten even the bleakest day?" an obtuse reporter asked her.

"I figure you'd suffer through it, Henry," and for dramatic effect she put the back of her hand to her forehead. Lila had thought to bring Iris an extra sweater for insulation against the drafts when the door was opened, but she wasn't wearing it when Lila came through with her tray, nor either of the two that Paulie had insisted she bring.

"You shouldn't be going in today," he had fussed. "Nobody's going to want to go out in the cold to go to the bakery."

"Paulie, Paulie, that's where you're wrong. Eight days till Christmas." Her good-natured grin indicated he didn't know what he was talking about. "It's going to be busy clear up to next Friday. Are you kidding? We can't stay ahead of the orders. Lila will really need my help today, and besides, what's a little cold? I'll take a break after the holiday, don't you worry. I promise I won't overdo it today." She'd been to the bathroom twice to throw up but Paulie was in the kitchen at the time making her oatmeal with raisins and butter and brown sugar and didn't notice.

"This will stick to your ribs and keep you warm," he vowed, setting porridge down in front of her. He hoped it looked inviting and appetizing because he had put it in a festive green bowl. He had made himself a promise to devote his energies to bringing her back to health with nutritious breakfasts so tasty she would not refuse them. She covered her mouth pretending mock surprise, encouraging him to think that he had hit the mark, and to hide the fact that she was about to gag. She took a few tiny bites, washed them down with great gulps of coffee, and smiled at him as he watched her every swallow. When he saw she had emptied her cup, he got up to refill it, and she dumped most of the oatmeal in the napkin in her lap when his back was turned. She teased him when he came back with a full cup.

"You're trying to make me fat, aren't you?" She pretended to be criticizing him for giving her too much oatmeal. "I'm going to have to leave some of it, Paulie, or else I'm going to bust. Besides, I'll be munching all day. You know how it is when Lila brings out a tray with warm doughnuts or cookies." She choked down the nausea that accompanied the thought. "Who can resist all that divinity and fudge?"

Paulie remembered when Iris could eat an entire box of chocolates while taking a puff on a cigarette between bites. "You need the oatmeal to stay strong. And it will keep you warm today."

She smiled at him, shook her head, and said, "And that's just what I am doing, Paulie. As you can see." She lifted her half-empty bowl to convince him. He stopped pressing when he saw how much of it she had eaten.

"You sure you're all right, Iris?" Lila asked again after she had the gingerbread men with raisins for tummies and eyes staring up from under glass.

Iris stuck her tongue out at them. "Will you stop with that question, Lila? Between you and Paulie, I'm beginning to wonder if everybody sees me as some kind of an invalid."

Lila shrugged, whispered, "Sorry," and walked over to the pie window. The glass was etched with fantastic patterns of lacy ice in the corners, while the rest of the window was steamed up from the still-warm pies. The two remaining red Christmas balls were brilliant against the white. Lila wiped the glass with her apron. The few people who passed by had their coat collars up, hats pulled down to their eyebrows, and scarves over their mouths.

"Did Willy come in this morning? I didn't see him," Lila asked across the counter. Flashes of coats, dark green or tomato red, flew past the window. Their owners hustled by as though the cold was pursuing them, and they had to rush to stay ahead of it. Most of the regular

321

bakery customers came in and bought their favorites but did not sit down to linger over coffee and the morning paper. It was too much effort to take off the winter layers, to get too comfortable for a brief moment, when they would have to put it all back on to go outside.

"No. I haven't seen the bum. He must have frozen that cute butt off in his icy truck." Iris chortled. But she wondered, too, where he was. He'd never missed a day. She turned her back so her sister didn't see her wiping her forehead with a paper napkin.

"You all right, Iris?" Lila shot her a look from across the room.

Iris turned around and smiled. She looked so pale. "What in the world are you talking about?" Iris asked to deflect her.

"I don't know," Lila said trying to sound cheerful and walking back toward the counter. "I hope you're not working too hard. It doesn't look like we're going to have a lot of customers today, what with the weather. You could go home if you're not feeling good. Johnny will pitch in where I need him."

"It's the lights here, Lila. That's what you're seeing. You think I look sick, don't you? But I can tell you. It's these lights. They wash out the color in your face. You should see yourself," she joked, "if you think I look bad."

Lila tried to laugh. She wondered if she should call Paulie. That would infuriate Iris. "You will tell me, won't you, Iris?"

"Listen, Lila." Iris was suddenly serious. "I want to ask you something."

"Okay, what is it?" The door swung open. The bitter breeze blasted ahead of the customer, and they both gasped from its sting.

"The regular," the jeweler said to Iris. The same two words he used every day.

"What are you thinking?" Iris suddenly blurted out, completely disarming him. His chin was tucked into the lapels of his dark woolen coat. He barely looked up at her, but turned his head around faster than he was used to doing—because jewelers use precise movements in their jobs—to see if he had forgotten to close the door behind him, and as if it was his mother who was bawling him out. He almost said, "Sorry," but when he saw the door was closed, as it should be, that he hadn't forgotten, he wondered what else he could have done wrong. He took another peek at her. Should he tell her he was sorry? Was she upset because he ordered the regular?

Even during the summer, he came into the bakery as if he was fighting against an Arctic chill, and although he wasn't wearing his winter coat, he moved like he was bundled in heavy cloth. He didn't look at or speak to anyone beyond ordering the regular. His assistant at the jewelry store did enough speaking for the two of them, for which, if he had considered that, he would have felt grateful.

Iris had always left him alone, no teasing or poking at him, trying to loosen him up. She could see it took some effort for him to place an order. He did not come across to her as fair game, and since he ordered the same thing every day, after a few times of telling him how much he owed, she stopped saying anything. It would be only a formality to continue doing so, and not necessary.

"What do you mean?" he asked, and she heard the shake in his voice.

"Do you realize how cold it is?" She shook her head, and the little bells on her cap gave a tiny tinkle. Lila watched the exchange, wondering what Iris was going on about, and then she got it.

"How cold?" He stared at her without blinking, as though she had introduced a problem that needed time to be processed.

"Cold enough to put on gloves so your fingers don't freeze. That's how cold it is," she proclaimed.

"Oh," he said and thought to look down at his hands. "Where are your gloves?" she demanded. He stammered and began to see why he was in trouble. "You are a jeweler, am I right?"

"Yes...yes," he stammered.

"Well, how are you going to do your work if those hands get frostbitten?"

"I...I see what you mean." He expelled the words with a huge breath.

"And it wouldn't hurt you to put a scarf around your neck, either," she added. "In fact, I think I have just the one for you." She walked away to the kitchen. Lila put together his order and gently handed it across the counter to him. He stood there not knowing what he should do next.

"Here." Iris pushed through the swinging doors and came to stand by him. He moved back a step, and she moved with him and then handed him an orange-and-black wool scarf that she wanted in the worst way to wrap around his neck.

"I can't—"

"Oh, yes you can. And you will. Didn't your mother teach you how to dress for the winter?"

"I...I..."

"Oh well, never mind," and then she did take the scarf out of his hands because he hadn't done a thing with it. She wrapped it around his neck. His cheeks turned bright red. "I decided not to give you a

Christmas scarf," as though this was something she had been puzzling over. "Heaven knows what would happen to it by the New Year. Besides, you look better in these colors," she explained as she tucked it into the front of his dark-gray coat. He was so flustered he headed toward the door as if his business had been completed.

"Haven't you forgotten something?" Iris asked.

He turned around in a daze. "Here's your order. Now sit down and drink the coffee while it's hot and get yourself warm. And don't you dare forget to wear that scarf from now on when it's this cold. Understand?"

He nodded like a dutiful son. "I understand."

Lila smelled the cinnamon rolls baking in the back and hurried to the kitchen to rescue them. Their aroma was changing and warning her they were about to burn. It wasn't often that happened. When they were cooled, she took a tray out.

"Willy didn't come by?" she asked Iris again. It was eleven thirty.

"I told you. He's got a frozen butt, Lila." Iris laughed. She mumbled under her breath when Lila moved away, "Where the hell are you, Willy?" He should have had his coffee and roll and been gone by now. Aside from the jeweler, there was no one else in the shop, and he was afraid to move beyond drinking his coffee or eating his pastry for fear that Iris would find something else to fault him for. Lila walked to the pie window and wiped the steam off again. More flashes of clothing went by. People were taking the lunch hour to handle their Christmas details. She suspected they would flood the shop soon. Maybe they would wait until next week, though.

The jeweler kept his eyes on his paper until he thought it was time to leave. He gave a furtive look around to see that Iris was not nearby and then jumped up quickly, wrapping the scarf three times around his neck and rushing toward the door. Iris had one eye on him while putting the cinnamon rolls in the display case. She stopped herself from telling him that he needed to wrap the scarf only twice then tuck the ends into his coat to keep his chest warm. He fairly ran for the door but didn't make it before she reminded him, "And make sure you wear your gloves next time. No need for frostbite." He nodded and fled.

Sixty-Five

"**Y**ou ain't seen this one yet," Mr. Griffiths stood beside Minna in the lunchroom the Friday afternoon before the winter solstice, holding a photo of one of his daughters.

"No, I haven't," Minna replied. "This is Louise, right?"

"Yeah, my youngest, and bright as a whip. First year of high school and she gets all A's so far."

"She looks smart."

"Maybe she'll come see you about a job when she gets done with her school."

"I'll expect to see her when that time comes. What are you doing over Christmas?"

"We are going to the missus's folks over there in Wenatchee. My Louise wants a pair of skates. I got 'em for her, too, and now I have to figure out where to hide them in the car so she won't find 'em."

Minna stopped to chat with all the managers and workers who were taking breaks. She wasn't afraid of them any longer. When she walked by Cosmo, he flipped the screen of his protective helmet back and shouted, "Good to see you, Miz Benoit," to which she replied, "The same to you, Cosmo."

Mr. Griffiths was taking vacation time, and she herself wouldn't be at work until the following Tuesday so she wished him well. "Have a happy Christmas," she said, surprised by her cheerfulness. But she couldn't feel grim if she tried, nor did she want to. She loved riding the bus back from work in the wintry dusky evenings, particularly when it was rainy, settling into a window seat midway between the front and back doors, and trusting the driver to be in charge. The blur of enchanting colorful lights in the festive window displays of the department stores made her feel happy. Through the drizzle she could see toys, beautiful clothing, and glittery decorations. Celeste would keep her busy, no doubt, starting this evening. By Monday the place would be in a flurry if Celeste had last minute preparations to fulfill. Minna hadn't had a day off since the time following Crystal's birth.

Before she left for the weekend, she finished her routine by heading to Mr. Bieber's office to deliver her reports. She hesitated outside his closed door before taking a deep breath and knocking. Since it was the end of the week she steeled herself to be patient and since she would be gone on Monday, she would humor Mr. Bieber with the talk he would deliver. There were the rare times she had been able to slip out before he got going, but she hadn't been able to figure out what would work each time because once something might be effective, but thereafter it wasn't.

He would be waiting for her, and she would hand him the week's reports. She had only been able to flee his weekly monologues a total of five times. Her weak spot was taking his offer to sit down. She didn't have a plausible plan and missed her usual bus and the evening ride home. She hoped he wouldn't start talking about the House Un-American Activities Committee again. The Friday before, he had asked her, "What do you make of this Red Scare, anyway?" pointing for her to sit in the chair opposite his desk. "Do you think Hoover knows what he's talking about?"

"I don't know much about it," she sat down to face him. She was longing to run for the bus that was already idling at her stop and would be pulling away from the curb shortly.

"Here," he handed her a cup of warm liquid. "It's damp and cold out there. This will keep a fire in your belly on the way home." He laughed, saying he had added a touch of whiskey to the coffee. "You're not opposed to a bit of alcohol, are you? A little pre-Christmas celebration." He lifted his cup in a toast, and she had sighed quietly, remembering her first taste of whiskey on Waterworks Hill that night with Archie. The bus would be on its way, leaving well before Mr. Bieber would put the period on his words that day.

"But you heard about the Hollywood Ten, right?" he had pumped her that week, testing her. There was a radio on his side table that he tuned into during the day to get the latest news. It was running as they talked, and in the background, Gene Autry was twanging, "Rudolph, the Red-Nosed Reindeer."

She knew quite a bit more than she was willing to say about the HUAC. John had just completed his final exam in a current events class, and the threat of Communism had taken up the major portion of the class discussion. During one of their Wednesday evening dinners they had splurged and ordered the breaded veal cutlet for $1.10 at Mr. Peterson's suggestion, which John most likely did not notice the flavor of, he was that immersed in the controversy. She could have passed the test on the Cold War and J. Edgar Hoover's impact on the US Congress, and his favorite target, Hollywood. But if she got to talking with Mr. Bieber about that, she would have missed even the last bus.

"Ah, there you are," Mr. Bieber swung open the door before she had a chance to knock. "I've been waiting for you, now, young lady," he announced without inviting her to come into his office. He must have heard her coming and gotten to the door before she did. On a typical Friday, she knocked, he invited her to come in, and she handed the paper work to him over his desk. He would be sitting in his high-backed office chair and in his pleasant way would invite her to sit and talk, and she was caught in his sticky but benign web.

"I'll take that from you," he said collecting her reports. "So you're going to be off on Monday." He wasn't asking, he was stating and at the same time moving back to lean against the wall outside his office. "Now, I'm not going to ask you to come in and humor an old man today with that fine listening ear of yours because this is the start of your holiday. That's wonderful!" He was almost shouting in her ear. In fact," he said, and the way he said it made her stomach drop, "this is your last day of work." He looked as proud as if he'd just completed a challenging crossword puzzle.

"What?" she cried. She couldn't help saying it, couldn't disguise her shock.

"What?" He looked hard at her. Then, realizing as he saw she was stunned that he had not communicated what he'd meant to say, he added, "This year, I mean." He slapped his head. "That didn't come out right, did it?"

"Not exactly." She mustered a half smile and didn't say, "Unless you are planning to fire me." Her stomach was in a knot. The last time she had feared she would lose her job was when Mary was still working there. It took her a minute to get her breathing back to normal.

"I was going over year-end employee records this week, and what did I find?" Mr. Bieber continued.

"I don't know."

"Well, first of all, I've been blind as a bat. Right before my eyes. Leave it to me to not see it."

"See what?" she squeaked. She still didn't know the direction the conversation was taking. Was he going to fire her, or was he not? Maybe it wasn't that bad. Maybe he was just going to move her back into her old position. It was possible he had hired someone older, who carried more clout. She couldn't change the fact that she was the age she was. Did it stand in the way still, even after all she had accomplished? It didn't seem like that these days, not for a long while, judging from the cooperation she was getting. She was afraid she had been glib and hadn't understood that Mr. Bieber was evaluating her skills all along and found her coming up short.

"Do you know you haven't taken a day off in three years?"

Well, of course it was true. She hadn't gotten sick enough to stay off work, not with Celeste shuffling in and out with some brew at the first sign of a sniffle. That's how it was living with Celeste. She just never let you get to the point of feeling so miserable you didn't think you could get out of bed, and Minna wouldn't take time off unless it would be to help Celeste or Cosmo or Terra. Otherwise, there was no reason she wouldn't be at work! What else would she be doing?

"Now how did we let this happen?" His eyes looked huge behind his glasses, and his eyebrows drooped over the top of his lenses. He seemed perturbed, like she had undermined him or failed him, and she didn't know how to answer or if she should reply. She had to think for a minute.

"Because I didn't need to?" she said finally.

"Not good enough. Not good enough!" he spoke so loud it reverberated down the hallway. "You know, before my wife died she used to tell me, 'Gordon,' she'd say, 'there's got to be something besides work in your life.' I didn't listen to her. I thought she was exaggerating. But you know what?"

"What?"

"She wasn't. I didn't listen to her, and then she died. After that, I worked even harder. Well, you can see how much of my life is here. I hate it when Fridays roll around. And I'm not going to let that happen to you."

"But I like to work."

"You see what I mean? You and me, we're going to start listening to Della, God rest her soul. Dear lady. No, I'm making you take the time off. Understand? You don't have one single argument that is going to change my mind. You better not show up here until January fifth. Can you believe it is almost 1948 already?"

"Yeah. This year went fast. But what am I going to do with all that time off?"

"You see, that's what I mean, and that's what Della was saying. You'll figure it out. Now head on out of here, little girl, and don't you think about this place until the Monday after New Year. After New Year, you hear me? And then you come back, and you be ready to go to work."

She hardly noticed the showy Christmas decorations that

evening on the bus ride. *What am I going to do with all that time?* She counted the number of days she was going to be off but refrained from multiplying the number of work hours that would make. She felt like Mr. Bieber was punishing her for being a conscientious employee. Wouldn't Lila be surprised to find that her daughter worked too much! She could hear Lila now, saying, "That'll be the day."

She fidgeted in her seat. It felt hard and cold. Her fingers and toes were icy. She tapped her toes on the metal floor, wriggled her fingers in her gloves, which didn't warm them up, so she slipped them in her pockets. She wondered if her nose was dripping, and why there was no heat on the bus. Her earlier cheery Christmas mood faded. She got irritated and almost snapped at shoppers who got on board outside the stores, and banged against her shoulder with their packages wrapped in red and gold. But, by the time she got to Celeste's she had devised an outline for the next two weeks. Celeste wanted her kitchen painted. She would do that for her, and she would make Crystal some new dresses. Terra couldn't keep up with how fast the girl was growing. Her legs were like a spider's; they kept getting longer. She was all head and legs.

"It'll be all right," she whispered by the time she climbed the steps to Celeste's porch. She had to stop herself from doing the calculating, adding the exact number of hours she would be away from the office. "It'll just upset you if you do it." There would be more hours than she'd want to know. *You're as bad as Lila, having to fill every waking hour.* "Oh," she spoke out loud at that realization. It was forceful as a smack up the side of the head.

"You're just in time," Celeste called out to her from the kitchen. "Come back in here with John and me." The light poured down the hallway. It felt so warm and dreamy inside the house. She hung her coat up on the rack, changed out of her shoes into her slippers, and moved toward the glow.

Sixty-Six

"What you doin' out here, Iris?" Johnny said returning from a delivery. She was sitting on a crate by the back door, bent over. She wiped the sweat off her forehead.

"Longing for the good ole days, Johnny." She attempted a nonchalant wave to her brother. "Wishing for a puff on a cigarette," she said wistfully. His oversized earmuffs were attached to the ends of his cap, which came down to meet his eyebrows. Frozen puff balls from their breathing suspended between them.

"Lila said they ain't no good for you. Them cigarettes." He kicked his boot against the brick wall and slapped his mittens together.

"Did she now?" She would have laughed that off at another time. "Well, as usual, Lila is right, Johnny," she looked down at the sturdy shoes Paulie had bought for her and insisted she wear, "so your back won't bother you." They were so ugly she wanted to cry. It seemed ages since she had dashed back and forth behind the counter wearing snazzy sling backs, never giving a thought to her back hurting or getting tired from the standing.

"Don'tcha wanna come inside, now?" his brow furrowed. Judging from the confused look on his face, something didn't make sense. He couldn't complete the thought, the question of why she was outside in the spitting snow and not wearing a jacket.

"In a minute, Johnny. You go on in." He hurried past her to get inside. His fingers were cold, and Lila had told him not to dawdle. He had five more deliveries to make, and then the pans and pots to scour. Lila said he could make them shine better than anyone she'd ever seen. He liked Lila, and he loved getting every bit of burnt sugar and butter unstuck. He wouldn't leave an intractable spot, even when Lila told him to ignore it.

Lila came out just as he went in. "The deliveries are ready to go," she sounded short-tempered. She wanted to see who he was talking with back there. When she saw it was her sister she snapped, "Iris! What are you trying to do?" She nearly added, "*kill yourself?*" It was astonishing that Iris had slipped out behind her back and had been sitting there in her shirt sleeves in the freezing cold. Lila always watched for Johnny to come back for his deliveries. That's why she'd come outside when she heard him talking. She watched over him, fearing someone, a bully perhaps, would approach him in one of the alleys and take advantage of him. More than one person had died from a knife wound in the belly behind the downtown bars.

"I wanna talk to you," Iris mumbled, still staring at her shoes.

"Fine. Let's talk. But let's do it inside." Lila's legs started shaking, and her arms prickled. "Come back in, please." Christmas was a week away, and Lila couldn't keep up with the orders for gingerbread men. She'd be relieved when she pulled the last batch from the oven. She thought the cookies had begun to spy on her, sneering even when she added the raisins to their round faces so they could see, and put on their belly buttons and gave them pants or skirts of icing.

"Look at you," Lila scowled, back inside. Without hesitation, she'd gone straight to the ovens to get warm, pulling Iris along behind. "Your cheeks are beet red," but the rest of Iris was white as the gingerbread icing. "I swear, Iris, I'm going to call Paulie and have him come get you if you pull a trick like that again. I can't be watching you to see that you're taking care of yourself." She didn't notice she was frantically rubbing her sister's upper arms to warm her up. "How long were you outside?"

"Stop it, Lila." Iris pushed her away. She was starting to sweat and moved to the other side of the kitchen. "I think I'm going to suffocate in here." She pushed through the swinging doors toward the counter. Lila went after her. She wasn't going to let her run off. She wanted some agreement. "Promise me," she said behind her, but Johnny had just been ready to leave with his arms loaded up when they came back in, and now he stood in the center of the kitchen frozen in place.

"Oh no," he cried. "Oh no." He was moaning.

"Oh Lord, now what?" Lila said under her breath and turned from pursuing Iris to go back to Johnny. She gently began massaging him on the shoulder.

"It's all right, Johnny. Everything is all right. Iris is fine." The swinging doors banged back and forth, and they watched them as they slackened and whimpered to a stop. Lila spoke quietly to Johnny and at the same time peeked over the doors at Iris. She saw someone at the counter who was ordering a variety of Christmas treats. Iris was placing them in a square box, tucking them in like fresh eggs. Under other circumstances, Iris might have suggested the woman tone down her lipstick and rouge. She wouldn't have said the word *tart*. She would have said something helpful like, "You know what would really make your beautiful eyes stand out?" then tell her the makeup was taking the attention away from them.

"No one is hurting her, Johnny. You don't have to be afraid." But Lila felt afraid and didn't notice she continued to rub his shoulder. "I think you need a gingerbread man before you go back out," she said, coaxing him over to the cookies on the cooling rack. If he stayed locked in one position, his terror would intensify. "See? Look at this one." She pointed to the fattest gingerbread man. "He looks like you, doesn't he?" She smiled and patted him on the back. "You need a glass of milk with that." She wished she could have a cup of coffee.

"I don't want no milk," he announced. "I gotta go do my deliveries," he said, taking the last bite, which happened to be the head. Lila saw it was indeed smirking. Johnny dismissed the scene after Lila led him away from the spot where he'd been fixed.

She peeked over the quiet doors. Iris was still putting pastries in the box. The customer said, "I'll have one of those," pointing toward a plate of small round nut cookies wrapped in powdered sugar. "No, they look too good. Make that, let's see, there are six of us tonight, better put in five more of those."

Poor Iris was tapping her right foot by now, but she smiled. "Okay, that's a half dozen of those. If you buy six more, I could throw in two extra ones. Men love these. They go down like melted sugar." Lila relaxed her shoulders and went back to decorating her last batch, she hoped, of gingerbread men. When she had put the last swipe of icing on the last gingerbread man, she shrugged as if she were talking to someone and took them to the front.

"Willy didn't come in today again, did he?" Lila said, half to herself. He hadn't been in since Monday, and Frank hadn't shown up all week either. She was putting the cookies on the bottom shelf. "I pray that this is the last of these buggers," she declared.

"I could send Paulie to do some snooping. Find out what Willy's up to. If he's sick or something."

"No. Best to let sleeping dogs lie."

"What's going on between you two?" Iris asked again. Lila had moved over by the window. It was steamed over. She plucked another of the red balls from the swag. "You undecorating the place for a reason?"

"Huh?"

"That's the second one you've taken down."

"It is?" She looked at the ball as if it was a mystery lying in the palm of her hands. "Oh." She hung it back up and walked back to the kitchen.

Johnny was flushed when he pushed the front door open a while later. "You should see your nose. You look like Rudolph with that shiny red nose. Come on," Iris called him over. "Sit down and have some hot chocolate. You have to go out again?"

"No. I done it all."

"Good thing, I'd say. Otherwise we'd have to thaw you out."

"Huh?"

She put a blachinda on a plate and handed it to him over the counter. "Have you seen Willy around? Take your cap off, honey," she reminded him. Leave it to Lila to dig in her heels and be stubborn, but Iris wanted to know where he was. There was a hole at the counter with him gone.

"No." Johnny often said no, even when he meant yes.

"Are you sure you haven't seen him driving around?"

"He's got wood in the back."

"Of his truck?"

"Yeah." He took a sip of hot chocolate and made a face. It was too hot. "Ouch."

"Sorry, honey. Let it cool for a minute. You want me to put some cream in it?"

"Yeah." He smiled when he took the next sip.

"Where did you see Willy?" Iris rested her elbows on the counter so she could be eye to eye with him.

"He honked his horn at me over there." He pointed in the direction of Front Street.

"When was that?"

"I dunno." He took a bit of blachinda.

"Was it today when you were making your deliveries?"

"Yeah. You was outside. Remember? Lila yelled at you."

"She wasn't really yelling. It's how she is when she gets worried. She does seem angry, I know." It was too bad for Lila that most things worried her. "She's not mad, Johnny. With me or you. Don't you worry about that. She didn't like me being outside with it snowing."

"Why?"

"She doesn't want me to catch cold."

"Are you goin' to the hospital again?" His mouth contorted, and she read the fear on him. She had more dread than fear.

"I'm not going to any hospital, sweetheart, so don't even let that cross your mind." She needed to talk to Lila about that. She was scared with things as hectic as they were, she would not get the chance. "What do you think you're going to get for Christmas?" She smiled tenderly at her handsome brother.

"I want a cherry pie." His face brightened. "Lila said she'd make me a big one, and I get to eat it all by myself. She said I done real good this year."

"I think so, too, Johnny. You are a big help to her. Do you get ice cream with that?"

"Yeah. Chocolate or vanilla."

"Ugh. Cherry pie with chocolate. If it was me, I'd go for the vanilla."

"Okay. Lila says nobody makes the pans shine like me. When is Minna goin' to come back?"

"Minna? What are you talking about Johnny?"

"Lila don't like it 'cause she ain't here."

"Well, you've got that right, Johnny. But we don't even know where Minna is. It's been such a long time," she whispered.

"Lila cries when she goes to bed. You won't say nothin', will you? I hear her." He frowned and shook his head. "She'd get mad like she did 'cause you was outside." He shrank back on the stool. "Maybe she's mad 'cause you are goin' to smoke them cigarettes."

"Oh. What? No, Johnny. I'm not going to smoke. When was she crying?"

"I dunno." He ate the last bite of blachinda and wiped his hands and face on his napkin. Aunt Catherine had taught him good manners. He picked up his empty cup and saucer and started toward the kitchen.

Sixty-Seven

"*I*'ve been waiting for you," Celeste sounded piqued. Cosmo's arms were full of juniper branches, and they screeched against the doorjamb as he carried them through the front door.

"Didn't you hear they closed the pass down for coupla hours this morning?" He had on an orange stocking cap, although it was forty degrees.

"It was snowing up there? Did you get stuck?" There was a hint of remorse in her tone.

"Cars was backed up a mile behind me. It looks like the whole city leavin' town this weekend, too. But I got everythin' you asked for." He paused a second and then added, "Didn't I?"

Celeste chuckled. "I'd say you did, judging from that armful you've got. Put it all back on the table in the kitchen. I'll get to it in a bit." He started down the hallway and she called after him, "Thank you, Cosmo." He nodded and kept walking.

"Guess Celeste keepin' you all busy," he said as he ducked under the ladder at the entry to the dining room. John perched on the third rung. Minna was underneath handing up sprigs of mistletoe. "You seen my Terra? I thought she'd be here."

"She left a bit ago. She made a list of things for you to pick up on your way home." Minna searched for it in her pocket. "Are you hungry, Cosmo?"

"Now you mention it, I guess I is *starving*." He tapped his belly. "I forgot all 'bout it till you ask."

"I thought you might be, considering you've probably been in the car all day. I'll be back in a minute, John," she handed him one more sprig.

"So what's you big plans, then?" Cosmo wolfed down the first half of a ham sandwich standing at the kitchen sink. Minna didn't think he even tasted it. "Now that boss don't let you come back to work for a while."

"Did you even notice what you just ate?" she asked sternly.

335

"I've made a list," she added but being reminded of it made her feel uneasy in the pit of her stomach. Already she feared she might not have enough things to do to get through the next two weeks.

"Well, that don't come as no big surprise." He stuffed the last bit into his mouth and grinned once he'd wiped his mouth on his shirt sleeve. "It tasted real good. Trouble with you, Miss Minna"—he wagged his finger—"is that you too busy all the time." He leaned over and said in a loud whisper, pointing toward the ladder on the other side of the wall, "Why don't you and that boy out there go and have youselves a good time? Take a trip. Do somethin' new. You get one them sleds like I saw the kids doin' today, and go up in them mountains. Have youselves a good time."

"Why would I want to do that?" she sounded annoyed. That didn't sound like fun. She remembered the cold, especially when snow got stuck in her pants, and her mittens were sopping wet. "He has his own plans, anyway, I'm sure."

"The two of you is a pair, you know that?"

"What's that supposed to mean?"

"Jus' like I says it, Minna. He got his nose in books all the time, and all you think about is work. Night and day." He nodded, agreeing with himself. "Night and day," he repeated. "I believe it'd kill you if you does somethin' else for a change."

"He's not my boyfriend, you know," she was flustered. "Besides, I do new things all the time at work."

"Yeah, I knows. And what I got to wonder is"—and here his eyes got huge like disks—"why ain't he you boyfriend? What you two waitin' for, anyhow?" Celeste would be shaking her head if she heard him. Thank goodness, she was preoccupied with her tinctures and spices.

"We're not waiting for anything. There's nothing to wait for," she snapped and wished he would keep his voice down before the whole world heard him.

He was irked. "Well, you sure said a mouthful there, sister. Yes, sirree," he said.

"What business is it of yours anyhow?" Minna fired back.

"Oh, I don't have no business." He put his palms up in surrender. He'd removed his jacket while he gobbled the sandwich, and it was hanging on the back of a chair. He grabbed it off and said, "I best be goin' 'fore I says more. I already say too much."

"You're right about that," she said to his back as he went down the hallway. She was so upset she was shaking. She heard him say something to Celeste, who was in the living room, decorating what she lovingly referred to as the solstice table. Then she heard the door slam shut.

"What was that all about?" John came into the kitchen. Minna started to scour the sink, punishing it as if it had deliberately gotten itself messy.

"What was *what* all about?" she retorted.

"I don't know. Cosmo sailed right past me like I was a ghost and said, 'I jus' don't get it.' Then he stamped off. You did hear him slam the front door, didn't you?"

Minna shrugged. "I don't know what got into him. He was bossy as anything. He made me mad."

"What'd he say to you?"

"Oh, I don't know. He said all I ever do is work."

"Oh," John said. "Do you want to hand me up the last of those sprigs? We've got two more bunches to do. Unless Celeste finds more places she wants them hung." He laughed. "With her you never know." The last thing he wanted to do on a Saturday evening was to get into an argument with Minna.

"Know what?" Celeste was behind him. How she'd come in without him hearing her, he couldn't figure out. "Are you making disparaging remarks regarding me?" she scrunched her face up under his chin.

"God forbid," he whispered and then laughed. "Hey, Celeste. I've got a question for you."

"It'd better be a good one if you're going to talk behind my back."

"Oh, I was joking about you finding more places to hang mistletoe. You're like my Ancient Egypt professor was, Celeste. He believed there's always more work to do. You have to look for it, though, like the archeologists who never quit digging around the tombs."

"Humph," Minna said attacking the sink as if it had become her personal enemy.

"He's right, you know. And, I do have one more place. Now that you mention it," Celeste beamed. "I wonder if, on your way home tonight, you couldn't run by Cosmo and Terra's and hang a sprig or two over their front door. Try to be unobtrusive about it, though. He wasn't in the best of humor when he left, was he?" She looked at Minna, not John. Minna went back to scrubbing the sink.

"Oh, sure," John agreed. "Anything to keep spirits bright." He smiled but didn't look at Minna.

"Maybe I asked too much having him go over the mountains for the junipers." She considered the idea. "Do you think he's upset with me?"

"I don't think so." John sneaked a glance at Minna, who had her head over the sink. "He's probably got something on his mind. Maybe it's about Terra. Or Crystal."

"Humph," Minna repeated without turning around. They looked at her and at each other, and John raised his eyebrows.

"Now, what was it you were going to ask me?" Celeste prodded.

"Oh yeah. Well, you know I had to ask time off at the bookstore for this Monday."

Celeste nodded. "You're not going to disappoint me now, John, are you?" She became somber. Minna stopped scrubbing and looked over at him.

"Oh, no. It's not that. It's Mr. Archer."

"Who's that?"

John looked at her wide-eyed, as if everyone was supposed to know who Mr. Archer was.

"He's my boss, Celeste. I'm sure I've mentioned him before."

"I'm sure you have, too." She patted his arm. "Go on. What about this Mr. Archer? He is going to give you the day off, isn't he?"

"Oh yeah. It's not that. But this is strange. First of all, Monday before Christmas is going to be very busy. I mean it always is. Seems like people wait until the last minute to buy books. They buy the neckties and socks and wool caps and scarves. Then, it's like the light bulb goes on, and they know they want to give one more thing, something that will last a lot longer than clothes."

Celeste and Minna were waiting. He considered his thoughts; he turned them over, studied them, and tested them like he was weighing them on a scale to see how they measured up.

"So I think you are saying, John, that you are going to have to work on Monday because it is such a busy time. I understand." Her disappointment was so palpable Minna wanted to put her arm around her. Now Cosmo was in a sulk, and John was backing out, and Celeste felt her detailed preparations suddenly turn into an old lady's fantasies that were essential only to her. Celeste looked like she was about to start crying.

"No. That's not what I'm saying. Don't you get it?" John could see he'd upset her when that was the least thing he meant to have happen.

"No, John. I don't get it," Celeste mumbled. She wanted to be kind and fair. She spoke a private sermon to herself, right there while they were talking. She told herself while John was finding the way to back out of the celebration to let go of the dreams she was holding on to, maybe holding too hard. Sometimes those higher powers don't let things go ahead like you want them to, and it doesn't matter how hard you wish and work for them.

"And neither do I," Minna shot across the kitchen table. "Just what is it, John Welles, that you have to say? Can't you see you're upsetting Celeste?" He could be so irritating sometimes. If he had something to say, why couldn't he just say it? It must be because he was raised in an orphanage, she decided, and this wasn't the only time she'd been frustrated by him not saying what he meant to say. He got her so riled she was ready to throw the scrubber at him.

He tried again. "All I'm saying is that Mr. Archer wants to shut the bookstore down on Monday."

"What?" Celeste and Minna said together.

"Well, that's good," Celeste said, smiling. "But I don't understand where the problem is then, John."

"There *isn't* a problem. I mean it's great for me. It's Mr. Archer's business that's going to suffer, though."

"Well, surely he can run it without you there," Celeste suggested.

"But he doesn't want to be there either. He wants to come here! He was finally able to say. "When he asked what I was going to be doing, you know, that I wanted the day off in the middle of the Christmas season, I told him. I mentioned we were having a winter solstice celebration."

"Well, John, that is not bad news, is it?" Celeste relaxed her eyebrows and her shoulders.

"I didn't know how you'd feel about him wanting to come," John said.

"My goodness, John. Do you think we are that exclusive? That it can only be our little group? The more the merrier." She clapped her hands. "Unless he is planning to be a troublemaker."

"I should have known better," John smiled. "He's not going to bring trouble. I promise you that. He's not that kind of man. He's curious. I think he's lonely, too."

"We welcome anyone who wants to join us. It can only add to, not subtract. Now, tell me a little about this Mr. Archer so I can prepare his special place at our gathering," she riffled through all the whatnots scattered about her kitchen to find her writing pad. When she found it, she said, "Go on. I'm ready now."

Sixty-Eight

"Where is everybody?" Fischer asked no one when he hung his fedora up inside the door and almost backed into the Christmas tree.

"Lila is working in the back," Stella said from across the room.

Fischer turned to see who the voice belonged to. He almost said, "Who the hell are you?" but he was in pretty good spirits. He'd had a profitable week and was feeling magnanimous. Instead he said, "Looks like the Rapture come and took all the customers to heaven," which he thought was awfully funny. He was addressing the swinging doors, not Stella. "Guess it didn't get everybody, though." He chuckled.

"'Bout time," he carped when Lila pushed open the swinging doors with her back end. She was hauling a tray of doughnuts. He never got tired of watching her rear end jiggle. It was still pretty good-looking for a woman her age. Not that he was going to get to enjoy it, except for the looking part. She couldn't do anything about that, thank God. He'd been waiting at the counter for all of two minutes.

She glared at him and started putting the doughnuts on a shelf. "What do you want?" she asked pointedly.

"Them doughnuts look good. I'm gonna have a couple of them. One chocolate. What's that other one?" pointing to the caramel-colored ones.

"Maple."

"Yeah. I like them, too. You got any of them ones with the peanuts on 'em? They're my favorite."

"I haven't finished them yet. I'll have them out in fifteen minutes."

"Well, here's what I'm gonna do, Lila. I'm gonna sit down over there at my table and drink my coffee. And I'm gonna eat these two here," indicating the doughnuts he'd already picked out. "Then, when you have 'em ready, I'll have one of them peanut ones and another cup of coffee." He looked pleased with himself. He didn't notice Stella smiling down at her slice of rye toast.

"Where the heck is everybody today?"

"How would I know?" Lila shrugged.

"Probably doin' their last round of shoppin', I suppose," he responded to his own question. "Spending hard-earned money they don't have. No doubt they'll be floodin' the place when they see the doughnuts are up."

"No doubt," she muttered.

"What 'bout Willy? Why ain't he over there on his regular stool? I thought he was permanently attached to the damn thing." The realization took him aback. "I never seen *him* miss a day."

"He's your brother. Why don't you ask him?" She hated it when he cursed.

"Well, dang it, Lila. You *are* in a great mood today. Somebody shoot your dog?" He chortled. "Oh, how could I forget? You don't even like dogs." She put the two doughnuts on the saucer of his coffee cup and left them on the counter on her way to the kitchen.

He whistled to himself, "Away in a Manger," as he collected the newspaper from another table and headed to his favorite spot. "Dang, this is good," he said, addressing the chocolate doughnut after he took his first bite. He didn't notice Stella smile again. He slurped his coffee. Lila had cured him of drinking it from the saucer while they were still married. He'd just gotten immersed in the feature about how the city was in the middle of making improvements to downtown.

"I hear the weather is going to be mild all the way through Christmas," Stella announced to the room, which had been silent except for Fischer's slurping, his flipping the pages of the newspaper, and his whistling. She must have thought Fischer had been wondering about the weather forecast, maybe looking for the report in the paper. Fischer was just to the point of getting worked up about the damn lady mayor he'd voted against in April. He rested his pointer finger to keep his place and looked up, then he looked over his shoulder to see who Stella was talking to. When he saw he was still the only other person there, he asked, "You talkin' to me, lady?"

"Well, yes, I am." She giggled like a girl and didn't take her eyes off him.

"You the weatherman, or somethin'?" He couldn't believe it when she actually laughed at that. He'd thought it would shut her up and she would stop interrupting his reading.

"No, I'm not." She giggled again. He stared at her for a full minute while she went on, for she had not finished what she was going to say. "That dip we had the other night...down to nine degrees?" She was jogging his memory in case he had somehow missed it. "That's as low as it is going to get. For a while, at least," she added. "Maybe that indicates we will have a moderate winter." He didn't take his eyes off her, and she didn't wiggle under his gaze.

"Did you hear what that dang lady mayor is going to do?" His mind was not on the weather but on the article. His finger was still pointing to the item he had been reading.

"I believe you are talking about the parking meters she's having put in."

"This dang city is nickel-diming us to death. She didn't get my vote. It's them damn college nuts over there

elected her. What's it gonna be next? We gonna have to pay a toll to get across the goldarn Higgins bridge?"

"It is unsettling, isn't it?" She smiled. He was surprised at how shapely her lips were.

"Huh?"

"It is difficult to adjust to change, don't you think?" She smiled again with her rosebud-pink lips. He could almost smell the perfume. He preferred fire-engine-red lipstick.

"What? You mean to highway robbery?"

"On the surface it certainly looks that way, doesn't it?" Fischer couldn't make out what she was telling him. What she said made his head feel funny. He kind of liked it but it gave him a strange tickle right where his neck met the back of his skull. He was relieved when Johnny came flying through the door just then. He didn't want to have to look forward to a headache this weekend.

"Hey, big fella," Fischer called out. Johnny was breathing hard. "Slow down, there, sonny boy." Fischer stood up and went over by him. "You all right?"

"There was...a d—dog," Johnny stuttered. Fischer caught sight of it out on the sidewalk. It was an ancient black lab and it was shivering.

"Yeah. I see him now. Don't worry about him, Johnny. He was followin' you 'cause he thought you had some food. Look at him. He's cold. Just look at him shake." Fischer couldn't walk by a dog in distress. He opened the door for him. "Come here," he commanded, and the dog came in and sat down right inside the door. He wasn't a rude fellow.

"Oh no," Johnny cried out. "He's gonna bite me." Stella rushed over to his side. "Here, Johnny. Just stand behind me." She moved between him and the dog.

"All he's doing is lookin' for food, Johnny. He ain't gonna eat you. You don't have enough meat on you." Fischer laughed, but he felt bad that he had scared the guy. "He probably smelled the bread you were out delivering."

"It would be a good idea to put the dog someplace else," Stella said gently to Fischer. "Johnny. I'm going to stay right here in front of you so the dog can't see you. Understand?"

"No," he said.

"That's okay. Fischer is going to take him out back now, isn't that right?" she raised her eyebrows at Fischer. He was puzzled that she knew his name, and it surprised him that he didn't mind doing what she asked.

"What's that filthy mongrel doing in here?" Lila banged the swinging doors. She was carrying in the peanut-covered doughnuts.

"I was just trying to get him warm, Lila. And…he's hungry."

"That figures. Well, get him warm and feed him at your place. Not mine. I don't want a filthy animal in my bakery."

"Can't he have a scrap of bread first?" Fischer whined. "Surely you wouldn't begrudge the poor fella that. Just look at him. He's scrawny as anything. Hell, I'd feed him my peanut doughnut if I didn't think he would die from the joy of it." He hoped she would find that as funny as he thought it was.

"Take him out back. I'll get him some scraps when I finish here. And stop scaring Johnny. I wish just once you'd use your head." She shook her own head and put the doughnuts in the case, leaving one on the counter for Fischer.

Stella stayed in front of Johnny until the dog was safely out of the shop. "It's all right now, Johnny. Why don't you just wait over at the counter. I bet you'd like to have a doughnut. Lila will be back in a few minutes." She walked beside him across the room.

"Is that dog comin' back in here?" Johnny wouldn't sit on the stool.

"No, he's not. Lila will make sure of that." Stella was firm. "You're safe now, Johnny." She gave him a very gentle tap on the arm.

"I put him in my truck," Fischer confirmed when he came back in. "I'll take him home with me. See he's got a place to stay." He wasn't speaking to Stella, but then he wasn't not speaking to her, either. No one else had come into the shop.

"Johnny, how about some hot chocolate." Lila came

in behind Fischer. "You need a couple of doughnuts, too. It wasn't too cold out there, was it?"

"Nah." He took a bite of a doughnut.

"Take your cap off, Johnny," Lila reminded him.

Stella had returned to her seat. She picked away at her rye bread. Lila refilled Fischer's coffee once he sat down again, then Stella's. Lila said, "Thanks for what you just did there for Johnny. He can get pretty riled up."

"I'm glad I could help."

"He wasn't gonna hurt nobody," Fischer said between them. "I felt sorry for the old feller." Lila shook her head and went back behind the counter.

"He did look like he needed help," Stella assured him. "It's good you will watch out for him now. Poor old dog. I wonder if someone threw him out." He was liking those rosebud lips more than ever.

"Well, Lila. I think I'll take another one of them peanut doughnuts," Fischer said across the room, jumped up to go get it, and gave Stella a big grin, deliberately going out of his way to walk past her table.

"Hey. I forgot to ask," he said to Lila at the counter. She had her back to him making a fresh pot of coffee. "What happened to the jerk you were hangin' on and makin' a fool of yourself over last Saturday?" For one second she didn't move at all, frozen solid like the backside of a snowman.

"Lila?" Her back started shaking like she was sobbing. "Lila?" he asked again, and the sobbing got worse, and then she was crying, but she did so without making a sound. She never did turn around. Somehow she managed to get through the swinging doors without him seeing her face. On the other side of the door, she shouted, "Leave me alone," and the hinges fluttered behind her.

"Now what the hell did I do this time?" Fischer directed his question to the pastries staring back. Johnny was eating his second doughnut with his head halfway down to the plate.

"Lila don't like it when you talk mean to her," Johnny said with his eyes fixed to a spot on the counter.

"What'd I say that was mean?" Johnny leaned away from Fischer like he had bad breath. "Sorry," Fischer said softly. The last thing he needed was to rile the guy a second time.

"Guess I'd best take the dog and shove off." He grimaced. "Not makin' no money here." He sounded sad, as though it was his feelings that had been hurt.

"I think Lila just needs some time, Fischer," Stella showed up at his elbow.

"Time for what?" What was this woman talking about now? How could she annoy him and please him at the same time?

She spoke almost in a whisper, "You didn't mean to upset her, but you know how people can take things when they are sad." He did? Well, maybe he did, but he hadn't spent his life thinking about that.

"You wanna go to a movie tonight?" he blurted. Between the two of them it was hard to tell who was the more surprised. He was having a heck of a time trying to figure out what she was explaining about Lila being sad. But it wasn't his fault those lips of hers were interfering with his thinking.

"Well," Stella said. "Well," she said again. "Well…" she said one more time, and then she beamed and added, "That would be just lovely."

Sixty-Nine

"Just point me in the direction you want me to go, little lady," Cosmo greeted Celeste the afternoon of winter solstice." He appeared on the front porch holding a sack full of items, things Terra had loaded him down with, and grinning. Towering over her, the magnificent raven Father Christmas looked down upon the elf decked out in a wintergreen vest over a long-sleeved white shirt, and red plaid skirt.

"Now what are you bringing that we don't already have?" Celeste peeked into one of the sacks, brushing her crown of mistletoe against the paper. "Oh, just leave it to Terra to think of one more thing we can use."

"She be cookin' half the night. I tell her to come to bed, but you know Terra when she gets her mind made up."

"Let's see what you've got in there." Celeste didn't wait for Cosmo to set the sack down. At the top was a covered pan. Inside were sweet rolls with raisins, in the shape of the letter "S" and the color of lemons. "Oh, she said she might make these. If she had the time. I've not eaten them before, have you?"

"Nah. But she smacked my hands when I saw 'em on the counter today. Said I have to wait jus' like ever'body else."

"They have a foreign name. I can't recall what she said they were. Something Swedish, I believe, that her grandmother made for her when she was a child. Take them out to the back. Minna's getting the table set up in the dining room." He was going down the hall when she added, "The largest mistletoe wreath back there is for you."

"You 'spect me to put one of them things on my head, too?" He made a face and stuck out his tongue.

"No arguments, Cosmo."

Minna heard him come in. She thought he might avoid her and go directly to the kitchen, but he didn't. He peeked around the corner and gleamed at her with an irresistible smile.

"There you is."

"There you is, yourself," she grinned back at him.

"You ain't still mad at me, is you?" He raised his eyebrows.

"I can't stay mad at you for long. Besides, you are my only brother and…it is the winter solstice." She was folding napkins and concentrated on that so she didn't have to look at him.

"Next time, you jus' tell me to keep this big ol' black nose to myself, little sister, okay?"

"Okay," she agreed, but she'd been thinking about it, couldn't stop thinking about it since he'd said it two days before. She felt awkward, but she decided to tell him what was on her mind. "Cosmo?"

"Yeah?"

"In case you're wondering, I think you were right."

"Right 'bout what?" He squeezed his eyes together.

"About me working too much. I've been thinking a lot about it since you said it. And since it's the solstice, I'll bet dollars to doughnuts, that Celeste expects us to find an answer to something we didn't know we even had a question about."

"What you sayin', girl? You as obtuse as that Celeste is, I swear. You been livin' here for too long, I 'spects."

"Are you serious? You know exactly what I am talking about. What do you have in that sack, anyway?" she asked, changing the subject.

"Peace offering," he joked. "Terra told me I better get it straightened out with you 'fore she come with Crystal. Is we okay now?" he was the one to feel shy.

"We're okay. Better than okay," Minna said. She ran her hands over the tablecloth searching for a wrinkle.

"You haven't made it back to the kitchen, yet?" Celeste passed him in the hallway. "Good. You can help me with the wassail pot, and we don't have to bother Minna. The table looks lovely, dear. I think that's a perfect spot for the soup tureen. You will remember to put the Yule log on the candle table, dear."

"That's next on my list. Do you want the small plates in there now, too?"

"My goodness. I forgot about them. Where is my head? I think this Mr. Archer that John is bringing for some reason has me in a bit of a tizzy."

The front door banged open, and in rushed Crystal down the hallway to throw her arms around Celeste. "Here, Auntie Celeste," she said, breathless. She shoved a small box wrapped with red ribbon into Celeste's hands. "It's fo' you!" she squealed. Her hair was in two braids. "I'm gonna have candles in my hair!" her eyes lit up. Terra came up behind her laughing. "That's all she's been talking about for days now."

"Will my hair burn?" Crystal quizzed Celeste. She looked very serious.

"Not at all, sweetheart. We will be very careful, and so will you, won't you?" Celeste expected and waited for Cosmo to comment.

"Brief, I believe, is the word," he muttered. He had made his objections known. "Lord knows how much I tell you, and you still don't listen." He would not put aside his fear. He was not in favor of yet another chance for someone to get burned. "Hello, my pretty angel," he took her in his arms. "You look like one of them decorations. Nice 'nough to hang on the Christmas tree. But then we need a bigger tree," he laughed.

"But I don't wanna be on the Chwistmas twee." Crystal's lower lip came out.

"You Papa is jus' teasin' you, sweetheart," he soothed her, patting her back.

"Min-nah!" Crystal shouted running from Cosmo to Minna's open arms.

"How's my special girl?" Minna hugged her and would have held her longer, but the girl was too excited to be still. "Papa's gonna make a big fire," at which everyone chuckled, even Cosmo. Crystal was standing on her tippytoes and making a big circle above her head with her arms.

"Maybe not quite that big, Crystal girl," he told her. "But big enough."

"Now put everything that we will bring together for our feast in the kitchen," Celeste said. "We have almost come to our time to begin. The sun is going to be setting soon. We are only waiting on John and Mr. Archer." She tapped her wrist where a wristwatch would be—if she wore one. Minna wanted to go to the porch to look for them. John prided himself on not needing a watch. "Set the train schedule by me," he often boasted when he arrived before she did.

"I'm sure you told him to be here well before sunset," Minna assured Celeste. "Don't worry. He's never late," she said, feeling anxious. She needed to pace. Cosmo came into the dining room with the wassail. Minna hurried to get the Yule log out of his way on the side table so he could pour the punch into the elegant bowl. She licked her fingers from the chocolate that had gotten stuck on the platter.

"Are you nervous about him coming?" Minna thought John should have been more considerate than to ask at this late date. For weeks, Celeste had been planning, organizing, and arranging. Minna didn't want anything to spoil Celeste's ceremony. However, she wasn't worried that Mr. Archer would cause a problem. She would have liked to assure Celeste. When she visited the bookstore, he always had a hearty handshake for her. His brown corduroy pants and shoes with soft soles blended with the deep-toned books lining his shelves, and his sweater was the same gray as his hair. An amiable imp lived behind his glasses, and although Minna didn't approve of how John delayed asking till almost the day, she felt Celeste would find the gentleman pleasing, and he would amuse her. She wouldn't have to crane her neck to look up at him to make conversation.

Cosmo was wiping the drips from the pot with a towel. Terra had cautioned him about spilling and making the table or the floor sticky. He paused to hear what Celeste would answer.

"No. In fact, I'm the opposite. I had been mulling something before John suggested bringing Mr. Archer along. I had the sense that something was, hmm, I don't want to say missing, because that's not the right word."

"Unfinished?" Cosmo offered coming over to her.

"In a way, Cosmo. I think you're onto to something. I don't know why I haven't been able to come up with what it is. Maybe my upstairs is slowing down." She tapped her head. "Oh, well. Not much to do about that, I guess. But now you've got me thinking." She paused and then said, "I believe the word I've been searching for is incomplete." The gleeful Crystal twirled by in the hallway, waving her pretend magic wand, and Terra came in with a tray of multicolored hard boiled eggs.

"Oh, aren't those lovely," Celeste noted. "Now that I say that, and I've put my thinking out in front of me, I feel a little self-conscious." She tittered observing the spinning angel circling down the hallway. She was flushed and seemed disoriented. Terra had come in on the middle of the conversation, but looking at Celeste she felt the urge to reach out and hug her.

"Wudolph, the wed-nose weindeer," Crystal sang and danced in the otherwise silent hallway. Celeste said, "I have to say this addles me a bit. You see, I don't think I've ever been more satisfied than I have since you wonderful people filled my life." She opened her arms to encircle the three, held them as best she could with her short arms, and thought of that pitch-dark night when two stragglers appeared at her door, limping and wounded and crying. With her arms around them at this moment it seemed a fantastic dream. She had gone into action immediately because it had been necessary. She had been needed, and without knowing it, she'd been waiting for them all along.

"Let's all get our jackets on for now," Celeste directed. "It's so

349

warm we probably don't need them until the sun disappears and it gets chilly." They collected their coats from the rack. Crystal hadn't taken hers off, which she pointed out to Celeste.

"That was very smart, Crystal," Celeste said. "You were thinking ahead." She looked toward the front door. "We'll wait a moment or two longer."

Minna decided if John Welles didn't show up by the time she counted to ten and put on her coat, she was going to give him a big surprise, and it wasn't going to be one he would like. It just wasn't like him to not come on time. It was practically a trademark to arrive ahead of time. She was, she realized, more than angry with him. She was agitated but wouldn't admit to being worried.

"Here we are." John came through the door without bothering to bang the knocker. "Sorry about the delay, Celeste." He kissed her quickly on the cheek. "We had to help a poor old dog. He got himself winged by a car."

"My goodness. Is he all right?" Celeste implored, eyeing the older man standing behind John. When John finished recounting the story, she scooted around him and put out her hand. "Hello there, Mr. Archer. I'm Celeste. We are so happy you could join us for our winter solstice celebration." It was a contest to determine who blushed more.

Seventy

"Well, just take a look at you," a customer remarked to Iris the Monday before Christmas. "You all fancied up for the holidays, are you?" He leaned over the counter to get a good gander at her legs when she went to the urn to pour his coffee. "Not bad," he muttered. "Not bad."

She had laced up her clunky shoes in front of Paulie that morning before they left home, the ones he had purchased for her while she was still in the hospital and insisted she wear while at work. As soon as he dropped her off, they were stowed in a cubby by the bakery's back door and exchanged for her red sling-backs. She'd manage to fit them inside her purse the night before. They complemented a blue-and-green-plaid long-sleeved wool dress that hugged her at the waist. With her apron over it, you couldn't really see how the bodice sagged unless you examined it closely. She didn't sew much now. It seemed too big an effort to make the necessary tucks to conform to her once buxom bust. The multicolored cap with the tinkle bells should have looked entirely out of place with the rest of her outfit, but Iris fashioned it so it set off her outfit. Some of the women who came into the bakery that day were even envious, and they all had their own hair.

"I hope you have more blachinda than the ones you've got out in the case," Iris said carrying an empty tray to the back. "I think everybody is going to be wanting them. No one wants to cook before Christmas if they don't have to." Not that she knew that for a fact. She'd never been one to cook if she could get out of it. She left that to Paulie, and if he didn't make a lunch for her before he went to work, she did just fine, she told him, "With my handy can opener." *Who in the world would want to waste their life sweating over a pan of gravy?* she mused. Lila and Paulie were the queer ones, not her, the way they fussed over ingredients and recipes. You'd think they were admiring a newborn baby, googly-eyed as they acted.

"Yeah. I've got some more coming up in a half hour. I thought that might be the way it would go." She couldn't get over how well her sister seemed. The Friday before, when she'd discovered her hunched over in the alley, she'd looked awful. It was a relief to see a nice rosy color in her cheeks, and her liveliness practically kicking her feet up. It was the old Iris. The red shoes sent happiness up her legs, and the clatter of their heels on the linoleum had her beaming. *Just let her have a good day today,* Lila whispered. *Let her get well.* "You look great today," she said.

"Not too much with this crazy cap?" Although Lila had not mentioned it, Iris wondered if she kept quiet so she wouldn't hurt her feelings.

"Only you, Iris. Only you could get away with it and make it work." Lila smiled. "Any sign of Willy out there?" It was useless to ask. He always came in through the alley. It was a week since he'd been there. It didn't take a genius to see he was making his point. They were crossing into unfamiliar and vexing territory because for the first time, Willy wasn't relenting. When they had a row, he was the one to say he was sorry. Her head hurt, and she was irritated. She hated that she felt guilty, but she set her mouth against offering an apology.

"I'm going to send Paulie on a mission if he doesn't show up today," Iris declared. "Enough of this nonsense."

"Just leave it, Iris."

"Are you serious? What if he's sick or something? You've gotta miss him. You know this is not like Willy."

"He's not sick."

"Then what is it?"

"Nothing I want to talk about." She grimaced.

"You going to let it go on like this? Mama said you're bullheaded. Boy was she ever right. God bless and save us, said Mrs. O'Davis. It's Christmas, for criminy's sake. Come on, Lila."

Lila shrugged and made a sour face. "I don't think he's coming back. Even if I asked him to. Christmas or not."

"What's that supposed to mean? He'd come back in a heartbeat. You know it, and so do I."

"Not this time."

"Why not?"

Lila frowned. "Because, Iris. Just because." She was exasperated.

"Come on, Lila. Time's a wastin', kid. Would you please, for my sake and *his*, fix this?"

"You think I can pull a rabbit out of a hat? Even if I wanted to?"

"You're crazy if you think you're the only two people with

problems. I bet you think it's peaches and cream with Paulie and me. Right? You think we haven't gone at it?"

"No. I don't think you have." Lila could not see Paulie losing his temper with Iris. Not the way he doted over her.

"Well you are wrong, wrong, wrong. I wouldn't want to count how many times he got my goat the way he clucks over me. It gives me a pain in the neck to think about it. Lord knows what I'd do if I didn't have the bakery to escape to."

"I didn't think you ever fought."

"We just don't hang out our dirty laundry." Iris could still astound Lila. "I'd like to pound him over the head more times than not. But sometimes, you just gotta give in."

"What's that supposed to mean?"

"What I mean is that Willy can't be the only one who does it, Lila, and he's done it plenty. I know that because I know you. Maybe you're the one who has to keep it going this time." Iris held her breath, expecting her sister to stamp off and slap a lump of dough around.

Lila's face was vacant, but she didn't move. Neither of them did. Then the bells on the front door tinkled. "Do you love him, Lila?" Iris raised her eyebrows. "'Cause if you do, he needs to know that. God knows I've done my fair share of things to hurt you, and I don't want to mess things up between us, but really Lila, you can't turn Willy on and off like he's a dial on your oven. I gotta go take care of a customer," she said and left.

"Now just look at you," Iris said beyond the swinging doors. This sister was the one Lila had fought with when they were young to see who was the tougher and would come out on top. They had bloodied each other because neither would concede. Where did Iris make the shift, find the way to give in without feeling she was losing something? Lila's shoulders sagged. She stood near the doors and watched her sister perform. All of life was her playground. She cajoled and teased, playing verbal tag, pulling the laughter out of the sourest of souls, and at this time of the year there were so many of them.

Lila felt hollow clear down into her legs. She had to grab hold of the wall, or she feared she would tumble down. She hated to think she might never have, not even once, told her sister she was sorry for something. She was frantic trying to remember such an occasion. Surely she must have said it at least once or twice. What about Willy and Minna and Fischer? *Oh Lord*, she cringed. The very words "I AM SORRY" would be bitter as vinegar on her lips and tongue, and in her throat. She felt her windpipe constrict.

"Now I got a serious question for you, mister," Iris spoke on the other side of the wall. "By the way, I'm glad to see you've got the scarf tucked in just like I showed you. And look at you. You're wearing gloves, too." She laughed and said, "But, hey, any chance you noticed the weather today? It's sunny!" she announced.

"Please God, let her live," Lila whispered from the other side of the door. "And bring Minna back to me. That's all I ask."

"How long you been coming in here for your coffee?" she asked the jeweler. He was stumped.

"I don't know," he said barely above a whisper.

"Well, guess what?" she asked and didn't wait. "I know. Even if you don't."

'You do?" his voice still at a whisper. Stella had come in behind him, and Iris said to her, "School must be out, huh, Stella? Vacation time?" Stella nodded.

"Hang on a minute, Stella. I gotta take care of this gentleman, and I'll be right with you. Now before you say you want 'the regular'"— she turned back to him—"I have a question for you." The jeweler studied the counter, searching for a diamond that had gotten away from him.

"You've been coming in here for three years and one month," she said. "Like clockwork." She reminded him he had first come in 1944, on the third Monday of November. "I don't remember the date, though. Do you?"

"No," he mumbled. Stella was enjoying the one-sided repartee. Iris resembled her wisecracking students, the ones who were too stimulated to stay at their desks for an hour and had very creative notions about how the class could be better spending their time.

"Well, you have. I'm telling you. You have. And you know what?" She leaned over the counter trying to get between him and his invisible diamond. "In those three years and one month I have yet to know if…you have a name," she announced. Stella studied the gingerbread men, and they studied her right back.

"Oh." He thought he'd been released from a trap.

"So…" She waited.

He glanced in her direction, wondering if they were finished.
"So?"

"Oh," he said as he began to comprehend. "Warner," he said and repeated, "Warner."

"No, no, no," Iris shook her head like he'd given the wrong answer and was going to be graded down for it. That's how it sounded to Stella, who was still eyeing the sneering gingerbread men.

"I mean your Christian name," Iris scolded. "What do I call you when I see you at a Christmas party?" That was a preposterous idea for all three of them, but seeing that he wasn't going to get his regular order unless he answered correctly, he finally said, "Jacob."

"Jacob?" Iris said, testing if he had answered correctly. He nodded.

"Well, all right then," she immediately filled his order. "Here you go, Jake. You don't mind if I call you Jake, do you?" He hurried to his table, put his coffee down carefully so it wouldn't spill, and then turned around and stunned her by flashing the biggest of smiles.

Lila heard and watched the spectacle from the back and then went to rescue her blachinda from the ovens. "And help me find a way to apologize to Willy that will make him forgive me," Lila whispered.

"So what are your big plans this week, Stella?" Iris was cutting a slice of rye bread for her.

Stella grimaced. "I've got a stack of essays to grade."

"Now that does not sound like an exciting way to spend your holiday, Stella," Iris half chastised her. "Can't you find something more romantic than that?"

Stella leaned over the counter and whispered, "Between you and me and the fencepost, I had a date Saturday night."

"Well, good for you, Stella. It's about time some man finally wised up. He won't be sorry. Whoever he is." Stella was talking like a real human being, not a schoolteacher.

Stella leaned farther over the counter and said more quietly, "You know who it is?"

"No," Iris whispered back. "But I think you're going to tell me, aren't you?" She tittered. "I'm all ears."

"It's Fischer." Stella beamed.

"What?" Iris gasped out loud.

"Hey, Iris, would you pull that tray out?" Lila said, carrying the latest blachinda to the counter. Stella looked like a deer caught eating a gardener's sprouts. She hurried off with her coffee and bread to her usual table. Iris winked at her while Lila loaded the blachinda into the case.

"Lila. Listen. I need to tell you something." Iris said softly. Other than Jacob and Stella, the bakery was quiet.

"Let's go in the back."

When they were behind the swinging doors, Iris said, "Will you promise me one thing?"

"What?"

"Will you promise not to let Paulie send me back to the hospital again?"

"Are you sick?" Fear flashed across Lila's face, and she didn't hide it.

"It comes, and it goes. I'm all right for now, but in case...you know—"

"But look at you. You look so good. You're great today. You are not going to be sick anymore," Lila insisted.

"I hope you're right. You looking into a crystal ball?" she joked, but then said seriously, "I'm asking, Lila. Please, if anything happens, let me die at home."

Lila pushed her fist against her stomach.

"You know Paulie. At the first sneeze, he's going to rush me to the hospital." If there was one more thing a doctor could do, Paulie would insist.

Seventy-One

"But please call me Arthur," Mr. Archer insisted when Celeste asked that he sit at the head of their table. Minna had sewn silvery stars into the red fabric of the tablecloth, and the candles glimmered and sparkled on it.

"Well, of course," Celeste answered Mr. Archer, gently touching the sleeve of his gray sweater. His wreath was cockeyed, not fettered by conventional practicalities, and she was tempted to set it right. He reminded her of Shakespeare's Puck, which wasn't at all an unpleasant sensation. He had presented her with a book at the doorway when he and John arrived, before the group had gone out to watch the setting sun. Minna and Cosmo shared a knowing glance because they caught the coy smile Celeste returned to Mr. Archer.

"Oh," she exclaimed after opening it, "I had planned to buy this for myself." She didn't sound as surprised as they were by his gift.

"What's the name of the book?" Everyone squeezed about Celeste's elbows in the hallway to peek at the title. "*Salmagundi: Being a Calendar of Sundry Matters*," she said reverently. John remembered having put that very book on a display in the bookstore that fall. He hadn't given it much notice then. The others nodded, figuring it was just the kind of book Celeste would like, but they hadn't heard of it, so they were just happy that it was something that pleased her.

They were pulling out their chairs when Celeste took the moment to praise Minna. "Just look at how festive she has made our winter table." It wasn't lavish or overdone, not ostentatious or silly. The beauty was in its simplicity, the manner in which the dishes communed and were in balance with the earth's seasonal elegance.

"You will notice, too, that we are not using artificial lighting this evening." They had noticed and already decided they favored it, and this was important for Celeste. For weeks the candle preparations had occupied the kitchen counters. They sat in various stages of completeness among the squash and corn and carrots and unwashed dishes. Now that they were lit, they gave a soft and calming golden glow to the room. Celeste had foreseen their essence long before they came together for this occasion.

"The candle light will help to remind us of how comfortable we have become since that wonderful invention of electricity." Celeste paused to let them consider that, and it raised in their minds the question of whether or not she valued it as an improvement. She continued, "And to consider the ancient dwellers living without our daily conveniences who waited expectantly for this particular day each year. The day the sun and moon stopped moving," she said. Then she abruptly said nothing more. When that concept had a chance to sink in, she added, "Or so they thought. It signaled the turning point, however. The end and its beginning, for the days would grow longer and the nights shorter. Imagine how they counted on and awaited this event."

"*Sol.* Latin for sun," Mr. Archer rumbled, and then added, "*sistere.* Also Latin," punctuating what he knew about the evening's meaning. "Which means to stand still. *Solstice.*"

Celeste beamed at him like he was a schoolboy who had done the unthinkable—his homework! "Yes!" she clapped her hands in delight. Perhaps her joy was due to the discovery that someone understood her and her motives. If she wasn't mistaken, Mr. Archer appeared to be moving in a familiar direction. Her shoulders sagged in relaxation.

The group had gone outdoors before their feast, but only for a short while. Daylight was dying as they gathered around Celeste. "Look at that wonderful sky blessing us," she said, her face full of childlike wonder. There were rich shades of orange mingled with black and gray that had grabbed ahold of the very tail end of the day. A prescient observer might see in those chromatic hues a celestial heaven returning to Celeste some gift that she had been cheated out of by dint of birth. As the day began to transform into night, Celeste was visibly moved. She spoke softly. "It is time to release our worries and troubles. Let them vanish off the earth and go with the light that leaves us quickly now. See how it runs from us?

"We who are born in imagination," she continued, pointing upward, "discover the latent forces of nature. Besides the stars that are established, there is yet another." They watched as she collected her words. "*Imagination!*" she said with emphasis, "that begets a new star and a new heaven." Once more she pointed to the sky. "Let us be silent for a moment and release our concerns and any regrets or sorrows." The light had hung precipitously at the edge of the sky, waiting for her to be done, and when she was, it got swallowed up by the darkness.

"Did you send your worries on their way?" John whispered to Minna at the back door.

"I don't know." She was puzzled. "I'm not sure which are worries and which are wishes."

Celeste overheard this and said quietly to them both, "Don't worry. We're going to make wishes before the night is over, too."

"Good!" John said softly. "I was hoping for that." Mr. Archer followed behind Celeste, and he nodded, although no one noticed.

✢

"Cosmo," Terra warned. Each of the savory dishes had been passed around, and all the plates were laden. He had just uttered, "Oh!" and she knew he was about to brag about her stew. She could predict what was coming next and frowned at him. When he added, "Mmm, mmm, this be the best..." after his first bite, and he was chewing a chunk of very tender beef, she stopped him. The others smiled because they had been waiting and expecting to hear him do that very thing.

For reasons other than its appetizing appeal, the stew had not gone unnoticed by Celeste. The inventive Terra had often displayed her skill for reading the tarot and for being able to discern undisclosed wishes. Still, it didn't stop Celeste from marveling again, to herself, that Terra understood how important it was to combine the appropriate colors—even in her stew—to honor the winter solstice. Red pepper glistened among the delectable bits of beef. Chunks of unmarred potatoes nuzzled pale-green beans and iron-rich kale. Part of Terra's genius was her ability to listen to what was said and also to what was not said. Celeste was her mentor but not pedantic. As the wizard with ancient knowledge to impart, Celeste disseminated her information in the form of vivid stories. Terra absorbed them in wonder and delight and felt privileged to receive the wisdom from her teacher.

Minna, too, had learned from storytellers. Her Boppy, in his sly and secretive way, slipped to her in whispers the tales of his pranks as a boy in Germany. He clammed up if Martha or Lila appeared. "Oh, Boppy." She was thrilled with each tale he told. The first one he shared was not so unusual, putting worms in a girl's sandwich. But the stories grew more fantastic because she enjoyed hearing them, and he could trust her not to repeat them to Martha or Lila.

"You were a very naughty boy," Minna wagged her finger at him. He liked that very much, although his wide grin was her only clue. His baker's hat predictably flopped over into his eyes.

Then there was Fischer, who enjoyed tremendous satisfaction in telling the most extravagant tales, real stories, but only the most absurd.

He liked to deliver them to whoever was at the bakery, as soon as he had absorbed new ones to tell, although they seemed disgusting to Lila. Minna listened but pretended not to while she cleaned tables or scrubbed the counter.

Celeste's stories, to be forthright, were best suited to agile thinkers who could instantly picture impenetrable forests with homunculus sprites dwelling amid viny vegetation, where they offered up commonsense tips about their herbs. When Celeste told her yarns, you could practically hear high-pitched voices behind her excitedly giving solutions to the most complex problems.

"I'm sure you will appreciate the greenery that John and Minna decorated all the doorways with," Celeste hinted. She merely glanced at Mr. Archer who was holding down his end of the table, studying the stew and appearing to not hear her comment.

"I sure 'nough noticed 'em." Cosmo laughed. "I got the scratches to prove it, too." He tapped the top of his head. In some places he hadn't avoided colliding with them. He and John were very attentive to the mistletoe dangling from all the door jambs. No one considered what Mr. Archer might be thinking.

Earlier, when Terra was rushing between the kitchen and dining room, Cosmo had grabbed hold of her. "Hey, you," he teased. "You notice somethin'?" A sprig of mistletoe was straight over their heads.

"Not now," she admonished. "There will be plenty of time for that." Her eyes twinkled. Mr. Archer squeezed past them, looking a bit red-faced as though he'd seen something he shouldn't, and glancing briefly up at the mistletoe. The entire atmosphere was filled with the scent of candles that had been tinctured with cinnamon and pine and cloves. Their exotic aromas were hypnotic, and confusing, for they calmed but aroused.

"Mr. Archer," Celeste said across the table, "I mean Arthur. Perhaps you would like to take the lead and show everyone into the living room." He looked like she had placed a crown on his head, one of gold and precious jewels, not wintry greens.

"It would be my pleasure." He jumped up from the table, almost pulling the edge of the tablecloth off at the same time. But then he didn't move at all. He stood by his chair as if he was lost.

"Yes, Mr. Archer?" Celeste asked, coming to his assistance.

"I'm not sure where to go. Is it the room near the front door? I don't want to lead anybody in the wrong direction." He laughed in a self-deprecating way.

"It certainly is, and you are most right about leading people astray. That room is right across from the front door, where you came in with John." She cautioned him. "Just to prepare you, Arthur"—she seemed to be very much enjoying saying his name—"the room will be in the dark. But don't you worry, Arthur." Again she said his name. "You will be able to find your way and lead the others because the candles are lit in the hallway. They will help you find your way," she promised, and she was correct. Everyone paraded out in single file behind Mr. Archer, automatically taking the hand of the person in front and behind them.

"Find a seat wherever you like," Celeste advised once they'd entered. "See, Arthur. You didn't lead us astray. And there are enough chairs for all of us lined up against the walls." The pale light coming from the hallway was not entirely adequate, and John took Minna's hand and together they found their seats. Mr. Archer followed behind and sat on John's other side while Celeste stood in the center of the room next to a large table.

"Our eyes will grow accustomed to the darkness in a few moments," she assured them. Terra and Cosmo put Crystal between them.

"We will sit in the darkness for a time," Celeste said simply and went to the empty seat next to Mr. Archer. Immediately, Minna had to wiggle her toes and her thumbs. She hoped Celeste wouldn't make the silence go on for very long. She heard the others breathing and shuffling their feet, shifting in their chairs. John stayed completely still beside her.

Crystal spoke in a very loud whisper, "Why is it dark, Papa?"

Terra softly explained, "Because we want to see how bright it is when we light the candles in a bit."

This sounded like a very fun game to Crystal and in a moment she whispered loudly, "When *are* we going to light the candles?"

Terra whispered, "Very soon, darling, but we must be very quiet so that can happen."

"Why?" Crystal asked.

"Because the light will make us feel happy. But first we must wait for it. Can you do that?"

"Yes," she said loudly. "But when do I get to put the candles on my head?" Terra said, "It won't take very long if you can be very quiet. When the darkness knows that we are waiting for the light, it won't be much longer."

"But how will he know?"

"He knows because it gets very quiet, and he thinks we have fallen asleep."

Crystal giggled and whispered, "But we're gonna play a trick on him, aren't we?" Then she became quiet.

Seventy-Two

"Lila!" Stella called out from behind the swinging doors. She didn't push the doors apart, and so it was to her advantage that she was tall enough to see over them. Stella assumed Lila's kitchen would be off-limits to customers, for she herself was a stickler about seeing that boundaries were preserved. In her classroom, no one was left to wonder about her position on intruders. She wouldn't go so far as to say that she considered the behavior dishonorable, but it certainly raised the question. No one was exempt from this, and thus it covered a wide range of people who might enter her room without an invitation, from the principal on down to a tardy student or a prying parent. Naturally she would assume Lila felt the same about her kitchen, and she came to the doorway only because it was necessary.

In other circumstances, had she been invited in to look around, she would have been the keen observer, immediately intrigued and fascinated, as any curious teacher would be. Lila was decorating popcorn balls at that moment, twisting red ribbon around cellophane as she looked up, and Stella was sure she had been right. Lila, however, heard the urgency and stress and was not reacting to a customer peeking over and calling out her name.

"It's Iris!" Stella warned. Lila knew that before Stella had put the punctuation on it. She got to the swinging doors so fast Stella had to jump out of the way to avoid getting knocked back.

"What happened?" Lila demanded. There was Iris, flat on the floor, and poor Jake, the jeweler, kneeling down next to her. She was out cold. He'd put the scarf she'd given him under her head.

"I…she…" he tried to explain but really he didn't know what had happened, and he was afraid Lila would think that somehow it was his fault.

"Iris!" Lila spoke somewhere between a demand and a plea. "Iris. Can you hear me?"

"I'll call the ambulance," Stella said gesturing to the wall. "I'll just use your phone." It was ludicrous to add, "If you don't mind," although she almost did blurt that out.

"No," Iris muttered coming around. She couldn't lift her head, but she did not want Stella to call the ambulance. She was groggy but attempted to get her jelly legs to move so she could raise herself up.

"Just lie still, sweetheart," Lila said soothing. If Iris wasn't lying on the floor in a muddle, she'd reply, "Are you kidding me, Lila? When did you start calling me, sweetheart?"

"How are you feeling?"

"Okay, okay." She let the jeweler support her when she couldn't get her legs to work the way she wanted and found she could not stand on her own two feet.

"Should I call the ambulance?" Stella asked again, thinking it was the right thing to do.

"I don't think so," Lila was hesitant. "Give it a minute, yet. Let's see how she does."

"I'm right here, Lila," Iris grumbled. "I'm fine."

"But what happened?" Lila asked the jeweler again.

Stella started to clear up pastries that had fallen along with Iris when she had gone down. She put them on the tray that had gone done, too, and grabbed napkins from the counter to clean up sticky stuff that landed on the floor.

"We just heard the crash," Stella answered for him. It was no use waiting for the jeweler to explain. "It happened so fast."

"It was my shoe," Iris said trying to sit up.

"Oh yeah. Right." Lila frowned.

"Well, it was. It got caught on the linoleum," Iris retorted and would have argued the point if she had a bit more fire to her. She sounded like a shadow speaking about herself.

"You...you've got an egg," Jake pointed to a nasty bump on her forehead. Her cap had slipped back, and he saw she had very little hair. He reached over and repositioned it without saying anything, and she didn't have the gumption to snap at him for doing so. A customer came in just then.

"Let's help her back to the kitchen," Lila said softly.

"I can do it myself," Iris insisted, but she relented when she tried to stand and got woozy.

"I'll take care of the customer," Stella whispered to Lila, and for the rest of the day, until closing time, she worked the counter, serving everyone who came in. The jeweler camped beside Iris in the kitchen for a time. He didn't want to leave her side. They'd propped her up in a chair, but he didn't trust her not to topple again.

"I'm fine, I'm fine, Mr. Jeweler," Iris said weakly. He scared her the way he studied her, evaluating her. She couldn't get her breath with him hanging so close. "Don't you have some rubies or emeralds that need you at your store?"

Lila giggled, in part from relief, and also from fear. "I want to call Paulie, Iris."

"No way. I'll get the business from him soon enough." Lila was in no mood to make more Christmas cookies. She wanted to get Iris home. If she couldn't get ahold of Paulie, she determined to call Willy. He'd have to come if she told him she needed his help. But Stella, who was wearing an apron, came through the kitchen like she belonged there.

She motioned at the empty trays. "I'm looking for refills if you've got any more." She was eager and looked expectantly at Lila. There would be no point in keeping the bakery open if they sold out.

"You're a natural," Lila said, surprised.

"I haven't had this much fun since, well, I don't know since when." Stella beamed.

"You're not taking over my job, Stella," Iris warned. Even her teasing sounded worn out. "So don't like it too much." The jeweler, at the urging of Iris and with Lila's approval, slipped out and went back to his store.

"I'll be back tomorrow," he promised as he fled.

"Well, what a surprise that will be." Iris poked at him. "Don't forget how to wrap that scarf," she said sadly. As soon as he was gone, she turned white.

"I'm calling Paulie right now," Lila said.

"Okay," Iris conceded. "Do me a favor first?"

"What?" Lila wished she could cross her fingers and make a wish. She knew what Iris was going to ask about not making her go back to the hospital.

"Help me put on those god-awful shoes Paulie got me," she said softly.

"Okay." Lila fought back a sob.

"And you do remember the other thing." Lila was kneeling at her feet, tying the laces on the matronly shoes. "You won't let him take me back to the hospital."

"But how can I stop him?" Lila cried.

"Just do it, Lila. Okay? You find the way. You always have."

Willy answered on the first ring. "I need your help right now." Lila made herself be calm. She spoke into the wall phone by the counter. Customers waited for their orders, but they weren't listening to her.

She'd tried to call Paulie but no one picked up at his work. She hadn't expected they would. It was a busy time of day for them.

Still she tried the number three times. Then, she tried Willy's number. She tried to keep her voice from going shaky.

"What's the problem, Lila?"

"It's Iris. She's very bad. Can you help me take her home?"

"I'll be right there. But shouldn't we go to the hospital?"

"I'll explain that when you get here. Hurry, please."

"I'm coming, sweetheart."

They waited for Paulie to come home. Willy had carried Iris up the stairs. Lila ran ahead of them to turn back the covers. Iris nuzzled her nose into his jacket collar where it met his neck. "You smell nice," she murmured. "I always knew you would." She seemed gay, euphoric almost, as if she was emerging from a very pleasant dream.

"I'll get those shoes off," Lila said.

"Yes, do. Throw them out the window," Iris said quietly. "Lila?"

"What is it, Iris?"

"Don't let Paulie see my red shoes. Okay? Hide them." Lila shook her head.

"I'll put them back in your closet. He doesn't need to know about today." But surely Iris was joking about the shoes getting caught on the floor.

Iris slept for a bit. Lila and Willy sat near her, watching over her. She seemed serene, not in pain.

"I'm sorry," Lila mouthed to Willy.

"I know," he mouthed back. They looked at Iris. She mumbled in her sleep but was not restless. Lila reached over to feel her forehead. She didn't have a fever. Willy was watching her.

"Will you still marry me?" she asked silently. He couldn't read for certain what her lips spoke.

"What did you say?" he asked out loud.

"What is it?" Iris opened her eyes briefly. "Paulie," she muttered before closing them again. "Turn off the light."

"Will you marry me?" This time she whispered.

"I want to see Minna," Iris called out.

"Yes," Willy answered.

The brakes squealed as Paulie pulled up by the house. Lila and Willy had tried calling several times, but there had been no answer at his work. He would have gone to the bakery when he came off shift to pick up Iris, and found Stella, instead. She would have delivered the news, words he could not be rescued from despite his vigilant efforts and valiant striving. Lila wished with all her heart that Iris had been right, and that it had been her red, floppy sling-back that made her trip and fall.

They heard Paulie grinding the gears, a sickening clank while attempting to find neutral, and then the front door slamming behind him. His footsteps stampeded up the stairs. He hadn't stopped to take off his work boots. They would be caked with mud and grease. The car engine rumbled in the driveway, chastened and purring.

Seventy-Three

"*I*'ve made a decision," Minna said, barely above a whisper.

The merrymakers were warming their backsides by Cosmo's small fire. They had tossed in their slips of paper with their wishes on them, and witnessed as the tongues of flames curled around their requests and devoured them. There was yet a song to be sung, the one Celeste had taught them during their candlemaking and decorating, and the bells to be rung. Celeste beamed. She searched overhead for Orion's belt, expecting its brightest star to seek her out from behind the frolicking clouds.

"Ringing out the old, ringing in the new." They'd each chosen from the candle table an odd-shaped bell that they would ring after their wishes had been offered up to the heavens.

"Out of darkness, new light is born," Celeste had said earlier to the shadows sitting on the chairs in the living room. They anticipated, longed for, the signal she would give to light the candles, one candle for each of them. But she didn't. Minna and Crystal fidgeted in the darkened room. Sitting there doing nothing was like holding your breath until you thought you would explode. Two times Minna choked back the urge to get up and scream. The third time she actually opened her mouth, was on the verge of standing and pronouncing, "Celeste, I can't take it anymore. What are we waiting for? Can we please light the candles now," when a strange, completely foreign feeling came over her. It was like a fog that was not there, and then it was. It enveloped her, settled over her. She stopped swinging her leg and twirling her thumbs. Her brassy everyday bustle let go its hold. It was dreamy, and she pictured herself leaning against the roots of a towering tree in a misty primeval forest. Cosmo cleared his throat. Crystal squirmed and whined a little. Mr. Archer was breathing deeply, snoozing perhaps, and Minna was certain she was in two places that came together as one.

"I never felt so...oh, what was the feeling?" Minna pressed John afterward. They were on the train by then, and it had stopped in Yakima to pick up passengers. They held hands and watched as a couple with two happy children got on board. They were a gleeful family, but the wife had to caution her husband because of the odd-shaped festive packages he carried. They looked like they were about to tumble, and the dazzling red bows and silver wrapping paper would be damaged.

"I'm not sure." John had felt it, too, he thought, but was hesitant to say for fear it might not match her feelings.

"Well, it was as if something that was holding on to me just let go." Raindrops splattered against the train's window, and she checked overhead to see that her purple umbrella was there. "Oh, I know what it feels like," she exclaimed, considering. "It's like a rubber band," remembering Mary Evans and the span of weeks when she snapped the one at her wrist over the course of the workday and winced.

"I thought I could sit there forever then. In the dark! You know what I mean? And it didn't matter if we ever lit those candles. Does that seem right to you, John?"

"You know what Celeste would say." He touched the top of her hand. He'd imagined doing so. Part of his wish was being granted, something he hadn't believed possible, sitting close, holding hands.

"Yeah. If I was feeling it, it must be right."

The group could have been sitting in the dark for two minutes, or a half hour. It was difficult to know how long it had been before Celeste got up and lit the large candle. There was no longer a measurement called time for it could have no meaning. It didn't matter.

"We bring back the light and come to the end of a great darkness." Celeste roused them. She was reverent and modest. The match hissed against the abrasive surface creating a spark—a beginning. The candle caught the flame, the wick flickered, not convinced it wanted to bring forth the promise of light. The flame captured their eyes. They stopped breathing until it shot upward and stood steady and promising, and they collectively exhaled.

"This candle"—Celeste stood in awe of it—"reminds us to honor the sun's promise that it will continue to light our way." In the soft golden light, she was bewitching and transformed. For a time she said nothing. She looked magnificent in the illuminated light. "Mr. Archer," she said then, "Would you honor us by lighting the first candle?"

He nodded but did not answer for he was transfixed by her beauty. He came to stand beside her, and from the large candle, he lit a smaller one.

"Stay here beside me," she whispered.

"We will arrange the candles in a circle around the large one," Celeste instructed, and she called Cosmo up next. One by one they came. Terra took Crystal by the hand. "Take Minna's hand, too," she whispered. Minna reached out to John with her other hand. Terra lifted Crystal up, and Minna helped Crystal light her candle. She giggled. "Daddy, look at that. I lit it all by myself!" Terra kissed her, and Minna squeezed her hand."

"They are like our spirits," Mr. Archer said shaking his head once all the candles were lit, "living and dancing before us." The flames flashed, darted sideways, stood soldier straight, and resisted being fixed or passive. It was mesmerizing, and they were mute, except for Crystal who had waited far too long and was getting cranky.

"Terra, it is time for Crystal to lead us, with her candles lighting the way, back to the dining room."

Crystal pouted. "I want some cake after my candles."

"You will have it, my darling," Terra promised. Crystal could not contain her exuberance. She wanted to run down the hallway with the lit candles on her head. Cosmo took one of her hands, Terra the other. They strolled with her carefully and explained how the ice queen with her sparkly crown would move so her admirers would have a chance to see her. "Wouldn't she?"

"Yes," Crystal said excitedly, trying to act regal. Once the candles were safely out and off her head, Cosmo gave Terra a relieved smile. Crystal was quite polite eating her slice of Yule cake, and then Terra took her to bed.

"Now for the wishes," Celeste said when Terra returned. She chuckled to herself. Mr. Archer had eaten three slices of Yule cake. If she were sitting next to him, she would wipe the chocolate at the corner of his mouth. *He has an unfilled longing.*

She had prepared square pieces of paper, which she handed out. "Use as many as you like. For all the wishes you have." She gave each a fountain pen and produced a sturdy square bottle labeled Dragon's Blood Ink.

"Now, what is this?" Cosmo asked her when he started to write his first wish and saw the ink was red.

"Not as bad as it sounds." Celeste had prepared for a comment from him. "It is used only to put down positive wishes."

"Where you find a willing dragon?" Cosmo laughed.

"My secret this time." She was ancient yet ageless, a prehistoric priestess administering a sacred rite. It sent a shudder of awe through Cosmo, and he bowed his head. Then her hand was patting his crown.

He allowed his tears to flow freely. She leaned over him and whispered, "We've so much to be grateful for. Haven't we?"

"When you have listed all your wishes," she said to the group, "we will move outside again and cast them into the fire to burn and be sent on their way to the universe, where they will be granted and returned to us." It was chilly, but the night air was not frosty. One at a time, they stepped forward to the blaze, a small fire, Cosmo affirmed, and said their silent prayers and tossed in their wishes. The pieces of paper flashed in bursts of light, and then they shriveled up.

"Did you make any other wishes?" John asked. They were somewhere on the Washington plains. He said it so quietly it threatened to be defeated by the clacking wheels, metal against metal, before it could reach its mark. They hadn't spoken since Yakima. After the train had picked up speed, Minna studied the landscape as if seeking some clue, a sign. Anything to confirm her decision to return to Missoula. She wanted to see trees where there weren't any. The land was so empty and barren it was alarming. She felt desolate, as though being forewarned about the reception she would receive. "We could get off in Spokane instead," she muttered.

"What did you say?"

"Did I say something?"

"I thought you did. Didn't you?"

"I don't think so."

"I did though. I asked you a question." He would have deliberated doing so if Celeste's words had not spurred him on.

"We begin again when we welcome the light." That sounded to him like permission.

"I asked if you made any other wishes."

She shook her head. The one she had made didn't allow room for any others.

"I did. I made more than one."

She looked preoccupied as she waited for him to say more. "Go on."

He chuckled. "I'm just thinking of Crystal in the hallway, grinning like a queen, lighting up the whole world."

"I know." She wasn't expecting him to mention Crystal. "I love being nearby to watch how they love her and help her grow." She glanced out the window. In the distance the mountains were rising up, crowned in snow. A few pine trees began to dot the barren fields.

"If it goes well there. You know"—he pointed in the direction the train was going—"maybe then I can tell you about my other wish." She looked at him again. He thought she was looking through him to his backbone.

"Yes. We'll see how it goes." She withdrew to her window.

"Spokane in twenty minutes," the conductor barked through the coach. The family with the pretty packages collected their coats, and the husband retrieved his fedora. The children were counting each of the buildings they passed. They had gotten to twenty-five when one of them asked, "Is Grandma gonna be waiting for us?"

The train moaned after it left Spokane. It objected to the strain on its engine climbing the pass on the border between Idaho and Montana. Minna started fidgeting with her gloves. She put them on and took them off. She crossed her legs and then uncrossed them. There were plenty of trees now, and they were wearing white skirts and dancing.

An hour outside of Missoula, Minna jumped up. "Bathroom," she whispered, climbing over John's legs before he could stand up to get out of her way. She was beet red when she came back.

"You okay?"

"I don't know. What if it's bad? What if they say they don't want to see me?"

"I can't imagine that. They're your family."

"I know. I just—"

"Remember what Celeste told you before we left for the train?"

"Yeah, but—"

"But?"

"Okay. She said I was in a lot of trouble when she met me."

"And..."

"She reminded me of how I doubted that anything was going to work out. It took me an awful long time to face things."

"And look what happened with that. What else did she say?"

"That she was glad I'm doing this, but not to expect it to be easy. She said that I can face whatever comes my way. She said that when you are in a dark place, you can find the light."

"Yeah. And she said you are strong. Do you remember? Stronger than you think."

"Yeah. She did." They were quiet for a bit. Things seemed murky. Even the gray sky.

John gave her a huge grin and nudged her. "However, you've got me beside you. I can always get you a hard-boiled egg and a glass of milk when you need it." She laughed from deep inside. They held hands and stared out at the snow-scattered fields blotched by an occasional ebony horse.

"Will Celeste be all right, do you think? We left in such a hurry, and I didn't think about it till we were talking about her, but she'll be alone for Christmas."

"You have my word on it. She's going to be just fine." He smiled and laced his fingers with hers. She'd taken her gloves off, and he began to hum. It was the song Celeste had taught them. When she realized what it was, she joined him. Less than twenty-four hours before, as they stood in a circle around Cosmo's fire, they'd sent their wishes on their way, and at the top of their voices they'd sung:

The holly and the ivy,
When they are both full grown,
Of all the trees that are in the wood,
The holly bears the crown.
Chorus:
The rising of the sun,
The running of the deer,
The playing of the merry organ
Sweet singing in the choir.

"Thank you, John." The train began slowing down, bleating its shrill whistle.

Mae Schick